Praise for the
Jayu City Chronicles

"*The Hermes Protocol* grabbed my attention from the get go. I found myself in a believable future world that left me torn between wanting to destroy the establishment and accepting my corporate branding in order to enjoy the enticing benefits available. Chris Arnone weaves a tale of intrigue wrapped around characters I found myself rooting for. As Elise revealed each layer of story and world, I lived the shock, anxiety, and everything else with her. Quynn and Bastion were a cyberpunk dream come true. If you're looking for a relatable adventure of cyberpunk mystery rather than misery, then this is the story you've been waiting for."

—H.S. Kallinger, *Author of the Lost Humanity Series*

*　　*　　*

"*The Hermes Protocol* has everything you could want in a story: adventure, mystery, and a heist! Following Intel Operative Elise through the twists and turns of her mission kept me on the edge of my seat, desperate to know what happens next. Movie material, for certain!"

—Stephanie Eding, Author of *The Unplanned Life of Josie Hale*

THE
CORDELIA
SOLUTION

CHRIS M. ARNONE

CASTLE BRIDGE MEDIA
DENVER, COLORADO, USA

CASTLE BRIDGE MEDIA
Denver, Colorado

Cover art by Adrian Marc and Cheng Feng/Unsplash

THE CORDELIA SOLUTION
© 2025 Chris M. Arnone

ISBN: 979-8-9917855-8-7

For Katie Salvo

For seeing my potential and taking the chance that launched a career.

Chapter One

I SHIFTED UNCOMFORTABLY IN MY seat, a folding chair. You'd think having cybernetic legs starting at the hips would nullify any discomfort from a chair designed for portability rather than comfort, but you'd be wrong. The too-tight dress and the room full of strangers did nothing to help.

"Huginn Industries citizens and honored guests," the magistrate said. They were dressed in flowing, black robes. Their dark head was bald and shining in the warm lights of the art gallery. "We are gathered here today to honor and formalize the corporate union of Isabel Huginn-Cyber and T'Kwe Huginn-Media."

The gathered crowd, about 150 of Isabel's and T'Kwe's closest friends, family, and coworkers sat in these cheap folding chairs, all dressed in suits, gowns, and every other variation of formal attire. And because they were Huginn Industries citizens, the colors were loud, often contrasting, and many were lined with glowing stitches and fabrics. Someone coughed. Children squirmed in their seats. I was seated in the back row, closest to the exit, trying to look as inconspicuous as possible.

"My name is Thewlis Huginn-Juris, she/them, and I will be presiding over this ceremony today," the magistrate continued, their voice booming in a room built for whispers and shuffling feet. This room was the largest in the Huginn 410 art gallery, so named for taking up several floors of building Huginn 410. Not very imaginative for a bunch of artists, huh? Supposedly priceless paintings hung on the walls, most dating back over a century, all painted on our little planet of Little Sekhmet Settlement, some 60 light years from Earth. At each corner of the room, a Huginn Industries security guard stood at attention. They were each dressed in heavy, gray uniforms with vibrant orange piping. They were modded for strength and speed, bigger than a normal person, and most had multi-lens ocular implants, giving them an insectoid appearance. They were keeping an eye on the art.

The security guards were paying particular attention to the large painting on the wall behind Thewlis, the backdrop for the ceremony. Three meters wide and two meters tall, it depicted a desolate landscape, a post-apocalyptic rendition of Jayu City in which we all lived. Hessod, my analyst, had told me there was some sort of political statement there, but it went over my head. At least, I didn't care enough to pay attention to that part of the briefing. I liked art as much as the next person, but I'm an Intel Operative, not an art critic. My job was to steal things for Corto Corporation. I was focused on the huge piece because embedded in the paint were three gigabytes of code. What was in the code didn't matter to me; I just knew I needed to get it. That was my job today.

"Corporate union is not entered into lightly, but with utmost care and dedication," Thewlis continued. "To that end, you will both repeat after me, the standard Huginn Industries loyalty pledge version 2.15.3."

Isabel and T'Kwe let go of each other's hands and turned fully toward the magistrate, who said, "I, state your name."

Isabel and T'Kwe did as instructed. I felt the instinctual need to sit up straighter even though it wasn't my corporation.

"Do hereby swear my legal and moral loyalty to Huginn Corporation."

"Do hereby swear," Isabel and T'Kwe said, "my legal and moral loyalty to Huginn Industries."

"I shall abide by the chain of command from my direct supervisor to the CEO.

"I shall work always toward the benefit of Huginn Industries, its subsidiaries, and its vested partners.

"I shall respect all Huginn Industries property, regulations, and codes of conduct."

The couple repeated every line. Then the magistrate smiled and said, "You've said these lines before, but now you say a new one. I shall ensure that my partner is as pledged to Huginn Industries as they are to me."

They repeated the last, new line for them, and then joined hands and faced each other again.

The magistrate moved their fingers in the air briefly, and they looked to the middle distance, surely pulling up documents on their display. By display, I mean their ocular implants, much like my own cybernetic eyes. Thewlis was navigating menus with modded or fully cybernetic hands via augmented reality. Everybody did it.

"Now for the vows," Thewlis said. "I will read each one, and you will say, 'I agree' afterward."

The couple nodded, smiling at each other like giddy children.

The magistrate started rattling off exhaustive legalese about Isabel's and T'Kwe's living arrangements, financial responsibilities, career paths, and even early agreements about children. It was all pretty standard no matter which corporation you belonged to. I couldn't help but smile, thinking of a similar ceremony with my own partner, Quynn Corto-Nano. Nearly ten years ago now, we'd held our ceremony on a rooftop garden surrounded by family and our closest friend. They'd looked absolutely stunning that day in a black suit jacket over black skirt, a smile never leaving their face, their mismatched eyes locked on mine. My own face was sore from smiling, too.

Not the time to get lost in a memory. I shifted slightly in my seat, careful to draw no attention, and brought up my AR keyboard. The person next to me, a holographic fish swimming on their dress, saw my hands and scoffed. Whatever. The keyboard appeared like a glowing, blue wireframe floating in front of my hands. As I typed, text appeared to hover above it on my display, and haptic feedback in my cybernetic fingers made it feel like the keyboard was actually there. To anyone else, they just saw my hands moving in front of me.

I texted my apprentice, Nox Corto-Intel, he/him, "Time check."

In a few seconds, his response appeared on my display. "2:12."

Two minutes and twelve seconds. I was going to have to duck out of here before the wedding got to the good parts. The signing of mutual NDAs. The agreements on the potential dissolution of the partnership. The kiss. That was always my favorite part.

The magistrate kept going over the tedious legalese, and I used my haptic keyboard to do a quick check of my loadout. I was in my work limbs, my cybernetic arms and legs specially made for what I do: breaking and entering. They were loaded with gadgets and tools, covered in carbon-polymer skin the deepest possible shade of black. I'd had to replace all four last year after massive exposure to radiation. Long story that resulted not only in new limbs, but a regular dose of anti-cancer meds built into them that I'd have for the rest of my life. I really needed to be more careful.

I'd had the new ones built with 30% more raw, physical strength, and reinforced with some new alloy that was supposed to be twice as strong as the previous skeleton and a third of the weight. They weren't cheap. My hands alone were loaded with lock picks, welders, EMPs, taser knuckles, data cables, and more.

The batteries in my arms and legs were all at 90 percent charge. The pneumatic pistons in my legs were fresh and ready. All of my emergency medical supplies were topped off, though this job shouldn't need them. I'd been wrong about that before. Very wrong. But come on, I was just here to scan a big painting. No big deal. I also had some new surprises for anyone who decided that I was a problem. But my preferred method was to never even be seen or suspected.

Finally, the arms and legs were loaded with compartments of various sizes, including one special compartment in my left shoulder. It contained a unique neural interface, a microchip designed to translate brain signals to cybernetic mods and back. But I kept it housed in my shoulder. I didn't want it installed as my own neural interface. Too experimental. Too talkative. My own neural interface worked perfectly, thank you very much.

"30 seconds," Bastion said directly into my ears via my aural implants. Bastion. An artificial intelligence developed by the CEO of Corto Corporation, my corporation. Bastion wasn't even supposed to exist according to Earth

Space law, but here he was, riding along inside my shoulder and talking to me. Yeah, that neural interface was him. It was an even longer story.

Of course, no one could hear him or see any of my mods. I was wearing a floor-length green dress, dark and heavily sequined, that hugged every one of my slight curves. The seams of the dress glowed a gentle yellow. While the dress was sleeveless, I had a meter-long cape and gloves of the same color, though a sheer satin, hiding my arms. Beneath the dress was my carbon nanoweave jumpsuit, a black getup that covered me from neck to the seams between flesh and mods at my shoulders and hips. That, at least, I was used to. Before the ceremony had begun, I'd spent an unnerving two hours milling about with the wedding guests, making small talk and keeping my specialized mods hidden. At least that was easier while sitting.

I counted to 30 in my head and then got up, heading for the nearest exit. As expected, the guard standing nearby stepped forward. They weren't as big as most security guards, but that didn't mean they weren't well-equipped with mods and weapons. They raised a hand toward me, palm out.

"Not this way," they said. "The rest of the museum is closed."

"I have to use the bathroom," I said, squirming a little for effect.

"There are restrooms the other way," they said, pointing to the exit on the opposite side of the room. Back that way was the room for the upcoming reception.

"If I go that way," I whined. "I won't get back until it's over. Isn't there a restroom just around the corner? Between the impressionist and expressionist exhibits?" I'd never been to this museum before, but my analyst, Hessod, had done his homework. I'd spent days poring over blueprints and planning for every contingency we could think of.

The guard glanced around, possibly at the other guests or guards, I wasn't sure. I just kept squirming and selling my desperation. Finally, they said, "All right. You know your way around. But be quick about it."

"Thank you!" I didn't wait for any further discussion, moving as fast toward the impressionist exhibit as my restrictive and itchy dress would allow. I felt like the innards of a sausage in its casing.

Except I didn't head toward that restroom, of course. Once I rounded the corner into the impressionist exhibit, out of the guard's line of sight, I hung a hard left, ignoring the various cameras. Several of them saw me, sure, but that wasn't my concern right now. I had the camera situation well under control already.

Just on the other side of the impressionist exhibit was a plain, white room. No paintings or sculptures. The only thing in the room was a white pedestal, waist-high, with a dozen simple data ports in a ring around the top. There was no stealing that big painting with over a hundred people looking at it. I needed to create a distraction.

"How's it looking?" I asked on my comms.

"The guards are still in place," Nox said. "No one is approaching."

I crossed to the pedestal as quickly as I could and then deployed my data cable. It was state-of-the-art, a thin cable that I could shift into dozens of different data port shapes. It even had a fiber-optic camera on the end. It was overkill since these ports were intended to be common, intended for any museum guest to plug in.

I did so, and all around me, a world sprung to life. I went from standing in the middle of a cavernous, white room to standing amidst the cosmos in AR. Not any real cosmos, though. A nebula shaped like a cloud of pinks and blues shifted into a butterfly and swooped across the room. Stars danced around a black hole. It was a beautiful piece of AR art. See, I do enjoy art. Too bad I wasn't here to just enjoy it.

"Hey Carbon, begin the package swap," I said aloud. Carbon was the name of my digital, onboard assistant. I'd disabled it when Bastion came along. He was much better. Since Nox didn't know about Bastion and I was on an open channel, I had to code my language.

On my display, two progress meters and a blinking CONNECTING appeared. One bar was a download of the AR art installation. Totally against the museum's rules and Huginn Industries' corporate copyright policies. There were digital security systems in place, of course, alarms that would sound, doors to slam shut, guards to summon. That's why another package was uploading first. It was a little something Bastion had compiled, something to give me a little time.

The blinking CONNECTING soon changed to a solid CONNECTED, and Bastion said, "I've got you linked up to the gallery cameras."

"The guard is starting to look nervous," Nox said.

"Hurrying," I said.

Bastion's package finished uploading, and the download of the art installation began, the progress bar taking much longer.

"Any idea how big this file is?" I asked.

"No idea," Nox said.

"I would estimate a little over three terabytes based on the size and fidelity of the AR projection," Bastion said.

Thirty seconds in, the progress bar was just hitting 15% done. I suddenly felt very exposed, a glittering green island in a sea of white. And tethered to a pedestal. I had to wonder if the guard had the patience to wait three more minutes.

"There's chatter on the guards' comms," Nox said. "They're wondering where you went, what's taking so long."

"Anything you can do to slow them down?"

"The guard who let you through just left the wedding," Nox said. "Looking for you. Nothing I can do now."

"Silent circuits," I whispered. The progress bar showed only 20% complete. Given what I had planned, I didn't want to be found anywhere near this pedestal. Time for one of my new toys. I reached down and pulled up the hem of my dress until my left thigh was exposed. Then, I opened a large compartment, the faux muscle sliding open on magnetic rails.

I reached in and pulled out a silver disc, 8 centimeters across and two centimeters thick. I tossed it out onto the floor, and just before it touched concrete, a little whirring noise started up and it bounced in the air, settling into a hover a centimeter off the ground.

"He's going to look for me in the bathroom," I said. "So let's give him something." I could have made a complicated gesture with my hand to pull up an AR joystick, but I didn't need to. Bastion started piloting the little drone since I'd already told him where to go.

"What are you thinking?" he asked as a picture-in-picture appeared in the corner of my display, showing a fisheye view of the drone zipping along the museum floor.

"We're going to park this in a stall and turn on its speakers as loud as they'll go," I said.

"So he'll think there's a fire alarm in just the bathroom?" Nox asked.

"Not quite," I said. The progress bar on the download passed 50% as the drone slid under the door to the bathroom. The room was nice, with rich, faux wood floors and wall paneling. The lighting was warm and dim. The drone breezed under the walls of the first stall and tucked in around the side of the toilet, out of sight of the door.

"Ready," Bastion said.

"Apprentice," I said. "Which camera?"

"22."

Bastion heard and put the feed from camera 22 in the lower left of my display. Sure enough, there was the guard, moving toward the bathroom door. I used my AR keyboard to close my comms to Bastion and Nox and instead opened a channel to the drone. I waited.

52%. I breathed in and out slowly, quietly.

53%. The guard was at the door. My carbon-nanoweave jumpsuit suddenly felt like it was too tight, too close, though I always vacuum-sealed it to my skin.

54%. The guard pushed the door open a couple of centimeters.

"By Huginn's eye," I yelled. "Don't come in here."

"A-a-are you all right?" the guard asked. I couldn't see his face, but his voice echoed into the bathroom.

"I pre-partied too hard," I said, doing my best to sound desperate. "I'm going to be a while."

"Do you need a medic?" the guard asked. "I don't even see your feet. Where are—"

"Don't look at me!" I screamed, way too loud for the empty room I was actually standing in. I hoped he wouldn't hear me in here over the speaker on the drone.

"I…you…you really need to get back with the rest of the wedding party," the guard said. "They're almost done, and this entire wing will be locked down once they move to the reception area."

I glanced at my progress bar. Almost 75%.

"I just need another minute or two, I swear," I whined.

"I'll just wait out here for you, then. Are you sure you don't need—?"

I faked a loud retching sound, and the guard let their question die in the air. They closed the bathroom door a moment later. That was one problem, though now I would have to exit a bathroom that I wasn't even in while a guard stood outside the door. Fun.

I disconnected my comms from the drone just as the progress bar for my download finished. The relief was palpable, like I could breathe fully again. I unplugged my data cable and waited. No alarms sounded. No hurried footsteps of guards. I reopened my comms with Nox and said, "We good?"

"We're good," he said. "What about your bathroom buddy?"

I hurried out of the white room as another progress bar appeared on my display. Bastion was copying the art installation files to a data drive stored in my right arm, just like we planned. I moved through the adjacent room and peeked around the corner to see what camera 22 saw: the guard standing right in front of the bathroom door, their back to it. They were tapping one foot and lazily looking around.

"Can you buy me 20 seconds?" I asked.

Silence.

"Apprentice?"

"Hold on."

I did, though my heart was hammering. This was taking too long.

"Okay, Star Girl," Nox finally said, using his nickname for me. I still hated it, but whatever. "Tell me when you're ready and then go when I say."

I moved back from the corner and said, "Ready."

One big breath. A second. I was about to inhale again when Nox said, "Go!"

People with biological legs and a little training can be pretty quiet. I had a lot of training and really expensive cybernetic limbs. So when I wanted to be quiet, even the best aural mods on the planet would have a hard time hearing me. That was a good thing because the guard was only a couple of meters down the hallway that led back toward the wedding. They were talking on their comms and had stepped away from the bathroom door. Nox, I was guessing, pretending to be one of the other guards. Yeah, 20 seconds might be a little generous. The ruse wouldn't last long. I sprinted past in utter silence, as fast as the dress would allow, reaching the bathroom right as 20 seconds was up. I opened the door and barely put one foot inside when I saw the guard round the corner, confusion all over their face.

"Oh, my goodness," I said, fully back in character and pretending to come out of the bathroom. "Thank you for your patience. That was…" I gestured wildly toward the bathroom. "Not good. Don't go in there."

The guard looked nervously at me and back over their shoulder. I felt a tapping at my heel just as the drone's fisheye camera feed reappeared in one corner of my display. Bastion reminding me to grab my expensive little drone.

"Right," I said to the guard. "We need to get back. Of course. Thank you again."

The guard nodded and led me back to the festivities. The moment they turned, I bent down and scooped up the little drone, stashing it in a pocket of my dress. Hey, I wouldn't have worn a dress if it didn't have pockets. I had a job to do.

The ceremony had a different feel from when I'd left. Everyone was on their feet, for one. A chant-like murmuring was moving through the gathered guests, though what they were saying, I didn't know. Admittedly, I'd stopped reading the briefing on Huginn wedding ceremonies once I got to the part when I knew I'd have to leave.

"Gathered friends and family," the magistrate said, bellowing over the crowd and silencing them. "With that, through the power vested in me by the Huginn Industries CEO, Rae Prax Huginn, and the Vice President of the Juris division, Otto Huginn-Juris, I now proclaim these two as bound corporate partners."

Everyone in the room stomped three times in unison. I moved up on my tiptoes to see the happy couple embracing and kissing. In spite of myself, my eyes were misting up. My favorite part of the ceremony. I took a deep breath and blew it out, hard. I was working, after all. No time for crying. I heard the guard next to me sniffle.

"What?" they said. "I always cry at corporate unions."

I shook my head. "No judgment here."

"Now," the magistrate continued, pointing to the back right corner of the room. "If you will all proceed out the back and to my right, the couple will join you soon for the reception. Thank you all for coming."

I snorted up a little snot, the last meager vestige of a cry, and focused ahead. The crowd was moving on, and I weaved in with them. Time for the real fun to begin.

Chapter Two

THE WEDDING RECEPTION WAS REALLY impressive. When Quynn and I had ours, we rented a big tent to take up one corner of the rooftop. It was strewn with twinkling lights and collapsible tables with fancy tablecloths. It wasn't much, but it was beautiful and everyone we loved was there. Best day of my life.

This Huginn reception, by contrast, was expensive. The huge reception room was the entrance hall to the art museum. Rather than hung with paintings or dotted with sculptures, the room itself was art. Oval-shaped, ornate pillars lined the walls, towering four meters before they started bending, twisting toward a point many meters above. Looking straight up was like looking into a conch shell or a screw turned inside out. And between the spiraling pillars, the ceiling seemed to glitter and shine between gold and silver. The effect was dazzling and dizzying.

A raised platform held a single, wide table draped in a gold tablecloth and shimmering dining ware. The rest of the room was filled with circular tables, smaller and just as shimmering with plates, drinkware, and utensils. A quintet of musicians was playing stringed instruments that I didn't know, and they filled the room with a beautiful, quiet melody. It was gorgeous if you liked that sort of thing.

"Do you see a likely target?" I whispered into my comms.

"I'm watching a couple of people," Nox said. "Oblivious. Close to the exits."

There were six cameras in the room, and Nox could watch them all. I moved farther into the room, keeping my head on a swivel while trying to not look like that's what I was doing.

"I see her," Bastion said via text on my display. Because I had access to the cameras, then so did he.

Before I could say anything, a hand lightly touched my right shoulder and a barely familiar voice said, "My, what a lovely dress."

I plastered on a pleasant face and turned to see my admirer. It took me a moment to recognize him since we'd never actually spoken. Dark skin stretched lean over sharp cheekbones. Close-cropped, salt-and-pepper hair. Obvious rejuvenation surgeries made it difficult to pin down his age. He was wearing a rather traditional tuxedo. No glowing seams or holographic cape in sight. Sinclair Huginn, one of the wealthiest and most powerful people in the city. He was also the father of Theo Huginn-Intel, whose death I was responsible for. Another long story. My stomach knotted up and heat flared in my cheeks. Did he know me? Was he here for me? For revenge?

I smiled and said, "Thank you."

"Here alone?" Sinclair asked.

I kept my smile, but my guts twisted up at the question. He must know me, looking to corner me on his home turf. "Looking for my partner," I said. "Lost them in the shuffle over "

"Can I buy you a drink?" he asked.

No name or introduction. No pronouns. I looked at him closely without making it obvious. He didn't know me. He was hitting on me. I said, "No, thank you."

He held his hands up as though I'd attacked him. "Hey. No need to take offense."

It took everything I had to keep my smile in place. On the one hand, I wanted to punch him for the boorish behavior. On the other hand, I wanted to run, to hide before he recognized me, not that I'd been closer to him than 40 meters the night Theo died. Instead, I glanced over Sinclair's shoulder and said, "Oh, there they are."

The fool looked that way, and I quickly darted off in the other direction, weaving through the wedding guests in a zig-zag manner. Losing a tail was something I was trained for. Thank Corto.

"Who was that?" Nox asked.

"A potential problem," I whispered. "Let me know if I get too close to him again."

"Got it."

That's when I saw my target. Rahima Huginn-Cyber. She was wearing a burgundy and gold sari with holographic cranes flying along the sash. Her ears, fingers, and wrists bore more gold and platinum than any human should be wearing at one time. Says me, who avoids wearing jewelry.

"I've got a likely drop-off in sight," I said to Nox.

"Where?" he asked.

"Northwest corner of the room, near one of the bars." I described her.

"Looking her up," he said. I hated this part, keeping things from my apprentice. He didn't know Rahima was a big part of this operation, that Hessod and I had researched her for weeks, learned everything we could. Married. Three children. Lead developer on an experimental leg modification that was supposed to produce short-term flight. That experimental leg modification was based on plans stolen from Corto Corporation.

"I've got her," Nox said. "Rahima Huginn-Cyber."

"She's on the way to my exit," I said. "That's what matters."

Rahima was involved in an animated conversation with someone who looked nearly identical to her but dressed in a blue and silver sari. Involved was good. I could easily work with involved, especially in a crowd like this.

I weaved through the crowd, careful to keep Rahima in my sights without looking directly at her or her conversation partner. I smiled and nodded at the people I passed, looking every bit like a happy reception guest. I looped around, not taking a direct path to Rahima, but several arcs. Soon enough, I was close. I pulled the data drive from its compartment, discreetly palmed it, and then made contact. It was light and timed with another guest bumping into Rahima. She looked over at the other guest, who apologized, but she never looked at me. The drive was in her pocket, and I was on my way toward the exit.

I held up a hand in front of my face and gave a thumbs up, which was Bastion's signal. Alarms started to blare. Red lights blinked in the corners of the room. Metal security gates started lowering over the entrances and exits as a dozen more security guards poured in. I ducked under one of those gates as I eased through to an emergency stairwell exit. A little rush of adrenaline accompanied me, the little rush I always got when a plan succeeded.

The door shut behind me, muting the alarms. I leaned up against the door and waited.

"Anything?" I asked.

Nox didn't say anything for several long moments. Then he said, "No. No guards heading toward your location. They're focused on the other guests."

"Good. On my way."

"Do you want a timer on your display?" Bastion asked.

I nodded, knowing he would see the gesture from the wobble of my eyes. In the upper right of my display, a yellow countdown timer appeared, starting at 15 minutes and counting down. It was roughly how long I had before security reinforcements might arrive. They might not come at all, depending on if the guards on duty felt the need, but better to play it safe.

I pulled the hem of my dress up around my hips and started flowing down the stairwell, which was concrete, gray, and absolutely plain. My cybernetic legs made easy work of it, though, taking the steps down three at a time. In less than a minute, I arrived at a secured door and said, "Let me in."

The door opened from the other side, and Nox poked his head out. My apprentice was a head shorter than me with much darker skin. He kept his head and face clean-shaven, which somehow made him look even younger than he was. I opened the door completely and nearly laughed. He was dressed in a Huginn security uniform, an ill-fitting gray thing that did him no favors. Nox had a particular sense of style, always dressed in crisp whites and unfaded blacks, always tailored. He looked ridiculous in this Huginn uniform.

As soon as the door closed behind me, Nox wrapped me up in a tight hug, his arms pinning mine in place. I let him. I hadn't seen him in a month, after all. That's how long he'd been embedded here at the art gallery, living and working as a Huginn Industries citizen. False name. False CV. False everything. And our communications had been sparse during that time before today.

After 30 seconds ticked off from the timer on my display, I said, "Okay. We have work to do."

Nox let go and smiled up at me. "Good to see you, Star Girl."

I shook my head. I still disliked that nickname, but not enough to make him stop. He was so happy every time he said it. I took in the room. It was large, easily 30 meters by 10 meters. A huge section of one wall was taken up by viewscreens showing dozens of camera feeds from around the art museum. It was how Nox was able to keep tabs on me and help. It was also why I hadn't been worried about cameras. Nox was the only one looking at them today. The rest of the room was dotted with empty workstations, a large stack of crates in one corner, and hundreds of tubes lining the walls.

Ever since I'd entered, I'd been hearing swishes and thunks registering from the tubes, which were an array of different sizes.

"The painting is on its way," Nox said in answer to my unasked question.

"Which tube?"

"One of these." Nox pointed to a bank of rather large tubes across the room. At waist level, each tube had a clear, polymer panel with a handle on it. As I was looking at them, one of the tubes made that swishing noise, and then an enormous, rolled-up canvas slid into view with a gentle thunk.

Set off the alarms, and an automated system rolled up the valuable paintings and sent them down here. Just like Hessod and I had researched. Just like we'd planned.

"Tube 48," Bastion said in my ear. "And one of the guards did call reinforcements. They're searching all of the reception guests, but they haven't gotten to Rahima yet."

"Tube 48," I said to Nox.

"How do you know?" he asked.

"Call it intuition," I lied. Then I looked at all of the big tubes. "It's the only one that's still empty."

Nox grumbled and then wandered back over to the wall of viewscreens. "How are things back in Corto?"

"Same as you'd expect," I said, staying near the empty tube. The countdown timer on my display showed less than 10 minutes.

"And my uncle?" Nox asked, his eyes on the screens instead of me. I could hear the hesitancy in his voice.

I sighed. Nox's uncle was Solomon Corto-Intel, the Cloak of Corto. That was a title for the absolute best Intel Operative in the company, a title that was more than symbolic. The Cloak was a leader in the field, a mentor, and didn't answer to any manager. It was a job I'd wanted since I started as an Intel Operative. The dream. Solomon was also a mentor of mine.

"He's not used to the wheelchair yet," I said, swallowing my feelings of guilt over the events that led him to that chair. "Grumbles and groans whenever he gets caught on the corner of a table or has to take the long way to find a ramp."

He let a long silence stretch between us before he asked, "Is he talking to you yet?"

"No," I whispered. Nox knew about the rift between Solomon and me, even if he didn't know all of the details. There was nothing I could have done to prevent what happened to Solomon, but Solomon didn't see it that way. He was trailing Tazia Toinette-Intel, the Ghost of Toinette, his counterpart at Toinette Holdings, and I was trying to get up the Offworld Relay. They fought. Solomon kept Tazia from her objective, but not before she slammed a handful of neuro disrupters into his neck. They'd damaged his spinal nerves beyond repair, even beyond what cybernetics could handle.

I'd seen it all happen, watched a video feed while I was away from him, ascending the Offworld Relay to chase a different lead. Nothing I could have done. Maybe if I kept telling myself that, I'd believe it. Maybe my mentor would walk again, too, if I kept saying it.

Nox turned to face me. "Are you ever going to tell me what happened? Why he's giving you the silent treatment?"

I shrugged. I wanted to, but I wasn't sure how. Before I had to answer, the big, empty tube 48 started to make that swishing sound. The biggest canvas of them all slid into view and made a bigger thunk than the rest.

"Help me," I said, opening the door and grabbing the bottom of the rolled-up painting, the same painting that had hung behind the wedding ceremony. Even with all four of my limbs replaced with cybernetics, the canvas was heavy.

Nox and I grunted the painting out of the tube and onto the ground.

"What's so special about this thing, anyway?" Nox asked.

"Unroll it," I said while I pulled a special tool out of my right thigh. It was a metal and glass rod that I extended from 10 centimeters to half a meter. It wasn't something I normally carried on me, but I didn't often need a portable molecular scanner.

Nox unfurled the painting, which took up a lot of floor space. It seemed even bigger laid out like a rug rather than hanging on a wall. Nox asked, "Is the painter famous? Is it really old? From another planet?"

"No idea," I said. "There's code we want in the paint, though."

"Code in the…" Nox seemed to muse this over in his mind for a bit. He'd been undercover for most of this operation, so he didn't know what we were after or why. Poor guy. It's never fun being the new person. "Code in the paint? Like, computer code?"

I nodded and started moving the scanner over the painting, a readout on my display telling me how fast I needed to go.

"This is going to take you more than 10 minutes to scan the entire painting," Bastion said in my ear.

That was a problem. I didn't have 10 minutes left before extra security arrived. Mother of Corto.

"What can I do to help?" Nox said, pacing one end of the room.

"Be ready to run," I said. "We'll want to put this painting back in the tube before we go, but we're going to be rushed. Security reinforcements may arrive before we—"

"Sec Room One," a gruff voice said through a speaker near the wall of screens. "You there?"

Nox ran over to the screens, pressed a button, and said, "Sec Room One here. Situation?"

"We need data drive eval," Gruff Voice said. "Six so far and counting. I'm sending Alexi to you with the drives."

I paused in my scanning. The timer on my display didn't matter if one of the museum guards was headed this way. Before I had a chance to panic or start forming a plan, Nox cleared his throat and told the other guard, "I have an onboard. I'll be right there."

"Thanks, rookie," the other guard said, "but museum protocol says someone has to be in the office at all times."

"I know the protocol, Seb," Nox said in a weird accent. "I've read the entire handbook three times. What do you think I do on those overnight shifts?"

"Watching the cameras? Reviewing the logs?"

"Sure, of course I watch the empty camera feeds. But our protocol also says that if we don't take care of this in the next ten minutes, Huginn Security is going to be crawling all over our museum. They're going to call the docents, and then we'll all be sitting in this office getting yelled at while a bunch of over-modded goons who don't know anything about art are rummaging through the Cadoth exhibit.

"Besides," Nox glanced at me and winked, "Everyone in this museum is in that room with you. And that room is certainly secure with all of you there."

I winced. It wasn't a bad play, but my apprentice was pushing too much. I couldn't say anything, though, couldn't risk being overheard.

After a couple of seconds, Nox said to the guard, "It's your call, though. I'm just the new guy who reads too much."

Maybe too little, too late, but that was more like it. Then my apprentice did something very smart. He shut his mouth and waited, letting all the implications just roll around in the guard's head. Sure enough, in less than a minute, the other guard said, "Fine. Get down here. But be quick. It would be just my luck that one of those lazy docents would actually come check out the alarm while the security office is empty."

"You got it," Nox said. "Be right there." He disconnected the communication and flashed his teeth at me.

"Well done," I said and continued scanning. "Now go and do it. Gloat later."

"How much longer will you need?"

"Seven minutes and 40 seconds," Bastion said in my ear.

"About eight minutes," I said to Nox.

"See you then," he said. And he was out of the door.

"He's improving," Bastion said.

"Still too cocky. But he's always been good at the acting part, at infiltrating."

"Better than you?"

"I'll never tell him that to his face," I said.

"He's getting better at thinking on his feet, though. Learning from you how to navigate a mark and gauge the appropriate level of response."

"It's almost like I know what I'm doing."

"As an operative or a teacher?"

"Why not both?"

"Now who's too cocky?" Bastion said with a chuckle.

I let my arm keep scanning, moving steadily and evenly across the enormous canvas, scanning every molecule of paint and collecting data. I glanced up at the wall of camera feeds just in time to see Nox enter the frame. He was walking differently. His shoulders were hunched a little, but he smiled the same. He pulled up one sleeve, opened a compartment on his arm, and took a data drive from another guard, probably the one he'd spoken with earlier. Nox plugged the drive into a port in his arm, and after a few moments, shook his head. He unplugged it and exchanged it for another data drive. On the fifth drive, his eyebrows shot up and he nodded.

The room went into a different sort of tizzy then. The guard with all the drives pointed at one person, Rahima, of course. The rest of the guards who'd been detaining other people released them and converged on Rahima. That'll happen when you're discovered with stolen art files on your person.

Four minutes to go.

Instead of coming right back, Nox stood next to the guard from earlier and kept making conversation, his hands gesticulating toward Rahima, the cameras, and the rest of the room. The guard wasn't quite paying attention to Nox, though, trying to shoo my apprentice away and survey the room. Nox was buying me time, I was sure. I didn't know what he was saying, but hopefully he was being tactful.

As Rahima was being bound, hooded, and escorted out of the room by two of the bigger museum guards, Nox left the room. Less than two minutes of scanning left.

"Anything from Huginn's main security force?" I asked Bastion.

"I've heard nothing on open comms, but that's no guarantee that they aren't on the way. They could be using secured, rotating comms channels."

I tried to focus on my task, though I couldn't make it go any faster. I kept glancing at the camera feeds, watching the wedding reception awkwardly return to a festive mood, though it was easy to see that everyone was uncomfortable. I caught a glimpse of the newlyweds. One was in tears. I'd ruined their special day. I felt sorry for them and made a mental note to send an anonymous gift if I could. Those two had nothing to do with this plan. They were just in the right place at the wrong time.

Nox entered the security office just as I finished the scan.

"Help me get this back in the tube," I said.

"Huginn Security just landed," Nox said. "We need to thrust."

"Thrust?" I asked as I started to roll up the canvas.

"Yeah. Like, to go quickly."

"Are you just making these expressions up?"

Nox shrugged, then we finished rolling up the canvas and wrestled it back into the tube. By the time we finished grunting and groaning, a handful of the heavily modded security folk were in the reception room, talking to the museum guards and failing to be discreet.

"They're going to come here," Nox said. "They'll want to commandeer the room and check the camera footage, not that I left any to check. We have to—"

"After you," I said, interrupting. "You know the building."

Nox led and I followed, out the door and up the stairs, both of us taking them two or three steps at a time. My heart was skipping a little. Everything had gone well. We were almost clear. The idea of a perfect, undetected job gave me chills, and we were about to pull off another one. Seven stories later, he scanned his palm over a panel and opened a door. The corridor beyond wasn't part of the museum, but an office of some sort. I followed Nox still, jogging around a few bends before he opened a door to a landing pad.

We burst through and nearly slammed into a hulking Huginn security officer. Their cluster of optical mods looking down at us, a sneer on their face.

Sparks. So much for a perfect, undetected job.

"And where are you two going?" the officer asked in an impossibly deep voice.

Chapter Three

BEFORE I COULD MOVE OR say anything, Nox pointed a finger behind the guard and said, "That way."

The guard grinned, but they still glanced over their shoulder. In that moment, Nox's other arm flashed out. Something small and metallic flew, flicked gracefully from Nox's hand to slap against the guard's neck with a clang. Then the guard went rigid, fists balled up and teeth clenched together. They seemed to be vibrating. After a few seconds of that, they slumped to the ground. Still breathing, but unconscious.

I wanted to ask what that tricky little device was but as the guard slumped to the ground, a bigger issue presented itself. Leaning up against a security vehicle on the other side of the landing pad were three more Huginn Industries security officers. They were just as big and modded as their friend that Nox had just dropped. And they were looking at the two of us.

"Have any more of those?" I asked.

"Nope," Nox said. "You have any ideas?"

"Not good ones." The three guards stood up fully, glancing at each other and their fallen comrade. I looked at them and yelled, "By Huginn's eye! What happened? Help!"

"Not a good idea," Bastion said in my ear.

"Elise?" Nox said, his voice shaking.

Yes, three large, armed and armored security guards were trotting over to me. And I was just an Intel Operative. We were trained to work a room, sneak into impregnable places, pick locks, crack safes, and hack computers. A job well done meant one in which our presence wasn't discovered until days after it was over, after we were long gone. Rudimentary self-defense was part of our training, but not full-on fighting.

But the last year of my life had been anything but rudimentary. I narrowly escaped an assassin. Twice. I'd won a fight with a superior foe mostly on luck, and then nearly been killed by a professional fighter. I'd gotten into a terrible habit of making enemies that saw violence as their first resort. So after all of that and terrible radiation exposure forced me to replace my work limbs, I made adjustments to my approach.

I twisted my wrists twice, sending a small current into the subdermal network of metal mesh that ran through my hands. Why? Cybernetic fingers can either be intricate and agile or sturdy and cumbersome. The former were dedicated to tasks that required finesse such as picking locks, like my hands. The latter were good for slamming into security guards. This subdermal mesh, when lightly electrified, turned my nimble fingers into blunt instruments. I couldn't grip anything as they curled into unmovable fists, but they would do more damage.

As the first guard reached their fallen companion and saw the little device that Nox had used, I moved, plowing one of those fists straight into the kneeling guard's ear. They sprawled, clutching their ear and screaming in pain. Oh, did I mention that I let out a sonic discharge from my wrist at the same time? Yeah. Two blows in one when aiming for an ear. Thank you, element of surprise. One down.

The other two shifted quickly into fighting stances though, both deploying stun batons from both forearms. Arcs of blue electricity leaped from them, threatening the air with light and heat.

But I never go anywhere unprepared. "Fuchsia," I whispered. Bastion knew what that meant, and the outside edges of both of my forearms lit up in vibrant, fuchsia light.

The guard on my right took a big swing, and I met their stun baton with that glowing forearm. Fuchsia and blue sparks flew, and the guard bounced away before they could bring their other baton around. I ducked, partly relying on my own recent training and partly assisted by Bastion. He had access to all my systems, aural and visual included. Even if I was focused on one thing, Bastion was processing everything, so we both anticipated the other guard taking a swing out of my peripheral vision.

Their stun baton flew over my ducked head, and I jabbed up under their rib cage. In that same moment, I deployed the pneumatic pistons from my legs, rocketing upward with the same trajectory as my fist. Despite the armor on the guard, I felt bones give. We both flew up over a meter, and the guard crashed down on their back, wheezing and writhing in pain.

I focused on the last guard, the one I'd parried before. They were moving one hand toward their ear, probably ready to engage their comms and call for backup. No, thank you. I aimed both arms at them and whispered, "Grapples."

Magnetic grapples attached to thin, strong metal cables shot out, magnetizing to the guard's shoulders a breath later. Then I jumped and reeled them in. Fast. The guard stumbled, sure, but they were a lot heavier than me. I was counting on that. As they stumbled, I was flying toward them. Before they knew what was happening, my cybernetic knee slammed into their face. Metal and blood and translucent polymer sprayed. Bastion released the grapples as the guard crumpled, and I rolled past them.

I turned to look back, hands still up and ready for a fight. All three guards were down. All three were still breathing. The only one conscious was curled up on their side, gripping their shattered ribs. I let my hands and forearms go back to my sides, blowing out a breath and powering down my defenses. I was breathing hard, every muscle in my body tense and shaking slightly. Adrenaline is useful in the moment but was about to be a problem when I crashed.

"Let's go," I said to Nox.

He nodded and followed as I started for the outer edge of the landing platform. The rest of the Huginn Industries borough splayed out before me. It was night, nearing midnight, and the forest of skyscrapers was aglow with towering advertisements, hundreds of vehicles flying by, and little dots of residences and offices.

"Where is she?" I whispered to Bastion.

In response, a green line appeared in my display, hovering a few centimeters above the concrete, leading off the edge of the landing pad a few meters to my right. Bastion said, "Two meters straight down."

I walked that way with authority, breathing in the night air. A little humid and a little crisp. The rainy season was coming soon. A few months of extra clouds, heavy rain, and slightly cooler air. I hated it, but what do you do?

"How are we—?" Nox started to ask.

I cast him a glance that told him to be silent. To act cool. One of those guards was still conscious, after all. Nox quieted, looking like a wounded puppy. I reached the edge of the landing pad a handful of strides later and walked straight off. Sure enough, two meters down, I landed astride my flying motorcycle. Matte black and highly customized with hyperthrusters and a couple of dozen other upgrades, I called her Poe, after the ancient Earth poet. It was pretty easy for Bastion to access her autopilot, which was handy for situations like this.

I looked up, and Nox was standing at the lip of the landing pad, looking down and squinting. For all his fancy mods, apparently he hadn't upgraded his night vision. I flashed Poe's headlight twice, and Nox's eyes widened. He jumped down, landing awkwardly, but catching himself. He started to wrap his arms around my middle, and I slapped them away.

"No need for that," I said. "Magnetize your feet and squeeze the seat with your thighs. What do you think mods are for?"

"Sorry, Star Girl," Nox said.

He leaned back, and I pushed a button that deployed a seat back for him. Quynn had insisted on that upgrade. Something about my flying.

"That's nice," Nox said.

I smirked. Nice. We'll see about that. I opened the throttle. Nox let out a yelp as we accelerated into the night, flying back toward the Corto Corporation borough. Mother of Corto, I loved this bike. I hated that the rainy season was coming. Nothing ruined a good ride like hard rain. For tonight, though, I was just enjoying it.

#   #   #

I offered to take Nox out for dinner, a nice little celebration after a successful job. In a rather out-of-character sigh, though, he said he just wanted to go home. To shower in his own bathroom and sleep in his own bed. Right. Of course. He'd been embedded in Huginn Industries for nearly a month. I had done a dozen or so embeds over the years, though none that long. Even if it was for only a few days, though, coming home was a welcome relief.

I dropped Nox at his apartment, lifted back off from the landing pad, and called Quynn.

"Dinner?" I asked.

"Sure," Quynn said, though it sounded like they were already chewing something.

"Noodles?"

"You always want noodles."

"And?"

"We had noodles yesterday."

"Pizza?" I asked, sweeping Poe up and around a building, then descending into a major traffic lane.

"We're having pizza tomorrow with the group."

"Ugh. That means we have to clean the apartment tonight. Why can't anyone else host?"

"Because," Quynn said and swallowed before continuing. "It's your obsession. We're all just helping you."

"And I like having my speakers," Bastion said to both of us.

"Fine," I said. "So, noodles?"

"Sandwiches or curry?" Quynn said.

"Sandwiches sound good," Bastion chimed in.

"You don't eat!" Quynn and I said in unison.

"No," he said. "But it's nice to be included."

Quynn snorted a laugh, which made me laugh. Then we were just setting each other off, laughing for a solid minute. After we both calmed down and I had my breathing under control, I finally said, "Sandwiches do sound good. Fine."

#   #   #

We ate our sandwiches while I told Quynn about the job, leaving out nothing. We'd had issues over the last several months with that. I should say, I've had issues with that. Between Bastion coming into my life, several people trying to kill me, and finding out that I had a brother I never knew about, I'd resorted to keeping things from Quynn from time to time.

Okay. Right. We'd been going to therapy for the last month, and apparently, I like to minimize. I had been lying to Quynn. Repeatedly. Quynn is my partner, my love. There's no excuse for lying. And yet, I'd done it again and again. Most recently, when Quynn wanted me to back off Tazia Toinette-Intel, the Ghost of Toinette, I'd gone straight at her. It felt like the right idea at the time. How better to get her off my back than to find dirt on her? Not only did I not tell Quynn about it, but it backfired. Of course.

Tazia's hired muscle nearly killed me multiple times, her plan succeeded, and she permanently paralyzed Solomon, the Cloak of Corto and Nox's uncle. So now, honesty really was our best policy.

We ate and then cleaned while I gave Quynn the download. Finally, I was ready for a shower, our bed, and sleeping until I woke up without an alarm.

"Are your dress limbs charged?" Quynn said.

"Of course," I said. I owned three sets of limbs. My work limbs, of course. My everyday limbs were practically the first limbs I ever bought. A little stronger and faster than biological limbs, but pretty cheap. Then there were my dress limbs. Heavy. Expensive. They looked very much like biological skin but with a little extra panache. I didn't know why Quynn was asking about them, though, so I said, "Why?"

Quynn smiled in a way that meant they were about to break bad news. "Tomorrow is your mom's birthday."

"No."

"Yes."

"That means…"

Quynn's smile turned a bit devious. "Brunch."

I loved my mom, don't get me wrong. After my dad left, she raised me in the face of that. I was who I was because of her. Still, sitting through brunch with her on her birthday was the ultimate test of my patience.

I whined, but then a message appeared on my display. CALL ME NOW. It was from the CEO of Corto Corporation, Dr. Ariela Corto. No hyphen or division in her name because she was over all of them.

Quynn must have seen my face fall because they asked, "What?"

"Our illustrious CEO needs a word."

"My creator calling in one of her favors, I'm sure," Bastion said.

I sighed, sat down on the circular bench in our bedroom, and called the CEO.

"My office," she said by way of greeting. "First thing tomorrow morning."

"Hello to you, too. I have a pretty busy day tomorrow. I can't just—"

"You can. You will. 6:00. My office."

"Listen," I said. "I need to—"

CALL DISCONNECTED flashed on my display. I groaned. I take it back. Dr. Ariela Corto was the ultimate test of my patience.

"That was quick," Quynn said. "What does she want?"

"A meeting," Bastion said over the speaker.

"A very early meeting," I said.

"Oh, we're definitely going to be late to brunch," Quynn said.

I sighed. "Yeah."

Chapter Four

DR. ARIELA CORTO'S OFFICES WERE a master class in understated elegance. Visiting her meant landing on her private landing pad near the top of Corto 1, the tallest building in Corto Corporation, a glimmering black shard at the very heart of the borough, though the glimmer was dulled today by the heavy, black clouds overhead. Not everyone was allowed to land on that pad, but since I'd been summoned, the security guards let my Stryder land and let me walk into the offices without a word. Yeah, a Stryder, the largest automated rideshare service in the city, rather than my bike. Between my brunch outfit and the looming rain, I didn't want to take any chances.

A long, arcing desk stood across from the doors. Strangely, there was nobody there. Usually, there were two or even three assistants taking calls, booking appointments, and guiding guests like me where they needed to go. Not today. That didn't feel ominous or anything. I knew the way in, so I took a left into the outer office. Again, there was nobody there. No one else was waiting for the CEO of Corto Corporation. Dr. Corto's usual legion of workers wasn't buzzing around. At least if the CEO had me killed, Quynn knew I'd been here.

"This is disturbing," Bastion said in my ear.

I agreed but said nothing. I had to assume that there were cameras and microphones everywhere.

"Be careful," Bastion said.

I nodded once, hoping he would pick up on the gesture.

One of two things was happening. This could have been a power play, some sort of maneuver to psych me out before meeting with her. She wanted me off balance so she could gain an upper hand in whatever negotiation was about to take place. If so, it was kind of working. The other option was that Dr. Corto was being secretive, which was in her nature, of course. In this case, being secretive about me. That made sense. She had developed Bastion in secret and in direct defiance of Earth Space laws. She had me in her pocket since she was letting me keep him, but that bit of information could be her undoing. Best not to have anyone, including her own staff, looking too closely at me.

So, I kept walking, keeping my strides even and my head high. Maybe I was a little rattled, but there was no way I was going to let Dr. Corto know it. I entered her main office, which was empty in a way that I expected. Her massive desk was made of real wood. Keep in mind that the local flora of Little Sekmet Settlement, our planet, couldn't be made into wood, so that desk was shipped in from off-world. Very expensive. Half a dozen empty chairs surrounded the front of the desk like cushy sentries. The CEO's chair, which looked more like an ergonomic throne, was also empty. Again, I expected that.

Dr. Ariela Corto was waiting for me on her balcony, just like always. Despite the altitude and lack of any visible windbreakers, there was only a warm, calm breeze blowing across the expansive balcony. Some fantastic technology at work, no doubt. Dr. Corto was leaning up against a railing overlooking the borough, the sea of skyscrapers that stretched out as far as the eye could see. She was a head shorter than me and very fit. Her brown hair looked picture-perfect as it cascaded halfway down her back in gentle curls. She was wearing an ivory suit, tailored perfectly without being showy. That was how she always appeared, precise and expensive, but never flashy. She was sipping from a tall glass of clear liquid.

"Nice day," I said.

"Not really," Ariela said. She waved a hand, and a portion of the clear, blue sky shimmered and revealed dark clouds blanketing the city. A cool gust of rainy-season air made me shiver. She dropped her hand, and the false weather returned.

"Neat trick." I joined her on the balcony, leaning against it with one elbow but keeping my focus on the CEO. "What do you need?"

"You're going to Necropolis Alpha after this."

"You know about—?" I started to say.

"Of course I know about it. Just assume that I know everything you know before you do."

I hated that thought with everything in me. I said, "Fine. I have to debrief. I have brunch with my mother first. It's her birthday."

Dr. Corto turned and looked at me. "That explains the outfit."

She'd seen me in only two different outfits before. She'd seen my work attire, the limbs and jumpsuit all black from the neck down, my hair shellacked to my head. And she'd seen me in very formal attire at the galas when Quynn was in the running for the director position they now held. Today, I was wearing a gray-green pantsuit, the V of the lapels creating a plunging neckline. My black hair was brushed entirely to the left side, the shaved side clearly visible and highlighting a dangling earring of steel and green. I was even wearing a hint of makeup. I felt ridiculous, but Mom was going to love it.

Dr. Corto didn't seem impressed by the outfit. She looked me up and down, quickly, her mouth upturned. She said, "You're going to be called to Necropolis Alpha along with half a dozen other high-level operatives. Things are happening with Kotega, things that accelerate our efforts."

I blew out a breath. Tazia Toinette-Intel's grand plan was to put a member of the Toinette faithful in line to succeed as CEO of Kotega Industries, which she'd done, at least in theory. She'd sabotaged a huge gaming tournament, ensuring that Orogen Kotega-Seventeen won. In a culture based around ceremony and honor like Kotega, that might have been enough to put Orogen at the top of the succession list. I'd been waiting for some official word from the current CEO of Kotega, announcing her eventual successor. Maybe this was it. I hoped this was it. I was tired of waiting. I asked, "What things are happening?"

Ariela waved a dismissive hand. "Your people will get into that. We're going to talk about what you're going to do."

"Me? I don't even know what's happening, so how would I—?"

"Stop talking," Dr. Corto said. There was no spite or malice in the words, but they put me on my heels and shut me up. She was more curt than usual today, and it made me want to scream at her. Oh, how I wanted this meeting to be over. "You're going to embed. Gloria Siwa Kotega has an opening for a new Daeli. Gloria's head of house owes me a favor, so the position is yours."

I blinked, trying to process all of that information. Gloria was the older sister of Orogen. She had long been considered the heir apparent to the CEO's office until the tournament. Both she and Orogen were overachievers and held in high regard, but the tournament win seemed to have nudged her off the top spot. What was I supposed to do, though? What was the angle?

I blurted out, "What is a Daeli?"

"A proxy. You can look it up later."

"A ceremonial position in Kotega Industries," Bastion chimed in. "They date back from more hostile, disruptive times in the company's history when rival families would assassinate each other and vie for power. Now, Daelis merely—"

"Tell Bastion that he can explain it to you later," Dr. Corto said as though she'd heard him, too. "I don't have much time. I can only keep my staff out and occupied without raising their suspicions for so long. Just lucky that one of them has some big work anniversary today. Easily bribed with donuts, the lot of them. Anyway, the head of Gloria's house is named Zhao. Xey're expecting you to contact xem using the name Xyla Kotega-Cyber. Do whatever else you need with the identity, but that's the name Zhao is expecting."

"How—?" I said.

"You were staring off. Since you weren't using your hands on a haptic keyboard, I figured our mutual friend had your ear. Now focus. This plan is your plan. Your contact. However you have to sell it, this is how you're going to deal with our Kotega problem. Understood?"

I nodded, though I didn't fully understand. I had a dozen questions, and they were creating a dozen more.

Dr. Corto took a deep breath, downed the rest of her drink, and then turned to me fully. "You're going to find someone." She worked her jaw for a moment before she spat out a name. "Gowran Kotega-Media."

"Who is that?"

"Searching," Bastion said. "He's an editor for—"

"Works in Kotega's media division," Dr. Corto said. "He knows… things. Things he should not know. I need you to find him and eliminate him. Make sure it cannot be traced back to Corto Corporation."

"Eliminate?" I stuttered.

"Don't play the fool," Dr. Corto said. "It doesn't look good on you."

"I'm no assassin."

A horrifying smirk pulled up one side of the CEO's lips. "Really? I think Theo and Vert might disagree."

The names were like a one-two punch to my gut. Both of those men were dead. Both were my fault. It didn't matter if a faulty neural interface had blown out of Theo's brain, it was after the stress of our fight. And it didn't matter that I didn't put a cybernetic limb through Vert's eye. I called in the assassin who did. I saw their faces in my nightmares, thought about them often. It wasn't fair that Dr. Corto could find my weak spots so easily, pierce them with so little force.

I growled, "I won't kill for you. For anyone."

Dr. Corto's face hardened. "Make it so he never talks to anyone. About anything. Ever. I don't care what you have to do but don't forget that I own you. That AI you're carrying around isn't legal. Be a shame if you or Quynn were suddenly demoted to cleaning out toilets."

"You created that AI," I said with as much venom as I could muster. Nobody owned me. I didn't care what she knew or how much power she had, I wouldn't let her own me.

Dr. Corto smiled. "We've gone over this before, Elise, you don't want to pit your word against mine. Even if you can somehow knock me down into a deep, dark hole, I'll make sure your hole is even darker. Even deeper. And I'll make sure everyone you love is down there, too. I have levers that I can pull that you've never heard of. Friends in very high places that would surprise you. I don't even need to touch Quynn. I knock you down far enough and their career would nosedive right along with yours. That's how partnerships work here in Corto. So be a good little thief and do as you're told. I'm giving you a gift with Zhao. Now leave."

"I won't—"

"This conversation is over," Dr. Corto said, picking up her glass and leaving the balcony. "If you and your ridiculous bike aren't off my landing pad in the next three minutes, I'll have my security toss both of you over the side."

Bike? Ha. See, she didn't know everything.

"Wait," I nearly yelled. I wanted to yell, to scream at her, to throw HER off the balcony. But she had the upper hand here. I took a breath and continued. "I have one question. Unrelated to any of this, I swear."

Ariela stopped just short of the door to her office.

"Gibbingson Holdings," I said. "Have you ever heard of it?"

Something passed over her face. She was really good at being unreadable, but there was something. I'd surprised her. Nevertheless, she said, "No, I have not."

I would have believed her if not for that flicker of recognition. She wasn't giving me any information, but at least I knew the lead wasn't worthless. At least something from this meeting didn't make me want to strangle her.

The CEO breezed back into her office without another word. I stood there, unsure what else to do.

"We should probably leave," Bastion said after nearly half a minute had gone by.

"Yeah."

"I know you like diving off of buildings, but—"

"Not the time, Bastion."

"We'll find a way."

"What?" I asked.

"We'll find a way to do this without killing Gowran," Bastion said. "And maybe we can find a way to bring down my creator without incurring her wrath, too."

"I don't see how."

A reminder appeared on my display, then. 10 minutes: Brunch with Mom. Right. Two and a half minutes to leave the CEO's office. Ten minutes to get across the borough for an uncomfortable brunch. Then, debriefing. And apparently, so much more, including selling the CEO's plan as my own.

Chapter Five

"WE'RE NOT LATE," I SAID as soon as I opened the door to our apartment.

"We're always late," Quynn said from back in the bedroom. I couldn't see them, but our apartment wasn't that huge. I had just walked into the living room, a nice-sized space with a wall of windows looking out over the Corto Corporation borough. The dark clouds had finally let loose, beginning the rainy season in earnest, dulling the sheen of the city. Our white, sectional couch pointed at the large viewscreen on one wall, surrounded by shelves of pictures and trinkets of our lives. The small kitchen was to my left, a nook with some appliances, really. To the right, the door to our enormous bedroom. Quynn's voice had called out from there.

"Not always," I said, hurrying through the living room and into the bedroom.

Quynn was already dressed in a ruffled lavender suit. They were nearly two meters tall today, their hair long and black, cheekbones soft and round, with a jutting chin. They'd opted for a blend of masculine and feminine today, with significant musculature around their shoulders and arms and a slight swell of breasts. Quynn was gender fluid, using nanobots each night to change every aspect of their body from day to day. Except for their eyes.

One lavender like their suit, the other aquamarine. No matter what else they changed, those eyes always drew me in like home. Right now, they were applying light eye shadow around those eyes.

"We'll never hear the end of this from her," Quynn continued.

"That would be true even if we were on time. For once, I'm not the one running us late."

"Is that what you're planning to wear?"

"I was thinking about my tattered overalls and a tube top," I said in answer to Quynn's question.

"Hilarious," my partner said flatly.

"Too dressy?" I said with a smirk.

Quynn really looked at me finally. "You look great. Perfect for a nice, dressed-up brunch your mom loves."

I double-checked myself in the floor-length mirror. Nothing had been disturbed by my early-morning trip to the CEO's office. Hair and makeup and suit were all good, even if they didn't feel much like me.

"Yes," I said. "She could just come over here for lunch. Or we could go to her. But she wants to lunch at Ballerina Martini's. She wants to be seen for some reason."

Quynn finished their eye shadow and then reached for the blush. "She's just proud of us," they said. "We're both successful. She's playing the game."

"She's retired. She doesn't need to play the game anymore. And she doesn't know what I even do except for the Intel in my name."

"It doesn't hurt us to indulge her a little," Quynn said and checked their blush, making funny faces in the mirror. "Corto knows we do way more to indulge our bosses."

I grumbled and ran a brush through my hair. Just in case. Maybe I needed a fresh coat of lipstick, too. Maybe. No, it was fine. "Okay," I said. "Let's go."

"Shoes?"

I frowned. Since my feet were cybernetic, shoes were an accessory, not a utility. I didn't even think about shoes most days. "Right. Ballerina Martini's. Shoes required."

Quynn grabbed a pair of strappy black shoes with baby heels from my closet and tossed them to me. I slipped them on. "Now you're ready."

\#   \#   \#

Ballerina Martini's wasn't one of the fanciest restaurants in the Corto Corporation borough. I don't think it cracked the top 50, even. It was one of the nicest restaurants for those of us firmly in the middle class, however. Quynn was a director, sure, but I wasn't even lower management. We averaged out to middle class.

The tables had white tablecloths. The cocktails cost at least three Corto credits more than they should. The butter arrived in the shape of flowers. The food was really good, don't get me wrong, but you went to Ballerina Martini's if you were trying to push out of middle management and into the upper echelons. Quynn and I walked up to the maître de, but before we even said a word, my mom waved from a table by the windows, a half-empty cocktail glass already in her other hand.

"Smile," Quynn said.

I did, and we walked over to meet my mom.

"There are my kids!" Mom said with a toothy smile. There was no denying that she was my blood. A scant two centimeters shorter than me, we had the same brown skin, same cheekbones, and same thin eyebrows. While her hair cascaded halfway down her back and mine barely past my ears, it was the same straight, black hair. Mom did have slightly more curves to her, but only slightly. Her face was like looking into my future. 23 more years of worry creased gently creased her face. Her brown eyes had seen 23 more years of heartache. She stood and said, "What took you so long?"

"Told you," Quynn whispered.

"Shut it," I hissed. Then to my mom, I said, "I was held up at work."

"I know how that goes," Mom said. "When I was reporting to Benjamin – you remember Benjamin? – anyway, they would set the most foolish deadlines, completely unattainable without spending extra time in the office. That Benjamin was a go-getter. Still is, I suppose. He certainly moved up and on fast enough, that's for sure. I didn't keep track of them after they made senior director. But there were months when I was staying late at work every night. You had to fend for yourself, but we got through it, didn't we?"

"We did," I said as I sat at the table. I didn't remember Benjamin or this particular swath of time. No point in telling her that, though.

"And I suppose you can't tell me anything about your work?" Mom asked.

I opened my menu and said, "Nope. Sorry."

"And what about you, Quynn?"

Quynn unfurled their napkin and draped it over their lap. "The next generation of nanobots launches next week, so everything is this weird sort of calm. The code is in, the builds are finalized, and there are ads all over the borough for the next launch."

"I've seen those!" Mom said. "Almost every stream. Seems like every other block has a big billboard. So fast, so slick, and no tingling in the fingers?"

Quynn nodded. "Yep. Along with a few dozen other upgrades."

"I'm surprised it's so calm at your office with only a week to go," Mom said.

Quynn opened their mouth to respond, but Mom just kept going.

"I remember when the 11th-generation neural interface was about to launch, the Mobius, I think we called it. Our labs and offices were like hives. Everyone was there nearly around the clock. Last-minute tweaks and bug corrections, changes to the manufacturing sequence, and even our marketing folks were buzzing around asking too many questions. Do you remember that year, Elise? I think you were 14 or 15. I felt like I was never home for almost a month."

I shook my head no, but Mom wasn't paying attention. This was probably the 50th time I'd heard this story, but I also knew it was best to just let her finish. I only half listened while I perused the menu.

"My area worked on the feedback loop between the hands and brain. Those are some of the fastest-firing nerves, you know. You're not just dealing with the sense of touch, but the signals for fine motor skills. Have you ever heard of proprioception? It's our inherent sixth sense, the sense of where our body is in space. Like if you close your eyes and move your arm, you know exactly where your hand is. That's the trickiest thing to get right in neural interfaces. You have to make sure that if the customer has a cybernetic arm and hand, they know where that hand is even if they're not looking at it. So challenging."

Quynn nodded while they looked at their menu. I didn't think they were listening.

"The Mobius was a big misstep for Corto Corporation, actually," Bastion said in my ear. "Lots of latency issues and reports of misfiring fingers. Probably why things were so hectic around your mother's office at the time."

I kept my face neutral. Saying anything negative about Corto's neuro division would be received as a personal slight even if she'd had nothing to do with it. In some ways, that made my inability to talk about my own work a blessing. Mom couldn't accuse me of comparing my successes with hers.

"What have you been up to?" I asked Mom. I figured that would send her on a rant giving Quynn and me enough time to figure look over the menus. And maybe give us a new story. Probably not.

Rant, she did. She filled us in on her daily walks around her building, visiting her handful of friends who had also retired. She complained about her favorite market no longer carrying her favorite nut butter, and how she had a 20-minute conversation with the market's manager, but to no avail. I promised to find her some and bring it to her.

Then Mom started talking about her sister, Emerald, the family flunkie, according to Mom. Emerald married young and to a man that my mom despised. Emerald never seemed happy, always complaining and never making changes to her life, and Mom couldn't seem to let go. Mom told us about my aunt's latest problems and then started retelling stories Quynn and I had both heard dozens of times. There was no point in stopping Mom, though, no point in telling her that we'd already heard the stories. Mom would keep talking until it was out of her system.

The rant did give Quynn and me time to pick out our drinks and meals, though. We both ordered mimosas and omelets, and Mom finally ran out of steam when the food arrived. We ate. We drank. I took a long look at Mom's face. We were so similar. Looking at her was like looking into my future, seeing where my laugh lines would appear and which parts of my neck were likely to sag first. But there were differences, too. My lips were fuller. My chin more pronounced. My hands weren't like Mom's at all. Those features came from my dad, the man who abandoned Mom and me when I was 12. He defected from Corto Corporation, was discommended, and we now no longer speak his name. The same was true with any discommendation, their names fell from Corto mouths.

I hadn't thought about him much in the intervening years until a couple of months ago. I had met and worked with a young man named Valdo, a hacker living in Toinette Holdings. I discovered that his dad was mine. My father left Mom and me for Toinette and made a whole new family. I had so many questions that I hadn't been able to get answered. And it stung that Valdo wasn't in my life, that I learned he was my brother right after he told me in no uncertain terms that he wanted nothing to do with me.

"Mom," I said, swallowing hard. "Do you know what happened to my dad?"

Quynn's eyes went wide, glancing at me with an oh, no, you can't ask that look on their face. Quynn knew about Valdo. We'd talked about it, and Quynn had told me that they thought it was a bad idea to bring it up around Mom. But I had to know.

Mom didn't even flinch. She kept chewing on a bite of waffle, glancing at us with a slight smile then out the windows at the skyscrapers of Corto Corporation glittering in the mid-morning light, and swallowed. She took a sip of her own mimosa and said, "No, I don't think I do."

Then she took another bite.

"That's it?" I asked.

"Elise," Quynn hissed.

Mom swallowed, set down her fork, and really looked at me. "That's in the past, Elise. He left us. He didn't want anything to do with us anymore. He didn't love me anymore. I thought about him for a long time, but it doesn't do me any good to dwell on it or think about him now. My life kept going. So did yours. No point in thinking about a man whose name I'm not allowed to speak."

"But—" I started to say. I'd expected some emotion, rage or sorrow, not this flat rejection.

"I don't want to hear any more about it," Mom said with a note of finality.

But I'd found him. Seen him. I wanted to tell Mom that, but what good would it do? Quynn's words from previous conversations echoed in my head. He broke her heart and ruined her career. What good would it do to know that he found love, found a whole new career, and is actually father to someone? That would just break her heart all over again.

I sighed and said, "You're right, Mom. I'm sorry."

Mom smiled, though it looked pained.

"We got you something," Quynn said.

The pain vanished from Mom's face, her eyes sparkling. She'd seen the wrapped box when we walked in, of course, but leave it to Quynn to find the perfect time to lighten the mood. Mom unwrapped it and loved her gift. A quartet of servers sang for her birthday, and we didn't speak of my father for the rest of brunch.

Chapter Six

THE MAIN OFFICES FOR THE Intel Division of Corto Corporation were secret. Not just secret from the other companies of Jayu City, but from most citizens of Corto Corporation. Up until a couple of months ago, I thought those offices were the epicenter of our Intel operations. Dozens of analysts worked to gather information for operatives like myself, who went out into the city to acquire intelligence and items as needed.

For most of my career, I never asked why I was stealing a particular file or piece of technology. I was given a target. I worked with my analyst, Hessod Corto-Intel, to gather information and execute my operations. Steal what I needed to steal. I dropped it off at the Corto Intel vault and went on to the next job.

I'd found information on Toinette's Intel operation that the brightest minds in Intel hadn't turned up, which prompted Gustin, my manager, to raise my clearance level. To read me in, as the saying went. So I was taken down, way down below street level, and into a room called Necropolis Alpha. That's where the real work of the Intel Division happened, where high-level operatives and analysts played an elaborate game of intelligence and counterintelligence with Kotega Systems, Toinette Holdings, Nexus

Neuronics, and Huginn Industries. I still didn't know if there were other rooms like it. Apparently, I didn't have high enough clearance for that. Though the word "Alpha" in the name certainly implied there were more.

Down in Necropolis Alpha, we discussed the moves and countermoves of our own Intel operations and our competition. It was eye-opening to finally understand why different items were stolen. More than that, I now had a say in those plans. I was pretty low-ranking in that room, but everyone was listened to. The best idea in the room always won.

I was still a little blown away that I was and had always been part of such a vast and elaborate intelligence operation. It changed how I saw Corto Corporation and the rest of Jayu City, and I was only scratching the surface so far. Like how sometimes, the real target of a job wasn't at all what the rank-and-file Intel personnel thought it was. Like the code embedded in that painting I scanned. There was data in it, sure. Valuable, even. But the real target had been Rahima Huginn-Cyber.

Through a number of confusing backchannels, we'd discovered that Rahima had been smuggling schematics out of Huginn Industries and selling them to Nexus Neuronics. This was accelerating Nexus' development of neural interface firmware. That was going to cost Corto Corporation a lot of market share. So along with the code for that art installation piece, the data drive that I planted on her also contained several of the schematics that she'd stolen and what we'd intercepted.

Huginn Security apprehended her with the data drive. She'd be in trouble for stealing copywritten art. She'd be in even more trouble for stealing company secrets. The kind of trouble that meant she probably wouldn't see sunlight again if I knew anything about corporate regulatory punishment in Huginn.

I'd just spent the last 40 minutes telling my manager, Gustin Corto-Intel, every relevant detail about the job in Huginn. Every major success and minor complication. We'd met in a small office down in Necropolis Alpha, not his office upstairs. The information on Rahima was eyes-only, after all.

"And Nox didn't suspect anything about Rahima?" he asked.

"Not that I could tell," I said. That had been a very tricky line to walk for the last two months. I knew about Necropolis Alpha and the secrets it entailed, but my apprentice was far from that level of clearance.

"Good," Gustin said. "Sounds like the job went well." We'd been on better terms ever since I started coming to Necropolis Alpha. Maybe it was because he saw me as less of a short in his circuits and more of a model employee. Maybe at my next performance review, I'd find out. Now, he glanced into the middle distance, seeing something on his display that I couldn't see. "I hope your afternoon is clear. I didn't tell you before since we already had this meeting on the schedule, but we're about to have a meeting in the big room."

"Movement on the Kotega front?" I asked. My conversation with Dr. Corto was still fresh in my mind.

Gustin's eyebrows raised. "How did you know?"

"I'd say lucky guess, but haven't we all been waiting for the other shoe to drop there?"

He chuckled. "Fair enough. Come on."

The main room of Necropolis Alpha was like a theater, but instead of rows of chairs, it was rows of desks dotted with workstations. An enormous screen covered the main wall. Right now, it was blank other than the interlocking Cs of the Corto Corporation logo. More people than I'd ever seen in there at once were filing in. I recognized some faces, analysts and operatives I'd worked with over the years. Other managers. And sitting in a sleek, silver and gold wheelchair by the screen was the Cloak of Corto, Solomon Corto-Intel.

Solomon had been a mentor to me, almost like a father. Through my own poor decisions, he was now in that chair. Unable to walk. I tasted bile every time I saw him or thought of it. I couldn't have helped him. I couldn't. That didn't take away the sting. At least he was still the Cloak of Corto, though.

"Sit down," his gruff voice boomed across the room. "Hurry up."

Everyone did as they were commanded. I spotted my analyst, Hessod, sitting in a seat halfway down the room, near the center aisle. He was a big man. Tall, wide, and reveled in his size. I slid into the seat next to him, and Gustin sat on the other side of me.

"How was your date?" I asked Hessod.

He blushed. "It was okay."

"What's her name?"

"His name. And it was Alexi."

"Oh, sorry for the assumption."

Hessod shrugged. "I've been married to a woman most of the time we've known each other. You didn't know."

"Was he nice? Handsome?"

"Very handsome, but he doesn't like kids."

I grimaced. Hessod's daughter just turned 13. Not liking kids was a definite dealbreaker. "So when did you tell him it wasn't going to work out? Did you at least finish dinner?"

Hessod blushed even more. He focused on the big screen, not looking at me.

"You didn't!"

Impossibly, his face reddened so deeply, I was worried that a blood vessel might pop.

"Did you tell him," I leaned in close and whispered, "after breakfast?"

The red stayed as his mouth curled up in a big, goofy smile.

"Good for you!"

Hessod just shook his head, the smile still plastered in place. His divorce had been rough with a big battle over custody of his daughter. He'd been so much happier since everything was finalized. He seemed pretty happy with a 50/50 custody split, too, though I knew he liked having his daughter around more.

Before everyone had stopped talking, the Corto Corporation logo faded away. The lights dimmed. What looked like a news stream filled the enormous screen. Tenisha Siwa Kotega, head of the Siwa family and CEO of Kotega Systems, was standing in front of a podium. She was wearing a high-collared vest the same color as her straight, silvery hair that stopped just below her ears.

Standing to either side of her were her children: Orogen Siwa Kotega and Gloria Siwa Kotega. The two weren't twins, but they were barely a year apart, Gloria the elder. They were dressed in identical black suits. Orogen had short, spiked black hair. His build was trim, his face similar to his mother's and cleanly shaven. Gloria, on the other hand, was almost like looking in a mirror. Similar build, height, skin tone, and even hair to me.

"Thank you all for coming," Tenisha said. "You honor me and my family with your presence and attention." She looked out across the room. Though I couldn't see who was sitting or standing before her, Tenisha's gaze slowly swept from right to left before she continued. "Today, I make an announcement that many of you have been waiting for. I have notified the Kotega Systems board of my pending retirement. In 30 days, I will no longer be CEO and will find my place on the board instead."

Any remaining murmurs in Necropolis Alpha went silent. We'd all been waiting for this and the announcement to follow.

"At that time," Tenisha said, her face as stoic as if she were reading a weather forecast. "The new CEO of Kotega System will be my son, Orogen Siwa Kotega. I will take your questions, honored guests."

The stream paused and then faded back into the Corto Corporation logo as the lights came up.

"Not everyone here was in the loop on this, but we suspected this was coming," Solomon said. Then he gestured to the big screen. Images of Orogen and Tazia Toinette-Intel appeared on the screen. "Orogen, the next CEO of Kotega Systems, is a devout follower of Ibhalism, the corporate religion of Toinette Holdings. He was evangelized by Tazia Toinette-Intel, the Ghost of Toinette. You may know her as Josephine Toinette-Deus, which was a deep-cover alias she was using."

A murmur rushed through the room. I knew all of this. I'd been in on trying to stop her, but this was news to plenty of people in the room. It would have made me feel special if it didn't make me feel like a complete failure. It was why Solomon was in that chair, after all.

"Two months ago," Solomon continued, bellowing to quiet everyone, "she orchestrated Orogen's win at the Dregs of Osiris tournament on Cirilla Island. She meant to do exactly this, to get a devotee leading a rival corporation. Our belief is that once Orogen takes the CEO's chair, he'll work to bring Kotega Industries under Toinette, consolidating the two companies and evangelizing the entire company.

"We don't care about the religion. We care about what happens when two of the five Jayu City corporations combine. Particularly with the evangelistic motive, the new and double-sized Toinette Holdings will certainly try to take over the rest of the city. This young man taking his mother's seat means that the entire, very fragile balance of power in our city will be disrupted. The Corto way of life as we know it will end, either by coming under Toinette's religion or by merging with Huginn and Nexus."

I sucked in air through my teeth. Corporate culture was everything, it was our way of life. Toinette had their big religion. Huginn had their boisterous, hypercompetitive…everything. Nexus was so laid back that I was perpetually surprised they ever got anything done. Kotega was big on honor. Corto? I felt like we were the only sane ones, the ones who balanced work and life just right. Then again, I'd grown up in Corto. I'm sure people in other companies felt their cultures were the right ones. Point being, if companies started to merge and gobble each other up, our way of life would never be the same. Even though I knew all of this, it still made my stomach tie in knots having the entire scenario laid out like that.

"As you all know, we cannot act directly against a CEO, not that Tenisha is our problem. Even with a future CEO, we have to be very careful. The risk of exposure is very high with targets at that level. It's harder to hide our actions when we act against high-level targets. They have better security, more public eyes, and more powerful connections.

"That said, we have to stop Orogen from taking over as CEO. Gustin?"

Gustin cleared his throat as he stood up, shuffled past me, and walked down front to join Solomon. The screen changed again. This time, there were six pictures on the screen, including my own. My heart leaped in my chest. Was I in trouble? What was going on? But the other five pictures were of other Intel Operatives, the best of the best in my opinion.

"We need our absolute best operatives and analysts on this." Gustin pointed at the right-most picture and worked his way through them. "Val, Elise, Akosha, Hillel, Penny, and Colm. These are our best operatives. Many of you don't know each other, and most of the analysts in this room have only worked with a few of them. From this point forward, you'll all be divided into teams supporting these six."

Gustin looked at Solomon. The Cloak's face darkened, but he nodded.

Gustin looked back at the room. "Solomon has decided that he is no longer able to fulfill his duties as Cloak of Corto."

My stomach came to my throat, and my vision went blurry. I wanted to leap to my feet and scream, No, no, no. I loved that man like a father, and it was my fault he was in that chair. My fault this terrible announcement was shredding me from the inside out. The voices in the room echoed my shock. Solomon was the best of us. I couldn't imagine anyone else as Cloak. Of course, there had been others before him. Others would follow. I wanted the title myself one day, but not yet. Not yet.

Gustin continued, "The decision was his. If you have questions about it, take it up with him. Corto Corporation cannot be without its Cloak, however. Whichever of these operatives manages to stop Orogen from becoming CEO of Kotega Systems will be our next Cloak. All analysts on that operative's team will receive bonuses and possibly promotions, as well."

What erupted from that was more than a murmur. Hessod's jaw dropped, his eyes wide as saucers as he looked at me.

"Mother of Corto," I blurted out louder than I'd intended.

"You could be the next Cloak," Hessod said, a smile growing with every syllable.

"Yeah," I said. It was exciting, my ultimate career goal right before me, but guilt ran through me like a fiery river. I couldn't celebrate a potential promotion, my ultimate career goal, when I was responsible for Solomon's paralysis. It was my fault that he was stepping aside. That I might be the one to benefit from it just made me feel even worse.

"Analysts, check your emails," Gustin said. "You've already been divided into teams. You'll be working through each operative's primary analyst. Those names are also in your emails."

"That's you," I whispered to Hessod, trying to cheer myself up by cheering him on.

"I'm going to have a team," he whispered back. I think he was in awe.

Gustin continued, "Val, Elise, Penny, Kosha, Colm, and Hillel, Conference Room A in 10 minutes." With that, Gustin stepped aside.

"You all know the stakes and the mission," Solomon said, quieting the room again. Then he looked directly at me with the darkest expression

I'd ever seen. Each word he spoke was like a dagger to my heart. "Work together. Trust each other and earn that trust by keeping each other safe. Whatever personal issues in your life, those take a back seat."

Then my picture and the rest of the operative pictures faded from the giant screen, replaced by three words in large, blocky font.

"This is our operational codename, The Cordelia Solution. Outside of this room, I expect no mention of Kotega Systems, my replacement, or anything else we've talked about today. Use the codename if you need to talk about it, but every aspect is eyes-only. We have 30 days. Let's get to work."

Chapter Seven

30 Days to Ascension

THE SIX OF US FILED into the narrow conference room around the even narrower, polymer table. The room was as plain as it was ugly. Blank, beige walls. The table was a tepid gray, and the chairs were a darker gray. They were more comfortable than they looked, at least. The other five Intel Operatives jockeyed for the chairs closest to where Solomon would hold court. I let them. I took the chair at the opposite end of the table. Solomon and I hadn't really spoken since Tazia paralyzed him. I'd tried to reach out, and he'd given me the cold shoulder. I could take a hint even if it stung.

Before we were all seated, Solomon entered and barked, "Sit down. I'm not going to be the Cloak much longer. Sitting closer won't do you any favors."

Everyone finally sat, though half of the room sighed. The door opened again, and Gustin strode in, taking the last seat, which was near me. Gustin and I had never been friends. Matter of fact, up until a few months ago, I was pretty sure he didn't like me. Our relationship had thawed significantly since he'd brought me down to Necropolis Alpha. Maybe it was because he saw me as more than just another Intel Operative. Maybe it had something to do with trust. I wasn't sure. He was still my manager, and Gustin kept all of his direct reports at a distance.

Solomon looked at everyone in turn. Nearly everyone, at least. His eyes skipped over me like I wasn't even there. "I know I just gave you all a lot of information," Solomon said. "And a big ask. I don't expect anyone to have solid plans for how to approach Kotega yet, but I'd like to work through some ideas. What are you thinking? What assets do you have that you can leverage? That sort of thing. You're competing with each other, sure, but this job supersedes everything, including your career goals. So let's hear it."

Most everyone looked down at the table. I followed suit. I needed to sell Dr. Ariela Corto's plan as my own, so I needed to look ponderous for a while.

Penny spoke first. "I've made contacts in Kotega's Security division."

Solomon raised an eyebrow. Intel and Security in any borough got along like CEOs and negative quarterly reports. Security felt that half their job was to stop people like us from doing our jobs.

Gustin said, "Do your security contacts have interactions with the Siwa family? Access to Orogen?"

"Maybe."

"What do I say about maybes?" Solomon barked.

"They're as useful as empty safes," all of us operatives mumbled. We'd heard it many times. Any intelligence that wasn't actionable wasn't really intelligence.

"A blunt way to put it," Gustin said.

Solomon shot him a warning look before asking the rest of us, "What else?"

"Is Dr. Corto doing anything? Talking to Tenisha about Orogen's religious affiliation?" Val asked.

"Gustin?" Solomon said.

"They've had conversations," Gustin said. "I'm not privy to them, but the short version is that we don't have solid enough evidence for our CEO to broach the subject with theirs. There are all sorts of other social codes that would be broken if Dr. Corto were to discuss Tenisha's successor with her, as well."

Val sighed.

"But that's why we exist," Solomon grumbled. "If we left everything to the bureaucracy, nothing would ever get done."

We all laughed a little at that, even Gustin.

I'd looked ponderous for long enough. I cleared my throat.

"Something to add, Elise?" Solomon asked.

I took a deep breath. "I have a contact in Gloria's household. Zhao, her head of house."

Solomon furrowed his brow. Everyone else's faces suddenly whipped over to face me. Right. No pressure.

"Gloria?" Solomon said. "Orogen's sister?"

I nodded. "There's an opening for a new Daeli. Zhao owes me a favor. A big favor."

"Are you suggesting…?"

"That I take the job? Yes. Embed in Gloria's household. Right in the inner circle of the Siwa family. I'll have proximity and access to Gloria, Tenisha, and even Orogen. Maybe I can find that evidence we need for Dr. Corto to intercede. Or just expose it directly to the Siwa family."

Solomon leaned forward, resting his face on his steepled fingers. After a long minute, he said, "You're not our best embed."

"But it's a good plan," Gustin said. It still felt strange for Gustin to speak up for me, especially against Solomon. It was like their roles had reversed. My once-confrontational manager was now backing me against my former mentor who was doing his best to avoid me. Gustin continued, "And Zhao can certainly get you in. Xey were Gloria's proctor starting when she was 12. Once Gloria came of age, Zhao became Gloria's head of house. There's some unbreakable trust there, which means some of that trust will pass to you."

"Maybe we can leverage that contact," Solomon said. "Embed Penny or Colm, someone better at that sort of thing."

"It's my contact," I said. "My plan. The best idea in the room right now. You can't just steal it from me."

"Stealing is what we do best," Solomon practically growled. "And what about your apprentice, huh? You can't spend the next two months away from him."

I opened my mouth to reply, but Gustin beat me to it. He said, "Actually, that's a good idea."

"What's a good idea?" Solomon said.

"Nox is excellent at embeds. He's a natural. If we can embed him in Kotega in proximity to Elise, he can help her. A little flip-flop of the mentor-apprentice relationship, but one that we can leverage."

"Nox isn't read in," Solomon said in a huff.

"He can be, at least for this," Gustin said. "Like you said, this mission supersedes everything."

Solomon glared back and forth between Gustin and me. My fellow operatives shrank in their seats, silently watching the confrontation. After several tense seconds, Solomon said, "You can't. Nox isn't ready. It's too dangerous, and we cannot compromise this mission."

Gustin didn't get angry. He rose to his feet, his face perfectly neutral. "I know he's your nephew. You're concerned. I get that. But Nox and Elise are my direct reports. It's my call. They're embedding. Both of them."

Solomon stared long and hard at my manager, who stood there and didn't flinch. It's like I was a kid, and my parents were fighting. Scary and exciting all at once. After a long minute or two, Solomon said, "Fine. What about the rest of you?"

#   #   #

"And this was Dr. Corto's idea?" Quynn asked after swallowing a bite of pizza.

I nodded and took a bite of mine, glancing out the windows. The rain was coming down in heavy sheets now, slowing traffic and turning the glowing city into a wet haze of muddle lights.

"I don't like it," Quynn said.

"I don't, either," Hessod echoed. We were all sitting in the living room of Quynn and I's apartment. Hessod, Quynn, myself, and Bastion's speaker was turned on. Ever since we'd brought him into our lives, we'd installed speakers so that he wasn't just a voice in my head when I was home. This

60

wasn't quite everyone that knew of Bastion's existence. There was Dr. Corto, of course. But also, Solomon and Valdo. Their absence from these weekly meetings pained me. Neither had wanted to talk to me since Cirilla.

"And you'll be there for how long?" Quynn asked.

I nodded toward Hessod.

He quickly swallowed and said, "It'll take at least a week to get Elise and Nox ready. We need to build the false Kotega identities for her and Nox, plus rigorous cultural training. We usually take a month or so for these embeds, but we don't have that kind of time. Gustin has given me nine days."

"Why nine?" Quynn asked.

"He wants it done in a week. I got a couple extra days out of it. Still gives Elise and Nox three weeks in Kotega. After that? Well, Orogen becomes CEO in one month. So either they prevent that from happening or come home once he takes that seat."

"A little over a week here, then up to three weeks in Kotega," I said.

"That's a long time," Quynn said. "Will you be able to contact me?"

Hessod shook his head.

"Why?" Quynn asked with sudden heat in their voice.

"I won't be able to use my normal communications array," I said in my most calming voice. "Hessod is building me a network tunnel so that I can communicate securely."

"We'll have to change out her comms array for a Kotega unit," Hessod said. "And given her proximity to Gloria, we have no doubt they'll be monitoring her comms traffic. The only problem is, we only have approval to build one tunnel, and that's to me."

"My only point of contact will be Hessod," I said. "And even that will be sparse."

"Through a coded, web-based system. There are about a dozen firewalls to deal with," Hessod said.

"I hate that," Quynn said."

"You have me," Bastion said.

We all turned to face the speaker.

"I can keep you two in contact with each other," he said.

"But my comms array—"

"I have other ways," Bastion said. "I can relay messages between you with relative ease, all without using your communications. I can use The Net."

"How does your access work, Bastion?" Hessod asked. "We have to assume that all Net traffic in and around the Siwa family will be closely monitored."

"Normally, I use whatever connection is available to me," Bastion said. "But I can get creative. Short of a Faraday Cage, I can gain access to The Net, bypassing whatever firewalls try to block me. I have full confidence that I can circumvent any Kotega Systems trying to monitor Elise. The two of you won't be able to speak directly, but I'll be able to relay messages between you. It may prove easier than the digital tunnel you're trying to establish, Hessod."

Hessod's eyebrows rose slightly as he took another bite.

A little tension left Quynn's shoulders. "At least there's that. I still don't like you being so isolated, so cut off from us."

"I'll have Nox."

"That doesn't put my mind at ease."

I sat my plate down and focused on Quynn. Lessons from therapy came to me. I needed to be present and really listen to Quynn's concerns. I was working on that. I said, "What would?"

Quynn glanced outside, gazing out at the waves of water painting the skyline gray. Eventually, they said, "You'll be able to stay in contact, keep me in the loop so I can help you plan. Both of you."

Hessod and I both nodded.

"And Nox will watch your back." Quynn sighed. "I guess that's not nothing. It's not like we have a choice."

"Not really," I said. "Dr. Corto didn't give me an opt-out clause."

After a few more moments, Quynn blinked and waved a hand in the air. "Enough of that. Any new leads? Anything on Gibbingson Holdings?"

"Nothing since I saw their logo at the Offworld Relay," I said.

"I have not been able to find any trace on the Net," Bastion said. "Not even a mention."

Quynn said, "All five companies of Jayu City are funneling their marketing information to this mysterious Gibbingson Holdings, but it doesn't seem to exist? That doesn't make sense."

"It could be a shell game of some sort," Hessod said. "A fake name for another entity. You'd still think something would turn up. I'm working on an algorithm to search for the logo in online images. It's a lot harder than searching for text, but it might point us somewhere."

"I did ask our illustrious CEO about Gibbingson Holdings," I said.

"She's never heard of it," Bastion said.

Fascinating. Bastion had access to most of my systems, including my optical mods. He saw what I saw. What's more, he could replay and zoom in on things I'd already seen. She'd said she'd never heard of it, sure. But that look that passed across her face told another story. And yet, Bastion didn't see it or didn't notice it.

"And?" Quynn said, breaking me from my thoughts.

"She's heard of it," I said. "I saw it on her face. She lied and said she didn't, but I saw the surprise on her face."

"So, it's real," Hessod said.

"In some fashion," I said. "It must be. Not that a wayward facial expression tells us much."

"After two months of nothing, that's at least some encouragement to keep looking," Hessod said.

"I just hope it's worth it," Quynn said.

That stung, but those were words I'd heard from them before. Theo's dying words about the five companies being connected still haunted my dreams. He'd felt it was important enough to mention to a stranger, an enemy before he died. It had to be important. And I'd sacrificed so much in pursuit of that connection. I'd found it, or some part of it when I went up the Offworld Relay and left Solomon to his fate.

"I can't stop now," I said.

"Which begs the question," Quynn said. "How do we keep looking into all of this with you embedded in Kotega?"

"I can keep working on my algorithm," Hessod said.

"And I'll be able to make sure your lines of communication remain open," Bastion said.

"It won't be easy, though," I said. "I don't know if or how often I'll be able to sneak away. And this job, stopping Orogen from taking over as CEO of Kotega, it really is important. I can't just ignore it."

"Although," Quynn said, chewing on the word. "You will be in much closer proximity to a CEO. There's no way you could ever poke around in Dr. Corto's files. She knows your face. Corto Corporation knows your biometrics and cybermetrics, might be tracking everything you do."

"But not Kotega," I whispered. "And if anyone in Jayu City will have information on any connections between the companies, it would be a CEO."

"I don't think that's wise," Bastion said. "You already know this job is flying dangerously close to directly interfering with a CEO. Your wings could melt, Icarus."

Hessod, Quynn, and I blinked at each other.

"Who is Icarus?" I asked.

"An old Earth myth," Bastion said. "The point is, you would put yourself and your career in serious jeopardy."

I shrugged. "This group, this entire inquiry does that. You know that, right?"

"You also have no idea what sort of security Tenisha Siwa Kotega has around her or her offices. I think you should stick to your given mission."

"Oh?" I said. "Which one? The one Solomon and Gustin gave me to stop Orogen from becoming CEO? Or the one our CEO gave me to assassinate someone I've never met? Or how about protecting and teaching my apprentice? Or keeping the secret of your existence safe? Which mission are you talking about?"

"How does that—?" Bastion began.

But I wasn't done. I was angry that he did this, kept getting in the way instead of helping sometimes. "I'm constantly juggling missions, goals, whatever. It's what I do, what I'm always doing. I'm not going to let this business with the five companies slide just because I'm stuck in a different company with a fake name."

Bastion was silent.

Hessod shifted in his seat, looking uncomfortable before he said, "Even if it is too dangerous - and I'm not saying it is - we're a team. We all pitch in.

We all help. You'll be in Kotega, but Quynn and I won't be."

"Just," Quynn said, "talk to me before you go breaking into another CEO's office."

I nodded to them. "Strategic, not just tactical. I got it."

Quynn smiled. We waited. I squished crumbs on my plate and ate them off my thumb.

"We're going to talk about this assassination thing, too, right?" Quynn said.

"Seriously…" Hessod said.

"I'm not doing it," I spat. "I'll talk to him, this Gowran. Find out what he knows, why Ariela wants him gone. If it's juicy enough for her to want him dead, then I really want to know it. It's ammunition I can use."

"And what happens when you get back and this guy is still breathing?" Hessod asked.

"I don't know yet. I'll figure it out." I glanced at Quynn, who looked worried. "We'll figure it out."

Quynn smiled again. See? Therapy was helping.

I said, "Bastion? Are you going to just stay mad and silent?"

"I'm not mad," he said. He sounded mad.

"I'm going to be careful," I said. "We all are. I'm not going anywhere near Tenisha if I think it might jeopardize the Cordelia Solution."

"I still think it's foolish to try," he said.

"Noted," I said as I stood up. "Anything else? I need more pizza."

Hessod hopped to his feet and darted into the kitchen ahead of me. He hollered back, "Pizza!"

"Nothing else from me," Quynn said, rising to their own feet.

Bastion said nothing.

"Did you two catch the last episode of Kaden Corto's Run?" Hessod asked. "The Face was a guest star. She was terrible."

"LeGrand Corto?" Quynn asked. "The CEO's pet marketing gal tried her hand at acting?"

Hessod nodded, piling three slices of pizza on his plate. "How is she supposed to act when her face can't even move?"

"And those ridiculous eyelashes!" Quynn said, moving into the kitchen next to him. "Elise met her once. Said every time LeGrand blinked, the wind nearly knocked her over."

We all laughed. It was an exaggeration, sure, but a funny one. I wished so much that Valdo was here, too, helping with our plans. Or just being my little brother. I wanted to get to know him so badly. I still couldn't believe I had a little brother. And he wanted nothing to do with me, didn't even know we were related. That didn't make me want him here less. Soon, I wouldn't even be here. Three whole weeks without seeing these faces, hearing these laughs, tasting this pizza. Sure, Kotega probably had pizza, but it wouldn't be the same.

"And her laugh…" Hessod said. "Mother of Corto!"

Chapter Eight

24 Days to Ascension

The next days were a blur. For 12 hours each day, Nox and I were together with Hessod and a half dozen other analysts in the main Intel Division office, tucked away in a specially secured conference room. We were cramming information that every Kotega Systems citizen would know by heart. Not just the stuff that I could find on the Net like the date of their Founder's Day, the different divisions, VPs, and so on. That stuff was easy to memorize. We needed to learn their culture.

I knew some of it already, of course. I'd done jobs in the Kotega borough. Dozens of them. Those were different. Get in. Get out. Try not to be seen. Easiest way to blend into a society that valued honor and did a lot of bowing? Cast your eyes down and bow slightly at everyone who comes near you. When everyone perceives you as a lower status than they are, their eyes pretty much pass over you.

As the Daeli in the greatest house of Kotega, however, my place was going to be very specific. Some people were going to bow to me. Being visible was part of the job.

"What is a Daeli, anyway?" I asked during one of our marathon cramming sessions.

Hessod tapped some keys on his workstation and said, "A proxy of sorts. The position dates back well over a century, to when the company was more feudal. Members of the major houses were known to assassinate rivals."

I arched an eyebrow. I wasn't going to jump in front of a bullet for some wealthy CEO's daughter.

"They don't do that anymore," Hessod continued. "The Daeli is part of the honor system now. You'll sometimes go to meetings in Gloria's stead. You'll taste her food at large functions. Occasionally, you'll work as a bodyguard. Most often, you'll be her body double."

I opened my mouth with a litany of arguments ready.

"It's ceremonial, I assure you. And you're roughly the same height, build, and skin tone as Gloria. Close enough that a little holographic distortion can handle the rest."

Speaking of skin tone, my normal work limbs weren't going to be able to accompany me to Kotega. They were black carbon-polymer. And I don't mean skin-tone black, I mean black as the night sky. Since my cover story had me coming from a low-ranking household and not an Intel Operative, those limbs were right out. Instead, our R&D people were creating a new set of limbs for me. They were going to look similar to my everyday limbs: cheap and functional. They were going to be loaded with tools, though. Not as many tools as my work limbs, though. So I was working through a list of everything I would absolutely need for the job. And nothing else.

I hated that list. I liked my tools. All of them.

I barely saw Quynn during those days. When I was home, I was either sleeping or running through digital flashcards, trying to absorb every ounce of information. Sure, I had Bastion. He would be a leg up. Throughout the training, he would frequently provide me with additional, helpful information. At first, it was just information overload, but he learned how to balance that load for me after a couple of days.

But I wasn't going to use Bastion as a crutch. He was fast. Intuitive. But I needed to behave as though I'd spent my entire life as a Kotega Systems citizen. If I was asked a question by Gloria or Zhao or, Corto forbid, Orogen,

I would need to answer immediately like the information was in my bones. I couldn't wait for Bastion to find the answer.

Six days in and just as I was about to head home for the day, Gustin stepped in front of me. "We need to go downstairs."

"Now?" I asked. I hadn't been sleeping well, and I really just wanted to go home, eat, and go to bed early.

"Unfortunately," he said.

I sighed, and we took the elevator down, down, down to Necropolis Alpha. The big room was mostly empty except for Solomon down by the big screen in his wheelchair. He was talking quietly with an analyst named Mione.

"What's going on?" I asked Gustin as we started walking toward the front of the room.

"We have a lead on another of Tazia's safehouses," he said.

"There are more?" I asked as Bastion said the same thing in my ear.

"At least one more," Solomon said.

Since the events on Cirilla Island and Tazia vanishing, I'd broken into seven different safehouses our analysts were able to identify as Tazia's. Spread out all over the Toinette borough, each one had been a bust. Four had been hastily emptied out, indentations still fresh in the carpet from where furniture had sat. The last one had been burned out, literally. I found traces of accelerant. The fire had taken out half of the apartments on the floor.

"Who are we sending in?" I asked.

"You," Solomon said.

"Kind of getting ready to embed in Kotega," I said. "I'm a little busy."

"This can't wait," Solomon said, turning his chair to face the screen, which changed to a map of the Toinette borough with a single building highlighted.

Mione gathered up a few devices and walked past me silently and out of the room, not even looking at me. Seemed that Solomon's hostility was rubbing off.

"I'm not in the mindset to—"

"It has to be you," Gustin interrupted. "Nobody knows Tazia like you do. Based on our track record with her other safehouses, we need to get in there immediately. It might already be empty, but we won't know until we go. We don't want to waste time reading anyone else in."

"Toinette Building 91," Solomon said without looking at me. "You'll be heading down to—"

Gustin inhaled sharply and loudly enough to stop Solomon. We both looked at my manager, his eyes wide. He was looking at something on his display, and then he started back up the stairs to leave the room. "I have to go."

"Gustin," Solomon said.

Gustin looked back, his eyes wide. "It's time. Elise, this is Solomon's op. Take his orders like mine."

Before I could say another word, Gustin was bounding up the stairs and out of the room.

"What was that about?" I asked.

"His wife," Solomon said as though I should have already known. "She must have just gone into labor."

"He's having another kid?"

Solomon smirked. "I may not like the guy much, but I admire his professionalism. He leaves home at home." He turned back to the screen. "As I was saying, Toinette Building 91."

I suddenly realized we were alone in the big room. Alone for the first time since Cirilla. I took a big breath, steeled myself, and said, "Solomon."

"Focus."

"Solomon."

"You have a job to—"

"I'm sorry." My voice cracked.

Solomon stopped talking. He was looking up at the enormous screen. After a few minutes, he said, "You abandoned me, abandoned the mission. You should have been there to back me up."

His words were like a kick to my gut, right on target. "I didn't abandon you—"

Solomon suddenly wrenched the wheels on the chair hard to spin on me. "Then what in the name of Corto were you doing up there? Shutting down the Offworld Relay? What part of that was supposed to help stop the

Ghost of Toinette?"

I didn't have an answer for that. Only guilt. Regret. I'd thought he'd stopped Tazia. I'd thought he had her in hand. And he did until he didn't. Through a security camera feed, I watched her beat him, plunge a handful of neural interface disruptors into his neck, and run away.

"I'm sorry," I whispered though those two little words felt so inadequate.

"Why?" he bellowed.

"Why am I sorry?"

"Why did you do it? Why did you go up the Offworld Relay instead of helping me?" There was a shakiness to his voice that I'd never heard. Solomon was like a rock, one of my mentors, and he'd always seemed absolutely unflappable. I didn't know how to handle this newfound vulnerability in him. I didn't like it. I was supposed to be the one to get emotional with him, not the other way around.

"Answer me!" he yelled.

"The Five Companies!" I yelled back, not meaning to. What was I doing? He couldn't walk because of me. He was giving up his dream, the Cloak, because of me. Why was I yelling at him?

Solomon's face twisted up in surprise and confusion.

"There's a connection between them, something I don't understand," I said, shaking and holding my voice as steady as I could. "And it relates to Bastion somehow. Theo Huginn-Intel, the man I…I killed, the man who stole Bastion's chip, he told me about it. Said it with his dying breath."

Solomon worked his jaw for a moment before he said, "And you thought that was more important than Tazia's plan? More important than me?"

"No," I said. "I—"

"Yes, you did. You chose to go up that tower while I was fighting for my life. She won. I lost." Another kick, perfectly aimed again, like the words from my conscience were coming from his mouth. Tears were hot on my face, falling unbidden.

"You can still be the Cloak," I muttered.

"From this chair?" Solomon said with a shake of his head. "I don't think so. The Cloak needs to be in the field, sneaking into buildings and going toe-to-toe with security guards. Those days are behind me."

"Did they make you—?"

"No one made me do anything," Solomon said. "This was my decision. My choice."

"A choice you shouldn't have had to make."

"No," he said. The venom was gone from his voice, replaced entirely with sorrow. Somehow, that hurt even worse. Solomon was gruff, not sad. Never sad. He said, "Was it worth it?"

I stood there, clenching my fists, trying and failing not to cry for him, for our broken relationship. Of course, it wasn't worth it. I'd seen that marketing data from our planet was all flowing to some mysterious company called Gibbingson Holdings. For that scrap of information, Solomon couldn't walk, and our relationship was ruined. After several long seconds, I said, "No. No, it wasn't. Where do we go from here?"

"You're going to Toinette Building 91."

"That's not what I mean."

"I know, but it's where you're going. Ask me again when this business with Tazia is done."

"I want us to be okay," I said, even if it made me sound like a simpering child.

Solomon gave me a look that made me feel like I was a brand-new Intel Operative again, a look of cold and dismissive assessment. "Wanting won't make it so. Prove to me you understand where your priorities need to lie, then maybe. Maybe. But don't get your hopes up."

I nodded and swallowed down the lump in my throat, willed the tears to stay in their ducts. Then, I looked up at the screen. "Toinette Building 91?"

Solomon said, "Ever heard of the Acolytes of Aphnette?"

#   #   #

According to Hessod, the problem with the Acolytes of Aphnette was the utter unpredictability of them and how little visibility we had into their quarters. Toinette Industries considered them to be a cult, so they suppressed most of the information about and from them. Identifying where they lived was easy enough, at least. The immense Toinette security presence right above might as well have been broadcasting their locations. It made me wonder if they were dangerous, though everyone who came and went down to those floors didn't appear any different from other Toinette citizens on the surface.

"What do they believe?" I'd asked Hessod.

The big man had shrugged. "Not completely sure. They lean more toward the Chaos part of Ibhalism, but other than that, there's only speculation."

"Hypothesis?"

"I think they thrive on the mystery, on most people not knowing what they're really about. Seems pretty chaotic to me."

"Anything more from you, Bastion?"

"Your analyst's efforts are sound," Bastion said. "There's very little about them with any credibility. Mostly just regular Toinette citizens throwing around theories online."

I repeated that to Hessod.

"We do have a few images, at least," Hessod said. He brought them up on a screen, and it was like a whole other world past those security guards. Whereas Quynn and I would get home from work and change into pajamas to get comfortable, the Acolytes of Aphnette members looked like they changed into costumes that blended homeless ragtag with old Earth Mardi Gras with 22nd Century space marauders. Chains and spikes and flashing neon and enormous feathers and pretty much anything and everything seemed to go.

Was there a method to the madness? Chaos and mystery, indeed. The more Hessod and Bastion and I dug into Acolytes of Aphnette, the more it made sense why Tazia had put a safehouse down there. It really seemed like the last place that anyone wanted to go while still being safely under the corporate umbrella of Toinette Holdings. I certainly wouldn't want to live where a mysterious, chaotic, and potentially dangerous cult had set up shop. And getting in seemed like no easy feat.

Fortunately, I had a friend who was an expert in such things.

#   #   #

I throttled down Poe as I descended into The Mist, both the bike and

I drenched in the nonstop rain. Why, because Stryders didn't fly down into The Mist.

The Mist hung over the streets of the city, covering the lower several dozen meters. It was some trick of sea winds and massive skyscrapers that kept The Mist perpetually in place. I was still in the boundaries of the Corto Corporation borough, but it was like a whole different city down here. These people, Mistwalkers we called them, didn't belong to any corporation. Without corporate support, they lived off the scraps of the world above. Clothes didn't match and often had holes. The ragged streets were lined with little food stalls and shops. I'd heard that illnesses ran roughshod down here, though I'd never experienced that part myself. I cruised along several meters above the street until I set Poe down on the familiar landing pad that arched over the street like a metal awning.

I approached a nondescript door that I knew well. After a very specific series of long and short knocks, a series that changed weekly now, a green light above the door lit, and I pushed it open. A basket of pink slippers sat nearby. Before anyone could even ask, I slipped a pair on.

"Feet, feet, feet," came the familiar voice from the back of the shop.

I moved through the towering and meticulously organized shelves until I found Echo standing behind his counter. Bald, thin, pale, and perpetually shirtless, his eyes were looking into the middle distance, and his hands were fluttering in front of his face, obviously doing something with his display and a haptic interface that I couldn't see.

"Hello, Echo," I said. "You won't believe what I need today."

"Operative," he said. "Operative. Operative. Easy to believe anything."

He was a pretty literal guy, no doubt. I kind of loved him for that, for how consistent he was in a world that seemed to be shifting under my feet. I said, "I need to blend in with the Acolytes of Aphnette. Need to spend a couple of hours amongst them and leave with my head still on my shoulders."

Echo shrugged and didn't stop what he was doing. "Easy. Easy. Easy. Just go."

"Looking like this?" I said, gesturing to myself. I was in my full work gear. Black, carbon-polymer limbs. Equally black, carbon-nanoweave jumpsuit that covered all of my biological skin from my hips to my neck.

"I've seen a few blurry images. They're wearing the most outlandish, wild outfits imaginable. I don't want people to notice me for being too…conservative."

"Chaos. Chaos. Chaos."

For once, it took me a while to parse out what Echo was trying to say. Then I got it. In true chaos, anything goes. You'd be just as likely to see someone walking around in neon feathers as someone in a business suit or buck naked. At least, that was my interpretation of what he was saying.

"I get that," I said. "But this is a job. I'm sneaking in, and I'd wager that someone is supposed to be on the lookout for someone who looks like me, someone out of place among the Acolytes of Aphnette."

Echo stopped whatever he was doing. He dropped his hands. He glanced at me three times, all very quickly, and never making eye contact. Then he nodded and started walking out from behind his counter. I followed.

Echo stopped just before the last aisle before the outside wall. I hadn't noticed this one before, but it was sectioned off with a huge, white curtain. His eyes focused on the floor, Echo gestured me to go through the curtain.

"What's back there?" I asked.

"Chaos. Chaos. Chaos."

"That sounds like an invitation to a very bad time," Bastion said.

I stifled a laugh. Normally, I would have agreed. But this was Echo. I trusted him. I walked through the curtain and immediately had a headache. Echo was organized to the degree that CEOs were wealthy. Echo's shop was more like a warehouse, shelves towering meters above, all filled with everything imaginable. Every item was meticulously cleaned and organized. And Echo knew everything that was in his shop and exactly where it was.

Except here, apparently. This aisle, cordoned off by a curtain, appeared to be where the strangest items came to end their time on the planet. That Echo didn't even bother to draw back the curtain himself spoke volumes. I couldn't always identify Echo's organizational rationale, but I could always tell it was there. Not here. Nope. A couch that appeared to have been sawed in half formed the bottom of a pile that included a dozen matching bird costumes, a fender from a BMW, a dozen busted neon signs, and the front half of a ten-year-old Stryder.

And that was just the first pile. Was Echo secretly messy? Was this on purpose?

"Echo," I hollered. "Are you okay?"

He didn't answer.

"This must be where he keeps things he cannot categorize," Bastion said.

"Or things that set him off? Trigger him somehow?" I said. "This is so weird."

"Very," Bastion said.

I raised my voice and said to Echo, "Are there clothes in here?"

"Four meters," he yelled back from beyond the curtain. "Four. Four."

Even in this mess, he knew where things were, it seemed. I weaved through the mess and roughly four meters in, I found several piles of clothing that appeared beyond categorization. I had to pull out a flap of sparkling blue fabric, unfold it, and turn it inside out, to find that it was a light jacket that stopped just below the armpits. A poof of orange wound up being green pleather pants with giant, velvety, orange butt cheeks. And this particular pile was taller than me.

An hour later, I walked out of the curtained area with the wildest outfit that I could fit into. Well, fit into and not drive myself mad if I glimpsed myself in the mirror. Black pleather pants studded with metal spikes that ran up the legs in a pattern that mimicked DNA helixes. A purple, shiny bustier, and an iridescent jacket that looked different colors in different light. A white cape was built into the jacket to hang off one shoulder. Finally, I found a wig that was blonde with large, pink stars like a very complicated dye job.

I sat them all on Echo's counter and winced when I saw them all in the light. Echo stared at them and made a similar face.

"Do you think it'll work?" I asked.

Echo shrugged again. "Chaos. Chaos. Chaos." He started to ring up my purchase.

"But is it the kind of chaos I'll find there? That'll let me blend in?"

Echo sighed, looked at each piece in turn, and said, "Chaos."

That was likely the best answer I was going to get. I imagined that chaos made very little sense to a mind as organized as Echo's. So I asked the question that was really bothering me. "Echo, why is that aisle so…different from the rest of your shop?"

Echo's hands froze halfway through his work. He stared at his hands, his lips curling into a snarl. He was starting to breathe harder.

"Okay," I said. I wanted to put a reassuring hand on his, but I knew better than to do that after years of working with him. "Okay. I don't need to know. If it works for you, it works. You, as always, have exactly what I need, and that's all that matters. Thank you, Echo."

Echo stayed frozen for a few moments before he resumed his work, carefully folding my new outfit and placing it into an organized stack. Once he was done, he extended a hand, palm up. I lightly tapped it with mine, the only physical interaction Echo seemed to tolerate, and transferred the appropriate credits to him.

"All right," I said. "Time to go join a cult!"

Chapter Nine

23 Days to Ascension

AFTER A QUICK TRIP HOME to drop off Poe and change, I landed on the 50th floor of Toinette building 91. It was the lowest possible landing pad for the midsize building on the lower east side of Toinette. I hopped out of the Stryder and fell into a comfortable, I-belong-here stride toward the building. Over my work jumpsuit, I was wearing gray slacks that flared out near the ankles over a pair of small, black boots. I wore a billowing lavender tank top that peeked out from under a gray blazer. I looked very in-fashion for any Toinette worker, including the lavender handbag slightly overstuffed with outlandish clothes under my right arm.

I strode into the building easily enough. It was just a residential tower, so there was no special security to prevent me from entering. People came and went all the time, including people who didn't live here. I wanted to look like I belonged so if anything went sideways, a review of camera footage wouldn't catch anyone's eye. I moved through the halls, following the green AR guidance line that Bastion had put on my display. Finally, I entered an elevator.

"Floor 20," Bastion said.

"I remember," I said aloud since I was alone.

"Just making sure."

I pressed the button for 20. Less than a minute later, the doors opened, and I stepped out and into a winding line of similarly dressed Toinette citizens. They were queued up to walk around the corner to a separate set of elevators, the elevators that would traverse below floor 20, down into the quarters for the Acolytes of Aphnette.

"Act natural," Bastion said.

I brought up my AR keyboard and texted him, "Why are you talking to me like I'm new? I've done this longer than you have. Are you nervous?"

"Tazia has proven to be more capable than we ever expected," he said. "She has always seemed to be two steps ahead of us, even ahead of Solomon. So yes, I think I am nervous."

"It'll probably be another empty room," I texted.

"Even worse. Two steps ahead and nothing for us to gain."

I wound through the line and eventually reached a security checkpoint right in front of another bank of elevators. The security guards seemed disinterested, though, like they really didn't care about letting people through. I looked around at all of these normal, everyday Toinette citizens. Were they Acolytes of Aphnette? Was Toinette forcing them to act and look "normal" throughout the day? That was the only thing that made sense, which meant that security was just trying to keep them contained. This was the end of the day, in which they all just went back to their chaotic, rarely photographed home. I could only imagine what things must have looked like in the mornings with everyone leaving to go to work among the regular folk of Toinette. If I was right, that's when the security guards were really working hard, making sure no wild outfits or raving cult members escaped the lower floors.

I walked through the checkpoint and onto an elevator without anyone giving me so much as a sideways glance. Easy enough. But once the doors to the elevator closed and it began to descend, that's when things got weird. Weirder than I'd expected.

"Blessed are we!" someone yelled from the back corner of the elevator, their voice deafening in the tiny space. "For we are the true children of

Aphnette. We embrace chaos, true chaos, as the only path to order. For Shainette and Aphnette created nature long before us, nature in its utter embrace of chaos. Nature in its unending balance. So we are blessed as we embrace that!"

"Blessed are we!" everyone else in the elevator yelled, and then they started taking their clothes off. Like, all the way off. Oh, no. No, no, no. Blood rushed to my face as my stomach twisted up. I fought to keep my revulsion from my face.

I'd expected people to get a little crazy in the elevators, sure, to spout some cultish nonsense, quote apocryphal scriptures, or something like that. I then expected everyone to go home, change into their wild and outlandish clothes, and then go about their evenings doing whatever cultish things they did. I did not expect for the chaotic embrace of the Acolytes of Aphnette to mean that they just got naked right in the elevator.

To be clear, I have no problem with nudity generally. Sex makes my stomach turn and twist, but nudity isn't inherently sexual. I don't even equate nudity with sex most of the time, but that doesn't mean I go around streaking. It also didn't make me comfortable with the proximity of all these bodies or the looks I felt on me. I knew I needed to blend in, though. I suppressed a whole-body shiver as I doffed my blazer and pulled my tank top off. I was intensely aware of how close I was to the flesh of other people. There were about a dozen of us with bare centimeters between us. Elbows and knees were bumping into each other and the walls of the elevator as everyone scrambled out of their clothes. A bare bottom grazed my forearm, and I recoiled. A pair of breasts nearly slapped me in the face when I bent to take off my boots. I pushed air out of my mouth and worked to contain my nausea. I didn't dare close my eyes, though, not only out of fear of falling into someone but because I needed to look like I belonged.

"Are you all right?" Bastion asked. "Your vitals…you're on the verge of a panic attack."

I gave no reply but glanced around at the eyes of my fellow passengers, hoping they wouldn't look on my jumpsuit with suspicion. A one-piece of carbon nanoweave definitely wasn't what anybody wore as undergarments. But everyone was too busy getting rid of their own clothes, stuffing them into bags and backpacks. So, I quickly did the same, shimmying out of my pants and even the jumpsuit before stuffing all of it into the already overstuffed bag I carried. All the while, I forced myself to take deep, steady breaths.

"No one is changing clothes?" Bastion asked. "What about those wild outfits we saw in the still images? I can find nothing on the Net about the Acolytes of Aphnette being nudists."

I couldn't respond. I didn't even have enough room in front of me to pull up my AR keyboard without touching someone else. I just clutched my bag in front of me, barely resisting the urge to hold it like a shield over my nudity. I had no response anyway. Hessod hadn't known. I hadn't known, but here I was. I guess I wasn't going to need the wild outfit from Echo after all.

But that's when it really started to get awkward. The elevator was still descending. I was standing there, completely naked and surrounded by naked strangers. I felt eyes on me, looking over me in a way that made bile rise in my throat. A person near the front of the elevator turned and looked around, their eyes traveling down from my face in that hungry way that I hated. I focused my eyes on the steadily decreasing numbers over the elevator doors.

Finally, the elevator stopped. The door dinged and opened, and I scurried out, doing my best to not touch anyone else. The elevator had not been an aberration. Everywhere I looked, people were going about their business without a stitch of clothing on. Everyone from babies to teens to the elderly was letting their skin show, weaving through the corridors of the building around potted plants, vines hanging from the ceiling, and the strangest olfactory cocktail of human biology and dirt. At least there was some space around me now.

"Where am I going?" I whispered to Bastion as I resisted the urge to cover myself. I needed to pretend to be as nude-happy as the rest of them, after all.

A green line appeared for me, winding through the halls as efficiently as possible. I'd expected this place to be a nonstop party or for violence to be breaking out in the hallways, but it was all surprisingly normal. Apart from the nudity, that is. People were saying hello, striking up conversations, heading to the store, or just going home.

It didn't take long before the AR line led me to a nondescript door at the end of a rather quiet hallway. Now was the first real trick of this job. So far, we'd found that every one of Tazia's old safehouses had been meticulously secured and often boobytrapped.

"Let's run through the optics," I said to Bastion. My visuals flipped first to thermals, showing the water pipes as cold and the electric lines as slightly warm. To my surprise, I saw what looked like a small server rack inside the room, running nice and warm.

"Perhaps this one isn't a bust after all," Bastion said.

"Maybe not."

My visuals then switched to X-ray, then spectrometer, and through half a dozen other modes. I was looking for anything dangerous or unexpected. Every visual just made me more curious about that server rack. There were all sorts of unusual conduits running to it and weird structures built around it. The door, however, appeared to be fairly normal. Normal for Tazia, at least. Reinforced titanium with a state-of-the-art cybermetric and biometric combination lock. Two of them, in fact, for redundancy. Once the first one was unlocked, the second one would slam into place. If the second one wasn't unlocked within five seconds, the first would relock. That cycle would continue up to three times before they both locked and seized.

Sounds daunting, sure. And the first time I'd seen that setup, I'd failed. We had to bring in a literal wrecking crew to break through the wall next to the door only to find an empty room. Now, though, I had no hesitation. I ran two data cables, one from each wrist, and plugged into both locks at the same time. I didn't have to even say anything. Bastion forced Tazia's data into both locks at the same time, unlocking both at virtually the same moment.

I disconnected both cables, reeled them back in, and gently opened the door. I was ready to duck, to roll away. Even though I hadn't seen anything visually, I always expected the worst from Tazia. Nothing happened. No explosions. No klaxons. I stood in the hall for a full minute.

"No silent alarms," Bastion said. "The Toinette Security feeds aren't talking about this building at all."

"All right, then," I said and stepped into the room, gently closing the door behind me.

Whereas the other safehouses had been empty of everything but dust bunnies and indentations on the carpet, this one looked like there'd been an attempt to clean it out but then suddenly aborted. A pile of disused servers was jumbled in one corner. They leaned against a power closet, which I opened to find one lonely arm charged and waiting. A desk was next to it with some holographic recording equipment and a holographic projector sitting next to a cold cup of tea. I opened the drawers on a tool chest to find several of her trademark neural disruptors, the kind that had paralyzed Solomon. There were also some mini EMPs, digital camouflage emitters, and various tools.

A small but very expensive 3D printer sat on the opposite side of the room, some object that I couldn't identify halfway printed. I took the object out and found a communications booster, a listening device, and a remote EMP half concealed in whatever it had been trying to print. The three had been cobbled together to use a single battery. She'd had plans for this… thing. Next to the printer was an industrial atomizer with a full bin. Tazia had been destroying some sort of evidence before she left.

Then there was that server rack. It was barely over a meter tall and a meter wide. I'd been right, though, it was boobytrapped so much that it barely even looked like a server rack. Most Intel Operatives preferred discreet traps on things like this. Tazia was no exception, but she'd made one here. The data ports were surrounded with electrified port mods, guaranteed to deliver a shock if someone tried to plug in. All of the screws and connectors were attached to small-yield explosives. A block of explosives big enough to take out half of the floor was attached to the power supply. Conduits and cables were running everywhere. Every bit of it was obvious, not just to an Intel Operative.

"Don't even touch that," Bastion said.

"I wasn't going to," I said. "Do you see any way to safely access this thing?"

"Physically, no. Perhaps with an explosives expert or five. It would take a team of analysts weeks to dismantle everything she's built around this. I've been trying to access it through the Net since we walked into the room, but Tazia set up several dozen firewalls. Each one is also a hydra. Break one and it's immediately replaced with three more. I don't have the resources readily available to break this."

"Whatever is on there, she really doesn't want anyone to even think about touching it. Or she wants it to take a very long time."

"Or it's a red herring."

"A what?"

"Old Earth saying. Meaning she wants people to spend time on it so that they ignore something of real value."

"Maybe," I said. "But THIS much security? There has to be something on it."

"Not anything we'll be taking with us today."

I shook my head. "No. But at least we didn't find another empty room."

I spent the next three hours working through what I could take. I tossed all of the clothes that I'd brought except for my jumpsuit, making room in my bag for the half-printed whatever-it-was, the arm, and Tazia's toys from the tool chest. I then plugged in each of the discarded servers one by one, downloading what data Bastion could find. Much had been deleted and what remained was heavily encrypted. For now, at least.

Just when I thought I was nearly done ransacking the room, something caught my eye, something down on the floor. Back in the corner, behind where the discarded servers had been haphazardly piled, was a data drive. A centimeter wide and three centimeters long, had it not been for the glint of light off of the silver case, I would have missed it entirely. Had Tazia finally slipped and made a mistake?

"Hello, there," I said as I picked it up. I plugged it into my data port and said, "Show me what we have."

"It's lightly encrypted," Bastion said. "Give me a moment."

And a moment was all it took. Soon enough, my display showed one folder titled SEC_OBJV. I opened it to find a list of files, all of them layered images. I opened the first one, and it was schematics for a microchip of some kind. I opened the next and the next, and they were all schematics of the same chip from different angles.

"This looks familiar," I said.

"It's a neural interface," Bastion said. "Nexus Neuronics design, I think. Nothing really special about it, though. It's a model that came out last year. Perhaps this is from an old job, maybe before it hit the market, she was supposed to steal the schematics."

"Maybe," I said. That did make sense, but that didn't feel like the entire answer. Why would some random Nexus Neuronics neural interface seem familiar to me? I'd stolen schematics from them over the years, but I'd never paid attention to them. I downloaded them, snuck away, and uploaded them to the Corto Intel office. Done and done. This was different. And it bothered me, but this wasn't the time or place to puzzle it out. I disconnected the drive and dropped it in my bag.

I looked around the room one last time, blinking rapidly to take pictures of everything there.

"I believe that's all there is to take," Bastion said.

"Yes," I said. "Now comes the fun part."

The primary way that Toinette Holdings kept the Acolytes of Aphnette contained was by means of a curfew. They also suppressed their public events and demonstrations, kept them from streaming their extremist beliefs, and apparently removed images of them roving about their halls in the nude. That curfew had begun two hours ago. The elevators would no longer take me up and out of their little enclave. The stairwells would be monitored by cameras and security guards. Unless I wanted to spend the night sleeping on the floor of this room next to a bomb disguised as a server, I needed to sneak out.

Chapter Ten

23 Days to Ascension

"LET'S GET OUT OF HERE," I said to Bastion.

"Do you have a preferred plan?"

"How do options one or two look?" I glanced around the room and found option number two, an air duct. It was far too small for me or any human to fit into.

"Visual?" Bastion asked.

"Yes, please."

Most of my vision was suddenly taken up with still images from when I'd walked the hallways earlier. Bastion's vision was limited to mine, but he was constantly recording my sensory inputs. That meant he could zoom in, enhance, and examine tiny details I might have missed. The first image was looking through an open doorway into an apartment.

"No external windows," he said.

"Just like Hessod said from our surveillance. That's so strange."

"Toinette must really like to keep the Acolytes of Aphnette concealed. As for option number two, none of the air vents are big enough for you."

"I figured based on the one I can see," I said, glancing at the one in the room again. There were also several images on my display confirming that.

"I would suggest option number five," Bastion said.

"Not if I can help it," I said. I stepped out of the room and back into the hallway, which was much quieter and empty now. It was nearing midnight at this point. I continued speaking in a whisper. "I'm going for option three or four."

I backtracked through the halls. Other than the copious potted plants and vines growing up the walls, it was much like walking through the hallways of my own apartment building around midnight. No one was out in the halls. Muffled sounds of conversations or video streams could be heard as I walked past doors.

Well, I didn't walk the halls of my own apartment building while completely naked. Somehow, not seeing another nude person made me feel even more exposed, more out of place. After a handful of turns, I found a stairwell door next to the elevator I'd ridden down earlier. I stepped through the door, let it close behind me, and started putting on my jumpsuit.

"Which are you trying first?" Bastion asked once I'd finished zipping in and magnetically sealing the suit to my shoulders and hips. The jumpsuit wasn't armored, but it felt like it in that moment. I felt complete again.

"Let's try The Mist first." I picked my loaded bag back up and started descending the stairs, taking them as quickly and quietly as I could. Hessod had found nothing about security between these floors and the feral areas controlled by Mistwalkers, so I didn't know what I would find. Twelve floors down, I discovered that my caution was unnecessary. Where there should have been a door to exit the stairwell or more stairs going down, there was only concrete. No cameras. No security guards. From the dust and grime, it looked like nobody had been down here in a while, either. A quick scan with X-ray found that the concrete was a meter thick, too, and reinforced with a grid of metal alloy.

"They really don't want Mistwalkers breaking through," I said.

"I would imagine that all of the buildings throughout the city are similarly reinforced," Bastion said.

"All right," I said and adjusted the bag on my shoulder. "Up we go."

The trek upward was longer and more arduous even with cybernetic legs doing most of the work. That said, it was also more predictable. Hessod had been able to find ample information about Toinette Security at the top of the Acolytes of Aphnette area. I knew that after curfew, there would be three security guards standing by the stairwell door and another dozen stationed throughout the floor.

As I approached the last three flights, I softened and slowed my steps, finally stopping one landing before the door in question. I took a few minutes to catch my breath and focus, then I whispered, "Twenty seconds."

"Twenty seconds," Bastion said.

I climbed the last flight of stairs in absolute silence. A few seconds after I stopped right next to the stairwell door, an alarm started blaring on the other side. Right on cue.

I heard no voices at first, just feet shuffling a little. Then a clear soprano voice said, "Understood. Jensen, rotate in on comms in the main office. Patel and I will stay here."

A pair of feet tromped away, likely Jensen, whoever that was.

"What do you think it is?" said another voice, this one a wispy baritone. Patel, I guessed.

"Might be another drill," the first voice said. "We're on door duty no matter what, though."

I sighed and descended back down the stairs, slowly and silently at first. Once I was two full floors down, I said, "So much for that. Leave it to Toinette to—"

A door bursting open two floors above silenced me. I stopped talking and walking, listening instead. Boots on stairs. And they were getting louder. Sparks.

"They're coming down," Bastion said.

I nodded and silently continued my descent. I wasn't panicking, not yet, but I certainly didn't want to get caught.

"If anyone is in the stairwell," that soprano voice yelled from above me, though the owner of the voice sounded more annoyed than threatening, "Go home immediately. We are sweeping the stairwell. Anyone caught will be taken into security custody and questioned."

"How about that?" I whispered. "They actually have really good security practices."

"Option five is still very viable," Bastion said. "I don't think you want options six or seven."

I sighed and whispered, "No. I don't want to stick around until morning or create some sort of evacuation. Those are just regular families down here. Families that don't wear clothes and love plants, but they don't deserve being evacuated in the middle of the night."

Bastion said nothing more as I descended two more flights back to the floor that I knew, the floor of Tazia's safehouse. He was waiting for me to say it, and the boots were catching up to me from above. Catching up fast. Not panicking, though. Not even a little.

"Fine," I said as I stood by the door to the stairwell and started to open the door. "AR guidance, please."

"Your clothes," Bastion said.

Right. By Corto, I really didn't want to get naked again, but I wanted to risk getting noticed as an outsider even less. I stripped off my jumpsuit as fast as possible, shoved it into the bag, and followed another green AR line. I did wind up seeing two other naked people in the halls, one who gave me a polite nod and the other a leering glance south of my face. Either way, it was good that I stripped down again.

I smelled my destination before I saw it: the refuse room. I stepped into the tiny room with a grimace plastered on my face. It was two meters square with shelves lining the wall to my right. On the wall opposite from the door was the garbage chute, a metal panel with a handle on the top and hinges on the bottom. It was half a meter square.

"That is big enough—?" Bastion started to say.

"For me to go down?" I interrupted. "Yeah. Silent circuits. You can bet your microchip that I'm not going down THAT naked."

I dropped the bag and put my jumpsuit back on. Again. This was exhausting. Once I was sealed up tight, I grabbed my overstuffed bag and deliberated for only a few moments. I didn't want to land on it and break anything. Better that I go down while holding it over my head. Even if I lost my grip, I could try to catch it.

"How far down does this go?" I asked.

"At least eight floors," Bastion said.

"At least?"

"It goes below the existing schematics for the building, the Toinette schematics. The chute may terminate at the top of the Mistwalker floors or go somewhere lower. No way to be certain."

"So we just throw our garbage into The Mist?" If so, that was awful. Quynn and I needed to rethink our recycling strategy.

"For nearly 90% of Jayu City, yes. Now isn't the moment to become an activist for Mistwalkers, though."

I sighed. He was right. I tapped the plate on the back of my neck, and nanobots deployed around my head, soon occluding my vision and air, but only for a moment. The nanobots solidified into a helmet, restoring my vision and breathing, albeit filtered. The smell was minimized, at least. I pulled the garbage chute open with one hand, holding the bag aloft in the other. Even with the helmet, the smell slapped me in the face. I gagged. Then, I awkwardly climbed into the chute and began to slide down, my feet pressed lightly to the sides of the chute to control my descent.

I tried to ignore the weird stains and liquids that were attaching to my limbs and jumpsuit as I went down. Every meter or so, one of my feet would find a wet spot, sliding instead of gripping. I tried not to think about that, either. If I worried about what had created those wet spots, I was going to have a panic attack for real.

Despite the filtering from my helmet, one terrible smell followed another, each seemingly more stomach-churning than the last. I slid down, trying to be as quick and quiet as possible, though I didn't think I was terribly effective at either. Then again, I was inside the chute, so every little noise I made echoed and reverberated back on me. I was certain that nearby neighbors were being roused from their beds by my descent.

I kept darting my focus between the dark chute below me and up at my bag, bigger around than me since I'd stuffed it so full. I kept getting hung up on it, having to yank on it or rotate it to keep going. I cursed repeatedly. This was worse than I'd even imagined. It was during one such yank that my feet suddenly slid free. I flailed, finding nothing to grab hold of. I fell a few meters before landing on my back with a soft squish.

It was dark. Really dark. And I now knew where every one of those terrible smells came to reside. They were all around me, mixed and remixed in the most horrifying way. I was torn between leaving my helmet on to filter what it could and yanking the helmet off so that I wouldn't vomit inside of it. I opted for the former and started rolling sideways while tightly gripping my bag. Again, I tried not to think too much about what I was rolling on. I didn't succeed, but I didn't vomit, either.

"Night vision," I said. Instantly, my vision turned from absolute darkness to shades of green. I was exactly where I thought I was, in a huge room taken up mostly by garbage. Only a third of the refuse was in bags. I tried not to look too closely at anything as I worked my way off the pile and toward a door.

I tumbled and twisted my way down from the top of the garbage heap to the floor, which was covered in several centimeters of dark liquid. I'd never seen so much refuse at once in my life. I, like everyone in Jayu City, threw my garbage bags down the chute on my floor. I never thought about where that garbage wound up.

"Hey," Bastion said, highlighting something to my right in yellow. "What's that?"

I moved close to it, turned off my night vision, and shone a pin light from my finger on…a used condom.

"Ack!" I yelled, tripping backward away from it.

In my ears, Bastion was just laughing.

"Whoever programmed you with a sense of humor can…" I started to say but then remembered that everyone in the lab that created Bastion was dead.

Apparently, Bastion wasn't thinking the same thing. He was still laughing.

"You're terrible," I grumbled and struggled back to my feet amidst the horrid slop. I brushed off wet polymer and a fruit peel before approaching the nearest door. There was no handle or dataport or scanner, only a large, red button next to the door. I pressed it, and the door slid aside with almost comical speed. I took a few steps up out of the muck and through the open door.

"Who are you?"

I nearly tripped back onto the garbage as the question was yelled at me. The speaker was obviously a Mistwalker, a person who looked older than any human I'd ever seen. They wore a wide-brimmed hat made of three mismatched fabrics. White, wiry eyebrows spread beyond the bounds of their face, nearly blending into their sideburns, which cascaded into a white beard nearly a meter long. Their mismatched shirt and pants were threadbare. My first thought was that he looked like some wizard from one of Quynn's video games.

"Are you deaf?" They asked. "Who are you?"

"Sorry," I said as I regained my footing and composure.

"What are you doing here? This is my inventory. How did you get in…?" They stopped talking as they looked me up and down. I didn't look like a Mistwalker, and I thought they'd just figured that out.

I pointed up. "I took the long way down. I'll be going now."

The Mistwalker sputtered as I squeezed past them and out into what looked like a store, jam-packed with refuse from the floors above, cleaned up and labeled with prices. The trash of the 150 floors above was now sold to the company-less people below. I wanted to be surprised, but I wasn't. Of course this was how it worked.

"Don't steal anything!" the Mistwalker yelled after me as I headed out and onto the street. For once, I was grateful for the rain. At least some of the muck that had covered me was being washed off.

I was in the borough of an entirely different company, dozens of kilometers from Corto Corporation, and yet you wouldn't have been able to tell down here. Every street in The Mist looked the same. It was the middle of the night, so the streets were mostly empty. Food carts were closed up and locked tight. Vendor stalls had curtains drawn, awnings folded down and padlocked, and I heard gentle snoring coming from more than one stall. The few people that I did see were running through the rain in makeshift ponchos. Mismatched polymers were hastily sewn together. Mods peeking out of sleeves looked homemade or decades old and in poor repair. Ten meters above the cracked pavement of the streets, The Mist hung thick, blocking out any view of the buildings above.

The rain, however, was undeterred by The Mist. It fell just as constantly down here as above. I was drenched in the first minute. Thank Corto.

"Poe?" Bastion asked.

I sighed. Stryders didn't come down below The Mist. "This is going to be a wet ride home."

#   #   #

The next morning, I sat next to Hessod at one of the workstations in Necropolis Alpha, four rows up from the bottom and far to the left of the room. Hessod kept shifting in his chair as he typed, obviously uncomfortable. He kept looking at me with his nose upturned and scrunched. Yeah. I still smelled. And I knew that he preferred his oversized, ergonomic chair upstairs. He liked his mechanical keyboard, surrounded by photos of his daughter and models of starships. But we were working on Tazia stuff, so we needed to be down here, away from the general Intel staff.

"Well?" I asked, sipping coffee both to keep my eyes open and because I still felt wet and chilled from the ride home six hours ago. An hour-long hot shower hadn't been enough for the chill or the smell.

Hessod blew out a breath between tight lips. "The downloads from those servers are going to take days to decrypt."

"Days?"

"The encryption is similar to the two-key system she used the first time you dealt with her, but not identical. Except we don't have the keys, so we're going to have to rent time on the Corto Omni to crack it."

"Yikes," I said. The Corto Omni was the primary supercomputer for Corto Corporation. Upper management loved to boast about how it was the most powerful machine on the planet, even if I knew it was the third most powerful. Nevertheless, it had massive processing power. Renting time on it wasn't cheap. I already knew that Tazia was a major priority for the Intel Division, but this just reinforced how major.

"The data drive, on the other hand," Hessod said. "Easy encryption there, as you saw, but it's a bit of a mystery."

"Those schematics are of a neural interface, right?"

93

"Yes. And the other files tell me that this was a priority target for Tazia, though I don't know when. It could be a job she's on now. It could be a job she had before she was ever the Ghost of Toinette."

"The files aren't timestamped?"

"Unfortunately, no."

"How do we find out when they were created?" I asked.

"That's not the mystery that needs to be solved." Hessod pointed to the schematic of the interface on the screen, specifically pointing at one end of it. "These are the receive circuits. Look how many there are."

I saw a large shape like a blown-up microchip. It was covered with lots of lines. That was the extent of my understanding of circuitry. "Hessod, you're going to have to explain it to me like I know nothing about neural interfaces. Because I know nothing."

"Okay. Of course, neural interfaces are how the brain communicates with cybernetic modifications, right?"

"Right." That much, I understood.

"Send circuits are responsible for translating signals from the brain to your mods as commands. When you want to move your hand, you don't have to use a joystick or give a voice command. The interface uses the neural pathways you already have to make that happen. Likewise, receive circuits translate feedback from your mods to your brain. They're how you're able to process inputs from your aural and optical implants. It's how you feel pressure on your limbs when there's danger."

"Got it," I said.

"This interface has almost 100 times the normal number of receive circuits," Hessod said, tapping on that same spot on the screen."

"So it's a big advancement?"

Hessod shook his head. "Recent advancements in neural interfaces have been in the shape of better materials, better processing power, stuff like that. The number of receive circuits hasn't really changed in the last 50 years. The neural pathways are pretty well mapped at this point. This is something else."

"Wait," I said. "Didn't this chip hit the market recently?"

"No," Hessod said. "I've never seen anything like it."

That didn't make any sense. "It's not a Nexus design?"

"No," Hessod said. "What would make you think that?"

"My mistake," Bastion said.

That was weird. Really weird. Bastion could process information and research anything on The Net faster than any human or team of humans. A mistake like this wasn't like him. Was he malfunctioning? Damaged? What was I supposed to do about that? That was a discussion we would have to have later.

"Why all these extra receive circuits, then?" I asked Hessod.

"That's the mystery. Does your little friend have any ideas?"

"First, I am not little," Bastion said. "I'm currently working 1124 different servers across the city. As for ideas, military neural interfaces are often more complex to account for more mods and higher workload."

I said as much to Hessod.

"Military mods have two to three times as many send circuits, a few more receive circuits," Hessod said. "Nothing like this."

"Starship pilots?" Bastion asked. "There's the Argus program being developed that adds a ship's sensors as extensions of the pilot's mods. Wouldn't that require more receive circuits?"

When I told Hessod, his eyebrows shot up and his eyes gleamed. "Like the Rozita-class frigates. Hmm." He started typing furiously, screens closing and opening in rapid succession before the schematics for another neural interface appeared on his screen. Then Hessod moved the schematics next to each other. He slumped.

Even I could see that they weren't a match.

Hessod shook his head. "Ten times the receive circuits, not 100 times. Any other ideas?"

"None," Bastion said.

"Sorry, Hessod," I said.

"I'll keep digging, see what we have in our files from Nexus Neuronics. Maybe they did make it or at least design it. I could be mistaken. We've taken enough of their files, I'm sure we have something on it if they did."

"How long will Omni take with the server files?" I asked.

"Days," he said.

"Maybe weeks," Gustin suddenly said from behind me. I didn't even know he was in the room. "Depends on where we are in the queue and how dense the encryption is. Either way, good job. It's the best haul we've ever had from Tazia, and you didn't even make a blip on Toinette's security feeds."

"Forget about that," I said. For the first time, I kind of wanted to hug him, but we didn't have that relationship. "How's the new baby?"

Gustin beamed. Genuinely. I'd never seem him smile like that, like his face just couldn't stop. "Great. 3.71 kilos. 45 centimeters. Baby and Mom are both doing great."

"That's wonderful," I said.

"Congratulations, Gustin," Hessod said with tears in his eyes. He shook Gustin's hand, and so I extended my own to my manager, which he gladly shook.

"Enough of that," Gustin said, though he was still smiling like a madman.

I nodded said, "What about the server in that room? It's booby-trapped to the hilt."

"We're going to send in a team of analysts with an operative or two. It's going to take us a while to get a team that size in."

"Make sure they're comfortable being nude."

Gustin smiled and shook his head. "I can't believe you did that."

I shrugged.

"Two days," he said, and I immediately knew what he meant. Two days before I began my embed in Kotega Systems. "Are you ready?"

"Doesn't really matter, does it?" I said. "I'm going in."

Chapter Eleven

21 Days to Ascension

"YOU HAVE EVERYTHING?" I ASKED Nox. We were in a cheap, black flying car built by a manufacturer I'd never heard of. It was operated by Stryder, the dominant rideshare service in Jayu City, but it was a much cheaper fare than I usually hired. The car was flying itself into the Kotega borough.

"For the hundredth time, yes," my apprentice said. He was dressed in drab, gray coveralls. His head, normally bald, was covered in half an inch of black hair. Intentionally bald was an uncommon fashion choice in Kotega, so he'd been instructed to grow it out. Between the hair and the outfit, he really didn't look like himself, which was the idea. He needed to pass as a low-born maintenance worker, after all.

"Sorry," I said. "How are the new limbs?"

Nox shrugged. "A little heavy. Slow. I'm still figuring out where everything is."

"I can relate." Like me, he had new limbs made to look cheap while still containing a small selection of our operative tools. And Nox really liked his fancy tools, so he'd had an even harder time picking the few that he really needed. I had a feeling that Solomon had helped him narrow down the list. Having the Cloak of Corto as your uncle had its advantages.

I stared out the window as the car passed out of the Huginn borough and into Kotega. I wondered how long it would be before I saw Corto Corporation or Quynn again. The full three weeks? Would I get this done sooner? I hoped for sooner.

"Don't forget about me," Quynn had said. They were teasing, but there was a note of sincerity there.

"Remember to leave the house," I said. "And eat real food."

Quynn barked a laugh. "You're the one who eats all the worst takeout unless I order something better."

"True," I said. "But I'm the better cook."

"That bar is very low."

We both smiled, tears in our eyes. I kissed them and we held each other for a long time.

"Three minutes," Bastion said in my ear.

"We're almost to your drop-off." I took a deep breath and kept my eyes on Nox. For once, he didn't have anything to say. "I'll see you in there?"

Nox nodded once. "We got this, Star Girl."

I hated that nickname, but it put me at ease just now. Maybe it was just his confidence. I said, "Yes, we do."

The Stryder touched down on a landing pad on the 50th floor of a low-rent apartment building in the northeastern tip of Kotega. Nox gave me one last nod and stepped out. Once he was a few meters away from the Stryder, it lifted off again, its cheap thrusters shaking the whole car. I suddenly felt more nervous now that I didn't need to keep a calm face for my apprentice. I was about to walk into the most powerful house in Kotega and pretend to be someone else. One wrong step would mean the end of my career. Possibly my life.

"How long to my fake apartment?" I said to take my mind of the weight of it all.

"Less than ten minutes," Bastion said.

"Not as exacting as you usually are."

"I've learned. Do you need the exact time?"

"No. Sorry. Just nervous."

"This isn't like you. Nox is more confident than you are, and you're the one in line to become the next Cloak of Corto."

"He's in his element. He's a natural at embeds. I haven't done one in a long time because I'm not very good at them. Of course, I can lie. I can sneak in anywhere. Pretending to be someone else for a long time, though? Makes me break out into a cold sweat."

"Breathe," Bastion said. "Trust your training, your hard work, and trust that neither Nox nor I will let you falter."

"Thanks." I did feel a little better.

A few minutes later, the Stryder touched down on a 100th-floor landing pad of an apartment building that wasn't quite as low-rent as Nox's. I grabbed my bags and stepped out, quickly moving to the doors that led into the building. The doors slid closed behind me just as the Stryder was lifting off again.

I stood there in the vestibule, quiet and patient. Totally patient. I didn't quietly kick my rolling bag or keep adjusting the straps on my smaller bag. Definitely not. And Bastion's unusual silence completely helped put me at ease. Yep. Very much at ease here.

I wasn't sure how much time passed before a sleek, gorgeous red car swooped down and landed softly on the landing pad. It was longer than most cars by at least half, with long, dark windows separating the front doors from the rear. A limousine. That was probably my ride. I remembered my instructions, though, and waited. A tall, well-dressed person in a suit stepped out of the driver's side. Yeah, a human driver. This was definitely my ride.

The tall person came into the vestibule and stopped when they saw me, looking down with a flat expression. Their skin was several shades lighter than my own. Their light brown hair was lawyer-boring, parted and combed neatly. Their chiseled jaw was clean-shaven. I bowed slightly.

They said, "Xyla Kotega-Cyber? She/her?"

"Yes," I said.

They leaned down and picked up my rolling bag as though it weighed nothing. "My name is Ridley Kotega-Gloria. He/him. I'll be your driver today. If you would follow me, please."

Ridley didn't wait for a response but spun on a heel and walked back out the door, carrying my bag. I followed, my head a little higher. The lessons on Kotega politeness were still fresh in my mind. Defer to anyone you don't know. Once you know their rank compared to yours, carry yourself accordingly. As Gloria's driver, Ridley was higher than Xyla in rank, but only until Zhao welcomed me into Gloria's house as the new Daeli. Then, we would be equals. Even now, he was only moderately higher in rank, so my head was slightly higher.

Ridley opened the rear door, holding out his open hand. I didn't know why. Was I supposed to take his hand? Did he want a tip? Neither of those seemed right. I glanced at his face, and he helpfully gestured to my shoulder bag with his eyes. Right. I placed the strap in his hand and slipped into the vehicle.

The seat practically devoured me. To call the inside of that car nice would have been like calling interstellar travel quick. Behold the understatement. The seats were plush and white. I could feel whatever they were made of conforming to my body while also supporting me perfectly. There were real wood inlays everywhere. The teal lighting was a vibrant color yet restrained in its deployment, accenting the lines in the car. I was sitting in a work of art. I didn't even feel Ridley stow my bags in the trunk, nor did the car jostle when he opened his door and settled into his own seat behind the wheel. It would be too easy to get used to this.

I barely felt the vehicle move at all. There was certainly no thruster noise infiltrating the cabin. I could have fallen asleep in that car, but I was on the job. And this job had a clock on it. I looked around until I found a button marked, DRIVER. I pressed it and said, "Ridley, if you don't mind me asking, how long have you been working for Gloria?"

"Three years next month," he said over a speaker that I couldn't even see, gingerly maneuvering the car into a lane of traffic.

"Do you like it?"

"It's a good job. Gloria is a good boss from an excellent family." Ridley didn't pause before he said it. The politically correct answer rolled off his tongue like second nature.

"I'm honored to be joining her household," I said. I wasn't going to push anything. Not yet.

"We're honored to have you," Ridley replied. The customary response to the customary statement. I was going to have to burrow through all these layers of honor and politeness, but not today.

As we neared the center of the Kotega borough, Ridley steered the car up and out of the traffic lane. And up. And still up. We soon cleared the tops of most of the skyscrapers. Only a stark handful in the very center of the borough loomed over the skyline. In the center, taller than the rest, was Kotega Tower. Slim and gleaming black for the first 220 floors, the last 30 were a flourish in red metal and black glass. Spires and friezes and all sorts of other embellishments burst out in every direction like gnarled, bloody claws reaching for the stars. My mouth dropped. It was gorgeous, unlike anything else in the city.

"Which floors are Gloria's?" I asked.

"The top thirty all belong to the Siwa family," Ridley said. "Our mistress's house is concentrated on 233 through 236. Zhao will give you more details when we arrive."

Thirty full floors for one family of just three people. Each floor was likely 40 or 50 times the size of my apartment with Quynn. The wealthy really did live in a different world. I knew Kotega Tower was the seat of power for Kotega Systems and the home of the Siwa family, but little else was known to the Corto Intel division. Since CEOs were generally off limits, we'd never had cause to infiltrate it, never needed to breach that red and black fortress. This was new territory.

Just as I was wondering how Ridley was going to land, a pair of large, leaf-like panels of red metal parted, swinging up and aside. They were roughly a third of the way up from the bottom of the Siwa residence and created an opening large enough to accommodate very large vehicles. Ridley carefully guided the car inside. No external landing pads to ruin the aesthetics of this tower. Instead, we entered a cavernous space, easily four stories tall and taking up the entire interior space of those floors. Dozens of vehicles were parked on a dozen spotless, semicircular landing pads along the walls. None of these vehicles were in my price range. Wealth dripped from every corner of the immense space.

"Wow," I said. I didn't mean to let the word slip, but at least it was in character for Xyla.

Ridley made no reply but silently guided the car to a landing pad near the back corner, sliding in between a vintage green car I was unfamiliar with and a new, dark purple Mercedes. The sales sticker was still in the window, and the thrusters were still wrapped from shipping.

Once the car was settled, both Ridley and I climbed out. As Ridley came around to remove my luggage from the trunk, I gawked at the enormous garage. I recognized most of the cars and really wanted to know about the ones that I didn't, but I wasn't sure Xyla would care, so I gawked in silence. Also, the entire garage smelled vaguely of cinnamon. Not oil or thruster fuel. I had no idea how they accomplished that, but it couldn't have been cheap.

"Xyla?" Ridley said. He was standing near a door to go inside, my luggage in his hands.

"Sorry," I said, bowing my head slightly again. "It's so…"

Ridley smiled a little. It softened him considerably. "You'll have plenty of chances to see it. We don't want to keep Zhao waiting. If you would follow me, please."

I trailed him into the building proper through a door labeled 232A. The 232nd floor, one below Gloria's floors. The show of wealth continued. Real wood floors and embellishments along the ceiling, all flown in from off-world, immediately spoke to the vast, generational wealth of the Siwa family. Every piece of furniture I saw would fit well in a museum or high-end showroom. I wasn't an art connoisseur, but I could tell the many pieces hanging on the walls and perched on pedestals were old and expensive.

Ridley didn't lead me very far before he approached a door that opened once he was near it. On the other side of that door was a completely different world. The walls and floor were white. Simple and clean. We turned one corner before Ridley set my bags down in front of an elevator and pressed the up button. As expected, we only traveled up one floor before emerging into an equally drab corridor.

While floor 232 had been empty, people were buzzing to and fro here on 233. Not a lot of people, but enough to make the place feel busy. All of their shirts looked to be the same metallic bronze color.

"This is the staff area," Ridley said. "This way."

He turned right and led me down the hallway. Simple, gray doors were mostly closed. The few open ones showed rooms just as white and plain as the hallway. Ridley gently sat my luggage down just outside a door and knocked.

"Come in," a flat, androgynous voice said from the other side.

Ridley opened the door and gestured for me to enter. I did, and he closed the door behind me. The room was small and decorated with only a few abstract paintings. A large desk took up half of the space and it, too, was sparsely decorated. Sitting behind the desk was a person who looked to be in their early 60s. Their skin was a little darker than mine, well-wrinkled, and a cascade of black and gray hair spilled halfway down their torso. Below the black eyes and serious face, they wore a high-necked, bronze shirt over black slacks.

"Xyla?" xey asked.

I bowed and said, "Yes." I was fairly certain this was Zhao, the head of Gloria's house, so I made the bow fairly deep.

"I am Zhao Kotega-Gloria. Xey/xem. I am the head of Mistress Gloria's house, as I'm sure you know. You will address me as Seon Zhao."

I stayed in my bow and said, "I am honored to be here, Seon Zhao."

"And we are honored to have you," Zhao said. The response was customary, but there was an edge to xyr words. Whatever strings Dr. Corto had pulled to put me here, they obviously hadn't set well with Zhao. I would need to be careful. I stood upright, though was careful not to look Zhao in the eyes. Not yet.

Zhao took me in, looking me up and down, though xyr interest looked entirely academic. Finally, xey said, "You'll do. Let me show you to your room."

Zhao came around the desk, and I bowed slightly as xey walked past me. Xey opened the door, and I followed, noticing that my luggage was gone. Zhao was walking fast, the walk of someone accustomed to people falling in line. "Gloria's house encompasses this floor and the three above it. Mistress Gloria does not like locked doors in her house, though you are to only go where you are reasonably expected. If you don't have a reason to enter our mistress's private chambers, for instance, then do not go there."

Someone who doesn't like locked doors? Sounded like a dream to me.

"We are in the staff area of the floor right now. You'll spend most of your time here, particularly during your off hours. If you wish to leave during your off hours, check with me first, and I can arrange a ride for you."

"We can't just hire a Stryder?"

"Other staff members? Yes. As Daeli, no. You are the mistress's proxy, so we must keep up appearances."

That was going to make things challenging.

We turned another corner, took three steps, and a door opened. Gloria Siwa-Kotega, daughter of the CEO and my new employer, swept through it, her head on a swivel. Her black hair was in a spiky bun atop her head, her features sharp, skin unblemished, and makeup minimal. She was wearing a jacket, pencil skirt, and pumps the color of a golden sunrise. She carried that same aura of authority that I'd seen so many times in Dr. Ariela Corto, though her resemblance to me was startling. Gloria spotted Zhao and her eyes widened.

"Is that my new Daeli?" she asked, her tone sharp.

Zhao bowed deeply, and I followed suit, nearly forgetting to do so until Zhao did.

"She is, Mistress," Zhao said. "Xyla Kotega-Cyb…I mean…Gloria. She/her."

"I need her now," Gloria said. "I'm sorry to cut the introductions short, but I need a double."

My heart skipped. Needed already? Needed for what? I was expecting at least a day to get the lay of the household and a sense of Gloria and the family dynamic from the other staff members. I wasn't prepared to get to work yet.

Zhao stood and said to Gloria, "We have not had time to calibrate the distortion, Mistress. We've not even had time to register her name change."

Gloria looked thoughtful for a scant second before she waved a hand and said, "That's fine. The point will be made without all that. And they won't know her name, anyway."

"Of course, Mistress," Zhao said.

Gloria smiled in the same pompous, everything-will-go-my-way way that Dr. Corto did when she said, "Good. Ten minutes. Thank you, Zhao."

Zhao bowed her head slightly, and Gloria turned and left through the same door she'd entered.

"Is this normal?" I asked.

"There is no normal," Zhao said through pursed lips. "Come. You need to get ready. Quickly."

We hustled through more corridors until Zhao opened an unmarked door. Inside was a narrow bed nestled among three walls of wardrobes. Xey didn't hesitate, going straight in and opening one of the wardrobes. Inside were dozens of outfits in the orange and yellow color range. Zhao immediately grabbed one, and it was an exact replica of what Gloria was wearing today. Xey hung the outfit on a hook near the bed.

I glanced around, noticing my luggage already at the foot of the bed. I watched Zhao close the first wardrobe and open another, this one full of pumps in different colors. Xey pulled out a golden pair that once again matched Gloria's. Zhao turned to me and said, "What are you waiting for? Change. We have eight minutes."

"Right," I said, giving a bow. "My apologies."

"Stop apologizing and change."

The next few minutes were a dizzying flurry of activity. While I changed out of my Xyla clothes and into the expensive yellow outfit, Zhao replicated the spikey bun of hair and simple makeup, all the while telling me to hold still while I was trying to change clothes. You try changing clothes while keeping your head perfectly immobile. For the second time in a week, I was naked in front of a stranger, and I didn't like it one bit. I was so close to Zhao, I could smell the oregano and soy on xyr breath from whatever xey'd had for lunch.

With two minutes to spare, though, I was hurrying behind Zhao through the maze of corridors and stairs. My sense of direction was all turned around until we came to a landing pad, a different one than I'd been brought in through. That pad and the red car Ridley had brought me in were on the next pad over to my left and a floor up. Now, Ridley stood next to a shining, black Kotega luxury limousine. The rear door was open. Ridley gestured to it.

I slid into the open door of the car and found Gloria seated directly across from me. Her fingers were flitting in the air in front of her, obviously interacting with something on her display. The door closed, and soon Ridley took his place in the driver's seat, the back of his head barely visible through the small, tinted window that divided the front seats from the compartment I shared with Gloria.

"I'm here," Bastion said. I'd started to wonder why he'd been so quiet. "It took longer than I expected to create my tunnel through their network. What's going on?"

I swept my gaze across the car as it slowly took off from the landing pad. Gloria was still working on something. This car was even quieter than the red one that had brought me here. Finally, I looked down at my own outfit.

"Already body doubling, I see," Bastion said. "Things are moving quickly. Who is Gloria going to meet?"

I made a small gesture with my hand that meant I didn't know. We'd worked out of few simple gestures that I could make in front of my own eyes so that I could silently answer some of Bastion's questions.

"I don't have access to her schedule yet. I think you'll need to physically interact with her household servers to get me access. The firewalls around it are impressive."

"What is your name again?" Gloria said, nearly startling me. She was still interacting with whatever was on her display, not looking at me. Yeah, CEOs and children raised to be CEOs all must have gone through the same lessons in cold detachment.

"Xyla," I said. "She/her."

"Since Zhao hasn't had a chance to teach you, I'll have to on the fly."

I bowed my head slightly in response.

"Stay one step behind and to the right of me. Say nothing. Stand up straight. Bow when and exactly as deeply as I bow. Walk through doors in front of me. Keep your disruptor on."

A holographic disruptor, she meant. They were devices worn around the neck or as headbands that projected a hologram over the face. While I'd heard of some that were good enough to fully replicate someone else's face and all facial expressions, Kotega Systems Daelis used them to create a blurry mask of the face of their employer. They weren't meant to be true disguises, but symbolic. Bringing a body double with a disruptor told whomever you were meeting with that you respected and feared them.

"Sorry, Mistress," I said, using the honorific I'd heard Zhao use. "I don't have a disruptor yet."

Gloria's hands dropped and she looked at me finally. Her eyes took me in from the matching shoes to my black hair in a bun like hers. Suddenly, it was like the coldness melted away. Her eyes lingered on my exposed calves. Gone was the piercing CEO gaze. This gaze was something that made me uncomfortable in an entirely different way. Her gaze was too hungry. I looked away. Then she said, "That's right. Zhao said that the disruptor isn't ready. A good match, though. Right build and skin tone. Surprisingly close on the face already. Shame about the disruptor, but that's Mother's fault for scheduling this so quickly."

"Who are we meeting?" I asked, trying to change the subject. Our physical similarities made her attention even more uncomfortable for me. Sexual attraction was strange enough, but wasn't it creepy to find your double attractive?

The response was silence, so I chanced a look at her face. Gloria's eyes had narrowed. I'd mis-stepped. That was fast. When she spoke again, her tone was clipped and firm again. "We are not meeting anyone. I am. And questions are not part of your job as a Daeli."

"My apologies, Mistress," I said, bowing as deeply as I could while sitting. By the time I looked back up, she was back at work, not giving me another glance. At least this silence was more comfortable than her gaze.

#   #   #

Twenty minutes later, the car landed on a pristine pad on the roof of a wide building that was only 100 stories tall. It was like one immense green space woven through with silvery walkways that looped and looped again, connecting one corner of the space to another. The constant rain only seemed to enhance the green against the concrete city. Even the landing pads at the four corners look like they'd been grown instead of built. Standing just off the landing pad as the car settled down, a group of six expensively dressed figures were waiting.

Ridley looked unhurried but was still out of his seat and opening the door for Gloria in a flash, a large umbrella in his hand. I sat there for a moment before Gloria looked directly at me. Walk through doors in front of her. Right. I climbed out of the car, doing my best impression of the woman still sitting in the car. I stood, the afternoon light harsh, and the skirt riding up from the ride in the car. I tried to adjust it as subtly as I could while I waited for Gloria to step out.

And step out she did, looking utterly unrumpled, making strides toward the waiting group before I knew what was happening. Ridley handed me the umbrella, and I took three quick strides to catch up, and then fell in line one step behind and one step to the right of her, holding my head up like I was Gloria Siwa Kotega myself. The umbrella was large enough to cover both of us, even with required distance between us.

Now that we were closer, I could make out the waiting group. They looked like they were attending a theme party together, all dressed in similar shades of silver and lilac. The designs of their clothes were similar, too. Stiff, tall collars sprouted out of quadruple-breasted jackets that didn't stop until nearly their knees. Below that were pants that seemed ill-fitting.

The two in the middle of the group looked like relatives. They shared similar enormous foreheads, sagging cheeks, and huge, expressive eyes. I could see now that the other four people wore clothes that weren't quite as tailored. The fabrics looked less ornate, though in the same style. These four were also all holding things in their hands. Handbags, a silver tray of cocktails, a small box lavished with ribbons, and umbrellas to keep the rain off the two in front. Servants, then.

The two in the front bowed deeply, their legs straight, but their torsos bending level with the ground. The servants all dropped to one knee and lowered their heads. It was going to take me a while to get used to all this bowing. It all felt so demeaning.

"Gloria Siwa Kotega," one of the pair said, "we are deeply honored and humbled by your presence. Our father sends his highest regards to you, your mother, and your brother."

Gloria bowed, her legs and back straight, bending roughly 45 degrees at the waist. Half the depth she'd been offered. A clear sign of the difference in rank. I matched Gloria as best I could. Gloria said, "Trillux Trystte Kotega and Mileau Trystte Kotega, I am honored to be invited and hosted by such a grand family."

The pair of Trysttes bowed again, acknowledging the compliment. Then one waved a hand, and the servant with the tray of drinks moved forward. The servant was tall with incredibly dark skin, a bald patch reflecting the glaring sunlight. Three delicate cocktail glasses held a pinkish liquid that barely moved as the servant stepped forward. Sitting in front of the three cocktail glasses was a tiny, empty glass. It looked like the galaxy's most expensive and ornate shot glass.

The servant stopped three steps shy of Gloria, bowed their head deeply, and stepped forward enough to put the tray at arm's length for the CEO's daughter. Gloria stood there, stock still, not reaching for a glass or saying anything. Was this a test? Some sort of code? Was she waiting for the servant or one of the Trysttes to say something?

"Elise," Bastion hissed in my ear. "You're supposed to—"

I lurched forward toward the drink tray, knowing what Bastion was about to say. I was Gloria's food taster, of course. That was part of the Daeli job. If someone offered her food or a drink, I was supposed to taste it first. I grabbed the closest cocktail glass and raised it only a few centimeters before Bastion yelled in my ear, "No! The small glass!"

I froze, holding the cocktail glass aloft, pretending that I was weighing it, examining it in the light. Definitely not seconds from putting it to my lips.

"Pour a sip into the tiny glass," Bastion said. "Drink from that."

A week of training wasn't enough to cover every aspect of Kotega society. It wasn't even enough to cover every aspect of a Daeli. And I'd been fed a lot of information in a very short time. I was nervous. I wasn't focused enough. I took a deep breath and kept the cocktail glass aloft for a few more seconds before nodding in approval and setting it back down on the tray. I picked up the tiny glass, the umbrella still in my other hand, and poured a sip of the cocktail into it. I picked up the tiny glass and downed my sip. The drink was powerfully sweet with a bitter finish. I swallowed it and counted to ten in my head, slowly, just like I'd been taught. Then I nodded slightly to Gloria and stepped back to my place.

Gloria swept up the cocktail glass I'd tested and took a long draw from it all in one motion. She smiled widely and said, "Rosewater and Cirilla One rum. Delightful. And so sweet. What did you use to sweeten it?"

The Trysttes bowed in gratitude, and then the one on the left said, "Sugarcane from Earth."

"Ooh," Gloria said, holding the drink up to the light. "How exotic!"

The rest of the meeting was less stressful, though just as inane. The Trysttes gave Gloria the ribboned box, which she accepted gratefully and handed to Ridley, who put it in the car, unopened. Then Gloria and the Trysttes moseyed around the top of the building, alternately talking about the future of Kotega Systems, the Trystte family's place in it, and the various plants and building techniques around us. Gloria was complimentary on the latter, but noncommittal on everything else. How was this important enough to require a body double? The conversation was vapid and pointless.

The Trysttes were obviously concerned about their place and where they stood with Orogen, the future CEO. I still didn't fully understand how the succession from Tenisha to Orogen was going to affect the Trystte family or the rest of the company, but it appeared that a power struggle was already taking place. I wondered if everyday Kotega citizens understood what was happening here. Were these the secretive workings of the upper echelon or just the obvious movements that happened with every change in CEO?

Xyla was supposed to be an everyday Kotega citizen. Born of parents who worked in manufacturing. Grandparents who did the same. A respectable family, but not one with significant means or a family name. Barely middle class in the Kotega hierarchy. I needed to determine Xyla's understanding of all of this before I could discuss it with anyone, even with the other lowly members of Gloria's household.

After two hours of meandering and talking, Gloria bid the Trysttes goodbye through another half dozen bows. More honorifics and compliments were paid. Then we were back in the car, flying back to Gloria's home.

"Odious prats," Gloria spat the moment the car doors were closed.

you. They'd rather a Daeli spend a few hours there than go running around the borough."

The garden was on a terrace deeply inset into the building several floors above Gloria's household. I wasn't sure if I was on one of Orogen's floors or what. The edge of the terrace, which overlooked the borough, was 60 meters away. I weaved through a diverse arrangement of flowers, shrubs, and decorative grasses that barely left room for narrow, stone pathways.

"Are we clear?" I asked once I reached the terrace railing, the wind from being so high up buffeting my hair and helping prevent any unwanted listeners from hearing me. The rain was meters away, though, the bulk of the building covering the entire garden.

"I detect no spyware on their network," Bastion said. "No listening devices since you walked onto this terrace.

I turned around and leaned against the railing, checking for people. I acted casually. I'd definitely seen a few cameras near the door when I'd entered the garden. The rest of the terrace was clear of people, though, so I turned back around to face the city.

"Make the call," I said. After several moments longer than it usually took, NARROW-BAND CONNECTION ESTABLISHING appeared on my display.

"Took you long enough," Hessod said a few moments later. His voice wasn't as clear as a standard comms call, but it worked.

"Hit the ground running," I said. I told him about my day, at least in an outline. Not much to really talk about.

"No suspicions?" Hessod asked. "No strange behaviors?"

"Not that I can tell thus far. The number two doesn't seem to like me, though. Probably has more to do with whatever our fair doctor said to get me in." I was speaking not quite in code but not using anyone's names. While the scans had been clear, you could never be too cautious.

"Likely," Hessod said. "You'll just have to earn their trust yourself."

"Xyr," I corrected.

"Zhao uses xem, xey, and xyr?"

"Yes."

"Noted."

"What?" I said before I caught myself. I braced for a dressing down, but none came.

Instead, Gloria typed on an AR keyboard that I couldn't see, and then she swiped my direction with one hand.

INCOMING FILE FROM GLORIA SIWA KOTEGA appeared on my display. I opened it and found a nondisclosure agreement.

"I already signed an NDA," I said as I skimmed through the document hovering in front of me.

"You did," Gloria said. "This one is a special version. I need you to sign it."

"It's more tightly worded than the general NDA you signed for the Siwa family for employment," Bastion said. "It prevents you from sharing anything that Gloria tells you in confidence, even with other members of her family or staff."

"Why?" I asked Gloria. What was I getting myself into?

She gave me a look that I couldn't decipher and then said, "Please, just sign it."

"I see no issue," Bastion said. "It's unenforceable outside of Kotega Systems and you're going to sign it with a fake name anyway."

He was right, so I swallowed hard and signed it as Xyla. I sent the file back to her.

Gloria took a deep breath and said, "The Trystte family barely deserves a name, let alone two hours of my time. A body double? What was Mother thinking? It's been a century since the Trystte name meant anything, back before their starship division collapsed from mismanagement. They've been begging for scraps from every family ever since. Mother should have just sent an email telling them to learn to marry better if they want to move back up in the world."

Yeah, there was that CEO voice. Gloria wasn't in line to be CEO of Kotega Systems now, not since Tenisha had announced Orogen as the successor. But Gloria had been raised to be CEO, taught to move in those circles and speak with that same cold precision I'd heard from Corto's CEO too many times. This was going to be a fun three weeks.

Gloria looked at me then, and that very look of fury soon turned to curiosity. It took me several seconds to realize that I was glaring at her.

"My apologies, Mistress," I said, quickly making my face neutral and bowing my head.

"I assume you're better at staying silent than you are at being a Daeli," she said, though there was no venom in her words.

I looked back up, and she was smiling slightly. It wasn't that predatory smile I often saw from Dr. Corto. Was it genuine? Amused? I didn't know what to say. Was listening to Gloria rant a part of my job now? How many Daelis had to sign those extra NDAs? Was there no one else Gloria could talk to?

After a few moments, her smile dropped. Gloria turned her gaze to look out the window and said, "Pay no mind to what I said. And never repeat it, obviously. I just need to get things out. You only just arrived. Zhao still has to train you. There will be many meetings like this in the next few weeks. Most with much more respectable families than the Trysttes. Orogen will meet with the greater houses, of course, so I'll be meeting with everybody else. You'll do better next time."

"Of course, Mistress."

"We have time before your kendo practice," Ridley said to Gloria over a speaker. "Would you like to go anywhere else first?"

Gloria pressed a button near the door and said, "Home. We can drop off Xyla." She released the button and said, "No need to try Zhao's patience."

"Yes, Mistress," Ridley said.

Her head still turned, Gloria leaned her head back. Soon, she was asleep as the Kotega skyline slid by outside.

Chapter Twelve

21 Days to Ascension

BY THE TIME I RETURNED to the residence, the place was a flurry of activity. A dozen people I didn't recognize, all wearing bronze shirts, were carrying trays of food, cleaning supplies, or walking in pairs while speaking in hushed tones. It took me several minutes to find Zhao, who paused mid-sentence with another staff member to tell me to change clothes and then wait in the staff cafeteria. Then xey were off down the hall.

Except I had no idea where the staff cafeteria was. I wasn't even sure where my room was in relation to where I was. And what was I supposed to change into?

I wandered through the staff hallways, trying to look like I belonged while looking for a sense of familiarity. Three times, I thought I had found my room but was mistaken when I opened the door. Once, another staff member was changing, and they turned red from forehead to heels at my mistake.

I finally found my room and exhaled hard once I closed the door. For the first time in hours, I was alone. I was myself, Elise. That's when I saw that the door didn't lock. They weren't just unlocked. None of the doors were even equipped with locks. Not a fan of that. I'd at least hoped that my room would be my one safe space in Kotega, secured from everyone else.

"How are you doing?" Bastion asked.

"Tired," I whispered, happy to speak to him with my voice again, though I wasn't sure yet whether the room might be bugged.

"Gloria didn't seem too put out by your faux pas."

"Seemed pretty put out to me," I said.

"She seemed frank and unflinching but not offended."

"There's still time." I took in my room, casing the place, looking in every corner for cameras or microphones. Once I was fairly certain that no digital eyes were watching me, I deployed a scanner from my right hand and ran it over every centimeter of the place while I continued to talk. "I don't know if Gloria does the dressing down herself or just has Zhao do it."

"As far as either of them know, you have no training as a Daeli," Bastion said. "A modicum of patience would be in order."

"I have no reason to believe that Gloria is patient with her staff. We've both seen how Dr. Corto handles her staff. And just look at how the staff here scurry about."

"That might be Zhao's doing, not Gloria's. Or it could just be a sense of dedication and urgency. You have no reason to believe that Gloria and Dr. Corto are the same."

But didn't I? I was going to err on the side of having offended Gloria. Better to be overly humble than not humble enough. After a few minutes, I completed my scan. No bugs. They were making it too easy on me, which made me uneasy. My trade was in locked doors and surveillance systems, the lack of them made me wonder what else was being employed to keep the staff in line.

"All right," I finally said. I opened one of the wardrobes and found dozens of dresses and outfits, carefully arranged by color. "What am I supposed to wear?"

"These appear to be duplicates of Gloria's clothes like the outfit you're in now."

That made sense. I closed the wardrobe and moved to the one farthest to the left. Since the body double clothes were arranged by color, I was guessing that my clothes would be on one end. I was right. I didn't find any of Xyla's clothes that I'd brought, but instead a variety of pants and skirts in black, white, and navy. Then there were tops in various cuts, all made from the same bronze fabric I'd seen the rest of the staff wearing. I frowned.

"Is this the Gloria's official color?" I asked as I browsed through them.

"It would appear so."

"Why can't they be black?"

# # #

I eventually found the staff cafeteria, a room roughly a dozen meters to a side with a large kitchen taking up one corner. The room was more sedate than I'd imagined. Less than a dozen people were in the room. A tall, ungainly person was obviously in charge of the kitchen, moving through the space with authority and occasionally snapping or clapping or using hand signals to order around the two other people. Ridley was sitting at a table on the other side of the room, chatting casually with someone. The stranger was more muscled than anyone else in the room. Judging by their stance, even relaxed and sitting, I was guessing they were security.

I didn't see Zhao, though a few other people that I didn't know were milling around the tables.

"Xyla," Ridley called, his face and voice still neutral. He was gesturing for me to join him.

I wandered over, trying to not look nervous, and gave Ridley a very slight bow.

"You don't need to do that here," Ridley said. "You're family now, and nobody is watching."

"Really?"

"Yeah. This is Thrace, he/him," Ridley said, gesturing to the broadly built stranger across from him. "He's our head of security."

Thrace rose to his feet, surprisingly a few centimeters shorter than me, but he was much broader. His shoulders seemed to be fighting to escape his uniform. Short didn't mean incapable, though. He held comfortable eye contact with his ice-blue eyes. His hair was gray and cut close to his head and

115

face, more like stubble. His skin was dark and leathery, like he'd spent too much time in the sun. He extended a hand, which I shook with a slight bow.

"I'm Xyla," I said. "She/her."

"Honored to have you," Thrace said with a rasp and a neutral expression. "And Ridley is right. You don't need to bow here, not to us. You're our Mistress's new Daeli?"

I nodded.

"You'll be spending some time with me soon. You're not officially part of the security detail, but there's some crossover. Body doubling is sort of an extension of security. Zhao will put some time on our schedules."

Finally, I saw an opportunity to start learning things. "Does the Siwa family have a large security force?"

I saw a flicker on Thrace's face as though I'd touched a nerve, but he quickly recovered. "I'm head of Gloria's household security. She prefers details about security and scheduling to remain close to the chest. Sorry. She doesn't even share that info with her family."

"Trust problems?" I asked.

Thrace's gaze didn't budge this time, but I saw Ridley glance at me over his shoulder before he glanced at Thrace. Definitely hit a nerve.

"It's not for us to talk about the family," Thrace said, his tone very serious. "Just protect them, drive them, serve them, and so on."

"Of course," I said. The silence that followed was awkward, and I didn't know where to look. I took in the rest of the cafeteria, watching the kitchen staff bustle. I didn't understand how the chef was communicating when they weren't even speaking. I chanced a look back to Ridley, and he still looked like he was avoiding my eyes. I looked away and wondered what everyone else's jobs were. When I was about to fidget and my gaze landed back on Ridley, his face was red, and he looked ready to burst.

"Are you all right?" I asked.

In answer, Ridley burst out laughing. Thrace just shook his head and smiled. In that moment, the broad shoulders, slightly crooked teeth, and off-kilter grin reminded me of Valdo, my brother. They had the same smile. The thought tugged at my heart.

"What?" I asked.

"Drive them," Ridley said in an exaggerated impersonation of Thrace. "Serve them. And I thought I was the funny one."

"I don't sound like that," Thrace said as he grinned.

"Of course you don't." Ridley turned to me fully. "We totally gossip down here. How else would we keep ourselves entertained?"

"So long as the gossip stays within our walls," Thrace said, and I didn't see one hint that he was kidding this time. Nevertheless, a knot in my stomach unwound. I let out a breath and smiled, even if it was half-hearted.

Since the ice was broken, I said, "I haven't seen many cameras around here. Kind of surprising."

"Mistress doesn't like voyeurs," Ridley whispered while grinning.

Thrace rolled his eyes. "Mistress believes in trust, not spying. She insists on very few cameras where people live."

Trust? Okay. That didn't sound like Dr. Corto at all. Had my first impression been wrong?

"Not sure it's best for Kotega, though," Ridley said to Thrace. "Remember Carmela's last sous chef?"

"I took care of that," Thrace grumbled.

Ridley shrugged.

"Come on, then," I said. "Out with it."

Thrace and Ridley exchanged a conspiratorial look, and then they did. It wasn't as scandalous as I'd hoped, just a former sous chef stealing knick-knacks from Gloria's residence and selling them. Pretty tame compared to my day job, but listening and reacting at all the right times was getting me in good with these two.

Suddenly, Thrace stood up straighter. Ridley sat up a little, too. I spun and saw that Zhao had entered the room, sweeping toward the kitchen staff without so much as a glance at anyone else.

"Carmela," Zhao asked the tall person in charge of the kitchen. "Three minutes?"

The chef answered with a stiff nod. Carmela. Got it.

Zhao turned and made xyr way to a small table close to the door. Carmela and the kitchen staff were suddenly moving much faster. Thrace retook his seat, and the rest of the household staff stopped milling and did the same.

"May I?" I asked Thrace and Ridley. They gestured to an empty chair next to them, which I took.

Sure enough, three minutes later, one of Carmela's underlings brought a plate of steaming food to Zhao. Then both underlings were buzzing around the room, setting down plates in some order that I couldn't immediately decipher. When the last plate was set in front of me, though, I figured it must have been a seniority thing.

The food was surprisingly good, if under-seasoned. The produce and meat were obviously fresh, which did a lot for the meal. The conversation was more interesting, but only slightly. Thrace had been Gloria's personal bodyguard since Gloria was 13, ascending to head of her security when Gloria established her own house. Ridley had driven for a few lower houses before coming on with the Siwa family. Frustratingly, they didn't have much in the way of concrete details that I could use. Jokes and anecdotes? Sure, but nothing tactical. This was going to be a long three weeks.

"So what are we allowed to do in our off hours?" I finally asked, tired of getting nowhere with my inquiries. We'd all finished our meals, and then Carmela's staff had quickly cleared and cleaned everything.

Ridley and Thrace glanced at each other, and then Ridley said, "We're allowed to go as we please on our own time, but I don't think things work that way for Daelis."

"Why?" I asked. Zhao had told me, but I wondered if the other staff members had a different view.

"Whenever you show up somewhere, it's a statement from Gloria, from the Siwa household," Thrace said. "It's not that you can't leave, but that we have to arrange things ahead of time and keep you a bit hidden."

"I'm starting to see why the last Daeli left," I said.

Thrace shrugged. "Nobody stays a Daeli for long. But it'll bring you and your family great honor, serving a Siwa so directly and faithfully."

"So I just come here and go to my room?" I asked.

Ridley and Thrace glanced at each other again, then Thrace said, "There's more to it than that."

Suddenly, the general murmur of the room fell silent. Thrace and Ridley both turned away and I followed their gazes to Zhao, who had just stood up.

"Staff," xey said. "We have a new Daeli, for those who haven't met her. The name change is official, so please welcome Xyla Kotega-Gloria. Gloria's first appointment tomorrow is at 8:30, so breakfast will be at 7:30."

Without another word or any reply, Zhao swept out of the room. The murmur in the room didn't just return but doubled.

"You're official now, newbie," Thrace said, his face breaking into a smile wider than I'd seen from him yet.

"Always good to have fresh meat for Zhao to pick on," Ridley said. "If you ever get tired of all that bowing and scraping xey'll have you do, I know a good chiropractor."

I was so caught off guard by how relaxed they suddenly were that I just stared at them both in silence for several long seconds.

Thrace leaned in closer. "That was a joke."

I smiled and sighed. "Had to wait for it to be official, huh?"

"And for Zhao to leave," Ridley says. "I think xey are allergic to jokes. Anyway, welcome to The Roost."

"The Roost!" Thrace yelled, holding his glass of water in the air.

Everyone else in the room raised their own glasses and shouted, "The Roost!"

"Back to your question," Thrace said, "Doing your job and sitting in your room? That's a lot of it. Sorry."

"And it's not like there's a nice garden a few floors up from here," Ridley said with a huge grin. "A garden that staff aren't technically supposed to be in, but nobody ever stops us. Nothing like that."

I smiled. "I didn't hear anything about a garden."

#   #   #

After what felt like an interminable walk through servant hallways and back stairwells, I opened the door as I'd been instructed and found myself in a beautiful garden high above most of the Kotega borough.

"We're not strictly allowed there," Ridley had said before I left the cafeteria. "But it's an open secret that we won't get in trouble. Especially

"Anything from my apprentice?" I asked.

"No. He doesn't have Bastion to help him, though."

"True. I should be able to start talking to him in a few days." I needed to create an obvious and organic-looking meeting between Xyla and Devon, Nox's cover name. Nothing wrong with a Daeli and a maintenance worker striking up a friendship.

"Good," Hessod said. "He has access privileges you could use."

"I'll need it. I'm pretty locked down. Sounds like I'm going to be busy, too."

"You'll figure it out. Be patient."

"I know," I said in a huff. Patience wasn't my strongest asset. "Any other updates?"

"We're next in line for Omni. Nothing else. Keep me posted."

"Will do," I said. I looked up, the stars intermittently visible between clouds. "Tell Q that I miss them."

After a few seconds, Hessod said, "I will," and then disconnected the call.

I missed him already. I missed Quynn even more. I stood there on that balcony for a few minutes longer, allowing myself to just be myself, before I turned and became Xyla again, striding back downstairs and to bed.

Chapter Thirteen

18 Days to Ascension

ALL I DID WAS LEARN and do my new job for the first few days. Between attending multiple meetings and meals with her, several car rides, and planning sessions in her residence, I was getting to know Gloria. The more I got to know her, the less she seemed like Dr. Corto. She was shrewd and had the same top-down view of her borough, but every time I saw an opportunity for a thread of cruelty to come out, Gloria chose diplomacy. Maybe even genuine kindness, I wasn't sure yet.

I was able to get to the garden twice more to check in with Hessod. No news from me though he had one bit of bad news. By the time our Intel team got into Tazia's safehouse among the Acolytes of Aphnette, that explosives-laced server was gone. The entire room had been cleared out. So much for that.

I'd finally made contact with Nox on our second day in Kotega. It was even truly organic. We ran into each other in a hallway and struck up a conversation, exchanging our Kotega comms information. And every night before I laid my head down, I chatted with Quynn with Bastion as a go-between. It wasn't the same as actually talking or even texting, but it was better than nothing.

On my second day, I figured out that Zhao definitely didn't like me. Since xey'd been blackmailed into giving me this job, though, I couldn't blame xem. Xey were terse with everyone, but particularly with me. Even Ridley and Thrace had noticed. For everything I'd learned in the nine-day crash course I'd been given before leaving Corto Corporation, I quickly learned how little I really knew. Fortunately, I didn't really have to convince Zhao that I grew up in Kotega. Xey obviously knew, and we never discussed it. It simmered between us, unspoken, constantly draping awkwardness over every interaction we had.

Gloria was consistently booked in meetings with different significant families in Kotega. After two hours of rough tutelage on meal and meeting etiquette with Zhao, Gloria had me accompany her to a lunch meeting, a walking meeting around a new arena, a dinner meeting, and cocktails. That had just been my second day. All four meetings were with different families. All required different outfits. And I did not get to eat beyond the tiny sips and bites to test the food. Every day had been like that.

Only 18 days left. I was beyond antsy or frustrated. I felt like I'd been wasting time for three days. By the time I returned to The Roost, my limbs were below 10% power, and I felt the same.

"It won't be like this all the time," Ridley said as I sat down next to him in the cafeteria. He was still in his uniform suit, but the tie was missing and the top few buttons of his shirt were undone. He and Thrace were playing some sort of card game. The cards looked similar to the standard deck used all over Corto Corporation, but a few cards were different. I didn't recognize the game at all.

"I hope it slows down," I said. "Or at least that I get some breaks here and there."

Dinner had ended long ago, but Carmela had set aside a plate of food for me. I'd learned that Carmela had been deaf from birth and chosen to remain that way. Aural implants could eliminate deafness, but she liked how she moved through the world. She communicated more with tastes and smells anyway and had been doing so since she was a child.

"Thanks," I told her as she brought it over. The steam from the plate condensed on my face like a fresh sheen of sweat. It looked like curry, though not one I'd had before. It smelled and tasted divine.

I took a small bite and was surprised to find the spice levels more to my liking. I looked up to see Carmela still standing there, an expectant look on her face.

"It's good," I said, trying not to sound too surprised.

Carmela smiled triumphantly.

"How did you know? I never said anything."

Carmela wiggled her eyebrows, shifted her smile to one more devious, and walked away.

"How?" I asked Thrace and Ridley.

"She's an enigma," Ridley said. "But she feeds me, so I don't pry."

"I think she's just great at reading people," Thrace said. "She also cleans us out at cards."

"Carmela the Card Shark," Ridley said.

"We don't call her that."

"I do."

"You don't."

"I'm going to."

"To her face?"

Ridley held up a finger and opened his mouth to protest but then let the thought die in the air.

Thrace chuckled and grinned that Valdo-like grin again. Why couldn't I go a day without being reminded of my absent brother? Thrace threw down a playing card, and said to me, "It's busy because of the ascension announcement." Thrace was in his full uniform, the standard Gloria bronze, though with extra armor-like padding around vulnerable areas.

I swallowed a bite and said, "Why would that make things different?"

"Every family has to fawn over the new CEO," Ridley said as he slid a card onto the table. "And they all want to be on his good side, to kiss the proverbial ring."

"Too many for Orogen to meet?" I asked.

"Partly," Thrace said. He threw down another card, though he didn't look happy about it. "And the boy has other things occupying his time."

Now we might be getting somewhere. I tried to look disinterested as I said, "Oh?"

Ridley glanced up at Thrace like a warning, but the head of security continued, "I'm not sure what. I just see his schedule blocked out from sunup to sundown, though he's not leaving the property for most of it. He's taking meetings with the really big houses, the ones that have always been close with the Siwa family. Probably meetings with Tenisha."

I nodded as I chewed. I let several minutes pass, watching the two play. I asked questions about the game, which they explained while they played. I didn't really care, though. Once I thought enough time had passed, I asked Thrace, "You know when everybody comes and goes, don't you? Staff, family, whatever?"

"Part of being security," Thrace said absently. "All of the household security teams coordinate."

That was useful to know. I was going to need to sneak into Orogen's floors at some point. And Tenisha's. Duplicating Thrace's access was likely going to be easier than cracking Orogen's. I finished eating quickly, and then begged off, claiming to be tired. I was tired, but I was also motivated to not let another day go to waste.

I stepped out into the hall and started walking to my room. Not seeing anyone, I whispered to Bastion, "Thrace's room?"

A glowing green line appeared on the floor in AR. While I hadn't done anything but work, Bastion had been able to map the staff hallways as I'd moved around them for the last few days, noting who was going in and out of different rooms. Bastion said, "Do you think you have enough time?"

"I just need to get in his room, see if he has a workstation, and get you access, right?"

"He is head of security. You're making some steep assumptions about how easy this will be."

"I get itchy when I haven't picked a lock in a while, assuming he even has one."

After a few turns, the glowing line stopped at a nondescript door. I was pleased to see, finally, a locked door. Thrace's was equipped with a Kotega ION 4 biometric lock. High-tech for these hallways, but the lock was three years old already. I glanced both directions. Coast was clear. Mother of Corto, this felt good. I deployed my combination fiberoptic camera and data cable, quickly connecting to the lock and bypassing it in a matter of seconds.

Thrace's room was the exact same dimensions as mine. It was just as beige, plain, and uninviting. His felt much larger, though, because there was only one wardrobe instead of the eight that took up residence in mine. A workstation was sleeping in the same place as mine, too, right next to the bed. While mine was pretty outdated and simple, Thrace's was newer and there were half a dozen screens connected.

"What do you need?" I asked Bastion.

"Connect to the workstation," he said. "I'll take it from there."

I sat down in front of the workstation, plugged my data cable into a port on the front of it, and sure enough, all of the screens flickered to life. On the screen right in front of me, dozens of windows started appearing and disappearing too rapidly for me to follow.

"Huh," Bastion said.

"Huh? Good 'huh' or bad 'huh'?"

"This is a security system I'm not familiar with. Not a standard, off-the-shelf build. It's very sophisticated, though."

"Is that good or bad?"

"Neither. I'm having no issues with it, just fascinating." Bastion was doing his work, indeed. The other screens were camera feeds. There were images from the garage that looked like still photographs because nothing was moving there. There were views of the glamorous living and dining areas that Gloria used. She glided through, still dressed in a lavish mauve suit, and sat down with a cup of something steaming. I envied her in that moment, just relaxing at home, alone, and being 100% herself. How I wanted to be cradling my own cup of something steaming, snuggling up with Quynn.

"Bastion, are these all of the camera feeds Thrace has access to?" I asked.

"I'm busy," he said.

"I know, but…" Then I heard footsteps in the hallway and shut my mouth. I sat frozen for a moment until I heard the footsteps stop just outside the door. I quickly stood and yanked out the data cable.

"I wasn't finished," Bastion barked.

I made a gesture in front of my face that meant I needed him to be quiet so I could focus.

If Thrace was here, I was too late. All I could do was hide. My head was on a swivel. One wardrobe. One slim bed. No room behind the desk. Nothing else looked usable. I heard the door lock click and I leaped up and atop the wardrobe. These weren't my normal work limbs, but they had enough power to do that. I curled in a ball, rearranging an empty suitcase and several lightweight containers that lived up there to block me from view. I settled in and stopped moving just as the door opened, my heart thundering.

Two quick footsteps sounded in the room and stopped. The door gently closed. I waited, barely breathing. My pulse was leaping against my throat and hammered in my ears.

After several long seconds, Thrace growled, "Come out now and I'll go easy on you."

He hadn't used my name, which told me he didn't know who had entered his quarters. I remained motionless and tried to breathe as deeply as I silently could. I'd been through closer scrapes. This was just another. Thrace wasn't my friend, not really. Right? No reason to feel guilty right now. None at all.

"Last chance," he said. After a few minutes of silence, he grunted and started moving around the room. I heard him check around the bed and the desk, of course, grunting again, surely noticing his workstation was awake when it shouldn't have been. I held my breath as he came close and opened the wardrobe with a flourish. One of the containers near my head started to rock with the motion, and I closed a hand around it as quickly and quietly as I could.

Don't look up. Don't look up. Please, don't look up.

Thrace slammed the doors of the wardrobe, making the empty suitcase teeter in front of me. I couldn't stop it, though, not without giving myself away. Panic leaped up in my throat, but after a few awkward moments, the suitcase and my panic settled back into place.

"Thrace to Siwa Control," Thrace said. "Possible breach on 233. Any external intrusions tonight?"

A few moments of silence passed, Thrace obviously listening to his comms, though I couldn't hear the response. Then he said, "No need. I'll check things on my end and report back. Thanks."

Thrace sat down at his workstation, the chair legs dragging across the floor before his fingers started to type on the keyboard. I hadn't seen any cameras in the staff hallways nor any feeds on his workstation, but what if I'd missed one? What if one was pointed at his door or even mounted in this very room? All I could do was wait and hope.

"You could use a distraction," Bastion said.

I couldn't respond. I couldn't make a sound and couldn't risk moving to type a message. And I wasn't sure I wanted a distraction. I didn't want to miss anything that Thrace was doing, a sudden cue that I needed to run. Or worse.

Fortunately, Bastion already understood that. He said, "Even though it was cut short, my intrusion into Thrace's workstation was not fruitless. There are eight cameras in Gloria's residence. There is only one in the staff area, and it is aimed at the door that leads to Gloria's private residence."

That was good. Thrace's room wasn't on the feeds. Neither was mine. I didn't think I'd walked past the door to Gloria's residence, even. I still didn't have a clear map of the place in my head, but there was a chance that I was all right. It also meant that I didn't know how Thrace had been alerted to a breach. It could have been on his door, on his workstation, or anywhere in this room. Hard to tell.

"Amberlee, Goren, Zhao, Xyla," Thrace mumbled. "In the residence but not the cafeteria with me. Could have been any of them. But to get past my door…"

"He might start to check with each of you," Bastion said in my ear. "I suppose I should give you a chance to get to your room in case he decides to start with you."

I blinked rapidly a few times. Since Bastion had access to my optical mods, that was the only response that I could give him, some acknowledgment that I was hearing him.

"You can never say that I'm useless," Bastion said.

A moment later, Thrace muttered, "What in…?" Then the chair legs scratched the floor again, and in a few steps, Thrace was out the door.

I slowly counted to five in case he ran back in, and then started unfolding my body and said, "What did you do?"

"Thrace has remote access to the camera feeds," Bastion said as I climbed down from atop the wardrobe. "Those feeds are actually less secure than most of the networks here. I just turned off a camera in the garage. It's three floors away."

"Thank you," I said as I carefully rearranged all the items on top of the wardrobe.

"Can you plug in a hidden data drive on his workstation?" Bastion asked. "Perhaps one of those micron-thin piggybacks? I could keep looking through things if—"

"I don't have any of those. Not in these limbs."

"You decided to leave those behind?"

I gently opened the door and looked out into the hall. Nobody was in sight, so I stepped out and hustled toward my room. I whispered, "I couldn't bring everything."

"You could have consulted with me on what to bring."

"Believe it or not, I prioritized life-saving measures and absolute necessities."

"We have very different views of necessities, apparently."

"Apparently," I said. I quickly made it to my room, changed, and got into bed. Less than ten minutes later, A gentle knock sounded. I used my best sleepy voice to say, "Hello?"

Thrace opened the door too wide, peering in like he was certain I wasn't actually in here. His eyes darted around the room before settling on me looking bleary-eyed over my blankets. His face softened before he said, "Nothing. Sorry."

He closed the door, and I said to Bastion, "Mother of Corto. At least tell me you got Orogen's schedule."

"No," Bastion said.

I cursed under my breath.

"But I did get access to some other workstations on the network. It looks as though Zhao doesn't trust Gloria's brother. I also have real-time tracking of Kotega's next CEO. Sleep well."

For the first time since arriving in the Kotega borough, I did.

CHAPTER FOURTEEN

15 Days to Ascension

THREE MORE DAYS HAD PASSED. In a blink, I was nearly a third of the way through my embed and had made virtually no progress. At least I'd discovered that Thrace's assessment of Orogen's movements was spot-on. He rarely left the family compound, taking meetings in his own residence, up on the roof, or in the offices on the penultimate floor of the building. I'd only noticed one helpful pattern when it came to Orogen. All three Siwas employed Daelis. The only meetings that we didn't attend with them, however, were when the Siwas met each other. Twice in the last three days, Tenisha had met with Orogen and Gloria. Both times, I'd been left behind. I'd asked Nox to stroll by the meeting room for the second one just to confirm that neither Tenisha's nor Orogen's Daelis were present.

So that was something. It was probably easier to track a Daeli than the future or current CEO.

Nox was struggling. Most of his work in maintenance was focused on the offices and Orogen's staff area. He didn't have a tunnel to contact anyone back in Corto Corporation like I did. He was texting me too much, more from boredom and frustration than need. I was trying to be patient about it.

I didn't have any leads for him to chase down while I was in back-to-back-to-back meetings. Even Hessod was growing frustrated with the lack of real information in my daily updates, and that man's patience is vast. I think it was compounded by how long it was taking the Omni to crack Tazia's server files.

In The Roost, I'd become friends with Thrace and Ridley and even the silent enigma that was Carmela. Maybe I should say they'd become friends with Xyla. Day by day, they were less guarded with me. Day by day, I'd become more comfortable with Xyla's backstory and more relaxed interacting with them. They'd even asked me questions about Gloria's meetings on occasion, but they also weren't surprised by my extra NDA or inability to speak. I wasn't the first and wouldn't be the last Daeli working under those conditions. Everything I could tell them, though, kept them on the edges of their seats.

Zhao remained as frigid as ever, and I did my best to avoid xem. There was no avoiding the head of Gloria's house forever, though.

"Xyla," xey said as xey seemed to appear from nowhere, standing in the entrance to the cafeteria. "Follow me."

"I told you," Ridley said too loudly, "don't go banging the maintenance staff in Gloria's bed!"

Thrace snorted a laugh.

"Hilarious," I said as I rose from my seat and followed Zhao. By the time I got to the entrance of the cafeteria, Zhao was down the hallway several steps ahead and not slowing down. I jogged to catch up. "Where are we going?"

Zhao threw me a venomous look but said nothing. Nevertheless, I followed around the corner and soon knew where we were going. I was finally getting a sense of where things were. The door to Gloria's residence came into view and we walked through it.

It wasn't my first time in Gloria's residence. On my second day, Zhao had given me a mostly silent and very uncomfortable tour. Once every other day, Zhao and I would meet with Gloria in her sitting room to look over the schedule and plan logistics. Gloria's home was enormous, of course, and very comfortable. Her furniture was plain in a way that showed she valued comfort and function over flair. In fact, her decor reminded me of Quynn and I's apartment. Well, our apartment if we had three full floors of a building instead of two rooms.

Gloria was standing in the sitting room dressed in a green, silky suit. That was odd since I was wearing a pale blue dress as instructed.

"Mistress," Zhao said with a bow.

I stopped and bowed as well, though I said nothing.

"Change of plans, Zhao," Gloria said. "Dinner with my mother and brother. I won't be needing Xyla after all."

"Have the Staffords been informed?" Zhao asked. The Staffords were another mid-level family. Gloria had plans to dine with them tonight.

"They have," Gloria said. "Orogen's house reached out, but I'd like you to follow up with the right level of apologies."

"Of course," Zhao said with another bow. "Will you be needing the car? Ridley is still standing by and ready for you."

"No need. We're dining at Orogen's tonight. Ridley can take the rest of the evening off."

Zhao bowed slightly in acknowledgment.

"Xyla," Gloria said.

"Mistress?" I said.

"Good job this week. You're catching on quickly," Gloria said to me. She'd actually given me pretty regular feedback during my first week, proving to be a very different person from Dr. Corto, indeed. She'd even been asking me a steady stream of personal questions and seemed genuinely interested. It had really put my memorization of Xyla's backstory to the test. Now, though, she was making a show for Zhao. She turned to her head of house and said, "My commendations to the staff. I know bringing on a new Daeli is a team effort."

Despite xyr best efforts to remain impassive, I saw a sparkle in Zhao's eyes and a hint of a smile. Xey didn't like me, but xey were proud of xyr work, no doubt. "Thank you, Mistress. I'll pass your praise along to the rest of the staff."

Gloria looked at me again. There was a sparkle there, one that had appeared occasionally in the last couple days. When Gloria looked at me, it was like she was really seeing me. Not just Xyla, but me. That look was compelling. It spoke to who she was, who I was learning she was. How she treated people. I wrenched my eyes away from hers. "Enjoy your night off. You joined at the busiest possible time. You've more than earned some downtime."

"Thank you again, Mistress," I said with another bow.

Gloria nodded once more to Zhao and then went through the door back into her residence. I didn't get a chance to feel any pride myself, however. Zhao spun on me and pinned me with a glare.

I held my hands up in submission. I glanced around. Seeing no one else near us, I whispered, "Believe it or not, we want the same thing." We both wanted Gloria to be the next CEO, after all. Maybe our reasons weren't the same, but the end goals were aligned.

"I highly doubt that," Zhao growled.

"Whatever is going on with you, I can probably help you if you'd let me."

Zhao's look somehow darkened even further before xey strode past me, each footstep assaulting the floor.

Once xey rounded the corner, I said, "Right. That ice isn't thawing anytime soon."

"It may not be worth trying," Bastion said.

I shrugged and started walking to my room. I whispered, "I don't like our CEO having leverage over anyone, frankly."

"I imagine she has leverage over more people than you could possibly know."

"I'm sure. But I'll take a victory lap for each one I can take from her."

"An evening off," Bastion said. "What will you do?"

I smiled and entered my room, closing the door behind me. "From my understanding, Tenisha won't be home for the next couple of hours. Dinner with her children."

"That's not a good idea," Bastion said.

"Well, I would prefer to get into Orogen's, but that's where dinner is happening."

"That's not my issue."

I unzipped the blue dress and wiggled out of it. "If anyone knows how the five companies connect or what Gibbingson Holdings is, it'll be a CEO. Probably all of the CEOs. I'm an elevator ride away."

"You should focus on Gloria and Orogen. Find the evidence you need to bring down the CEO-to-be."

"That is my focus," I said as I hung up the dress. "But I can't deal with either of them at this moment. This, I can do. At least some recon. Walk around, get a feel for the place, see what's hidden. There might be nothing. There might be loads of evidence or even something to help me get at Orogen. All the good stuff might be in her office near the top of the building, but I won't know unless I look."

"This is an unnecessary danger."

I ground my teeth. I hated when Bastion got like this. He could be so intransigent sometimes. I took a deep breath and said, "Agree to disagree. I'm going. Are you helping or—?"

"Of course I'm helping," Bastion interrupted. "I'm not going to let us get caught or hurt if I can help it. But I have my opinion."

"Which you've made very clear and very obvious." I pulled on my gray uniform pants and a bronze tunic. Not my preferred outfit for work, but it was my best option here in the Siwa compound. "Your opinion is noted. And ignored."

"You are infuriating sometimes."

I zipped up my bronze uniform jacket and checked myself in the mirror. Oh, way too much makeup for this drab outfit. That wasn't going to help me blend into the background. I grabbed the makeup remover spray from my desk, held my breath, closed my eyes, and sprayed it generously all over my face. I kept holding my breath while the nanobots did their work, tingling slightly as they devoured the cosmetics. Once the tingling stopped, I brought a small metal rod close to my face and let the little bots fly away, leaping magnetically from my face to the rod.

I checked myself again and ruffled my shoulder-length black hair. There. Much blander.

"Do you have a plan?" Bastion asked.

"Have I had time to make a plan?" I asked. "And no, that's not a reason to reiterate your complaints. We're going. We'll be careful and figure it out as we go."

"Quynn would hate this."

I sighed and stopped, my hand on the door. I thought about that, really thought. Tried to put myself in Quynn's frame of mind. "They wouldn't like me going up there without prior recon, but there was no getting around that. I needed to slow play this. Make sure I left no trace of my presence, be ready to run at the first hint of trouble. Quynn would want me to take advantage of an opportunity, but I needed to treat this like research instead of a heist. I didn't know what I was walking into up there."

"You don't," Bastion said. "We have no intel on what Tenisha's security is like or what the inside of her home looks like."

"So that's all this is. We're getting that intel. I can share it with Hessod. Make a plan for the real job later."

"Sensible. Still more of a risk than you should be taking."

Good enough. And if I happened to see something that connected the five companies while doing my research? Maybe I wouldn't need to go back. I left my room and made directly for the northwest stairwell, the least used of the stairwells.

#   #   #

Twelve floors later, I slowly opened the door into the staff hallways on floor 244, the lowest level of Tenisha's floors. It had been quite a trek through the rest of Gloria's floors, Orogen's floors, and some mechanical and staff floors, but I was here.

I looked around the door, checking for anyone walking by. Seeing nobody, I opened the door more, and then immediately heard a pair of voices approaching. I recognized one as Nox. I drew back, closing the door as quickly and quietly as I could, but the click of the door latching sounded far too loud. I stood there, waiting and listening as the two voices kept getting closer. Closer. Too close.

"Elise," Bastion said in my ear.

Yeah. They were coming right this way. I looked up to gauge my jump, then leaped straight up, gripping the ceiling with one of the few tools I made sure these limbs had: a goo that became powerfully adhesive when a small electric current ran through it. Barely a breath later, the door opened and someone in a khaki maintenance uniform walked into the stairwell. Right behind them was the dark head of Nox.

I held my breath. I was heading into Tenisha's to follow a lead that had nothing to do with our embed here in Kotega. Nox didn't know anything about my hunt for a connection between the five companies. He'd never heard of Bastion. He didn't know about my fight with Theo Huginn-Intel or his dying words that sent me on this path. I had to do this without Nox, and wouldn't you know it, here he was. As the other maintenance worker started walking down the stairs, talking about air filters, Nox stopped in his tracks. He looked around slowly and then looked straight up at me.

His brow furrowed. His head tilted like a confused puppy. Then he glanced at his fellow maintenance worker before looking back to me. Finally, he just shook his head and continued on his way, answering the question his coworker had asked.

I breathed out slowly, but I knew it was a temporary reprieve. I'd avoided being spotted by the actual Kotega maintenance worker, but I was going to have to tell Nox a plausible story later. I hated lying to him almost as much as I hated lying to Quynn. And since Nox wasn't read into Necropolis Alpha, I had to skirt a lot of truths with him. That didn't make it any easier.

I dropped back down and eased through the door into the maintenance hallway. I whispered to Bastion, "Guidance?"

"I don't have schematics on this floor," he said.

I nodded slightly, knowing he would see the movement of my head as he looked through my ocular implants. Then I started moving through the hall, trying to look like I belonged there. All the while, I was looking for a door larger than others, probably recessed, and very likely watched by a camera. Basically, just like the door to Gloria's residence from The Roost.

In fact, that was what made it easy. The staff hallways here were the same as The Roost. The rooms were used for different things, but the layout was identical. There were a lot more cameras here, though, so I was glad I'd chosen to act casual instead of sneaking. Soon enough, I was looking at an extra-large door watched over by a camera. The door used a simple combination lock, but the camera was the real problem. A Kotega Phalanx 9. Four lenses. Fisheye, infrared, mass spectrometry, and the last created depth of field for the other three. Also electromagnetically shielded. I'd read about them but had yet to see one in the field.

"Thoughts?" I asked Bastion.

"No known exploits yet. The power and feed are hardwired in. No external data ports. You just may have to abort."

Infrared was a real problem. Smoke was an easy way to move past a lot of cameras, particularly if I could create a plausible explanation for the presence of smoke. And I had smoke bombs in my left elbow. But the infrared would see right through it. The only way to blind infrared was to either become as cool as the wall or to overload it with heat.

Wait.

I turned and hurried back down the hall, taking a right until I came to an open janitor's closet that I'd passed earlier. I walked in and looked around at the various cleaning chemicals neatly arranged on shelves. Some were store-bought with professional labels. Others were reused bottles with hand-written names on them. I had no idea how any of them might interact with each other.

"I need to make a fire," I said.

"Why?" Bastion said.

"The infrared. I need to make something hotter than me. Doesn't need to last long. Better if it doesn't, really. Surely there's some catastrophic way to mix some of these chemicals."

Bastion sighed. Yep, I still hated it when the AI made that sound. Then he said, "The window cleaner, the adhesive ice melt, and the general nano-infusion."

"Got it," I said, grabbing all three bottles and putting them on a small, wheeled cart. I grabbed a smattering of other bottles and cleaning supplies to load up the cart, too. Then, I checked my corners and wheeled it all back over to the camera, stopping just outside its view.

"Careful," Bastion hissed.

"Does the order matter?" I whispered.

"No," Bastion said. "Just—"

I didn't wait for him to continue. I unscrewed the adhesive ice melt and sloshed half the container in a long, glistening streak down the hall. I put the container back on the cart but left it open. I repeated the process with the window cleaner. A pungent odor and a hint of steam started to rise from the mixed chemicals. Finally, I opened the general nano-infusion, which was in a large bucket. The mixture inside was clear and shimmered with nanobots.

"You have a plan to not burn yourself?" Bastion asked.

In answer, I grabbed a plunger and tossed it just inside the camera's view, then immediately shoved the cart toward it. Hard. The cart rolled, hit the plunger with one wheel, and as I'd hoped, tipped over. The bucket of general nano-infusion dumped out along with the other open bottles, everything scattering. In moments, every bit of the general nano-infusion lit up in violet flames, tall and hot.

I moved quickly then, staying low and running for the door, the blaze making a wall between me and the camera. I plugged into the door's lock, bypassed it in moments, and rushed into Tenisha's residence.

"Now what?" Bastion asked. "That's going to draw some attention."

"Now I hide," I hissed as I looked around. The space was cavernous, at least two very tall stories high. It was a room for entertaining, if I had to guess, but it looked like it hadn't been used in quite some time. The place was clean, of course, but the furniture was stacked in one corner and draped in white cloth. In fact, that would work. I hurried across the room and ducked under the cloth, squirming in between a couple of plush armchairs.

"What if they come in here?" Bastion asked.

"That's why I'm hiding."

"You don't think they'll look under the cloth?"

I opened my mouth to argue, but he was right. I went to the first and most obvious place. I crawled back out quickly and scanned the room. I could run deeper into the residence, sure, but I needed to know if and when people came in. I just needed something less obvious, or to make my hiding spot less obvious. I darted over to the wall of sliding glass doors overlooking a huge balcony. I unlocked and opened one of them, but only by half a meter, and then I rushed back under the cloth just as the big door opened.

"Is someone in here?" a voice said.

"Mistress is at dinner with Orogen," another voice said.

"That fire blinded the camera," the first voice said.

"And I told you, it was just a stupid janitor."

I took slow and steady breaths in and out. No fear or panic, just focus. This, I was used to. Even if things went sour, I knew I could handle whatever came next.

"Look, that door is open," the first voice said.

"So?"

"Did you leave it open?"

"Of course not. It must have been—"

"Mistress hasn't even been on this floor in three years. She didn't leave it open. I'm going to check."

"Fine. You check. I'm going to find out which clumsy janitor I'm firing."

"Wait. Scatter the drones to look at the outside of the house."

Drones? That was going to add a wrinkle. Nothing I couldn't handle, though.

"Should…should I alert the family?" the second voice asked.

"No," the first voice said quickly. "In fact, keep the drones away from Orogen's dining room. No need to worry them if it was just a lazy and stupid janitor."

One set of footsteps walked away. The door opened and closed. I waited, hearing the other set of footsteps walk out onto the balcony. After a couple of minutes, they walked back in and the door to the balcony closed. Then the footsteps retreated, sounding angry, and went through the door back into the maintenance hallway.

I sat there under the cloth, wedged between two chairs. I let five minutes go by.

"What are you waiting for?" Bastion asked.

"Just making sure," I whispered.

"If they haven't come back in here by now…"

"It makes me feel better, okay?"

"Fine."

Five more minutes went by before I felt reasonably sure that nobody was coming back. I heard the slight buzz of a drone flying close to the building, significantly quieted by very good windows. Finally, I emerged from the cloth.

"What now?" Bastion asked.

"Now? We explore."

Chapter Fifteen

15 Days to Ascension

I'D BEEN IN PLENTY OF big, expensive homes in Jayu City before. I'd broken into the apartments of vice presidents, powerful directors, and some people with generational wealth. But Kotega Systems set the standard for generational wealth. The Siwa family was the oldest, most powerful family in the company. Their lineage was unbroken running back to the founding of the company around 200 years prior. I should have guessed that Tenisha's home would be expansive given that each of her children had four full floors.

Tenisha had five. And she lived alone. I couldn't quite wrap my head around the place as I walked through it, either. Half of the first two floors were just that one room I'd walked into, a grand ballroom for entertaining. I wasn't sure why it hadn't been used in so long, though. The rest of the first floor didn't seem like it was really for living. There was a huge, commercial kitchen that was equally unused. Two large bathrooms with multiple stalls, half a dozen smaller bathrooms, powder rooms, and several lounges finished out the floor.

"Nothing suspicious or hidden," I said to Bastion.

"Only the disuse is suspicious," Bastion said.

"Seems like only the cleaners walk through this floor. Whoever came to check my entrance said Tenisha hasn't been in here for a few years."

The second floor was a little different. I found a dozen guest bedrooms, all resembling hotel rooms more than rooms in a home. Matching white linens, nondescript wardrobes, and identical plain desks were in each one. Obviously, much of the primary Siwa residence was designed hosting, not living.

I took the stairs up to the third floor, having to bypass a small lock to get in. Finally, it looked like somewhere that people lived. Sort of. A kitchen, two living rooms, two dining rooms, and what looked like a study occupied this floor, but something was off.

"It feels…empty," I whispered.

"Why are you whispering?" Bastion asked.

"Feels like I'm creeping through a museum." The place was downright austere. All the furniture was simple. Minimal. But also looked unused. The entire place smelled of nothing but faint cleaning products. "Does Tenisha actually live here?"

"I don't have access to a camera network or anything up here, but there's nothing on the Net or in Corto research to suggest otherwise."

"Just this weirdly empty place."

I wandered from room to room, keeping my aural sensors up a little higher than normal just in case. Everything was boring. Plain. Clean. Virtually unused. There was no sense of personalization, no pictures or décor to speak of. Almost an hour into my infiltration, I finally reached the fifth floor, and at least there was something to look at. There were a few dirty dishes in the sink of the kitchen. The fourth kitchen, if I was counting correctly. I found what looked like Orogen's and Gloria's childhood rooms, still plastered with posters, shelves covered with tchotchkes and trophies from their youths.

Directly above the ballroom below was something I hadn't expected, something that looked like an actual museum. Though only one floor tall, the room was the same square footage as the ballroom below, though it was filled with a maze of glass cases containing old and rather sturdy-looking items.

"What are these?" I asked.

"They appear to be mining relics," Bastion said.

"Mining?" I looked at one of them, which was made of slightly rusted metal and nearly the size of Poe. In fact, it closely resembled a bike, complete with handlebars. Instead of a front thruster, there was an enormous, spiked drill. Instead of rear and vertical thrusters were treads.

"From back before Jayu City existed, of course," Bastion said. "Back when the planet was founded as a mining settlement. Don't you know all this?"

"I didn't pay a lot of attention in school. I remember something about mining. Some rare elements or something."

Bastion sighed. "Sterlium 4. It was originally a lab-created element critical to the old Gibson drives."

"The what?"

"The first hyperlight drives for starships. Despite how far this planet is from Earth and the core colonies, the founders discovered that Sterlium 4 was being naturally produced in the core here. It was the richest find in the history of Earth Space at the time."

"But then the tech moved on, right?"

"The Raj-Lu drive? Double the speed and only a quarter of the energy use. And it used an entirely different fuel. Sterlium 4 went from the most valuable element in the galaxy to…well, considerably less so. Certainly not worth what it cost to mine and transport it 60 light-years back to Earth."

"And these are from that time? Then they must be over a hundred years old."

"Nearly 300, actually. I didn't realize this many of them were still around. There are more here than in the Stephenson Museum."

"Never been," I said, moving to look at another case that contained a dozen small artifacts.

"Of course you haven't."

"What's that supposed to mean?"

"You don't strike me as the museum type."

"I…" I stopped short. He was right. No adrenaline spikes happened inside a museum unless I was robbing one. My adrenaline did perk up a little when I heard the buzzing of a drone. I ducked behind the case and waited for it to pass. "Fine."

I stopped short when something caught my eye. It was on the largest piece in the place, a hulk of complicated metal gears and plates, twice the size of a car. It was also the only piece not behind glass. None of that was what grabbed my attention, though. Rusted and difficult to see was what looked like a logo. An interlocked G and H.

"Could it be?" I whispered.

"Could what be?"

"That logo. Gibbingson Holdings?"

"It's not the same, though," Bastion said. He was right, of course. It was cruder. A different font and different placement from the logo we'd seen in the Offworld Relay, but it did have a resemblance. I'd first seen the logo on a server terminal there. We'd then heard the name from the Relay's operator. Most of the data streaming off our little planet was going to Gibbingson Holdings in the form of marketing data with no differentiation between companies. Bastion, Hessod, Quynn, and I had all been looking for anything on Gibbingson Holdings since, but we'd found nothing.

"Maybe this was their logo 300 years ago," I said.

"You think this company that we can't even prove exists was doing business three centuries ago? And here, of all places?"

"It can't just be a coincidence," I said. I blinked rapidly, triggering the cameras in my optical implants. I took a few images from different angles, then continued to move through the space, looking at the other artifacts for the logo. I found it on only three different pieces, all on the larger side. None of them spelled out exactly what GH stood for, but it was a lead. A possible connection between the Offworld Relay and the pre-Jayu City past of the Little Sekhmet Settlement. I didn't know what it meant, but I was going to find out.

"This is a waste of time," Bastion said.

"Or it's exactly what we've been looking for," I said. "I'm almost done."

Bastion was finally silent as I finished looking for and taking pictures of those GH logos. I really wanted to pop open some of those glass cases and see if I could disassemble the artifacts to find more information, but Bastion wasn't entirely wrong. I was on a clock, and I still had halls and rooms to look through before Tenisha came back from her dinner with Orogen and Gloria.

I moved down the last hall that I hadn't explored yet. An old playroom. An empty office. Three more guest rooms with only minor splashes of personality. Then, at the end of the long hallway, I finally found Tenisha's bedroom.

It was the biggest bedroom in the residence, though still only a quarter of the size of the mining museum room. The enormous bed was unmade. A large desk by the windows was covered in polymer pages. There were piles of clothes in different corners of the room. A huge viewscreen was on and muted, showing half a dozen news streams at once. After the disuse and austerity of the rest of the residence, the mess here was shocking. There was even a faint sweat smell in the air.

"She definitely lives here," I said.

"Apparently," Bastion said. "The desk."

I nodded and crossed the room to it. I took a quick picture of the disarray, then started carefully riffling through the different pages. Spreadsheets. Corporate memos. Notes from Tenisha's staff and house maintenance. Nothing mentioning any of the other four companies or Jayu City generally. The only thing I found with any value to me were printouts of the Siwa family's schedules for the next three days. I took quick pictures of those, ducked behind the desk briefly when another drone flew by outside, and then carefully arranged everything so it was back in the mess I'd found it in.

As I did, though, something fell off the desk with a surprisingly heavy thump. I bent down and found a personal tablet.

"I haven't seen one of these since I was a kid," I said.

"The last personal tablets went out of production nearly 20 years ago," Bastion said.

I suddenly wished I was in contact with Valdo, that he was taking my calls. If this old thing was secured, I didn't have algorithms to crack it. My hacker brother would be able too, though. I took a deep breath, and I pressed the button on the front, and the screen came to life. No password or any other security. The OS made me nostalgic, even if it was a Kotega OS. It reminded me of the OS that ran on my parents' tablets when I was young.

"Why does she have that?" Bastion asked.

"Who knows. My mom kept her personal tablet for several years after they left production. She just liked it. Could be the same for Tenisha." There weren't many apps, but I tapped through them anyway.

"What are you looking for?" Bastion asked.

"She still keeps this charged and in use," I said. "Might be something…oh."

An unsecured memos file, directly tied to Tenisha's security account.

Mistress,

Here are the direct intranet addresses to their calendars, as requested. We've put in place the keyword searches you've requested as well, and you'll be sent a digest of hits twice daily. Please do not hesitate to reach out with questions or adjustments.

Below that were long strings of letters and numbers. The strings were labeled Gloria and Orogen. The memo was signed by Gordion Kotega-Tenisha, chief of security.

"That's useful," Bastion said. "One moment."

"What are—?"

"One moment."

I sighed and put the tablet back from where I'd bumped it.

"We now have direct access to Orogen's and Gloria's schedules," Bastion said as two calendars for the week appeared on my display, one for each Siwa child.

"Just like that?" I asked.

"Those numbers are impossible to guess, even for a supercomputer. Too long and complicated. But they're backdoors if you already know them, which we now do."

"Not a wasted trip after all, then, huh?"

"If you're planning to follow this with, I told you so, don't. This was pure luck."

He was right, but I wasn't going to tell him that, either. I turned and stood there, scanning my eyes across the room, seeing if there was anything I'd missed.

"We should go," Bastion said.

"I know," I said. I walked around the perimeter of the room, looking for any obvious signs of a safe or hidden panel, but nothing jumped out at me. As I walked around the bed, I spotted something that looked thoroughly out of place. It was a small shelf near the door to the en suite bathroom. Atop the shelf was a gold cloth. On that sat a framed image of a man, lean and dark of skin. Several extinguished candles surrounded the image.

"An altar," Bastion said.

"Oh," I said. "For Halse, her husband. Gloria's and Orogen's father." I didn't say it as a question. I'd read about the use of family altars in Kotega, but I hadn't actually seen one. It was odd here both in its cleanliness and overt sentimentality. Halse had died nearly a decade ago from a brain aneurysm. Very sudden. He'd been the public face of the Siwa family. Tenisha had inherited the CEO position from her father, and Halse had taken the Siwa name when they married. He was a gifted public speaker, a natural publicist for the company and the family. His death had rocked the entire company, but Tenisha had kept a firm hand at the till, guiding the company through it. But he had been her husband, her love, after all.

It made me think of my own father, the man who'd left when I was 12. I knew where he was now. I had a brother. Did I want a relationship with my father? Could I forgive him? I didn't know. I'd been so shocked by the revelation that Valdo was my brother, I hadn't processed what finding my father in the Toinette borough meant. I hadn't needed him for a long time. I didn't really need him now, did I?

"Elise?" Bastion said. "We're closing in on two hours here."

That shook me from my reverie. "Right," I said. I walked back to the door of the room, taking one last look around before turning to leave.

"Done?" Bastion asked.

"One last thing," I said as I took one step down the hall. "Switch to thermals."

My vision instantly changed from normal colors to a high-contrast view of the hallway. The warmer the object, the brighter it appeared. I only saw that for a moment before my vision went completely white, however. Blindingly white. I blinked, but it made no difference. A moment later, everything went dark.

"Ah!" I yelled. "Back to normal! Back to normal." Nothing happened.

"Bastion?" I whimpered.

"Working on it."

Then my normal vision was back, though I was having trouble focusing. "What happened?"

"Alarms and countermeasures," Bastion said. "You need to leave right now."

"What?"

"An infrared detector, I think," Bastion said. "A silent alarm went off the moment you started projecting infrared light, then some systems in the house started flooding your mods. I could have prevented this if you installed my chip as your neural interface."

I stumbled, the floor going in and out of focus as I tried to walk. "Something's wrong."

"Your optical mods rebooted," Bastion said. "No damage. Get moving, they'll be back to normal once they finish some calibrations."

Easier said than done. When optical implants were calibrating, it was usually in the presence of a technician. You just had to sit down and look at things as you were told. Look at this eye chart. Look out the window at the ad across the street. Look at your hand. After a few minutes, you were done. I was trying to move as quickly as I could down the hall while my depth perception kept changing and my focus wobbled. It all made my stomach churn as I kept tripping over my own feet.

"Any help?" I asked as I bounced off the wall. Again.

"It's almost done," he said. "Keep going."

I groaned, but as I reached the end of the hallway, my vision finally stabilized. Great. My relief was huge and immediately deflated. I still needed to leave Tenisha's apartment before it was flooded with security personnel. Every exit I could think of would be monitored. Doors to the maintenance and staff hallways, elevators, and the main stairwell were all watched by cameras.

"I don't have nearly enough repelling equipment for this," I grumbled.

"On the second floor, there's a garbage chute."

"You and garbage chutes! We'll call that a last resort." I looked around, desperate for any exit that wouldn't leave me smelling like sewage. Then I heard a familiar buzz. I hurried to the outside wall to get a good view while staying out of site. The drone was round, half a meter wide, with a small trio of thrusters on the bottom. A cluster of cameras were pointed at the building.

"Those drones hackable?" I asked.

"Those are Kotega Sparrows, sixth generation. They can't support your weight for flight."

"That's not what I asked." The drone was moving slowly, looking over the building. Once it moved past the nearest sliding door to the balcony, I edged over and opened that door.

"I can hack them," Bastion said. "The port is on the back side, but you'll never—"

It was about to fly out of range. I looked around and grabbed the first thing I saw, a small pot from the nearby kitchen. Then I moved onto the balcony and tossed the pot right over the drone. The drone stopped moving and spun away from me, looking up and following the trajectory of the pot as it fell into the street. I took two steps and jumped, landing on the back of the drone, which immediately wobbled and started to lose altitude.

"What are you—?" Bastion yelled in my ear.

I deployed my data cable while struggling to keep hold and stay away from the trio of cameras on the front of the drone. Surely only a few seconds passed, but the struggle made it feel longer before I plugged my data cable in. Moments later, the drone stabilized, though it was still shedding altitude. A lot slower than if I'd just jumped, though.

"Move closer to the building," I said.

"Someone might see," Bastion said. "Or hear."

"Let me worry about that. Get us down to Gloria's floors."

The drone and I kept descending. It wasn't built to be ridden, so there were no real handholds. I kept having to adjust my grip on the sides, still trying to avoid the front cameras in case a Kotega security person suddenly retook control.

"Three more floors," Bastion said.

We were descending quickly. It was tempting to watch the floors go by, to see if anyone saw me, but I knew the better plan was to hide my face. It might not do me much good if someone saw me out the window, but it was all I could do.

"One floor."

"Nice and close," I said. I looked at the building. Another balcony went by, and then the one that I needed was fast approaching. In one movement, I braced my feet against the top of the drone, twisted, and leaped. That drone wasn't meant for human weight, and it pushed away from the building as much as I pushed away from it. I landed short, grabbing the balcony railing under my arms. I quickly lost my grip, slipping to my elbows and finally grabbing hold with the goo on my hands. The sudden stop jerked my shoulders where flesh met cybernetics. I let out a curse.

"Get inside," Bastion said.

"I'm fine," I said, doing as he said. "Thanks for asking."

"I have access to your diagnostics. I know you're fine. You need to get inside before that drone comes back. I programmed my hack to self-delete the second you disconnected."

"Sparks," I grunted as I hauled myself over the balcony railing, landing clumsily on the balcony floor. Then I got to my feet and hurried inside, scooting away from the window just as that familiar buzzing came back.

"Where am I?" I asked as I looked around. It was Gloria's apartment, obviously, but I'd never been inside. There were three chairs, a couch, and a long wet bar against the far wall.

Suddenly, I was on the ground, a heavy weight on top of me. It was a person, definitely, and they were trying to pin me to the floor. I struggled and squirmed, wishing once again that I had my work limbs. They were stronger and built to help me in a fight.

"Stop it!" a familiar voice said, too close to my ear.

"Get off me!" I said.

A hand clamped over my mouth as I was forcibly twisted around to see my captor. My stomach dropped. It was Zhao.

Chapter Sixteen

15 Days to Ascension

"NOT A SOUND," ZHAO SAID in a whisper. I was still pinned to the ground with xem astride me. My hips were facing the ground, and Zhao had used one hand to cover my mouth while the other arm was wrenching my face and shoulders up to look at xem.

I wanted to fight. To struggle. To run. But Zhao was surprisingly strong, obviously modded more than I'd thought. And if Zhao wanted to rat me out to Gloria, xey could. So instead of fighting, I gave a curt nod.

Zhao let go of my face and slowly got off me, staying low and moving behind a counter. Like xey knew what xey were doing.

Zhao said, "This way."

I got up, mimicking the head of house's movements. Zhao hated me, obviously, but this seemed almost gentle. Xyr face was still stoney, xyr tone terse, but there didn't seem to be much anger, either.

We moved quickly, staying low until we were out of sight of the windows. Sure enough, the familiar buzzing of the drone came back. It seemed to be hanging out on this floor, slowly moving around the perimeter.

Once Zhao and I reached an interior corridor, xey assumed xyr normal upright, brisk step. I followed xem down the hallway and through a door back into the staff quarters.

One of the maids was hanging out in the hallway, and he took one look at Zhao and made himself scarce. Thing was, he didn't look at me at all. Perfectly normal behavior for the staff, in other words.

"Keep up," Zhao barked in xyr normal commanding tone.

I did, and soon, we were in xyr office. Zhao pointed to a chair and closed the door behind me. The moment the door latched, xey said, "Where were you?"

I took a deep breath before answering. "It's better you don't know."

"I'm sure it is," Zhao said. "But when the security reports start coming in and Thrace starts asking me questions, I need to have a viable story."

"You're not angry?"

"Of course I'm angry," Zhao hissed. "With you? Always angry. Now. Where were you?"

I shook my head and leaned back in the chair. "You have training."

"Planetary defense," Zhao said without emotion.

I wouldn't have thought that. The planet hadn't faced a threat from space in centuries, but there were still several thousand people who served at any given point. They came from all five companies and even the outlying regions and they were all trained just in case. I'd known very few people to serve, and none of them had personalities like Zhao's.

"I repeat," xey said. "Where were you?"

I said nothing.

Zhao's face set, xyr jaw working. Xey moved around the desk and slowly took a seat in xyr own chair. Then, xey said, "Fine. How will this blow back on Gloria?"

"It won't."

Zhao leaned forward, elbows on the desk. "I don't believe you."

"Believe it or not, we're on the same side."

"Not. I don't believe it. I don't believe a word you say about anything. You shouldn't be here. None of this should be happening."

"Agreed," I said.

That took xem by surprise. Xyr eyebrows shot up for a moment before xey leaned back.

"I'm here because there's a threat to the entire city."

"That's your defense? Melodrama?"

"I wish it was just melodrama, but I'm serious. Do you really think the CEO of a rival company would call in her favor and send me in for something less?"

"Your CEO?" Zhao said with a derisive laugh. "Absolutely. She would do it just for spite."

I opened my mouth to object but thought better of it. "You're probably right."

"Do you have an actual explanation? Anything concrete?"

I blew out a breath and stood up. I needed Zhao on my side, but I needed to be careful. I started pacing as I spoke, thinking and speaking as carefully as I could. "Look, I know you don't want me here. I need to be here, but we both hate how it happened. Dr. Corto uses people. She's using you, obviously. She has something on you, and I promise you, I don't know what. Here's the thing, though, being here wasn't my idea. It was hers. We're both being played here."

"Enemy of my enemy?" Zhao asked.

"Exactly."

"Not exactly, though. Not even a little. My loyalty is to Gloria. The Siwa family, of course. Kotega. But above all, to Gloria. Can you say the same?"

"No, of course not." I stopped my pacing, putting my hands on the desk and leaning in toward Zhao. "But I want Gloria to become the next CEO. And I have no loyalty to Dr. Corto."

Zhao leaned back, but xey looked unmoved. "And you're willing to leave a trail of bodies to make that happen?"

Xyr words were like a punch to the gut. I stood back and stumbled a bit. "Bodies? Is that what you think? Did Dr. Corto insinuate…?"

Zhao's face twisted in surprise for just a moment before the anger came back.

"That's not me, Zhao. I'm no assassin. I'm not here to hurt anyone.

Silent circuits, I'm trying to avoid hurting anyone."

Zhao looked away in silence. I sat back down, wondering what Dr. Corto had told Zhao to get me here. Eventually, the head of house broke the silence. "Why would Corto Corporation want Gloria to be CEO?"

I blew out a breath as I considered my answer.

"You're playing a dangerous game," Bastion said. "You have no idea if you can trust this person, no idea where xyr true loyalties lie."

He was right. All I had was xyr word on xyr loyalties, but Zhao could also be very useful on my side. Maybe a trickle of the truth would do. "We don't necessarily want Gloria as CEO, but we don't want Orogen."

"Why?"

"He's compromised."

Zhao opened xyr mouth to speak, but I held up a hand and said, "I won't get into specifics. Not without solid, incontrovertible evidence, which I don't have yet. I know I'm right. I've seen it. But I need more. I'm here to get that very evidence. We want the same things, even if not for the same reasons."

"I have no reason to trust you," Zhao said.

"No, you don't," I said just as an idea struck me. "But maybe I can help you and earn your trust."

Zhao barked out a laugh. "And how would you do that?"

"I'm here because Dr. Corto has both of us over a barrel. Not just you. Whatever she has on you, I don't care what it is. I don't need details, but maybe I can help you with it. Because I promise you, Dr. Corto will never let go of it. She may have said that if you bring me in, you're square, but that's not how she works. So long as she can hold it over your head, she'll call in as many favors as she needs."

"No," Zhao said, shaking xyr head. "She is a CEO. There is honor there. She would destroy…she said she would get rid of any evidence of my dishonor."

"She won't, though. No one in Corto talks about honor. She doesn't care about honor. That's not how she's wired. It could be years. Maybe decades or next week, but the moment she has a need for you, she'll call in another favor. But blackmail only works when the victim has something they're desperate to hide."

Zhao stared at me long and hard for a while, xyr face giving away nothing. Eventually, xey let out a long breath and said, "No. I don't trust you. If you knew, then you could destroy me just as easily as your CEO. How better to dishonor Gloria than to bring low her head of house?"

"That's not what—"

Zhao got to xyr feet in an instant, cutting me off. "I said no. Go back to your room. Go to bed. You have a busy day tomorrow as Daeli."

"Zhao—"

"Go before I lose my patience."

I closed my mouth and rose from the chair, moving through the door that Zhao opened for me. Before xey could close it, though, I turned to xem and said, "Just think about it. We don't need to be friends. You don't have to like me. But I can help you."

Zhao closed the door in my face. I turned and started back toward my room. The journey up to Tenisha's hadn't been entirely fruitless, at least. I'd learned a bit about Tenisha. And there'd been the mining equipment. And calendar access.

I walked past the cafeteria like it was just another day when Thrace's voice stopped me.

"Xyla," he said from the cafeteria.

I stopped in my tracks. Gloria's head of security. My pulse leaped in my throat and warmth flooded my face. Surely he knew about the alarm upstairs. Had anyone seen my wild ride down the side of the building? Anyone other than Zhao? I made my face neutral and turned to face him. He was sitting across from Ridley like normal. Carmela was just sitting down to join them. "Yeah?"

"You all right?"

"Yes," I said. "Why?"

"You look like you stood in a wind tunnel," Ridley said with his trademark smirk.

Carmela gave me a quizzical, empathetic look.

I touched my hair, and it was a wild mess atop my head. Right. Riding down the building on a drone. Being tackled by Zhao. I straightened my hair as best I could without a mirror.

"Deal you in?" Thrace asked with my brother's smile, holding up the deck of cards.

I nodded vigorously.

Ridley leaned in. "Did you hear about Orogen's driver? Put in three days' notice. Three days! Say goodbye to a Siwa family recommendation. I should apply, right? Drive the CEO around? It would be a step up for me."

I let out a breath, smiled, and focused on my cards. Mother of Corto, somehow, nobody here knew.

Chapter Seventeen

12 Days to Ascension

THERE WERE KNOTS OF TENSION in my shoulders for the next two days that I just couldn't shake. I was constantly worried that Thrace or some other security guard was going to drag me away. But I heard not one mention of the silent alarm in Tenisha's. Thrace gave no indication that he was even aware of an alarm anywhere in the Siwa residence. It was downright strange.

Nothing from Gloria, either. We were right back to our long days of meetings with brief conversations in the car. I would have thought that Gloria would have heard about the alarm from her mother, but she made no indication. Then again, those next couple of days were even busier than normal, so we didn't talk much.

I got an early start the third day, waking before dawn to a knock at my door. I groggily stumbled over to the door, opened it, and found a tray with breakfast sitting in front of the door. Coffee, toast with plenty of butter, and a cloud-like quiche. Carmela really was the best. I'd barely picked up the tray when Zhao appeared.

"25 minutes," xey said.

I wanted to say something snarky, but after our conversation the other night, I just nodded and brought the tray inside, going to my desk as Zhao followed. We were silent, xem doing my hair while I ate my breakfast and then started working on my makeup, a sketch sitting next to my mirror showing me exactly how I needed to do it to match Gloria. The look was tamer than most days. Simple eye liner, eye shadow that added a simple bronze to the eyes, same with the blush. There were multiple outfits in play today, multiple color palettes, so we needed a neutral look. Only the lipstick would change with each look today.

"Ten minutes," Zhao said as xey finished spraying my hair in place. It was up in three large curls that ran from the front to the back of my head. It did look cool even if it wasn't my style.

"The light blue?" I asked. Four outfits were hanging on small racks around my room, ready for the day's rotation.

Zhao glanced back at them and then looked back to me in the mirror and nodded. Xey stood there for a moment, still looking at me.

"Anything else?" I was hoping maybe our conversation had sunk in, had made the wheels turn in xyr brain, inching closer to letting me help xem.

Instead, Zhao's face turned stern. "Don't be late. You want trust? Show me you deserve it."

Without another word, Zhao swept out of the room.

"Well," I said aloud to the empty room. "I suppose it's a start."

#   #   #

Ridley was standing next to the open door of the car, and he smiled broadly when he saw me hurrying toward him, a pair of too-tall blue heels hanging from my fingers.

"Only one outfit?" he asked.

"For now. Am I late?" I whispered once I was close enough.

"Nah, she's not here yet."

I exhaled and let some tension out of my shoulders.

"You look a little rough. I didn't think you knocked back that many with us last night."

"Didn't sleep well," I said. It wasn't a lie. Once I got to sleep, I'd slept fine, but it took me too long to find my dreams. I'd been so worried about the alarm in Tenisha's residence and my conversation with Zhao, I'd tossed and turned for a while. It had been the same for three nights running.

"There's coffee in the car," Ridley said, tilting his head inside. "And some hair of the dog in the center console if you need a little help."

"Ancestors, no," I said, grateful to remember the Kotega slang. I climbed into the car and helped myself to a cup of coffee. The smell of fresh brew filling the cabin was a nice pick-me-up, too.

I took only a few sips before I heard Gloria say, "Good morning, Ridley."

"Mistress," he said with a slight bow.

Then Gloria slid into the car, always more graceful than me in our matching outfits. The outfits wore me, Zhao had told me, whereas Gloria wore them. I couldn't agree more.

"Good morning, Xyla," Gloria said, helping herself to a cup of coffee. At least she didn't ask me to serve her, not in here.

"Mistress," I said, bowing my head as Ridley closed the door.

"Busy day today," Gloria said. That glimmer in her eyes was back again. Each day, I'd seen it more and more. Each day, I felt like I was getting to know her more.

"Yes, Mistress. What's first?" I asked like I hadn't already reviewed her schedule. She didn't know I had full access.

"Breakfast meeting with the Greenway twins" Gloria said as Ridley guided the car out of the Siwa garage and out into the pouring rain. "I've actually known them since we were children. I like them, even if they're just begging for scraps from the Siwa table at this point. Their mother lost our Security division a lot of credibility years ago. The entire family fell from grace. Still, it will be nice to see the two of them."

"Why have the meeting if they're so far down?" I asked. In the last week, she'd become freer with her words and more accepting of questions. I had the sense that Gloria was a bit lonely, that anything close to real friendship was rather transactional for her. She tried to keep the staff at a distance, too. But here in the car, she would sometimes ramble on at length about the people she interacted with. Very little about her family, though. Nothing useful to me. I wasn't pushing for what I really wanted yet, but if

I kept asking innocent questions like an inquisitive Daeli, it would make things easier when I started asking questions I needed answers to.

Gloria sighed. "If my mother had her say, I wouldn't be meeting with them at all. But they're friends, real friends, and they asked. I hate what's happened to them. Maybe if some of the bigger families see them having breakfast with me, it'll help them."

"How generous of you, Mistress."

"How very un-Siwa-like," Bastion said in my ear.

How very un-CEO like, really. It was the most un-Ariela thing I'd ever heard her say. In fact, it reminded me more of Quynn than Dr. Corto. While we didn't rely on honor in Corto Corporation, your reputation was important. During our first year dating, a friend of theirs named Kal went through a scandal. I don't remember the details, but everyone else was distancing themselves from Kal. Not Quynn. Quynn, my love, had recently been promoted to manager, and their first act as manager was to have lunch with Kal. Not just anywhere, mind you, but at a restaurant frequented by managers and directors in their division.

"I wish I could do more for them," Gloria said. "Real friends are such a rare thing in this family, in this life. Seems like everyone smiling at me just wants something." She fidgeted with her hands for a moment, lost in thought, before she cleared her throat and then looked at me with those sparkling brown eyes. "I'm just going to enjoy this breakfast. The rest of the day is going to be purely business, I assure you, even the visit to the temple later this morning."

For the first time, I didn't look away from her gaze. There was warmth there, familiarity. It surprised me. Then it worried me. There was a warmth in my chest the puffed out with each breath and spread to my cheeks. Oh no, Elise. No, you don't. There's no need for that here. Job to do. Partner back home. Focus. I looked out the window and let the conversation die in the air.

Ridley landed the car smoothly on the landing pad of a posh-looking diner, which seemed like an oxymoron. It was like the restaurant was trying to capture a greasy-spoon vibe, but everything was too nice. The booths weren't lined with dock workers or laborers, but with executives in posh suits. Diner was just the theme. For someone who'd frequented actual greasy spoons, the effect didn't work.

I walked in and held the door for Gloria, then moved one step to the right and behind her, as always while I shook off and put away the umbrella. The Greenway twins were nice, very nice. They seemed downright normal, in fact. They both had jobs. They didn't use family names. They also asked Gloria questions about her life, about her rather than her family. Not once did they ask for a favor. I could see how relaxed Gloria was, how relieved. How nearly happy she was. I tasted Gloria's omelet, sweet potatoes, synthetic mimosa, and toast. No poison. Also, not at all what diner food tasted like, though it wasn't bad.

#   #   #

Two hours later, we were on our way to a temple, which was something I'd only read about. Okay, skimmed over. I knew that most Kotega citizens honored their ancestors, but formal temples were rare.

"They're a relic of old Kotega," Bastion said in the car. I was glad he thought to tell me because there was no way I could ask Gloria. Xyla would surely know about the temples. "There used to be ancestor worship instead of just honor, and weekly trips to temples were common from the highest to lowest of Kotega citizens. The company had become more secular over time, but a few of the very nicest and largest temples are still around as landmarks and for public shows like I'm guessing this is."

Ridley's voice over a speaker broke in, "Mistress, I've been instructed that we're picking up your mother."

"Thank you, Ridley," Gloria said. Then she sighed. "Of course she wants to check in and make sure I'm not making any rash decisions or taking unnecessary risks. This should be fun."

Fun. Right. I'd just been in Tenisha's home and set off alarms. I'd stayed clear of cameras as far as I could tell, but I'd been wrong before. What if she'd seen me? What if this was an ambush? I didn't relish being in the same room as Tenisha anytime soon, let alone the cramped cabin of the car.

Ridley made a wide turn, moving us toward a landing pad on a nearby building. The Kotega Systems CEO and her Daeli were standing there, just by the door to the building, both dressed in matching gray suits. As the car descended, Gloria pointed to the seat opposite her, telling me to scoot over instead of sitting diagonally across from her.

Within moments, Ridley opened the door to the car, and Tenisha Siwa Kotega entered, taking up the seat next to Gloria. It was my first time seeing Tenisha in the flesh. She was taller than I'd imagined, nearly as tall as Gloria. She bore more resemblance to Orogen than Gloria, though. Curly hair instead of straight, and Tenisha's was a beautiful silver. She carried more weight and quite gracefully. I had the distinct impression that Tenisha was rather strong. She was dressed in a plain but well-tailored suit the color of the gray sky. Her Daeli, whose name I didn't know, slid into the seat next to me. Apparently Tenisha's Daeli didn't go through all doors first.

"Good morning, Mother," Gloria said.

"Good morning," Tenisha said, bending sideways and placing a light kiss on Gloria's cheek. "You look tired."

"Staying busy is all," Gloria said.

"Doing your part is all," Tenisha corrected her.

"Of course."

Then Tenisha looked at me, her eyes starting at my toes and working their way up quickly. Oh, Corto. This was it. She surely recognized me. She'd seen footage of me creeping through her home or riding a drone down the side of the building. I held my breath.

Eventually, she said to Gloria, "Your new Daeli is a good match. Better than the last one. Almost doesn't even need the holographic mask."

"Thank you, Mistress," I said with as deep a bow as I could manage while seated. Once bowed, I let out a shaky breath.

As I looked back up, I saw Tenisha's eyes narrowed at the same moment that Gloria's went wide. Then Tenisha said, "It seems you haven't finished training her, though."

"Apologies, Mother," Gloria said. She gave me a look that said both I'm so sorry and please stop talking. Since when did I understand that kind of complexity in Gloria's looks? Mother of Corto.

"No speaking to the CEO?" Bastion said in my ear.

Apparently not. I bowed my head and looked away from the Siwas, casting my gaze out the window and trying to hide my sigh of relief. I'd mis-stepped, sure, but I was more relieved that Tenisha hadn't said anything about the break-in. A tap on my wrist pulled me back into the car. It was Tenisha's Daeli, a hand extended in the common gesture offering to share contact information. I was surprised but tapped my hand to theirs.

Nadia Kotega-Siwa, she/them, appeared on my display, and then she was texting me, "Tenisha isn't as progressive as Gloria. She prefers we don't speak unless spoken to."

"I noticed," I texted back. I glanced up and saw that both Tenisha and Gloria were using their AR keyboards as well, probably texting each other based on their frequent glances toward each other.

"Your first time to temple?" Nadia asked.

"Yes."

"Has Gloria told you what to expect?"

"No."

"We hang back farther here, five full strides straight back. We don't follow them into the temple, however. Once they go inside, we're to take up positions outside the doors like sentries."

"Guard duty?"

"More ceremonial. There will be a lot of press when we land. Once the Siwas come back out of the temple, they'll speak to the press for a while. We'll stay at the standard one-and-one position while they speak, then drop back again when following them to the car."

"Easy enough," I said.

"Oh, and no masks."

"No?"

"So as not to confuse the ancestors."

That seemed wild to me, but I didn't think Xyla would find it so, so I said nothing.

"Any questions?" Nadia asked.

"No. Thank you," I said.

The temple trip went exactly as Nadia described, and it was one of the least unnerving things I'd done as Daeli so far. The only annoying part was standing outside the temple for nearly half an hour while a mob of press lingered outside, casually vaping and chatting, waiting for the Siwas to emerge. They looked pitiful, huddled under their little umbrellas while Nadia and I stayed dry under our oversized ones. Once the Siwas had spoken to the press and we were all back in the car, Tenisha and Gloria were back to silently typing.

I took the opportunity to text Nadia, "Busy day for you?"

"Always," was the response.

"What do you think of Orogen?"

"Careful," Bastion said.

Nadia cast me a quizzical glance before she texted, "He is the honored son of Siwa, the next CEO of Kotega Systems. He will make a great leader."

That was a company line if I'd ever read one. It was probably best to let that one lie, but I had a rare opportunity here, so I pressed on. "A better leader than Gloria?"

Nadia cast nervous glances around the car at both Siwas and me before responding, "What are you playing at?"

"You don't have an opinion? I am Gloria's Daeli. I will always favor my mistress. Don't you?"

"Naturally. My loyalty is to Tenisha."

"And mine is to Gloria. She would be an incredible CEO."

"Of course she would," Nadia texted back quickly. "She is a Siwa. She's been trained since childhood to lead. As has Orogen. It is not for us to debate Tenisha Siwa Kotega's decisions."

"Of course," I said. I could see when I'd run into a wall. "My apologies."

Without another word, Nadia looked out the window, purposefully away from me, I thought. That was fine. I wasn't getting anything useful from her anyway. Ten minutes later, Ridley lowered the car down on yet another landing pad and Tenisha and Nadia left us. I said nothing but bowed as deeply as I could.

Once the door was closed, I said to Gloria, "Was that as awkward for you as it was for me?"

Gloria barked out a laugh before she said, "Probably not. Sorry. I should have warned you about Mother. Nadia isn't the warmest person, either. Makes her the perfect Daeli for Mother, though."

"I just hope I didn't make things harder for you," I said. It wasn't completely true, but it felt like something Xyla should say.

Gloria smiled in a way that made my nerves flutter. "Thank you. I'll be fine."

"Board meetings next?" I asked, desperate to get the subject back to business.

Gloria nodded. "Three of them. Which means three different outfits. Zhao will be meeting us there."

I didn't understand the need for clothing changes, but I didn't say that. "Anything special I need to know?"

"Just prepare to be bored."

That was an understatement, I would learn. After landing, Zhao met us with the next outfits. We entered a bathroom and changed into matching lavender suits. I wiped my lipstick off and redrew my lips in a purple so dark it was almost black. Gloria and I checked each other's hair and makeup, and we entered the first board meeting, though calling it a board may have been a misnomer. The first meeting was in a large room at the top of the tower that housed the Cybernetics division of Kotega. The so-called board was a collection of senior directors, all those that report to the VP of the division. As I stood there against the wall behind Gloria, I soon realized that this was a sort of job interview. They would ask Gloria questions about her vision for the division, what she thought the priorities were, and probe her knowledge of the industry.

In turn, Gloria asked questions about them, easily citing cost and production numbers without any documentation in front of her. She could have been pulling that information up on her display, of course, but I never saw her fingers move. Unless she had some interface tech beyond my ken, she'd memorized all of that information.

After an hour, Bear Kotega-Cyber, the current VP of the division who had remained silent the entire meeting, thanked Gloria for her time. Everyone rose to their feet and bowed to Gloria. She stood, thanked them all collectively for their time and attention, and we left.

Ten minutes later, we were at another tower changing clothes again, and then the entire process repeated for the Propulsion division. After that, the Healthcare division. Only once that was over did we both practically fall back into the limousine and relax.

"I don't know how you can sit through one of those, let alone three," I finally said.

Gloria sighed. "We won't have another day with three of them, but there are more of these meetings coming. Only two of the divisions have relatively new VPs, new enough that Mother doesn't want to see any changeover there. Though, it's already a foregone conclusion that I'll be taking over the Aerospace division."

My eyes widened. I couldn't help it. Which division Gloria was going to be leading was a frequent topic of conversation in the staff hallways.

"The NDA, remember," Gloria said. "It won't officially be announced until after Orogen takes the CEO chair. Though anyone with eyes and half a brain could figure it out. Our Aerospace division has been lagging for nearly a decade. Three VPs haven't been able to bring about any meaningful change. That'll be my job."

"That division is on the verge of economic collapse," Bastion said in my ear. "Their last major launch, an interstellar frigate, was plagued with shoddy work, cheap parts, and buggy software. It was shelved after six months, losing Kotega nearly 14 billion credits."

"Are you excited for that? For Aerospace?" I asked.

Gloria shrugged. "My brother always cared more about spacecraft and whatnot, but it's all just business. I've spent the last six months familiarizing myself. I'll do what Siwas always do. I'll turn it around and move on to the next problem division."

I bowed slightly. "The company is blessed to have you."

"I miss coding."

"Coding, Mistress?"

"My favorite hobby as a child. And a teen. I won some awards, even, built some entire systems from scratch. Until Mother said it was time to stop, to focus on learning to lead. Let the grunts do the grunt work."

"She…" I asked cautiously. "She said that?"

"No, no. She actually has a lot of respect for the working class of Kotega. But that was the gist."

"You could do both. Lead and code on the side."

Gloria waved a hand dismissively. "That's thinking strategically, not tactically. That's what mother says, at least."

I barked out a laugh.

"What?"

"My…" I almost said partner, but Xyla didn't have a partner. Quynn was all about strategic thinking after all. One of our frequent arguments. I cleared my throat and continued, "…mother says the same thing."

"Tactical is just more fun, right?" Gloria said.

"Oh, not her to," Bastion said.

"Tactical is absolutely more fun," I said, and I couldn't help but smile.

"Are you hungry? It's nearly 14:00, and we haven't eaten since breakfast." Gloria tapped a button near her hand. "Ridley? What's good to eat around here?"

"Not my neighborhood, Mistress," Ridley said over the speaker. "I'll check with the staff."

"I would do obscene things for a great pizza, but you can only find those in the Nexus borough," Gloria said.

"Why not go there?" I asked.

"No time," Gloria said. "And not good for a Siwa to be seen patronizing a rival company."

An image suddenly appeared on my display, almost making me jerk in my seat. Then I realized it was a screenshot from a news stream. Nezzus Pizza opening in Kotega on Friday. It promised Nexus pizza at a convenient Kotega location. The date was from a month ago. Another image appeared showing several very good reviews. Tactical advice, combat assistance, and food recommendations. Why was AI illegal in Earth Space again?

"There's a place not far from here that makes Nexus-style pizza," I said.

Gloria's eyes went wide and seemed to sparkle more than ever. "Well, don't keep us in suspense! Give Ridley the address!"

I did. We went as fast as Ridley could safely fly, urged on by Gloria's insistence as her fingers flew in the air. "What do you like on your pizza?" she asked Ridley and me. "Both of you. We'll have to take this to go."

The pizza was good. Very good. As good as Bella's or Fuselli's in Nexus? No, of course not. There was no better pizza on the planet than Bella's or Fuselli's, depending on my mood. But it was on par with the couple hundred other good pizza places in the Nexus Neuronics borough. That meant it was better than any other pizza place outside Nexus.

What was even more addictive and more dangerous than the pizza, however, was the look that Gloria kept giving me. It wasn't predatory, though she did sometimes glance at my exposed legs or minor cleavage. No, not that. I ignored those glances. I was seeing affection. Attraction. Not good. And yet, I wanted more of it. Really not good.

"What's next, boss?" I asked, trying to keep my voice light and steady. My view of her calendar just said, Practice.

"Kendo."

"Still squeezing it in even on a busy day?" I asked.

"It's busy days when I need it most. Too much sitting and talking. I need to just move my body, sweat, and swing a sword for a while, or I'll go mad. Can't be losing my cool in these meetings."

"Mistress?" Ridley said over the speaker.

"Yes, Ridley?" Gloria said.

"Your sparring partner had to cancel. Family emergency."

"Silent circuits," Gloria hissed. It was the first time I'd heard her curse.

"The facility can provide a replacement—"

"No," Gloria said. "Anyone who doesn't know me will just lose on purpose rather than actually hit me."

"Should I cancel, Mistress?" Ridley asked.

Gloria's face darkened.

"I'll spar with you," I said before I'd thought too much about it. "I don't know kendo, but I've done some sparring. I'll hit you if you want."

Chapter Eighteen

12 Days to Ascension

"WHERE DID YOU STUDY?" GLORIA asked as she walked into the large rectangle drawn on the floor and I followed. We were both wearing padded robes and mesh masks.

Bastion came through again, throwing up the names of three Kotega dojos that taught the same martial arts I'd been learning in Corto Corporation. I rattled them off, hoping that I got the pronunciations right.

"But none of them teach kendo?" Gloria asked.

No appeared on my display.

"No," I said. "I took classes for self-defense. I don't usually have a sword in my hand, so not as useful should something happen."

Gloria hummed in response.

"Apologies, Mistress." I wasn't entirely sure what I was apologizing for, but since I couldn't see her face, it seemed like a prudent thing to say.

"No apologies necessary. Kendo was never about self-defense in my family. It was about sport. Competition. I had to follow in Mother's footsteps in something."

"Of course, Mistress."

"Walk up to the white line," she said as she walked up an identical line about a meter from the one in front of me. She held up the polymer sword directly in front of her, hands a dozen centimeters in front of her waist, with the sword angling slightly up. I mimicked the stance and approached my line. She said, "Your part of the borough was dangerous, then?"

"I think every part of the borough is more dangerous than here," I said. "Though not particularly dangerous, no. I just like to be prepared, to feel like I can handle myself."

"I can respect that." Gloria rolled her shoulders. "When I yell, ha, we begin. Ready?"

"Don't I have more mods than you?" I knew that I did. I'd been briefed on them back at Necropolis Alpha. Her mods were minimal and very expensive. She couldn't mod her strength or speed without disqualifying herself from competition. But she had very good comms, optical, aural, synapse, and structural mods.

"Use your mods," Gloria said. "Help offset the difference in experience. Ready?"

I nodded. I totally wasn't ready, but I needed to do this. I'd learned from my time studying Corto Capoeira and Jeet Kun Do that combat was a language all its own. Movements were like words and punctuation. A fight was a conversation. I'd seen many students break down in tears not because they'd been hurt on the mat, but because they'd learned something about themselves, broken down some emotional wall while sparring. Maybe I could break down some of Gloria's. She'd been warming to me, but I was on a clock. The sooner she fully trusted me and opened up to me, the more information I could get from her and maybe convince her of what Orogen was up to.

"Ha!" Gloria yelled and stepped forward in nearly the same breath. She brought her sword straight down in a swift strike, which I barely deflected before stepping back. She was on me again, though, chasing me with quick steps and even quicker swings of her sword.

"Out!" she yelled. She lowered her sword and casually walked back to her line.

"What?" I asked.

"You're out of bounds. Point for me. Not that we're keeping score."

I looked down and saw that my right foot had stepped over the line of the rectangle drawn on the floor. It suddenly didn't feel so huge. I said, "Sorry, Mistress."

"Don't be sorry," she said as she assumed her ready position at her line. "You said you would hit me. So hit me."

I returned to the line, put my sword in position, and we went again. I tried to move sideways instead of just backward, searching for an opening, but Gloria was relentless. I couldn't find a window to take a swing between her quick strikes.

"Go left," Bastion said as I was already doing so.

"Press forward," he said a few seconds later as I was backpedaling and doing everything I could to deflect Gloria's blows. Really, not very helpful. Eventually, I stepped out of bounds again.

"You said you trained," she said as she returned to her line.

"I have," I said. "I did."

"Then use it. You don't know kendo. Fine. Use what you know, though, just with a polymer sword."

"Yes, Mistress," I said. She was right, after all. I did know how to fight, how to survive. I had to stop trying to fight like she was. This wasn't a kendo tournament. No judges were looking for particular forms or strikes. This was a sparring match between two people with very different training.

"I'm not helping, am I?" Bastion asked.

I shook my head slightly.

"I'll be quiet, then," he said. "Just don't get "

"Ha!" Gloria yelled.

I rushed forward, dropping low and to my left as Gloria stepped forward again with a simple downward strike. I wasn't there, though. I rolled, came up, and swung the sword at her thigh. She was already there to meet me, though, parrying my blow hard enough to put me off balance, and then there was a smack on my shoulder.

"Point!" she said.

I groaned.

"That felt more like sparring," she said, ignoring my complaint. "Don't overextend with the sword, though. Try to keep your balance, and as fast as you strike, pull the sword back to ready twice as fast. Again."

We went again and again, each clash lasting a little longer than the last. I tried to ply what I knew from my studies, though the sword still felt unfamiliar in my hands. Gloria kept giving me pointers, though, helping me learn sword technique while never discouraging me from using my non-kendo moves in the gym. After the dozenth or so round, I nearly landed three consecutive hits before Gloria finally landed the tip of her sword between my shoulder blades.

"I almost got you," I said between heavy breaths, smiling wide behind my mask.

"Almost," Gloria said through her own labored breathing, and I thought I heard a smile in it, too. "Again."

We circled each other, each making an occasional strike. I'd learned how she moved and how she fought, and she'd learned some of how I fought. The conversation was progressing. She moved right, but I knew it was a feint. I faked up and moved my sword to parry the blow that went left. It all felt familiar, like an extension of the closeness we'd been developing since I'd arrived in Kotega. It also felt a bit like fighting myself. Some people are very matter of fact when they fight, predictable, though often effective. I liked to be playful and creative in my fighting, to wing it as much as I relied on training. Gloria felt the same way, improvising flourishes and spins, then coming back to her ingrained stances.

Back and forth we went, circling, closing the distance, striking and parrying, and moving away. As she came in, I barely blocked one of her strikes to my knees, then shoved her away with a hip check. I heard a very un-Gloria-like laugh come from behind her mask. We went again, back and forth, eventually pressing sword to sword before she took my wrist in one hand and spun me away. The move was oddly gentle.

"Are you allowed to take a hand off your sword?" I asked.

"In a match? No. Here? Why not?" she said.

We exchanged blows again. I got the distinct sense that she was toying with me. She'd been studying kendo her entire life. I'd only tried it today, and my martial arts lessons hadn't been going on for a full year yet. I was trying to land a blow, when suddenly one of her feet was behind my ankle, and down I went, Gloria following me to the ground, her legs astride me.

"Elise, breathe," Bastion said. He knew me too well.

I lay there, pinned and as uncomfortable as I'd ever been in my life. Gloria's knees were on either side of my hips. Her pelvis was resting just below my own. This position was too much like sex. The sweat and heavy breathing weren't helping my discomfort.

"Please let me up, Mistress," I managed to grunt.

I couldn't see her face, but her posture suddenly stiffened like she was surprised. She tossed aside her kendo sword and then yanked her mask off. The brown of her cheeks was reddened with effort and a glisten of sweat stood out all over her face. The eyes. The smile.

"What's wrong?" she said between heavy breaths. "Don't like to lose?"

"You're on the verge of a panic attack," Bastion said. "You can throw her off with your legs."

"Please, Mistress," I said. It was all I could muster, trying as I was to contain my discomfort and growing anger at the position. I couldn't get enough air. I didn't want to throw her, though, to hurt her. My stomach was churning, and heat was flooding my face that had nothing to do with the effort of exercise.

Gloria must have noticed something was off. The playfulness suddenly fell away from her face, and she stood up off of me. Immediately, it felt like a weight had come away from my chest. I could breathe properly again, and my stomach started to calm. Gloria extended a hand to help me up, but I just rolled over and slowly came to my feet.

"Are you all right?" she asked.

All I could do was shake my head, still recovering. My back was to Gloria as I removed my mask, taking deep and steady breaths.

"Are you hurt?"

I shook my head again as I gathered myself up. Then a hand was on my shoulder, and I instinctively jerked away from it. A breath later, I realized how that must have looked, how impertinent it was. I quickly spun and bowed my head. "My apologies, Mistress."

"No, no, please," Gloria said, backing away with her hands raised. "Is there some PTSD that I don't know about? What's wrong?"

I shook my head, keeping it bowed. It wasn't trauma, though I could see how she might think that. Telling her that I was asexual, that the very idea of sex turned my stomach in knots, was too personal. Too real. Too Elise. It felt like violating myself to share that. But what was a reasonable lie, a reasonable excuse for my behavior that wouldn't put her off from me after all the work I'd done to ingratiate myself? Here she was, dismissing my apology and seeking answers like she was my friend. Like she wanted to be more.

I risked a glance at her face, and the look there confirmed it. Eyes wide. brow furrowed. Lips pursed and pleading. She was worried about me. She was worried that she'd done something wrong. But she hadn't. She just didn't know.

"Please," Gloria said.

And that broke my resolve. "I'm asexual, Mistress."

"But," Gloria sputtered, looking confused. "We didn't—"

"I'm sex averse. It makes me terribly uncomfortable. Sick to my stomach. When you had me on the ground, astride me, both of us sweating and…" I couldn't say more. I just stood there, shaking slightly, and bowed my head again. It was too much to look at her.

"Oh," Gloria said tentatively, and then she got it. "Oh. I'm so sorry, Xyla. I had no idea."

"No, Mistress," I said. "I don't share that information freely. People don't always react kindly."

"Xyla," Gloria said softly and sweetly, a tone I'd never heard from her. I looked up and once I did, it was Gloria who bowed to me. A sign of deepest sympathy and apology in Kotega. "I apologize. I was caught up in the moment and didn't think. I made…assumptions. Please forgive me."

Assumptions? What kind of assumptions? Had I missed something? What was she saying? Her eyes had drawn me in since we first met. Her wit and intelligence reminded me of Quynn in many ways, but her irreverence in private was more like me. I had a part to play here, to be Xyla, and the love of my life was back home in Corto. Had my work to ingratiate myself been going too well? Had Gloria Siwa Kotega caught feelings, deep feelings, for me?

"Of course, Mistress," I managed to whisper.

She stood upright, her eyes locking on mine. Those eyes of hers were full of understanding and apology. No judgment. No hostility. Mother of Corto, I'd never been compelled by her as I was at that moment. Not good.

\#   \#   \#

The car ride back to the residence felt different. Sweatier, sure, but also comfortable. Gloria's and Xyla's places in the hierarchy of Kotega Industries hadn't changed, but my footing with her had. Gloria seemed more comfortable, which made me both more comfortable and wary. I didn't know how Xyla would react to this newfound dynamic in the relationship. And how to react without betraying my own real-life partnership with Quynn made my head spin. I needed to focus. If she was comfortable, it was a good time to see if I could dig in deeper.

"So," I asked. "What happens once you go pro?"

"Pro?" she asked.

"At kendo."

Gloria looked at me and smiled weakly, but then her face twisted up. "I always thought I would start competing in the circuit, the tournaments that take place all over the city. But now…"

"Now?"

"Orogen is going to be CEO. I'm going to be head of Aerospace. That won't leave time for competing. Strategy, remember?"

"And being CEO would have let you compete?"

Gloria chuckled. "True enough, though I would have been in charge of my own schedule, at least."

"Do you think going pro would really change things with your mother?"

Her smile faded. "Probably not. Orogen has always been closer to her. They see the world the same way. I see a problem, and I look for a solution. Multiple solutions. I gather the smartest people that I can to help create those solutions, and we make them happen."

"Seem like a good way to approach things," I said.

"You should remember that," Bastion said. "Talking to the smartest people before you act."

"If I don't, I tend to make decisions with my gut. Works most of the time. My mom and Orogen, though, they're pure logic. Don't get me wrong, they have emotions, but they always lead with the logical approach. I've never been able to do that. I'm more like my father in that way."

"You must miss him," I said.

Gloria smiled, but it was a smile of remembrance flavored with sadness. "I do. Every day. Orogen will be a great CEO. I would have been a better one."

I wanted to tell Gloria about Tazia, about Orogen's conversion to Ibhalism. A tendency toward emotion and inspiration certainly made his conversion make more sense. But Gloria had already told me that anything that could stop Orogen's ascension to CEO would need incontrovertible evidence. I didn't have it, at least not anything that I could share without blowing my cover. I couldn't have her looking too closely at me until I had every shred of evidence that I needed.

"There's still time," I said instead. "Don't give up hope."

Gloria smiled, leaned forward, and squeezed my hand. She said, "Thanks."

Warmth flooded my cheeks, and I looked out the window as we pulled out of the rain and into the garage of the residence.

Chapter Nineteen

12 Days to Ascension

ONE MORE EVENT THAT DAY, and this one was black tie, so we had to go back to The Roost to get ready. I sighed when I walked into my room and found a floor-length, sparkling gown hanging from a dress form. I didn't sigh because it was a gown or because it hung off one shoulder, but because it was finally in my favorite color: black.

Two quick knocks hit my door. It opened before I could say anything. It was Zhao, of course.

"You haven't changed yet?" xey asked. "What are you waiting for?"

"I just walked in the door," I said.

"Change. Now." Without waiting, Zhao crossed to my desk and started pulling out and arranging various cosmetics and hair products.

I wanted to protest, but I was growing accustomed to Zhao. Asking xem to leave while I changed would have been a waste of breath, so I went ahead while xey were in the room. It wasn't like Zhao was even looking at me even while I was stripping down to literally nothing. Fancy gown meant fancy underwear and bra, after all.

Just as I was working on the last zipper, Zhao was suddenly behind me, batting my hand away and zipping the dress the rest of the way up. I didn't need the help, but Zhao was unnerved by how my cybernetic arms could twist around and zip a dress all the way up without assistance. Then, I was soon sitting at my desk chair as Zhao got to work on my face.

"Any trouble today?" Zhao asked after a few minutes.

"No," I said.

"Don't move."

How was I supposed to answer and not move?

Zhao continued, "Ridley said you helped Mistress with sparring."

"Mm-hmm," I intoned without moving my mouth.

"I wasn't aware that you are practiced in kendo. Someone named Xyla from that corner of Kotega would certainly be unfamiliar, I would think."

"I don't know kendo," I mumbled. "I know some other things. She taught—"

"Mistress," Zhao commanded.

"Mistress taught me some kendo. Mistress wanted the workout more than anything."

Zhao grunted as xey put a finishing flourish on my eyelashes, then moved on to my cheeks. "Mistress is not your friend."

"Mistress can make up her own mind."

Zhao stopped and took a step back from me. "You are deceiving her. She doesn't know who you are. I can barely tolerate your presence, but I will not tolerate you hurting her. Mistress doesn't deserve that."

I pictured Gloria's eyes, the way they looked at me with a sparkle that made me flutter. I had to keep ignoring it. And that laugh of hers during our sparring was too familiar, too easy. I needed to ingratiate myself with her, but it had gone too well, apparently. Gone too far. I needed to reel her back in or redirect her to someone else.

"I have no intention of hurting her," I said. "More than that, I'm actively trying not to. If I do my job right, I'll be helping her. Helping all of Kotega."

Zhao stared at me, xyr eyes burrowing into me for several long minutes. Without another word, xey continued to work on my makeup. I didn't know what else to say, but at least Zhao wasn't saying anything, either. That just left me with my thoughts and the fresh bruises to gently remind me of a delightful afternoon spent with Gloria.

"Stop moving," Zhao barked.

"I…" I started to say, then realized that I'd smiled. I hadn't realized. Just thinking about Gloria made me smile. That was bad. Very bad. I had Quynn, my love and partner. Gloria was part of the Siwa family. If I had anything to say about it, the future CEO of Kotega. She was destined for great things in a company that wasn't mine. She was a job. Not even that. Orogen was the real job. Gloria was a piece of the puzzle, a lever to pull to get the job done. I had to keep focus on that.

"There," Zhao said. "Done. Turn around."

I did so, and Zhao got to work on my hair. The moment I glanced in the mirror, I didn't see myself. For a split second, I saw Gloria staring at me. I blushed before I recognized that those weren't her eyes. The cheekbones were slightly different, and the slope of the jaw was different. That was my face made up to look like Gloria yet again. I sighed. Right. Focus. I just needed to focus.

# # #

The gala was a fundraiser for…something. I wasn't really paying attention when Zhao mentioned it. Something about children, I think. Orphans? There was a lot of Kotega lingo, and I was still thinking about Gloria and Quynn and my stupid heart fluttering at the wrong person.

And it did it again when Gloria slid into the limousine opposite me. She smiled, that new familiarity in her eyes. She seemed more comfortable around me after our sparring. Well, that had worked well. Good job, me. Too good. Job to do. Focus, Elise.

"You look great," Gloria said.

Oh, come on. "I am merely a reflection of you, Mistress," I said with a slight bow of my head. "Literally."

The laugh returned. "I suppose that was a rather self-serving compliment, wasn't it?"

I smiled in return, but a reserved smile. I didn't want to lead her on. "Anything special I need to know about tonight?"

180

"Lots of very important people tonight and people who think that they're important. Stay close, taste my drinks, all the normal stuff."

I nodded.

"Oh, we need a signal."

"A signal, Mistress?"

Gloria sighed. "I need to keep moving and making the rounds. If I get stuck with someone, I'll signal you to make up some excuse to move me along. Just lean close and whisper in my ear. I'll make something up."

"Scratch your head?" I suggested.

Gloria furrowed her brow for a moment and then smiled. "No. If I quickly down the rest of my drink, bottoms-up, so to speak, that's the signal."

"Sounds like a fast way to get drunk," I said.

Gloria's smile took on a wicked tinge. "Why, Xyla? You must have been to one of these before," she said with exaggerated sarcasm. "How else does one get through an evening with all these self-important people?"

#   #   #

The fundraising gala was held in a huge, opulent hotel ballroom near Drakon Bay. The flight in provided a great view of the sun setting over the bay. I swear, I could almost see Cirilla Island and the Offworld Relay from the landing pad high up on the towering hotel. I knew I couldn't really, the island was much too far away, but it felt like I could.

The single ballroom was three stories tall with hundreds of glittering, sparkling chandeliers hanging from the ceiling like a dense constellation of overblown stars. Floor-to-ceiling windows ran the entire perimeter of the room. There were doors at regular intervals leading to wide balconies, giving guests the opportunity to step outside and take in the views of the bay and the Kotega Systems borough. By the time we arrived, the gala was well underway, of course. The Siwas were the most powerful family in the company, so they needed to arrive fashionably late.

The attendees didn't realize how tightly scheduled the Siwas were to arrive in such fashion, though. Gloria and I arrived 42 minutes after the gala began, with Orogen to arrive 12 minutes later, and finally, Tenisha would walk in 20 minutes after that.

That evening was like a parade of all the people I'd seen over the last several days as Gloria's Daeli. The Trystte twins were dressed in matching silver, asymmetrical suits. Bear Kotega-Cyber and their partner came in coordinating floral outfits, obviously custom-made. The Aerospace, Media, and Nano VPs all vied for attention from higher-ranking families like the Siwas. And those familiar faces were only a slice of the people in attendance. Bastion helpfully highlighted faces and put their names and relevant details on my display. Still, they all started running together soon enough.

Fortunately, my job was to be silent the entire night. I just had to stay close, stepping up and sipping drinks a couple of times each hour, then diligently trailing Gloria around the room. Three hours into the evening, the room quieted as someone walked up to a podium and started speaking about the charity and thanking everyone before introducing Tenisha.

That was the first time Gloria suddenly turned her drink upside down, pouring more than half a martini down her throat in one go. I took the cue, stepping up and leaning in close to her ear. I whispered, "I believe that was my cue, Mistress."

Gloria nodded as I stepped back, and then she turned to the man who'd been talking to her and said, "If you'll excuse me."

"Of course," he said.

Gloria walked confidently out to one of the balconies, which was empty because Tenisha was speaking. I let the door close behind me, and then stood near the door, giving the CEO's daughter some space. She walked over to the railing and leaned against it, gazing out over the bay silently for several minutes. A large awning kept the balcony dry while the rain was still cascading in sheets. The rain smell filled the air, fresh and wet, and brought a chill along with it.

"What's it like where you grew up?" she asked.

"Mistress?" I asked.

"Do you need briefing information?" Bastion asked.

I gently shook my head and joined Gloria at the railing. "Where I grew up?"

She nodded. "Southeast Kotega. Not far from here, right?"

"No. Not far." According to my briefing, the fictional Xyla had been raised less than a kilometer from here, in a heavily blue-collar part of the borough.

Gloria looked down and I followed her gaze. She wasn't looking at the bay or the waterfront, but the low buildings that sat back from the waterfront. The constant wind from the bay kept The Mist at bay for nearly half a kilometer, and that area was dedicated to shipping, receiving, and manufacturing. The tallest buildings down there were only a dozen stories tall, nearly imperceptible from here, particularly with all that rain.

"Did you ever think about my family or any of us when you were growing up?" Gloria asked. "Do any of these people matter to people down there? The people doing the hardest, dirtiest work the company demands?"

I sighed, buying myself a little time before answering.

"This is an opportunity," Bastion said. "Make her think those people prefer her as CEO. Sow the seeds of discord, maybe even plant the seed of distrust in Orogen."

He was right. This was real vulnerability, what I'd been working toward with Gloria for weeks. Her walls were down. But I also just wanted to comfort her, to let her know that those people down there could never forget about the Siwas or other people in power. Their names and faces dominated news streams. They saw the corporate emails written by assistants but signed with those names.

But then, that had been my experience in Corto Corporation. I didn't work in manufacturing there like Xyla's fictional parents did here. I hadn't been the child of low-level, blue-collar parents. Maybe they really never spared a thought for their CEO or her children. Or any of these people up here.

I swallowed. None of that mattered. I needed to focus. A job to do.

"Of course we did," I finally said. "We watch the streams. We get emails. Things are hard down there, sure, but we're still Kotega citizens. My parents don't make as much as some others, but they belong as much as anyone up here. Always food on the table, healthcare, the promise of a pension when they retire at 80. Just like everybody living high up in the towers."

"Really?" Gloria sounded genuinely surprised.

"Decisions up here affect all of us. When the company is struggling, we feel it acutely. Hours get longer. Pay raises stop happening. We're all guaranteed jobs as citizens, but I knew neighbors who were pushed into even worse jobs when the good or easier work dried up." I didn't know if that was true, but it sounded like it could be.

Gloria just silently nodded, her eyes fixed far below.

"May I be frank, Mistress?" I asked.

Gloria looked at me then, curious, before she said, "Please."

I took a deep breath. "People down there, people I grew up with, are afraid of Orogen."

"Afraid?" Gloria stood up from the railing, shock plain on her face.

"Yes, Mistress. There are…" I paused, focusing on my fingers and doing my best to feign nervousness. "Rumors about his allegiances."

In the corner of my vision, I saw Gloria turn away from me, looking out at the bay once again. I'd expected incredulity or a gasp or something. Instead, she just signed and whispered, "His allegiances."

"My apologies, Mistress, I don't mean to—"

"No," she said, suddenly stern. "Go on. What are the rumors?"

I took a long pause, wondering how far I should step, how gentle or direct to be. Ultimately, I knew that my time was limited. I had an opportunity here, so I needed to take it. I said, "He's spent an inordinate amount of time in Toinette, in the time of a preacher from there, a woman on a lot of streams. Many people say—"

"Stop."

"Mistress?"

Gloria turned fully toward me, and I met her gaze. "I know about the preacher. So does Mother. Orogen hasn't seen her in months. That's all over."

They knew about Tazia? Or, they knew about her as Josephine, at least. Either way, I couldn't keep the surprise from my face.

"Don't be so shocked," Gloria said. "He's a Siwa. His every move, like mine, is closely watched. I'm surprised people heard about it down in the blue-collar levels. I suppose our security isn't as tight-lipped as we'd hoped."

"My apologies, Mistress," I said again.

"Nothing to apologize for. I gave you leave to be frank, and you did. I appreciate that. As much as I may not want my brother to be the next CEO, you don't have to worry about his allegiances. He's Siwa. He's Kotega, through and through."

Mother of Corto, if only that was true.

"Come on," Gloria said. "I need another drink and to be seen mingling again."

We rejoined the gala just as Tenisha was finishing her speech to rousing applause. I kept my head down and voice silent, staying on my best behavior. I wanted what I'd said to stew in her. I didn't want to step out of line and undermine my work.

"I thought that was going to work," Bastion said.

I smiled in spite of myself but couldn't reply. It didn't look good for a Daeli to talk to themselves, and it would have been terribly rude for me to start texting while working.

"This would have been a good opportunity to have Nox do some snooping," Bastion continued. "Everyone important is in this room. He should be poking around in their homes while they're all occupied."

He was right, of course, but it was too late. I'd been so caught up in the Daeli work and trying to get close to Gloria, I'd not given Nox a thought for several days. He was in the residence somewhere, cleaning toilets or fixing doors or whatever it was they had him doing. He was probably going crazy pretending to be a maintenance worker and waiting for me to give him something to do.

What did I want him to do, anyway? I pondered that as I took a sip of a fresh drink, this one minty and slightly sour. I nodded to Gloria and stepped back into her shadow again. I needed to go visit Gowran, the target of Dr. Corto's ire. I couldn't send Nox to do that. I was tempted to infiltrate Tenisha's again, though I wasn't really looking for evidence against Orogen there, I was looking for a connection between the five companies. Again, not a good use of my apprentice, who didn't know about any of that.

There was Orogen's place, though. Getting in there was one of the top priorities for our shared mission. I'd been focused on getting myself in there to look around, but Nox would be less conspicuous. If something broke, he could go right in. Even if he was sneaking in like a proper Intel Operative, a maintenance worker missing for a few hours wasn't going to raise as many eyebrows as Gloria's Daeli.

Gloria upended a drink, and I came up and leaned in close to her ear. She excused herself and moved away from that group but was quickly stopped by another. Once again, Bastion put the names of the four people in my display in AR. One of them ordered Gloria a drink, something smoky, which I sipped and stepped back again. That one was potent. I was feeling a touch tipsy, and I was only taking one sip from each of her drinks. I wasn't sure how Gloria was still upright.

"I'm still not sure how getting close to Gloria helps you with the Orogen situation," Bastion said. "She's the sister, sure, but she puts her family before anything. She's not going to go against him without solid proof that Orogen has betrayed Kotega Systems. And if you get that proof, taking it directly to Tenisha would be the better plan."

I ground my teeth. Partly because I couldn't say anything to argue and partly because he was right.

"No matter how close you get, how much trust you gain, she's not going to permit you to go snooping in Orogen's residence. She's not going against her mother's decision. Your time would be better spent focused on Orogen."

He was ignoring that most of my time spent ingratiating myself with Gloria was during my working hours as Daeli, hours when I couldn't do anything about Orogen anyway.

"She's not going to be your friend. She might be becoming friends with Xyla, but Xyla isn't real. Eventually, this job will be over. Gloria will probably figure that out at some point, and she'll hate you for the betrayal. It's never wise to earn the hatred of powerful people."

That…stung. As I followed Gloria to the next group of somewhat powerful people begging for scraps of Gloria's attention, I thought about it. Bastion's line of thinking didn't really hold up, though. Okay, it held up halfway. If I succeeded in helping her become CEO, I'd have her gratitude or at least indifference. If I failed, and there was no way I was going to let that happen, then she might hate me.

But I had an exit strategy. No one remained a Daeli for long in

Kotega. It was a difficult and degrading job, one often taken by people like the fictional Xyla. People with meager beginnings who were leveraging a passing resemblance to someone more powerful to give them a boost in life. And if they served well for at least a few months, it worked very well. That was our exit strategy. After the next CEO took the office, whether Orogen or Gloria, I would tender my resignation. Xyla would move on to another job and soon be forgotten by the Siwa family.

And in my years as an Intel Operative, I'd learned from experience and Solomon's teachings that getting a target to let down their guard could often pay dividends. Maybe not always in the expected ways, but the effort usually paid off at some point.

So, what was Bastion after? Why was he trying to dissuade me from getting close to Gloria? I wasn't wasting time on her. I was using the schedule put before me to maximum use.

Gloria knocked back yet another drink. I leaned in close again and she stumbled slightly against me. I held her, keeping her upright, and her eyes lingered on mine, far too close and for far too long before she made her excuses and moved away from the group.

"Mistress," I said. "It may be time to go home."

"We go home when I say," she hissed, slurring her words slightly.

I wanted to argue but didn't get the chance.

"Gloria," an unfamiliar voice said from behind me.

Gloria was steady on her feet, so I quickly and silently dropped back. The new person was half a head shorter than Gloria with black hair trailing down their back in thick locs. Rebecca Kotega-Sec, she/her, director of the Counter-Intel Section of Security. Thank you, Bastion, for the info. She walked toward Gloria with an exaggerated swagger, swaying her hips in a velvety silver dress.

I swallowed hard at Rebecca's title. Counter-Intel. Rebecca's eyes were focused on Gloria, though, not me.

"Hello, my old friend," Gloria said, the slur still there. There was a coldness to her words, though, something I'd never heard.

"Old?" Rebecca asked. "We're the same age. And what kind of friend never calls anymore?"

"Uh oh," Bastion said. My thought exactly.

"Drink!" Gloria said far too loudly while waving a hand in the air.

It took considerable effort not to look around the room with an apologetic face. That was not a Daeli's job or place. A server arrived in a blink with Gloria's preferred drink, a martini made with a botanical from near the southern pole. Before I could even step forward to take my sip, Gloria took the drink from the tray, drained it, placed the empty glass back on the tray, and sent the server to get another.

Rebecca just smiled. I didn't like her at all.

"What are you doing now, anyway?" Gloria asked Rebecca. "Still barking orders at security managers, screaming at the sky as Intel Operatives steal our secrets?"

Rebecca blanched but set her jaw. "We stopped six intrusions last month, I'll have you know. I've been personally responsible for—"

"And how many got away? You know what? Don't answer. I know. 30. That's it. 30. Maybe I should take over Security. You can clean my toilets. How's that, Re-becc-a?" Gloria pronounced her name like each syllable was its own word, spat with equal venom.

The server was approaching again with another of Gloria's martinis but stopped cold when Orogen stepped between Gloria and the server. He was dressed in a smartly tailored black tuxedo, trimmed in sparkling silver lapels and cufflinks. He was wearing a touch of makeup to smooth out his features. I couldn't see Gloria's face, but her shoulders fell.

"Sister!" Orogen said, smiling broadly and walking up to Gloria like nothing was wrong. "The life of the party, as usual."

Gloria said nothing, just stared at him. I could only imagine the daggers coming from her eyes.

Orogen put one arm around his sister and gently moved her toward me. I kept my head bent, eyes on their feet, his strides and hers shuffling toward me. "I know you have a full day tomorrow," Orogen said more to the room than to Gloria. "We're all so sad that you'll be leaving the party so early, me especially."

Once those feet were right in front of me, Orogen's voice was suddenly very quiet and very close to my ear. "Get her out of here, Daeli. Now."

"Yes, Mister," I said with a bow.

He placed Gloria in my care, slipping her arm into mine, and spoke to the rest of the room. "My sister has insisted on a 500,000-credit donation from the Siwa family in addition to our regular giving, and I couldn't agree more. To Gloria!"

I hurried to the exit, Gloria's arm looped through mine, her hand gripping my forearm tightly, as the crowd called back, "To Gloria!"

I half-walked, half-wrestled Gloria out of the ballroom, into the elevator, and down the hallway to the landing pad. Fortunately, no one except a few stoic security guards were to be found as we were exiting, and none of them paid us more heed than a cursory glance. Once we emerged on the landing pad, Ridley spotted us and sprinted over, helping me get Gloria into the car.

Instead of sitting across from her as I usually did, she clung to me after I lowered her into her seat, leaning on me so that she didn't slump completely over.

"They're horrible," she muttered once the car had lifted off.

"They are," I said.

"Rebecca…we used to date. She was so nice before…before I broke her heart. It's my fault."

"That doesn't give her the right to be cruel to you," I said even though it had been Gloria who'd been cruel tonight.

"Maybe," she said.

"Can I get you anything, Mistress? An electrolyte injection? A tablet or three of—"

"No," she said, suddenly sitting up and looking at me, her entire body weaving in place. "I'm drunk. I want to stay that way. Kotega take them all."

"Of course, Mistress."

"Don't call me that," she said, nearly in a whisper, her eyes darting between mine and my mouth. A warmth filled my chest, a warmth that shouldn't be there.

"But I'm supposed—"

"Say my name."

My face was suddenly warm. Gloria's face was drifting toward mine, close enough that I could feel her breath on my face, practically taste the martinis she'd been drinking. She was staring at my lips, drifting ever closer. My heart hammered in my chest.

"Say my name, Xyla," she whispered.

That broke the spell. I turned away, exhaling a shaky breath. Xyla wasn't real, wasn't me. Gloria was drunk and out of her mind with anger. My name was Elise. Quynn was at home, my love and partner, and they were waiting for me. I didn't need to cheat on them to accomplish my mission.

"You need rest, Mistress," I said, and I crossed the limousine to sit in my normal seat.

Gloria's eyes were on me as I sat back down and looked at her again. She looked surprised, pouty in a playful way, but the playfulness soon dropped away. She didn't look angry, though, only disappointed, though perhaps more with herself than me. At least, I hoped that was the case. We survived the rest of the ride to The Roost in silence, Gloria drifting in and out of consciousness, and when we arrived, Thrace and Ridley scooped her out of the car and whisked her away.

Chapter Twenty

11 Days to Ascension

"SHE DIDN'T!" RIDLEY SAID AT breakfast the next morning when I told him what Gloria had said to Rebecca. "What an embarrassment, though. I heard Orogen and Tenisha were making apologies all night."

"I knew she and Rebecca didn't get along," Thrace said, "but that's not like Mistress."

"Those muckety-mucks must have loved that," Ridley said. "Watching Mistress skewer Rebecca like that. Rich people have an extra gear when it comes to being nasty. It's like they can afford to buy those premium insults."

"I wouldn't know," I said. "I kept my head down. I'm hoping somebody took a video, though."

We all laughed until Ridley suddenly swallowed his laugh and discreetly pointed. I followed his finger to find Zhao walking toward us, xyr normal intensity silencing the room with each step.

"Xyla," xey said.

"Yes?" I said, getting to my feet.

"Mistress isn't feeling well today. Enjoy the day off." Zhao looked around at our trio, xyr gaze lingering on Ridley, who was struggling to keep a straight face. "Not too much."

Zhao spun on a heel and walked out of the room with no less intensity, and the three of us cracked up again the moment xey were out of the cafeteria. Carmela strode over, head shaking as she served us second helpings of potatoes, but she was smiling the entire time.

"An unexpected free day?" Bastion said in my ear.

I put my hands under the table and texted him, "Best not let it go to waste."

"Tazia? Orogen?"

"Not yet," I texted. "Gowran."

#   #   #

I knew from a bit of research that Gowran worked for the Media division as an editor for a morning news stream. I wanted to pay him a visit in the afternoon, hopefully before his wife came home. After my breakfast, I went back to bed and took a nap. Despite Bastion's protests that I could be more productive, I'd been sorely lacking in sleep since arriving in the Kotega borough. After a couple of hours, I made my way to the gardens to call Hessod, filling him in on everything that had happened in the few days since we'd last spoken.

"I haven't been able to find anything else on him," Hessod said, meaning Gowran.

"So he's either very secretive…" I said.

"Or he's absolutely clean."

"Nobody is that clean. I'm assuming secretive."

"Usually the better approach. How are you?"

I blew out a breath. I didn't want to mention any of my recent issues with Gloria. I didn't want it getting back to Quynn. That made me feel entirely new levels of guilt. I said, "I'm struggling, but there's a job to do. Several jobs, it seems."

"Anything I can do?"

"You're already doing it," I said. "Thanks."

"Should I pass along anything to Quynn?" he asked.

My mind immediately went to last night, to Gloria's eyes fixated on my mouth. That unwelcome warmth flooded my chest again. I swallowed down the guilt and said, "Tell them that I love them and miss them. I can't wait to be home."

"Will do," he said. "I do have some good news."

"Oh?"

"The Omni finally cracked those servers wide open."

"Finally," Bastion said.

"And?" I asked.

"Very little is actionable," Hessod said. "Some random information on jobs that Tazia ran years ago. Outdated intel stolen on jobs."

"None of that is actionable," I said. "So what else did you find?"

Hessod sighed before he said, "Personal files on her family. Spouse. Kids. Even her "

"No," I said without thinking.

"No?" Bastion said. "That could be the key to stopping her. Go after those people, her weakness."

"Are you sure?" Hessod asked. "You know she's not afraid to go after people we love."

I was sure. It wasn't about fear anyway. It was about right and wrong. What Tazia was trying to do was wrong. Going after her family? Also wrong. I knew it in my bones. I didn't always do the right thing, I knew, but I wouldn't do this. Not ever.

"Delete those files," I said. "I'm sure."

"This might be the stupidest thing you've ever done," Bastion said.

"Got it," Hessod said. "Glad you're still the same Elise I met a decade ago."

"You're both naïve," Bastion said.

I disconnected the call with Hessod and said to Bastion, "For once, you're absolutely wrong."

"Oh? How's that?" Bastion asked.

"We're not the villains here. Going after Tazia's family? Going after innocent people that just happen to be related to her? That's what villains do."

"The entire city is threatened. Doesn't that make it worth it?"

"Nothing makes it worth it, Bastion. Nothing. The ends don't justify the means. I've lost sight of that from time to time, but we all have lines we won't cross. There's one of mine."

"It's naïve."

"Then I'm naïve," I said with extra force, hoping to end the conversation. "But I'll be able to sleep tonight."

A few minutes later, Nox joined me in the garden, and we debriefed. He'd been gently poking around the security systems of the residences and Orogen's specifically but had no big revelations. I could tell he was getting antsy, but I reassured him that he needed to remain patient and keep his eyes open. By the time we were done talking, I was a little late for lunch in the cafeteria. I'd never been around for lunch before, and it looked like that was true for most people. Carmela was there, of course, silently guiding her kitchen staff, but Thrace and Ridley were both missing. Working.

I took lunch to my room, ate while discussing my approach with Bastion, and finally, began the tedious task of sneaking through staff and maintenance corridors, working my way down while avoiding being seen. Dr. Corto really couldn't have chosen a more inconvenient cover for an Intel Operative. Everyone was watching Daelis.

Roughly 20 minutes later, I was standing with my umbrella on the landing pad 100 floors below the Siwa residence waiting for a Stryder. Admittedly, I don't remember much of the ride. It was raining, of course. It seemed to never stop raining this time of year. I leaned my head back, watching the rain hit the window, and then I woke up when the car touched down on another landing pad.

"Now," I said. "Where am I going?"

"Apartment 11344," Bastion said.

"Thirty floors down," I said. "That's what, southwest corner?"

"It is. What's your plan?"

"I'm going to take the elevator down," I said as I started walking in that direction.

"Obviously. And then?"

"Walk through the halls to apartment 11344."

"Oh, pedantry. How exhilarating," Bastion said without sounding the least bit exhilarated.

I pressed the button to call the elevator. "I'm going to knock on the front door."

"Knock? Now you're just messing with me."

The elevator opened and I stepped on. Since I was alone on the elevator, I asked for floor 113. No need to obfuscate. I said to Bastion, "This guy doesn't know me. Never met me. I'm not here to steal from him."

"You're supposed to kill him."

"I'm supposed to keep him quiet," I said.

"So you're going to knock on his door and then jump him when he opens up to you?"

"I'm going to talk to him," I said. "Find out what Dr. Corto is so afraid of."

"She specifically told you not to talk to him."

"I know," I said as the elevator came to a stop and the doors opened. "Might as well be dangling candy in front of a toddler. This guy has something on Ariela. If the CEO wants to keep me over a barrel for carrying you around, I might as well find a barrel of my own to point at her."

"That's…" Bastion stopped short.

After several long moments, I asked, "That's what?"

"That's very smart, actually."

"Don't sound so surprised."

"He might be dangerous," Bastion said. "The way that Dr. Corto talked about him—"

"I'll be careful," I said. I saw the door labeled 11344 just ahead. "I'm not exactly a defenseless creature. But I also don't trust anything that Dr. Corto says."

That said, I primed what weapons I had. I charged the taser in my palm. I spooled up the limited pneumatics in my calves. I balled my left hand into a fist and knocked on the door, then I kept the balled-up fist ready behind my back.

I heard voices that I couldn't make out from the other side of the door. Voices, plural. That was exactly what I was trying to avoid. Then the lock gently released before the door opened a dozen centimeters. A face peered around the edge of the door, masculine with a bald head and gray beard, at least a dozen years older than me.

"Hello," they said. "Can I help you?"

"Hi," I said as innocently as possible. "I'm looking for Gowran. Is he here?"

"Oh," they said but were interrupted by the squeal of a young child, who suddenly appeared, colliding with this person's leg while gawking at me. Oh, silent circuits, I didn't know about a child. I let my fist uncurl and fall to my side.

"Who's that, daddy?" the child asked.

"A visitor," they said and looked back at me. "Sorry about that. I'm Gowran, he/him. This is Charlotte, she/her, at least for now. Can I help you?"

"Ah," I said. I let the charge on my taser dissipate. The pneumatics would unspool in a minute or so. "I'm here to…" I looked at Charlotte. I heard another child say something from farther in the apartment, and another adult voice, too. None of this was going to plan. "I have some questions for you. They're important, I'm afraid."

Gowran furrowed his brow, looked back into the apartment, and back to me before he said, "We're about to sit down for dinner. Can you—?"

Gowran was interrupted by Charlotte, who was repeatedly tugging on his pant leg while staring at me. He opened the door a little more as he knelt down with her. "What, Charlotte?"

"Is this your friend?" Charlotte whispered as though I couldn't hear her. "Is she staying for dinner?"

Gowran cast me a quick glance before telling Charlotte, "We don't know their gender, do we? So what do we say?"

Charlotte's eyes grew wide, and then she looked at me and said, "I'm Charlotte, she/her. And you are?"

I knelt to her level and said, "Xyla Kotega-Gloria, she/her."

"Nice to meet you," Charlotte said to me and then promptly turned back to Gowran. "We're friends now. Can she stay for dinner?"

"Why don't you go ask Mommy if that's okay?"

Charlotte smiled and nodded. Gowran kissed her forehead, and she scampered away. He stood back up and looked at me, his face suddenly more serious.

"Gloria?" he said. "Does the Siwa family want something? Are we in trouble?"

"I…" I was about to say no, that this had nothing to do with the Siwa family. But Siwa was power in Kotega. I'd stumbled into an opportunity. "No trouble. No trouble at all. Quite the opposite, in fact. You've been doing an admirable job, and Gloria Siwa Kotega has taken notice."

Gowran's apprehension suddenly evaporated. A smile swept up the corners of his mouth. "That's…wow. I mean, how did she even hear about my work?"

In an instant, the corners of my display were filled with images and words. Bastion doing what he did better than anyone, anticipating my needs. The images told the story of Gowran's work. Nothing flashy, to be sure. He worked in the Media division as an editor for a morning news stream. A good worker from what I could see, but he'd been doing the same job for nearly 10 years. No ambition, no innovation. I was going to have to spin this. Hard.

"Sunrise Kotega has made great strides in the morning news market," I said. Immediately, several of the images and text dropped away, replaced with a few graphs to show that Sunrise Kotega had, in fact, risen from 5th to 3rd in viewership among morning news programs in the borough. "Third place is nothing to scoff at, particularly in such a competitive industry."

"Third?" Gowran said. "I didn't realize we'd passed Mornings in Kotega. That's great."

"It is. And Gloria has an eye for editing, for live program direction. She's noticed your work."

"Wow. I had no idea," Gowran said, his cheeks red and the words fumbling from his mouth. He suddenly remembered himself, straightening and opening his door wide. "Please, would you join us for dinner? Any member of the Siwa household is always welcome at our table."

"I'd love to," I said. "Thank you."

Gowran's apartment was humble and lovely. He and his family had put a lot of thought into the arrangement and choice of furniture and art. The living room was a tasteful blend of blues and greens. Moving into the dining room where the family was adding a setting to the table, the greens gave way to gold. In the kitchen beyond, I could see that the gold continued with a purple so dark that it was almost black.

"That's Daddy's friend," Charlotte said in a loud whisper to another child, though one that was half a head taller than Charlotte.

"Everyone," Gowran said as he led me into the dining room. "This is Xyla Kotega-Gloria, she/her. She works for Gloria Siwa Kotega."

"The CEO's daughter?" the other child asked. They were trying to look unimpressed, but the excitement bled through their words.

"That's right," Gowran said to her, then turned to me. "You've already met Charlotte. This is our other child, Jackson, they/them."

"Nice to meet you," I said.

Jackson looked unimpressed and said nothing.

"And I'm Xiaofang Kotega-Sec, she/her," a woman said as she came from the kitchen. She was tall. At least a head taller than Gowran, who was already several centimeters taller than me. Her black hair was cropped close to her pale head, her sharp features sharpened even further by heavy makeup. She extended a long, thin hand to me, which I took and shook.

"Nice to meet you," I said. "All of you."

"You work for Gloria, then?" Xiaofang asked. "In what capacity?"

I smiled and said, "Oh, nothing you've likely heard of."

Three images of me standing a step behind Gloria suddenly appeared on my display. Bastion said, "These are just from today. The Daeli is no secret in Kotega."

"I'm her Daeli," I said quickly. "Though tonight, I'm just here to make sure that your husband knows that Gloria has taken notice of his work."

"Not part of the conventional Daeli work, then," Xiaofang said. It wasn't a question, and she was still gripping my hand and giving me a hard look.

"No," I said, pretending to be demure. "But conventional isn't a word I'd use to describe my Mistress. Innovative. And at the moment, spread rather thin with the Ascension coming up."

Xiaofang finally released my hand. That answer seemed to have appeased her. "Please," she said. "Join us for dinner. I hope you don't mind a vegetarian stir-fry. Not exactly the sort of dinner you get in the Siwa house,

I'm sure."

"I'd love to join you," I said. It was early for dinner. Very early. Nevertheless, I said, "And stir-fry is one of my favorites."

Dinner was a polite enough affair. Charlotte seemed to delight in my company, taking the chance to brag about her friends and school and everything else she could think of. I had a feeling she was like that whenever anyone came to their table. Jackson was mostly silent, only asking questions about the Siwa family that they probably thought were very witty or insightful in the classic preteen way. I made sure to answer them as seriously as I could.

Xiaofang kept trying to poke holes in my reason for being there. Whether she saw through my lies or was just that much of a skeptic, I wasn't sure. Fortunately, Bastion kept feeding me information to keep delivering convincing answers. When I was able to find common ground complaining about the recent lack of funding for upgraded armor for the Security division working along the border with Toinette, that finally got Xiaofang on my team.

Gowran was strangely silent, using his few words mostly to encourage Charlotte to let other people talk. It seemed to reinforce what Dr. Corto had said about Gowran being a former Intel Operative, keeping his own council and quietly assessing me. Everything else about his life, however, made me think that Dr. Corto had been lying. The Intel Operative life was an addictive thing. I'd never known one of us to give it all up and settle for a boring life behind a desk. And the way his family behaved didn't tell me that they were guarding Daddy's secrets.

"Do you like your dad's show?" I asked both of the kids once everyone had finished eating.

Charlotte nodded vigorously.

"You don't even watch it," Jackson said.

"I do too," Charlotte whined.

"Just because it's on when you eat breakfast doesn't mean you watch it."

Charlotte looked to her parents, her face pleading for help.

"Jackson," Gowran said as a warning.

"Whatever," Jackson mumbled.

"We're all very proud," Xiaofang said rather pointedly to Jackson.

"As you should be," I said.

Gowran blushed and looked at both of his children with a look I didn't understand. He looked constipated, frankly.

After casting her gaze across every member of her family and me, Xiaofang said to Gowran, "Why don't you show our guest your office?"

"Hmm?" Gowran said.

"You two can get into more detail about your work," Xiaofang continued. "Jackson and Charlotte can help me clean up."

Both kids opened their mouths to protest.

"And then we can have ice cream after," she said before any words could come from her children. "All of us."

Jackson shut their mouth. Charlotte lit up with a smile. Gowran still looked confused, but only for a moment. Then, he pushed back from the table. "Right," he said. "My office. Xyla?"

"Sure," I said and followed him down the hallway to a closed door. I wondered if I needed to ready my weapons again and be prepared for an attack, but everything about this man told me that he was exactly who he appeared to be.

We both stepped into the room, which was indeed an office. It wasn't a large space, and half of it was taken up by a desk. A fairly new but inexpensive workstation was set up there. Lots of family photos surrounded it along with a handful of plaques recognizing Gowran's long and undistinguished career.

15 years of service? That didn't sound like a former Intel Operative at all. He wasn't that much older than me by the look of him. More and more, it seemed like Dr. Corto had been lying to me.

"I'm sorry," Gowran said after he shut the door. "I…just don't understand why you're here. I do a good job, I think. I've been doing it a long time, but I'm not ambitious. I'm not the sort of person someone notices like this. I didn't want to say that in front of my kids, though. I want them to be ambitious, to chase their dreams, and—"

"I'm not really here for Gloria," I blurted out. I had to break this ice at some point, so why not go ahead and shatter it?

"What?" Gowran said in utter confusion.

"You know Dr. Ariela Corto," I said. It wasn't a question.

Gowran's face darkened.

"That's what I thought." I held up my hands slowly and gently. "You're not in any danger from me, but she sent me here to…hurt you."

"Kill me," he whispered.

"Yeah," I said. "I'm not going to. I want to know why, though."

"Why?"

"Why does she want you dead?"

He narrowed his eyes and really seemed to look at me for the first time. "What did she tell you?"

"A string of lies, I think. She said you're a former Intel Operative, that you basically seduced her assistant and stole a bunch of sensitive files. Then you went into hiding."

Gowran burst out laughing. Not a quiet, subdued thing, either. A full belly laugh. I didn't interrupt. When he finally had his breathing under control again, he said, "Intel? Seriously? That's rich."

"It never sounded quite right," I said. "And seeing you, meeting you and your family, I knew it wasn't true."

"Thank heavens you aren't some no-questions-asked assassin," Gowran said, wiping tears from his eyes and still recovering from the laugh. "Intel. Wow."

"Why does she want you dead?"

"She…" he started to say and stopped, eyeing me. "Why do you want to know?"

I only debated for a moment how much I should tell him before I said, "She has me under a barrel, so to speak. I'm no assassin, but she thought I would do this because…she knows things about me."

"Blackmail," Gowran said. "Sounds like her."

"One of her favorite pastimes."

"And you're hoping for some blackmail to use against her."

"It sounds so crass when you say it like that."

Gowran gave me a pitying smile. "You do realize that me telling you is exactly the sort of thing Ariela is terrified of, right? It's a genie that doesn't go back in the bottle."

"It's that bad?"

Gowran smiled. "It's not bad at all, but that's not how Ariela sees it." The smile fell away from his face. "She won't stop with you, though. She'll send more people. My family…"

"I'm sorry," I said. I didn't know what else to say. He was right. If Dr. Corto was willing to have him killed to protect a secret, she wouldn't stop trying. They would have to move, to leave Kotega and the life they'd made. I couldn't imagine doing that myself, and I didn't have children.

Gowran paced around the small room for a few minutes, staring at his feet. I let him. It was a lot to process and think about. Finally, he stopped and said, "We dated."

"We?" I asked.

"Ariela and I. This would have been, I don't know, 30 years ago? It was serious, as serious as you can get while living in different boroughs, working for different companies."

"That must have been challenging."

"Sometimes. We were both early in our careers, so it wasn't that tough."

"Why would she care about that staying secret?"

"At her level," he said, "Company loyalty means everything."

"I see," I said. I hadn't even considered what dating outside Corto would mean to a future CEO. It seemed harmless enough, but perhaps the board didn't see it that way.

"You don't see," Gowran said. "That's not the part she wants secret."

"Okay…"

He opened a large drawer in the desk and started pulling out lots of old, outdated electronics and cables. Once it seemed like the drawer was empty, he pushed down one corner and pulled away a false bottom. Then, he pulled out a folder stuffed with polymer printouts. He set it on the desk. He took a deep breath before he opened it and spread out a handful of sonogram images.

I looked at them for a moment, confused, until it dawned on me. "She was pregnant?"

"She was," Gowran said. "We were. She terminated the pregnancy."

"I'm sorry," I whispered.

"I'm not. I mean, I do wonder about that child, about who they might have been. At the time, though, it was the right decision for both of us. Neither of us was ready. But this is the big secret. Dating someone from another company? That's a little problematic for a CEO, but easy to sweep under the rug. But this? Potentially having a child with split corporate allegiances?"

"Then the child would choose a company at age 17, just like every other kid in that situation. Why would anyone care?" I asked.

"That's my feeling on it, but not everyone sees it that way. The corporate bloodlines run deep and strong. I would never tell anyone else about this. Xiaofang knows, of course. But I know what this would do to Ariela, and this…this was a difficult time in our lives. It still hurts a little. Why would I air that out?"

I nodded silently, thinking on it.

"This cannot become public," Bastion said.

I didn't entirely agree, but it gave me an idea. I turned fully to Gowran and said, "I'm going to help you. I don't like that Dr. Corto is doing this to you. Blackmail seems to be her modus operandi, so it's past time she feels the sting of her own tactics."

"You're not going to hurt her, are you?" Gowran asked, his eyes pleading.

"Not if I can help it," I said. "But she doesn't get to hurt you, either. And you shouldn't have to uproot your entire lives because of this."

"You can do that, help us?" The look on Gowran's face broke my heart. So earnest. So pleading. So hopeful.

"I think so," I said. I had the beginning of an idea, a plan. It was enough of a spark, though.

Gowran took a deep breath, sweeping his eyes back to the picture of the ultrasound before he set his jaw and said, "What do you need?"

Chapter Twenty-One

8 Days to Ascension

THE FOLLOWING DAYS WERE MOSTLY uneventful, even if they were both a relief and frustration at the same time. Meetings blocked out my days again. Gloria had been utterly silent toward me, hence the relief and frustration. In the morning several days after meeting Gowran, I slid into the limo for another day of meetings. Gloria was already there.

As soon as the door was closed, she said, "I need to apologize for the other night."

"No apology necessary, Mistress," she said.

"No, there is. I was unprofessional."

I bowed my head, hoping that would be enough.

"Did we…?" Gloria said, her eyes averted from mine. "Not sexual, of course. I remember what you said when we were sparring. But…?"

"Nothing happened, Mistress." I said quickly. We'd come close, though, far too close to kissing.

"Not nothing," Gloria said. "Not according to my brother."

"After the gala, I helped you to the car. Our ride back to the residence was uneventful, then Ridley and Thrace took you to your bed."

The relief was plain on her face. "Good. Good. I only made a fool of myself in public, at least."

I looked out the window, hoping once again that was the end of it.

"Xyla," Gloria said, the authority back in her voice.

I looked back at her. "Mistress?"

"We've become too familiar. It's my fault, not yours. But I would appreciate a return to professionalism. I'll do my part. I expect you to do yours."

I bowed my head. "Of course, Mistress." I was at once relieved, some of the guilt over my feelings draining away. But it also meant her walls were back up. Not great.

There were a lot of meetings that day. And the next. And the next. While standing there one step behind and to the right of Gloria, I had plenty of time to think. To plan. To prioritize. So on the following day, when I had a few hours between meetings, I arranged to meet Nox in the Siwa gardens, glad the area was set back in the building and entirely kept out of the rain. I couldn't imagine the water bills for irrigation, though.

"Hey," he said as he joined me on the balcony. There seemed to be no energy in his voice. His usual exuberance was completely missing.

"You okay?" I asked.

He looked out, leaning on the balcony for a while before he answered. "This feels pointless."

"It's not."

"I know, but I've just been cleaning and fixing things for days now. I hate it."

"I know how you feel," I said and let the silence stretch between us.

"You ever going to tell me what you were doing clinging to the ceiling of that maintenance stairwell a while back?"

"I wish I could," I said. I'd debated for a long time what to tell him whenever he asked. We'd talked several times since then, and I hadn't brought it up. I certainly wasn't going to. I could draw a shaky line between what we were here to do and breaking into Tenisha's. Really, though, there was no connection. That was all me. Nox didn't know about Bastion or my investigation into how the five companies were connected. In the end, I decided this was the best approach. "You know there are things I can't tell you. This is one of them."

"That's not fair."

"Maybe. It's how it is, though."

"Because I'm an apprentice?"

"Our job is secrets. Not just the secrets we steal, but the secrets we keep. And those above us are keeping layers and layers of secrets. I know more than you. Plenty of people know more than me. I'll tell you what I can when I can."

"Promise?" Nox looked at me.

I couldn't hold his gaze for long, looking out over the borough and swallowing before I lied, "I promise."

"So," he said after a long silence. "Why are we here?"

I looked at him and couldn't keep the smirk from my face.

"Is this some sort of hazing? I don't think it's funny if—"

I shook my head.

In an instant, Nox's eyes brightened. "You have something?"

"We need to get into Orogen's."

"Okay." Nox was obviously waiting for more.

"You're going in." I watched his face absolutely light up, the smirk returning to where it belonged.

"When?"

"Not sure yet. I need you to be ready, though."

"Today? This week? You gotta narrow it down for me, Star Girl."

"This week, I hope. It'll be when I'm out of the building as well as Orogen. I'm going to be your analyst."

"The great Star Girl is going to be my Hessod? That's bragging rights when we get back."

"Don't let it go to your head. But you've earned it. I trust you."

"I'm just happy to do some real work," he said, practically bouncing on his cybernetic toes.

"Get it out of your system now," I said. "And like I said, be ready."

#   #   #

206

5 Days to Ascension

Three days later, the moment finally arrived, though quite unexpectedly. Gloria was waiting in the car when I slid in, and Ridley closed the door behind me. She was being coldly professional, just like she'd been ever since the gala. I was being patient, not trying to push back into her graces, but I saw she was still casting me more familiar glances.

Gloria cleared her throat and said, "There's a new addition to the schedule today as well."

I used my fingers to pull up the official schedule on my display, the one coordinated with Gloria and Zhao. Then I waited.

"I have a date tonight. I sent the details to Zhao a few minutes ago. Xey'll be putting it on the schedule and sending you special instructions for how to act as Daeli."

"Understood, Mistress." A date. Good. Shut up, heart. I flicked my fingers, pulling up Orogen's calendar. He, too, was going to be out of his residence until late. I'd been prepping Nox for the job for two days, just waiting for the right time. Me being out of the residence? Perfect cover.

I flicked my fingers more and texted Nox, "Tonight. You're a go for O's."

#　　　#　　　#

When Zhao knocked and entered my room that afternoon, xey were probably prepared to do my hair and makeup, to make sure that I was wearing the right outfit the right way for Gloria's date.

Xyr eyes widened when they saw that I was already ready.

"Oh," xey said. "Good. I'll just—"

"Please, Seon Zhao," I said, gesturing to the chair by my desk.

"We have nothing to discuss."

"We do. I promise."

Zhao worked xyr jaw before xey closed the door and sat in the chair, looking uncomfortable and unhappy.

I sat down on my bed and said, "I cannot stand Dr. Corto."

"So you've said."

I grabbed the data drive sitting on a nearby shelf and held it out. "You feel the same. And there's someone else who is being threatened by her, another Kotega citizen. You can help each other."

Zhao stared hard at the data drive, not reaching out to take it.

"I don't know you very well," I said. "But what I've seen of you is a ferociously loyal and honorable person. And I've done my own digging. You're squeaky clean. Is this about your father?"

Zhao's gaze flicked to me with newfound anger. "My father's death is none of your business," xey hissed.

"It's public record. And in Kotega, suicide is often a matter of honor, right? He…he did it to protect you. Protect your family."

Zhao looked away, still working xyr jaw.

"Look, you don't have to tell me. It's terribly painful for you. I can see that. But if you can write about how Dr. Corto blackmailed you, record it or however you want to tell it, and put it on a data drive like this, I have a solution, a way to get Dr. Corto to never leverage you again."

"A drive? So you can know my…my…"

"I will swear on anything that I won't look at it. It's not for me to know. It's not for anyone to know."

"And this…other person. How can I trust them?"

"Because they're willing to trust you." I held out the data drive even farther.

"Why?" Zhao's stern mask cracked just a little, real vulnerability seeping out.

"Because you're the head of Gloria's household, and he holds the Siwa family in the highest regard. If Gloria trusts you, then he does."

Zhao stared at the data drive for a long while before xey reached out and grabbed it. "What is his name?"

"Gowran Kotega-Media."

"And I just…"

"However you want to tell it, whatever you need to put on a drive to tell the world about Dr. Corto, and I'll get it to him."

"You promise this will work?"

I smiled. There was no way I could promise it. Dr. Ariela Corto was a CEO. Powerful. She had strings to pull that I couldn't even imagine. Nevertheless, I said, "I promise."

Zhao set xyr face and shoulders, xyr mask of sternness returning, then looked squarely at me. "We aren't friends, but all right. Tell me how this works."

Chapter Twenty-Two

5 Days to Ascension

IT WAS A SIMPLE ENOUGH plan that evening. Get in, see what there was to see, and get out. That didn't put me at ease, though. Why? Because I wasn't the one doing it. I was sending my apprentice in. I told him that I trusted him, and I did. But I had to play the role of analyst this time, which was not a role I was made for. Doing research and then sitting back while someone else did all the fun and dangerous work? That wasn't why I became an Intel Operative.

I wasn't going to be just sitting, of course. No. I was going to be standing one step behind and to the right of Gloria all night while she went on a date. A date. Those flutters in my stomach? The warmth I was having in my chest when I looked at her? I didn't want those feelings, but those feelings really didn't like the idea of Gloria on a date. With me standing around and watching. I would rather have been skulking around Orogen's. While it was on fire. And submerged in acid.

As I climbed into Gloria's limousine wearing a sparkling magenta dress that showed too much leg and too much cleavage for my taste, Nox's voice was suddenly in my ear.

"Stepping onto the elevator now," he said.

I didn't need a moment-by-moment update, but I couldn't tell him that. Couldn't even text while sitting in the limo across from Gloria. So I just sat there, one knee draped over the other. Gloria glanced at me with another look that carried too much familiarity, so I looked out the window as the limo rose from the landing pad and started moving through the expansive Siwa garage.

"I'm nervous," Gloria said.

I gave her my attention. She was pulling off the same magenta dress with far more style and panache. She was obviously not put off by the amount of skin she was showing, though I kept my focus on her eyes. They were far more enticing to me than the rest of her, anyway. I asked, "Why?"

"I always get nervous on dates," she said. "I know I'm being judged every time I walk into a room. Part of being a member of the Siwa family. But a date? That's like asking to be judged."

"At least you get to judge right back," I said.

"I'm not sure that makes it better."

"Stepping off the elevator," Nox said. A few seconds passed before he said, "All clear. Proceeding to the maintenance door. Plugging in and running my supervisor's code. Here's hoping she's still asleep."

"Are you all right?" Gloria said.

I was still looking at her. At those eyes. I was staring, in fact. I hadn't even been aware, too focused on what Nox was doing. "Yes," I said. "Sorry. Just remembering back when I was dating. I hated it, too."

"Back when you were dating?" she asked. "You don't date anymore?"

Sparks. Xyla was supposed to be single. She wasn't in a committed relationship like I was. "Before I started working for you, I mean," I said. "I haven't had time since. I don't mean to sound ungrateful, of course. I'm so sorry, Mistress. That's not what—"

Gloria held up a hand. "I understand. It's a busy time to join my team. I'm only going on this date because Mother insisted. Lynn's family is an important ally to ours."

"Is that all your social life is worth?" I asked. "Political alignments and maneuvering?"

Gloria glanced away from me. When she looked back, she looked much sadder. "Not all. Most, though. For now, at least."

"For now?"

"Once Orogen is CEO, once I have my vice presidency and the families have settled into their new normal, I'll have a little more freedom." Something else came over Gloria's face, then. It softened. Her eyes drifted down my body for a moment before locking on my eyes again. Then she quickly looked outside, watching the buildings move by. "Only a little, though. I'll still be a Siwa, after all."

I didn't want to think too much about how she'd looked at me before turning away. Fortunately, Nox's voice was in my ear again. "I'm in. All quiet and dark inside. Starting visuals…"

A rectangle appeared in the upper left of my display. It was a well-appointed living room, barely visible in the dim, amber lights in the corners of the room. The wall to the right was glass, looking out over the Kotega Systems borough. What furniture I could see was expensive and looked like the sort that you displayed rather than sat on.

"Moving in," Nox said.

And the visual on my display moved, streaming from Nox's optical implants to mine. He weaved through the furniture, his head on a swivel, which was disorienting. I moved my gaze to look outside the limo just so Gloria wouldn't see my vacant gaze again.

"This room is clear," Nox said. "Moving to the next."

"I'm recording and reviewing everything," Bastion said via text on my screen.

Nox moved into the next room, which looked remarkably like the last. Not in content, but in quality. More expensive furniture, barely lit.

The limo pulled out of the main lane of traffic and started descending. Ridley said to Gloria over a speaker, "Landing now, Mistress."

"Is Lynn here yet?" she asked him.

"Yes, Mistress."

"Anything special I need to be doing?" I asked. I'd read Zhao's instructions, but I found it best to ask Gloria, just in case.

"Once Lynn and I are seated, find a nearby wall to lean against," Gloria said. "I don't want you to be in the way of the servers. Plus, it would look awkward if you were just hovering over me."

"Yes, Mistress," I said.

"And no tasting tonight. I know Zhao probably said to, but I don't want to insult the restaurant. Lynn would understand, but I've heard the chef is sensitive."

"Yes, Mistress."

The car landed and we both stepped out, me first as usual, opening the giant umbrella and giving a quick visual sweep of the landing pad before I stepped aside to allow Gloria to exit the car. We both walked into the restaurant while in the corner of my display, Nox was moving through Orogen's dining room.

Going somewhere truly public with Gloria was an experience unlike any I'd had. I'd been in the room with celebrities before, even broken into their homes while they were gone. But being in a very nice restaurant when Gloria Siwa Kotega unexpectedly walked into it was something else entirely. People stopped mid-chew to gawk. The host suddenly started fidgeting with their cufflinks and lapels, plastering on a wide smile that didn't even look fake.

They bowed deeply before saying, "Good evening. We at the Suydan are so, so honored that you decided to dine with us tonight. If you would follow me, your table is ready, and your guest is already seated."

They bowed again before backing away several paces. Only then did they turn and lead us deeper into the restaurant. Pristine, white tablecloths. Shining silverware that might have actually been made of silver. Every meal was plated like artwork deserving of a gallery. Every diner was dressed in sharp formal wear. No casual wear in sight. I recognized several faces by now, Kotega families of some renown that either Gloria had met with, or I'd at least read up on.

Finally, we arrived at the table. Lynn, she/her, stood. Her blond hair was cropped short, which helped her large, brown eyes take all of the attention. She was wearing a tuxedo. White jacket, black pants, black shirt, and a white sequined tie cut to resemble a lightning bolt.

She bowed slightly and said, "Gloria. So nice to see you."

Gloria barely inclined her head as she said, "Likewise."

The host pulled out a chair, and Gloria sat in it. Only then did Lynn sit back down and the sounds of people eating resumed.

"Will your Daeli be requiring a table or anything to eat tonight?" the host asked.

"No," Gloria said. "Just a place to stand that will be out of your way."

The host bowed deeply once again and said, "Of course."

I backed up until I was leaning up against the wall behind me. It was less than two meters from Gloria and seemed out of the way enough. A few diners cast me curious glances, but soon enough, they were all ignoring me.

"Orogen has too much stuff," Nox said. His voice seemed too loud, too close. I had to remind myself that he was alone in Orogen's quarters. No need for him to whisper. "I don't see anything suspicious, though. Nothing that would point to Toinette or Josephine."

I glanced at Gloria. She was looking over the menu while nodding along to something that Lynn was saying. I brought up my AR keyboard and, with my hands behind my back, texted Nox, "Keep looking. Plenty of rooms to go through."

"I still don't understand why you suspect Orogen," Nox said.

"Need to know," I texted back. "Sorry."

While Nox kept moving, I stood next to the wall. Servers would occasionally move past me, always saying excuse me as if they were in my way, not the other way around. Every table was full, I noticed. Plenty of wealthy people eating expensive food. They all kept casting glances at Gloria, of course. A server came by and took Gloria and Lynn's drink orders after spending far too long telling them about the chef's specials. From what I heard, every other sentence was thanking Gloria for simply being here.

Once the server left, I focused my aural mods on their conversation while keeping my eyes roving around the restaurant.

"Sorry about that," Gloria said.

"About what?" Lynn asked. She sounded genuinely confused.

"I can't go anywhere in Kotega without attracting this sort of attention."

"That's the game, though, isn't it?"

"The game?" Gloria asked, but I knew she knew what Lynn was

talking about.

"Why you agreed to this date," Lynn said. "Doing my family the honor of being seen in public with me."

"It's not…well…"

"It's all right. I understand. But, I really did want to ask you out myself. My brother insisted we go through these channels, though, jump through all these political hoops."

I dared a glance toward their table, and Gloria looked uncomfortable. Lynn was saying the things that they'd both been raised to never say out in public. This was the sort of conversation reserved for the car and under the strict tenets of an NDA. Definitely not the sort of conversation had in range of so many aural implants.

"I'm sorry," Lynn said. She'd obviously picked up on Gloria's discomfort, too. "I just hate the games. And I genuinely like you. I have since we were in fourth year together."

"Fourth year?" Gloria asked, obviously happy for the redirect.

"You sat in front of me in interstellar geography. You probably didn't even know I was there. I remember how you used to cock your head to the left a little when you were really listening. You loved learning about the stellar pathways between Little Sekhmet Settlement and Earth, all the colonies and other settlements a ship had to stop at along the way."

Gloria smiled. "Back then, it used to take ships almost a decade to make the trip."

"It still takes a few years, I hear."

"It does, yes. The Raj-Lu drive is a wonder of engineering."

I'd never heard Gloria talk about interstellar travel or geography. I had no idea it was one of her interests. The way she lit up when she talked about it, though, the light she was shining on Lynn was delightful. I felt jealous. Then I felt stupid and ashamed for feeling jealous. I looked away, doing my job and scanning the restaurant again.

"Kitchen is clear," Nox said. "Moving on to the hallway and bedrooms."

While I had my head turned toward the restaurant's kitchen, I focused on the visual coming from Nox. Even Orogen's hallway was as wide as my bedroom. The hallway was long and well-appointed with artwork. I recognized some pieces from famous Little Sekhmet artists, mostly from the Impressionist period nearly a century ago. No photos of family or friends.

Nox turned into a room that looked like a guest bedroom. Like the rest of his quarters, it was overstuffed with expensive and boisterous furniture. It didn't feel personal enough to be Orogen's room, however. It looked like it had been designed to look nice and hold Orogen's stuff, not to be the place he or anyone else put their head down at night.

Nox started checking drawers, flicking switches, and shifting paintings aside.

A server pulled my attention back, stopping at the table with Gloria and Lynn to deliver their drinks and take their food orders. They walked away, and at that moment, I saw Lynn reach across the table and slightly intertwine her fingers with Gloria's. My heart leaped. It shouldn't have, but it did. And it did it again when Gloria quickly pulled her hand away and glanced at me, her cheeks red.

Why did she look at me? It was one thing for my stupid heart to flutter like this, but she was Gloria Siwa-Kotega. She was part of a dynasty, and I was just her Daeli. Not really, but that's all she knew. She shouldn't be looking at me like that. But maybe I was just a reassuring presence. Just a familiar face in an uncomfortable situation. That had to be it. She wasn't looking at me anymore, but I gave her a reassuring smile anyway.

"What was that?" Nox asked.

For a moment, I thought he meant Gloria's look and my awkward smile. But how could he know? Then it set in: he didn't. Something was going on at Orogen's.

"I heard something," Nox whispered. "Did you hear that, too?"

I didn't. Whatever it was.

"Minor background noise on his end," Bastion said on my screen. "I need more time to analyze, but I believe it might have been Orogen's private elevator."

"Hide!" I texted Nox.

"Mother of Corto," he whispered while he shimmied his way into a closet that was overstuffed with Orogen's clothes. Of course, the rich guy had enough clothes to likely fill every closet in his residence.

I had to remind myself to keep my face neutral even though my heart was racing. I was still standing in a fancy restaurant, obviously Gloria's Daeli and security for the evening. But at that moment, I only cared about my apprentice. He was alone in Orogen's quarters. What if he was found? What could I do? If my cover was still secure, I couldn't risk blowing it early. I wasn't sure Corto Corporation would do anything, either, so long as I was still embedded.

"He's back," Nox whispered, barely audible. "And he's not alone."

By then, even I heard what he was hearing. Voices. I couldn't make them all out, filtered as they were through Nox's aural implants and comms, but there were multiple distinct voices.

"What's going on?" I texted him. "What are they saying?"

"He sounds drunk," Nox said. "They all sound drunk. Most of them, anyway. A dozen of them, I think?"

"I can make out 14 different voices," Bastion said. "I'm running analysis to identify them."

Nox's feed was dark while he huddled in the closet. The voices were getting louder, but there was no way I was making out any of them from here. Bastion was on it. I dared a glance back at Gloria and Lynn. Things had gone rather cold, it seemed. Lynn was talking sales numbers for Kotega's Neuro division, of all things. And Gloria was asking follow-up questions. Unless the upper 1% did dates WAY differently than the rest of us, it seemed like the date had morphed into a business meeting.

The food came far faster than I would have imagined, probably another perk of being a Siwa, and then my display was filled with more than a dozen photos with names listed under them. I didn't recognize any of them, though I noticed more than half of them had a family name to go with their corporate name. No surprise that Orogen had elite friends.

"What's going on?" I asked Nox via text.

"They're partying, I think," he said. "Just having a good time. Orogen walked down the hall, right on past this room, and then rejoined the group a couple of minutes later. Nobody has come in here, but I think I'm stuck."

"Been there," I said. "Try to get comfortable. Stay quiet. Stay vigilant. Make an escape plan."

"I think I can just duck out and run down the hall, away from the party. One of these rooms is bound to have a window."

"No. Stay put. Mission…" I was about to write mission first, but that wasn't quite right. I deleted the last word and typed, "Complete the mission if you can, but your safety comes first," before I sent the message.

"Okay," Nox said in a shaky whisper. "Okay."

The next hour was tense in the most relaxed way possible. Nox settled into the closet, whispering to me almost nonstop. At first, he was just making an escape plan out loud. Once that was done, he started talking about music, his favorite artists, and soon moved on to his favorite streams. I replied little, not wanting to look like I was constantly texting while I was playing the security guard. That and I understood Nox well enough to know that when he was nervous, he talked. He just needed someone to listen.

Gloria and Lynn ate their dinners, drank some wine, and even ordered desserts. After the misfire with the handhold, they'd been friendly enough, catching up and talking business, but certainly not date-like. Finally, after they finished their after-dinner coffees, Gloria rose to her feet. Lynn stood with her.

"This was very nice," Gloria said. "So good to catch up."

"Thank you," Lynn said. "It really was."

"Send all my best to your father and brother," Gloria said loudly enough for the entire restaurant to hear. Still playing the game. Always playing the game.

"I will," Lynn said and bowed at the waist.

Gloria inclined her head slightly and then looked at me. I removed myself from my perch on the wall and fell in step behind her as we made our way out of the restaurant. Nox's visual feed was still dark. The voices of partiers were still active in the background.

Then, two of the voices on the feed were growing louder. Two voices that I recognized. They were entering the same room as Nox, separated only by a closet door.

"Are you hearing this?" Bastion asked.

I had no way to respond, but I was certainly hearing it. One voice was Orogen. The other was Tazia.

Chapter Twenty-Three

5 Days to Ascension

AS I FOLLOWED GLORIA OUT of the restaurant and onto the landing pad, sticking close to keep her under the umbrella, the vast majority of my focus was on the feed coming from Nox. His visual was still dark. He was still hiding in a closet. But just on the other side of that closet door, Orogen was speaking with Tazia. Tazia, the Ghost of Toinette, who'd seemingly vanished after she crippled Solomon. She was here. She'd probably been here since that day on Cirilla.

"Are you having fun?" Tazia asked Orogen.

"Of course," he said. "Aren't you?" Several moments passed before he said, "Don't worry. This room is soundproofed. That bed has seen a lot of fun and sleepless nights for my friends."

"Delightful," Tazia said flatly.

"I like to be a good host. So, aren't you having fun in my borough?"

"Living in one of your spare rooms? Barely getting to leave? No. But I'm not here to have fun."

Living in one of Orogen's spare rooms? That was useful to know. Very useful. The most damning evidence I could use against Orogen was living right there in that building.

"You're here. You're safe. And we're together, right? Everything is going well. That's all—"

"I don't need you to worry about my safety. I didn't come here to be safe. I came here to advise you."

Orogen sighed. "You're my spiritual advisor. I've never felt more spiritually sound in my life. Am I not including you enough?"

"Don't treat me like a child," Tazia spat. "These days are the most crucial for you, leading up to the transition of power. Your dalliances with these…these…"

Ridley brought the limo around right as Gloria and I reached the landing pad. The large vehicle landed almost soundlessly. I opened the door, and Gloria climbed in. I followed close behind.

"They're my friends, Josephine," Orogen said. So he only knew her by her cover name. That was another question answered. "They've been my friends since we were young. We all went to the same school, and all of our families run in the same circles. These aren't dalliances. Jean oversees the temple restoration project. Alex and Rahne are both managers in Intel. And Kweenie was just made a VP in Security. You know we need her. This is me keeping my allies close."

"Speaking of Kweenie, is our contingency in place?" Josephine asked.

A contingency plan involving a Security VP? That didn't sound good.

"She confirmed with me this morning," Orogen said.

"Fine," Josephine said after a long pause. "But I can be of more use to you."

"How? I'm still just the heir right now, and I have to give everyone the Kotega party line. Once I'm in the big chair, then you'll become my official spiritual advisor. You can start preaching openly here. Until then, what can you do?"

They were silent then. I could imagine the wheels turning for Tazia. She was protecting the Josephine persona, the persona who was only a preacher of Ibhalism. Orogen had no idea that she had innumerable skills as a thief, spy, and so much more.

"That was pointless," Gloria said, and I nearly jumped. Gloria noticed and asked, "Are you all right?"

"I'm fine, Mistress," I said. "My apologies."

"You seem distracted."

"I…" I tried to come up with a convincing lie, but nothing came to mind. I was too engrossed with what was happening with Tazia and Orogen. "Yes. I'm sorry. It won't happen again."

Gloria gave me a tight and unconvinced smile. "That date was certainly a waste of time, wasn't it?"

"Mistress?" I wasn't sure what she wanted me to say.

"There was no spark, no fire, for sure. Not on my side, at least." Gloria was looking at me as she spoke, maintaining eye contact with far too much ease. "So many people don't see me as more than a Siwa, as a path to power. Did you see her reach for my hand?"

"I did, Mistress."

"Our food hadn't even come. She'd asked me nothing about myself, my interests, or my thoughts. It was all talk about the Ascension, about our futures in Kotega, and then she tried to hold my hand." Gloria shook her head.

"You don't think she was genuinely attracted to you?" I asked.

Gloria blew out a breath. Her cheeks reddened, and she finally turned away from me to look out the window. "Maybe superficially. But she didn't even try to get to know me."

"She probably thinks she does," I said. "I imagine you could live anywhere in Jayu City, maybe in Earth Space, and easily look up pages and pages of information on you."

"Of course, but—"

"But that doesn't mean they know you, the real you."

Gloria looked back at me. Those eyes were like land mines. Now, it was my turn to look away before I continued.

"I think that's something you'll have to work against. Force the conversation to something real, to something they cannot look up online. It'll make people uncomfortable, but it also might make someone start asking the right questions."

"That's not fair," Gloria whispered. "Other people don't have to do that."

She was right. It wasn't fair, but it was who she was. Famous. Powerful. Influential. Everyone she went on a date with was probably trying to leverage her name, but she already knew that. I didn't need to say it.

I turned my attention back to Nox's feed as Tazia said, "I can help you lay the groundwork. Get people talking about spirituality, talking about order and chaos at least in the abstract."

"And risk exposure? I know the plan, Josephine. We're less than a week out from the Ascension. We bide our time. I'll shake hands and structure my organization just like every CEO before me. Once I'm in charge, nobody will stop us from spreading Shainette's and Aphnette's messages."

Tazia sighed again, and I heard what sounded like the squeak of someone sitting on the bed. "At least give me something to do. I can't just wait around for your call all day."

"You have a Kotega name and ID. You can go wherever you want."

"I don't use that Kotega name. It's flimsy and won't hold up under scrutiny."

"How do you know that?"

"I just do," Tazia said. Because any Intel Operative with any experience would know at a glance how good a fake ID was.

"With me greasing the wheels, though," Orogen said. "I could make it work, help you get a job or something. A Kotega job. I have pull. A nice desk job, maybe even with a view."

I wished I could see the look on Tazia's face. She must have been fuming at the idea of taking on some menial job in the Kotega borough. The Ghost of Toinette reduced to filing reports and watching the same billboard out of an office window each day. It made me smile.

"Something funny?" Gloria asked, shaking me again back into my own reality. She looked so sad all of a sudden. Maybe it was the terrible date, likely the latest in a string of similar experiences. Maybe it was something else she wasn't saying.

But in the corner of my display was a dark feed with Tazia and Orogen talking. This was the break I'd been looking for, and I had access to it in real-time. But Gloria was right in front of me. She needed cheering up. And with a party at Orogen's likely to last well into the night, Nox wasn't going anywhere anytime soon. And he was recording everything. Whatever was said there, I wasn't going to miss it.

"Your schedule is clear for the rest of the evening, right?" I asked.

Gloria briefly looked into the middle distance before she said, "It is."

"You should do something fun."

She was still looking out the window and tried to hide it, but I saw the corner of her mouth creep up in a smile. "Fun?"

"You ever been flying?"

#   #   #

It took about twenty minutes to convince both Gloria and Ridley that it was a good and relatively safe idea. After all, while Elise had her own bike and had hundreds of hours of flying under her belt, Xyla did not. Once I found a rental place and convinced them to at least go there, I knew I could get Gloria on a bike.

"These are pretty basic," I said. Gloria was straddling the Kotega SkyGlide, a recent and low-end model that I was pretty sure was basically the same bike as the Corto StarClash. A good, reliable starter bike. Easy to ride. Nowhere near as fast or fun as my Poe, but I expected that. "Turn the right handle for thrust. It has auto-brake enabled, so just letting off the thrust will slow you down. You can also squeeze the lever on either handle to brake faster."

Gloria's eyes were wide. She was nervous, no doubt. She was also listening intently. "And how does it stay in the air?"

"Those are the vertical thrusters. You don't need to worry about them. So long as the bike is on, those thrusters will keep her in the air. Pulling back on the handles will make the bike ascend. Pushing forward makes the bike descend."

"What if the vertical thrusters go out?" Gloria asked in a rush.

"The backup thrusters will kick in. She also has more than a dozen stabilizing systems, backup systems, and even a remote pilot feature to bring you back here. Perfectly safe."

Gloria blew out a breath through her teeth and nodded. "Mother would hate this. Let's do it!"

I straddled my own rented Kotega SkyGlide, ran through my pre-flight checks automatically, and hit the start button. The bike lifted off the ground, kicking up some dust from the landing pad. The entire bike felt light and fragile beneath me, but I was used to Poe, which was much heavier. I looked at Gloria, smiled, and nodded.

She returned the smile, though it was plainly nervous. Then she turned her bike on. I watched her wobble in the saddle a bit as the bike rose, but the bike wasn't wobbling at all. Then, I gently twisted the handle on my bike, slowly accelerating into the open air of the street. The rain had backed down to a drizzle. We were going to get wet, but not terribly so. Even more slowly than me, Gloria followed, her eyes wide.

As I pulled away from the landing pad and waited for Gloria to catch up, I spared a glance at Nox's feed. Still dark.

"Everything all right with Nox?" I whispered to Bastion.

"Yes," he said. "Orogen and Tazia left the room several minutes ago. The friends are still there in the residence. Nox has been watching an entertainment stream to pass the time."

"Good," I said. "Alert me if anything happens."

"Of course."

"Come on," I said to Gloria over comms. "We'll stay out of the main traffic. Just keep up, get used to the bike, and tell me how it feels."

Gloria nodded and didn't say anything. I urged my bike forward and after a moment, she followed. We settled into a gentle cruising speed of 60 kph, which felt depressingly slow. Even this basic bike was built for more than that.

"How are you doing?" I asked.

"Good, I think," Gloria said. "Good. Is this supposed to be fun, though? It's just…scary right now."

I slowed down until I was right alongside her. Both of us slowed completely until we were hovering near the corner of a building. Her knuckles were tight on the handlebars. She kept looking over the sides of the bike to The Mist hundreds of meters below.

"Stop looking down," I said. "Look around. Take it all in."

In fits and starts, Gloria looked up, still glancing down a lot, before she settled her gaze on me for a few seconds. She seemed to relax and then really looked around. "Wow," she said.

"Right? It's not the same as when you're in your limo. To feel the wind whip by, to smell the city, to feel it on your skin."

"I get it," she said before she looked down again. "It's not much different than standing on my balcony, really. Except scarier. A lot scarier. Why do you do this?"

"I don't do this," I said. "Not just hovering or cruising along like this."

Gloria looked at me again, curiosity plain on her face.

"I do it for this," I said and twisted the thruster control hard. The bike lurched forward as fast as it could, and then I pulled on the handlebars, steering the bike into a steep climb. Safety lights blinked everywhere on the bike.

"This is not Poe," Bastion said in my ear.

Obviously, I twisted the bars and let off the thrusters, enjoying the few moments of zero G while the bike tried to right itself. The moment the front of the bike was pointed downward, though, I pushed the handles forward and twisted the thruster control again, forcing the bike into a steep dive. I twisted so that my dive became a spiral.

"This is why I do it!" I yelled over my comms. My demonstration complete, I pulled the bike out of the dive, which took much longer than when I was riding Poe. Once the alarms stopped going off and the thrusters stopped screaming, I heard Gloria laughing over my comms.

"You're crazy!" she said.

I brought my bike back alongside hers. "That wasn't crazy. You should see me on my bike back home. I like to have fun."

"Show me how?"

I did. Her speed wasn't as intense. Her angles weren't as sharp, but I showed Gloria how to push the bike, how to find that moment of zero G and the thrill of a steep dive. She giggled as her stomach wobbled, but she was stern like I was. Some people couldn't handle those moves, their stomachs threatening to vomit everywhere with the slightest change in elevation. Not me. I loved that feeling, the little flutter from my abdomen. It seemed that

Gloria was the same way.

Her brow was covered in sweat and rainwater, her grin wider than I'd ever seen it as she pulled up alongside me again. "What kind of bike do you have?"

I opened my mouth to talk about Poe, my pride and joy but remembered that I was Xyla. "Oh, it's not much. Not as nice as this."

"You said you did crazier stuff on it, though. Faster than these, then?"

"Yeah, but these are electronically limited," I said. I had no idea if that was true. "They're rentals, after all."

"Oh," Gloria said and looked embarrassed, though I didn't understand why. "Okay. So—"

Before she could say another word, though, a pair of heavily graffitied drones zipped by, both of them probably pushing 200 kph, and far too close to Gloria. Her bike didn't rock or wobble, the stabilizers doing their job, but she panicked. Her hands went up off the handlebars, she leaned away, and between the rain and her lack of instincts, she didn't grip the bike with her thighs. Before I could say one word or reach out a hand, she was screaming, her legs were above her head, and she was falling, tumbling toward The Mist.

Chapter Twenty-Four

5 Days to Ascension

I'D BEEN FLYING MOTORCYCLES ALL my adult life. So when the rental agent asked if we would sign liability waivers, I didn't even give it a second glance. When they asked if we wanted parachutes, I rolled my eyes. Now, Gloria was freefalling from just under 1,000 meters up. Right. Hindsight 20/20 and all that.

I pushed the bike into the hardest, fastest dive that it could handle. If I'd been on Poe, she would have soundlessly accelerated into a perfect vertical. I would have been able to catch Gloria before she even realized she was in danger. This bike? This lame bike started screaming at me, every alarm blinking and wailing at the same time. She wouldn't go fully vertical, so I had to pull her into a tight, downward spiral and keep my eyes on Gloria.

And then the handlebars started pushing against me, pushing the bike back to level. Seriously, the safeties on this thing must have been designed for toddlers.

"Where's the port?" I yelled at Bastion over the wind and screaming alarms. "I need you to bypass the limiters and safety systems!"

"Under the battery array," Bastion said. "Twelve centimeters behind the forward thruster."

I pulled my data cable out and reached down, feeling around the battery array while fighting the handlebars and trying to keep Gloria in sight. I was gaining on her, but only just. The bike's limiters were actively trying to slow me, so I was barely going faster than the terminal velocity of a falling human.

After what felt like an eternity, I found the port and plugged in. I sat back up, leaving the cable plugged in, and put both of my mediocre cybernetic arms to work fighting the safety systems. I didn't have to fight long, though, after about a dozen seconds, all of the alarms stopped flashing. The bells went silent, and the thrusters suddenly opened up.

"Done," Bastion said.

"Too right," I said as I pushed the bike into a proper vertical. I caught up to Gloria in a hurry. She was screaming her head off, her hair flailing around her head, the pins holding it in place long gone. The hem of her dress was in tatters. I moved past her by a meter and matched speed.

I looked straight up at her. Her eyes were wide, but she'd stopped screaming when she saw me. I yelled, "Grab hold!"

I eased off the throttle millimeter by millimeter and shaved off enough speed for Gloria's scrabbling fingers to take hold of me. She gripped and clawed at my shoulders, each finger like a knife. Her whole body shook as she pulled herself onto my bike. Only when I knew I had her safely did I level out and let the bike slow fully.

My heart was pounding. Despite all of my antics on and off of motorcycles, rescuing someone else from a big fall had taken a lot out of me. Then I realized I wasn't feeling only my own heartbeat. Gloria was pressed against my back. Her head was on my shoulder, her entire body hugged tightly to me. Even her thighs were squeezing me. She was shaking. Her own heart was rattling so near that I felt it on my spine.

"You're okay," I said. "You're okay."

"Thank you," she said through whimpers.

"I'm so sorry," I said. "So, so sorry."

Gloria stayed pressed to me, shaking. Her warm breath hit my neck in short, intense bursts. It was nice. Too nice. And uncomfortable, too. It wasn't sexual, of course, but the matching dresses we were wearing were thin. There was too little between us, and I was suddenly far too aware of her body. I swallowed and gently gave the bike some thrust, pulling back on the handlebars to climb back to Gloria's rented bike.

"Don't," she suddenly said, too loud and too close to my ear.

I released the throttle. "Don't? Don't what?"

"Just…just hover here for a minute. I need…I need to not move. Please."

I swallowed again. My mouth was dry. There wasn't enough room on this bike, not by far. I needed her to be on her bike while I was on this one. I at least needed her to lean back, but what could I say? She was terrified. She'd probably thought she was going to die down in The Mist below. Right now, all she wanted to do was sit here, not moving, and press every part of her up against me. I hated it and didn't all at the same time.

Mother of Corto, I'd just ingratiated myself with Gloria better than I could have hoped for. The walls she'd been putting back up had all come tumbling down. That was useful to me. Despite that, I just needed her to stop touching me. So, I breathed. Slow and steady. In and out. I thought about Quynn, about being home with them. They were probably sitting in front of their gaming station right now, just like they were so many nights. If I were home, we would be watching some movie with too many explosions and too little dialog. I missed them so much. I imagined sitting on our big couch, sharing a bowl of chips or caramel drops, holding hands or leaning up against each other. Just being home. Living my normal life. Our normal life.

Finally, Gloria sat up. She was still shaking, still squeezing my shoulders with her hands, but the air between us felt like a weight lifting. I looked at her over my shoulder. She was a mess. Her hair was going every direction. Her face was streaked from tears.

"Are you ready?" I asked.

She took a few moments, but she eventually nodded.

"You sure?"

"Yes," she whispered.

I wasn't sure that I believed her, but I gently twisted the throttle and pulled back on the handlebars. I put the bike into a slow and sure ascent.

I looked up and clocked her bike, still hovering a couple hundred meters above. There was no way I was getting her back on a bike alone tonight, but I could at least set the autopilot on it and get us both back to Ridley.

Chapter Twenty-Five

4 Days to Ascension

THREE DAYS PASSED BEFORE I was able to meet up with Nox for a proper debrief in the garden. I'd reviewed the footage that I hadn't watched in real-time, of course, but it was still good to get Nox's impression. He'd been in the room.

"Josephine is frustrated," Nox said. It was strange to hear her cover name. Strange that Nox didn't and couldn't know.

"Obviously," I said. "It's nice to hear her annoyed."

"Better than her trying to kill us."

"It's a big win. We need evidence that Orogen is compromised, and the evidence is literally living here."

"Why is she here and not back in Toinette, though? She's not doing anything here, just waiting around. She could be back home leading her flock or whatever."

"That's…" I said, absorbing his words. "A really good question."

"A very good question," Bastion said in my ear.

I pulled up Orogen's and Gloria's calendars on my display before I said, "Tomorrow night, they're both occupied. Late-night meetings upstairs.

No Daelis."

"Okay?" Nox said. "You have something for me to do?"

"Not you this time," I said. I'd gotten lucky that Tazia had been with Orogen when Nox was listening. She'd stuck to her Josephine cover, and I didn't need to read Nox in. "Josephine isn't going to be here unless she has a very good reason, maybe a reason she's keeping from Orogen. You did great in there the other night. It's my turn."

\#   \#   \#

I've had a recurring nightmare since my mid-twenties. I'm sneaking into a highly secured facility. Maybe it's a server farm or an R&D lab or a CEO's office. In any case, the locks are cutting-edge technology, but I bypass them. The cameras are multi-spectral and mounted in surprising locations, but I manage to move around and disable them. There are pressure plates and laser grids and all sorts of contraptions that they put in heist movies, but I've never seen in real life. Whatever, I get past them all. Finally, I'm at The Door.

You know, the final door standing between you and the thing you're going to steal. You can feel the capital letters threading through the air. The Door. Next-generation biometric, cybermetric, and encrypted locking mechanisms. I'm sweating, but I finally get through it. I open the door, sneaking gingerly into the room.

And every light turns on, bright as midday. There are dozens of people staring at me. Sometimes Quynn or my mom or Gustin or Solomon are there among them. In recent months, Valdo and a nebulous, person-shaped presence that I know is Bastion has joined them. Sometimes, it's a sea of strangers, however my subconscious manages that. They're all staring at me. It's in that moment that I realize I'm stark naked. Not only that, but I don't have my work limbs. In fact, I have my biological limbs, the ones I had removed in my early 20s. They're heavy, sweaty, and don't behave the way they should. They shake in fear and cold. They ache from tension. They fail me.

That's almost how it felt sneaking into Orogen's floors. I didn't have my helmet. These limbs weren't my normal work limbs. They were three

232

times as heavy, slower, weaker, and carried less than a fifth of my normal tools. I wasn't even in my carbon-nanoweave jumpsuit, but the basic uniform provided to me. It fit loosely, and every shift of my body made a soft rustling sound. Every movement sent a slight breeze down the collar or up the sleeves. It all felt wrong.

But now was the time. Orogen and Gloria were on the top floor in a late-night meeting, one that didn't require me. I slipped down the hallway of Gloria's staff quarters, acting naturally. Then I doubled back, darting down a side hall, and stopped beside a maintenance door. It was locked, but I expected that. I tapped on the door, three times rapidly, twice with a slow drag of my knuckle, and then once more. The door opened. Nox was on the other side. He didn't say a word but inclined his head for me to follow him.

We climbed six floors before striding down an empty hallway. There were racks of tools every 10 or so meters. I peered in an open door and saw what looked like a small machine shop, like a low-tech version of the shop at the Corto Intel offices. Finally, we stopped by a door as nondescript as all the rest, and Nox opened it. He looked inside, the door only cracked open before he looked at me and said, "Looks clear."

I nodded. "Will you be here when I'm done?"

Nox looked into the middle distance, viewing something on his display. "I have to be two floors up to fix a toilet."

"New guy gets the shit jobs?"

"Literally," he said without humor. "Message me when you're done and ready to go back downstairs. Something—"

"Something innocuous?" I cut him off. "Like I've taught you? You're still the apprentice, remember?"

Nox smiled but looked embarrassed.

"Good work," I whispered, taking the door handle from him. "See you soon."

He smiled with genuine pride this time, nodded, and walked away. I opened the door more and slipped into Orogen's residence, which was, just like I'd seen from Nox's feed, far more lavish than what I'd seen of Gloria's. Where Gloria had simple and elegant furniture, Orogen's was ornate with scrollwork and patterned cloths. The walls were covered in an alternating pattern of mirrors and sculpted metal or wood. Real wood, I was sure. Every surface was overpopulated with statues or strange art pieces or small display screens showing Orogen with numerous celebrities or hoisting trophies.

The young man was about a decade my junior, but his possessions in one room were worth more than I'd made in my entire life. It was ridiculous. I didn't even know where to look, the entire place was so overwhelming. Finally, I closed my eyes and took a deep breath. Tazia was living here, too. She might be here at this very moment, so I needed to be extra cautious.

"What am I seeing?" I asked Bastion.

Quickly, little labels began to appear in my display next to each little sculpture or photograph or whatever. Statues of ancient Earth gods like Zeus, Bast, Heimdall, Jesus, and Hachiman. Expensive collectible sculptures of characters from dozens of video games. Historical figures like Gandhi, Bill Gates, the founder of Kotega Systems, and Angela Merkel. On and on it went. As I passed my eyes over the room, the labels kept popping up, too many to keep track of.

"That's enough," I said.

"It's more than enough, I think," Bastion said. "I'm not sure if Orogen is a hoarder or just has terrible taste."

"I'd say both."

I thought I'd be able to look for obvious evidence of Orogen's faith in Ibhalism, the religion of Toinette. After all, it was Orogen's conversion that was the problem. Maybe I would find statues or tapestries depicting Shainette and Aphnette, the twin deities of fate and chaos. Perhaps religious texts. But this place was so cluttered with statues and tapestries of every variety, it wouldn't matter if Shainette and Aphnette were among them. Just part of the collection.

So I kept moving through Orogen's overwhelming home. While staying on the lookout for Tazia, I was looking for a workstation. Maybe he would have files or communications with Toinette, something that I could use against him. Not seeing anything in the living room, or whatever he called this room, I moved on. I was more cautious than I'd ever been, peeking around corners with my fiberoptic camera before proceeding, sticking to walls and shadows. I found two similar rooms to the first. A sitting room? A parlor? More couches, chairs, and statues. No workstations.

I moved down the hall and found a bedroom. It was just as overstuffed as the other rooms. I only knew it was a bedroom because of the bed, but it was still twice the size of my entire apartment with Quynn. I kept moving through, keeping an eye and ear open for Tazia as I found the bedroom that Nox had hidden in, bathrooms, and a small kitchen that was entirely free of clutter. Or anything else that a kitchen needs. Orogen obviously didn't cook his own meals.

I went up a floor, finding more of the same. I did find several statues of Shainette and Aphnette, but as I feared, they were mixed in with all the other religious paraphernalia that he collected. More guest bedrooms, mostly filled with more of Orogen's stuff, but the fourth bedroom on that floor was different. The statues and things were shoved against walls or off to the sides. The bed was made, but not pristine. I walked in and smelled Tazia. Not that she had a particular perfume or musk, but the light smell was familiar. It reminded me of when I'd cornered her in a hotel room on Cirilla Island, the same hotel room that Vert, her bodyguard, had thrown me out of. Through the window.

At least Vert wasn't a problem anymore, though I regretted how I'd handled that. His dead eye staring at me still haunted me at night, even if I hadn't been the one to end his life. I played my part.

I blinked rapidly, taking pictures from every angle in the room. Only after that did I start opening drawers, looking through them without disturbing anything. I carefully returned everything to exactly where I found it. If a drawer had been slightly ajar when I entered the room, I made sure it was exactly that much ajar after.

Nothing. There were clothes. Limbs in the power cabinet. A few personal care items. Nothing incriminating. Nothing useful to me at all. Tazia was being careful.

"You should bug the room," Bastion said. "Maybe multiple rooms."

"No way," I said. "I'm not going to risk it. She's too good, too paranoid."

"You can't waste this opportunity."

"Plenty more rooms to look through," I said as I left Tazia's room, looking back once to make sure I'd left no trace of my presence.

Finally, I found Orogen's room, half of which was dominated by a workstation. Well, a gaming station, to be more accurate. And it was the type of system that Quynn dreamed about. The workstation was built into the desk, which was so large that I was sure it had to be constructed in the room because it wouldn't fit through the door. Three enormous, curved screens were mounted above the desk. The chair looked like it could double as a captain's chair on a starship. The décor in here was simpler, the walls lined with shelves of gaming trophies and collectibles. Orogen's life as a professional gamer on display.

It seemed like a good place to start, though I was thoroughly unfamiliar with this design of workstation. "Bastion," I said. "Where do I plug in?"

"It's a custom machine," he said. "I don't see any ports on the front. Have a look around."

I did, eventually finding a bevy of ports hidden behind a panel on the right side. I plugged in, and all three screens immediately lit up. The room was suddenly filled with loud orchestral music and the sounds of a battle. I covered my ears, and the sound went away after a few seconds.

"What just happened?" I whispered, uncovering my ears and listening intently for anyone running this direction.

"There was a game suspended," Bastion said. "As soon as I accessed the machine, the game resumed. I shut it down."

I nodded and then just listened, not daring to move. That had been loud enough to be heard several floors away, or at least it felt like it. If the staff was nearby or, Corto forbid, Tazia was somewhere in the residence, I needed to run.

After several silent minutes went by, I let the tension out of my shoulders and said, "Where even are the speakers? That was deafening."

"In the walls. There are 16 of them, according to the audio settings on this machine."

I still didn't hear any footsteps hurrying this way, so I sat down in the chair. Of course, it was the most comfortable chair in which I'd ever placed my body. The cushions actively changed shape when I sat, molding around me and adjusting to relieve some nagging pains I didn't even realize I had in my lower back. The headrest and armrests adjusted as well, perfectly placing themselves behind my neck and bringing my arms to the perfect level.

On the screen, several dozen small windows appeared. Text scrolled faster than I could follow. Lines of code danced around on command prompt windows.

"Anything?" I asked.

"Not yet," Bastion said. "His personal communications were easy enough. The official communications as the future head of Kotega Systems are using stiffer security."

I sat there for a few minutes, lost in the extraordinary comfort of the chair and the mesmerizing scroll of code. Then Bastion said, "I'm in. But there's nothing."

"Nothing at all?"

"Some curious facts and figures, certainly useful things for Corto's Intel operations, but nothing on Toinette Holdings or Ibhalism or anything of that nature."

"Silent circuits," I muttered.

"Do you want me to download…"

Bastion stopped talking as we both heard something. A door closing, from the sound of it. I turned up the sensitivity on my aural implants, and sure enough, I heard footsteps. Quickly, I flicked my fingers on my haptics and brought up the real-time tracking on Orogen. He was still upstairs. It could have been his staff, but at this time of night? Unlikely. The hairs on the back of my neck stood on end. I knew who'd entered the residence.

Tazia.

All of the windows on the giant screens closed and the screens went black. Bastion knew what to do to cover our tracks. I unplugged from the workstation and started running through my quick tour of the apartment. My best option was to run, to get out of here before Tazia spotted me. My next option was to hide.

Or was that my first option? If I hid, maybe I could eavesdrop, find out why she was here and what she was hiding. The chances were slim, of course. From what I could hear, she was alone. She might just plop down on a couch and watch a stream.

Nevertheless, I had to try. I was great at escaping, sure. I was almost as good at hiding. Came with the job. I silently slid out of the room and started working back down the hall, closer to the footsteps that I'd heard only moments before. I ducked into every open door, using my fiberoptic camera to check that the coast was clear before advancing. I had ducked into the bedroom closest to the living rooms when sure enough, a viewscreen turned on. Local Kotega news.

"Hiding place?" I texted Bastion.

An image immediately appeared on my display of a very large HVAC access hatch in the ceiling of the hallway I'd just left. Bastion said, "It's just outside Tazia's room. A press-and-release latch."

I moved as silently as I could in these limbs, the sound of fabric moving with me felt deafening, though I knew it was far quieter than the news on the viewscreen farther down the hall. I found the hatch, gently pressed it, and it swung down with a click. Climbing up into the vent without making a sound felt like one of the hardest things I'd ever done. The limbs didn't twist the way I wanted them to. Every little tap of toe against vent echoed. Finally, though, I pulled the hatch closed.

That's when the viewscreen fell silent.

"Sir?" Tazia said, suddenly much closer than the living area.

Was Orogen here? He wasn't supposed to be back for hours still. And since when did she call him sir?

"Tazia," an unfamiliar voice said, a voice resonating with the familiar hum of a holographic comm projector. "Report."

"Everything is proceeding on schedule," Tazia said with a reverence I'd never heard her use.

"And Orogen?"

"He's ready. He's been preparing for this his entire life."

"No. His faith. How is it?"

"His doubts are rarer and rarer," Tazia said.

I couldn't see, but the telltale blue-green light of a hologram passed below the hatch, sneaking in through panel gaps and painting the inside of the vent in that sickening light.

"You were right," she continued. "Being here with him has been helpful."

"Good."

Then I couldn't hear any more. I heard voices but couldn't make out what they were saying. She'd walked down the hallway too far. That light that spilled through the gaps around the hatch, though, and that gave me an idea. I pulled out my fiber-optic camera, one designed to change shape to fit in different spaces. I made it as thin as possible and was able to shimmy it through the gap, folding it close against the ceiling and pointing it down the hallway.

After several minutes, Tazia reappeared with the bust of a holographic figure projecting up from her hand. I couldn't make out the holographic face from here. Where she'd come from, I certainly didn't remember there being a door right there.

She was walking this way, back toward the living area. It was the first time I'd seen her since on Cirilla Island. She seemed diminished somehow. She was still tall and lithe, but her white hair was pulled up in a bun and looked dirty. She was only in her early 40s, but she'd always looked younger. She looked her age now. Her voice and the mystery voice returned. It took a while before I could make out the words, though.

"How is my family?" Tazia asked in a whisper.

"They're fine."

"My disappearance, has it…?" Tazia wasn't able to finish the sentence.

"It's raised eyebrows, of course. I won't lie to you. I've made sure they're protected. My personal secretary visits them each week to check in. I have a security detail on them as well. They've been able to keep the press hounds at bay for the most part."

"Thank you, sir."

"It's the least I could do," the mystery voice said. There was something slightly familiar about the voice, now that I was hearing it more. I couldn't see the face, though, facing toward Tazia. "What you're doing is important, the most important work of either of our lives. You're saving the planet, Tazia."

"I know, sir," Tazia said. "That doesn't make it easy."

"No," the unfamiliar voice took on a tenderness. "The greatest causes are usually the hardest."

Saving the planet? Greatest causes? None of this made any sense. This woman had tried to kill me multiple times. She'd shown no remorse in any of her actions, no sense of righteousness, only single-minded resolve. But then again, when people thought they were doing the right thing, it wasn't hard to be single-minded.

"Is there anything else, Tazia?"

"No, sir. Thank you."

The unfamiliar voice sighed. If Tazia would only walk a little closer, right under me so that I could see properly.

"I don't know if Shainette and Aphnette are real," the hologram said, "but you are serving them nonetheless. You are serving the people of Toinette and all of Little Sekhmet Settlement. Everyone will know who their savior is, Tazia. I swear it."

"I don't need the recognition, sir," Tazia said. "Only for it to work."

"I understand. If there's nothing else…"

No. Not yet. I needed to see the face.

"Nothing else, sir. Thank you again."

"Of course."

Then it happened. Tazia took a few more steps, passing directly under the hatch, directly under my camera. Then I could see the face clearly. I'd seen it on news streams. CEOs were often on news streams, after all. It was Pablo Toinette, one of the two CEOs and so-called prophets of Toinette Holdings.

Which meant he and Tazia were keeping this from the other Toinette CEO.

Which meant that Tazia's orders weren't going through the standard Toinette Intel chain of command, but directly from Pablo. That was the only reason she would be talking directly to Pablo and not her VP. But why?

"Tazia out," she said, and the hologram disappeared a moment later. She sighed heavily and walked down the hall, back toward Orogen's room. I heard a click and then a swishing, sliding sound from down the hall. I hadn't heard that before.

"What do you make of that?" I texted Bastion.

"Toinette seems a house divided," he said.

"Right. But why? Why would one CEO keep this from the other? Why the end-around?"

"It could be a power play, trying to consolidate to one CEO. Or perhaps Pablo Toinette is trying to oust Zurian Toinette, the other CEO, in favor of someone else. Honestly, there are any number of political motivations for this. There's a long history of betrayals and power plays between the dual Toinette CEOs. It has never been a good system."

"But what about the whole planet-saving angle? Tazia obviously believes, which explains a lot of her behavior. Does Pablo?"

"I have no idea. I cannot even begin to compile a list of threats to Little Sekhmet Settlement that could possibly be thwarted by a religious corporate takeover."

"I need to let Hessod know," I texted. "Get the rest of the Intel division working on that end of things."

"Strategic thinking," Bastion said. "You still surprise me."

"Very funny. I'm just stuck here and not able to do it myself."

"Alas. What about—?"

He stopped talking when I heard the swishing, sliding sound again and a light thunk, then Tazia's footsteps coming back up the hallway.

"Don't worry," she said to someone on her comms. "I'll be right there. No, you won't see me, but I'll be nearby. Just keep your comms open and I'll help you through it."

I couldn't make out the rest of what she said as she kept walking out into the living area, and then the door leaving the quarters opened and closed. I slipped out of the vent, gently lowering myself so as not to make a sound. I was fairly certain Tazia was gone, but I could never be too careful when dealing with the Ghost of Toinette.

I wasn't leaving, though, not yet. I wanted to see where Tazia had gone and what she'd been doing. It was time to find that swishing, sliding sound.

Chapter Twenty-Six

4 Days to Ascension

I CREPT DOWN THE HALLWAY, still nervous that Tazia could come back in at any second. I reached the door to Orogen's room again, but this time, I looked right. There was no visible door, but this was where I'd seen Tazia go. Twice. A slide and thunk. A secret door, then. There were paintings and pictures, but nothing looked suspicious. I felt around for a switch but found nothing.

"How did she open it?" Bastion asked.

"Nothing obvious. Probably a scanner or remote code. I need a deeper look to know."

"Which vision setting?"

I was nervous after what had happened up in Tenisha's residence. What if all the Siwa residences were equipped with those alarms?

Apparently, Bastion wasn't as nervous as I was, or his impatience outweighed any nervousness. My vision suddenly switched to thermal. I gasped in surprise, waiting to go temporarily blind again and told to run. But that didn't happen. No alarms. The thermal vision was stable and normal. Water pipes and electrical conduits all terminated or moved around a space exactly the size of a door, cleverly hidden to look like part of the wall. On the other side of the wall next to the door was a box roughly the size of my palm. I recognized the size and wiring schematics.

"Remote access," I said. "Based on the Toinette Vanguard system. Modified, of course. Run the algorithm for Toinette Vanguard. Run three of them at the same time, actually."

My vision returned to normal, and I aimed my palm in the direction of the box on the other side of the wall. That was where my radio antenna was housed, and Bastion would be broadcasting to the box based on the algorithm I described. Three times, since I was sure the modifications were to add extra layers of radio signal. After about 30 seconds, a previously seamless section of the wall moved inward and then swept aside.

A light automatically flicked on as I entered. The small room was austere. One small desk. One uncomfortable chair. One workstation that looked like it was older than me. It looked familiar, and then I remembered when I'd first met Tazia, at least when I ran into her as Josephine. She was using equally antique equipment there.

"It would appear that Tazia has added her own touches to Orogen's residence," Bastion said.

I said, "My thoughts exactly. Doesn't look the same as the one in her office, though."

"No. It's even older. You should be able to bypass the security in a similar fashion, by holding down certain keys and rebooting. Just give me a moment to look it up."

I should have let Bastion do just that. But a memory was dominating my thought. It was a memory of the day I'd first met Tazia. It was the day I'd come across a similar workstation. The day I'd met Valdo. He hadn't been taking my calls or returning my texts.

A plan started to form. A seed of a plan. I could have let Bastion find the right sequence of keys, but I had a better idea, one that might break the silence with my brother.

"We're leaving," I said to Bastion and left the room, signaling the door to close before heading straight down the hallway and out of Orogen's residence.

"Leaving? Why? You just need to hold down space, ampersand, and the Kotega logo key while you reboot the machine. If there is anything incriminating on Orogen, it'll surely be on that workstation."

"I know," I said. Bastion wouldn't approve of my plan. Admittedly, I knew it was selfish, but I wanted Valdo in my life. I knew where this workstation was. And I knew in my bones that everything I needed was there. I still had time before the Ascension. Not much, but I knew I could get back here in a flash. But from what I knew of my half-brother, he would have a hard time ignoring me if convinced him that I needed him.

"What are you planning? What's going on?" Bastion sounded desperate.

"Don't worry," I said as I worked my way back to the maintenance corridor. "I have a plan. We'll be back. Tell Nox it's time to go."

"There are only four days to the Ascension. This is idiotic. Care to share this plan of yours?"

"You'll hate it, so not really. Where is Nox?"

Bastion cursed before he said, "He's already at the door."

I hurried back down the stairs and to the door I'd entered earlier. I gave the same sequence of knocks I'd used earlier, and it opened a moment later. There was Nox, my suddenly reliable apprentice.

"Any luck?" Nox asked once the door closed behind me.

"Hardly," Bastion said in my ear.

"Oh," I said to both of them, "I think this was a very productive trip."

#   #   #

I know you're angry, I typed once I was back in my room. Or rather, Xyla's room. *But this goes beyond any of that. I need your help. I've found Tazia. There's still a chance to stop her, to fix this. I know you don't trust me, that I made a mistake with Vert. I'd love to earn your trust, but I'll take your help in stopping Tazia in the meantime. I can't talk directly, but please reply to this account.*

"Send that to Valdo," I said. I couldn't send the message without risking Kotega security intercepting it, but Bastion could with his network tunnel, the same way I'd been messaging Quynn.

"No," Bastion said. "This is a terrible idea."

"You never like it when I involve Valdo," I said.

"No, I don't. He's an innocent child."

"He's 17."

"That's still a child. And you don't even need him. I already told you how to get past the security on that old workstation."

"What was that old Earth saying you told me once? The one about birds and stones?"

"Useful for accomplishing two tasks and minimizing effort or risk. This is just putting Valdo in danger and to accomplish what I could do."

"I'm not going to take him in there with me," I said. "He'll tell me what I need to do—"

"I already told you—"

"And I'll get to connect with my brother in the process."

"Connecting with your half-brother who doesn't even know he's related to you? I don't see why that should make a difference. You were perfectly happy before you knew about him. Better to let him live his life and forget about you. Seems that's what he wants, anyway."

That stung. For all of Bastion's intelligence and research capabilities, basic relationships and emotions still seemed to escape him with alarming regularity. It baffled me. "Quynn would understand. So would Hessod. It's just you that doesn't get it."

"I doubt Quynn would agree with this plan of yours."

I was tired and bored of his repeated arguments, so I blurted out, "Then why don't you ask them about it?"

"Fine."

I sat there in my room in silence.

After nearly a minute, Bastion said, "They aren't pleased, either."

"But?" I knew my partner.

Bastion didn't say anything.

"What did Quynn say?"

"They said that was really stupid, but that they understand, too. They wish you'd asked before leaving Orogen's, but now it's too late. And to keep Valdo safe. Don't lose sight of your objectives."

I leaned back on my bed. I couldn't help the smug smile growing on my face. "Send the message to Valdo."

"Fine," Bastion said with a growl.

Just as I was starting to drift to sleep, Bastion said, "Valdo responded."

"And?"

"He's asking why he should believe you and why this time is different."

A great question. When he'd been with me on Cirilla Island, going after Tazia the first time, she'd been accompanied by a retired professional fighter named Vert. He'd nearly killed me more than once. In response, I called an assassin. She also wanted to kill me out of professional revenge, but I created an opportunity that was better for her career: taking down Vert on a live stream across the planet.

She did. She killed Vert right in front of me and with millions watching. But that meant Vert's blood was on my hands. And Valdo walked away from me. I couldn't blame him.

I brought up my keyboard again. I could have just spoken a response, and Bastion would pass it on, but I wanted to word things just right. *I made a mistake with Vert. I shouldn't have brought in Roxy. I knew, even if I pretended I didn't, that one of them would wind up dead. And that's on me. I don't want to be someone who makes decisions that get people killed. Quynn is helping me with that. I'd like your help, too. I want to stop Tazia without anyone dying.*

The paragraph took a few stops and starts, deletions and rewordings, but I was eventually happy enough that I asked Bastion to send it. A few minutes later, Valdo replied again.

"Just two words," Bastion said, keeping me in nervous anticipation. "Where and when?"

Chapter Twenty-Seven

3 Days to Ascension

ARRANGING A TIME AND PLACE to meet Valdo took some work. Having to go through Bastion didn't make things any faster. Eventually, we settled on a food stall in the Kotega DB, or Down Below. Every corporate borough had a DB, the lowest floors of the buildings before The Mist. We would meet for lunch on my day off, which was tomorrow. That gave me today to plan an escape route.

"What is this thing on the schedule tonight?" I asked as Zhao was making up my hair. The day looked fairly light for Gloria and me, only a few meetings before an appointment called Roundtable Reception with no other information. I was only given full visibility to the schedule each morning, so even though I'd seen it on Gloria's calendar for weeks, I couldn't ask until now. I'd also been so consumed with meeting Valdo tomorrow that I hadn't given much thought to today.

"The other CEOs are coming in for drinks," Zhao said. "It's tradition. They are here to meet the incoming Kotega CEO."

I blew out a breath. "Then Dr. Corto will be here."

"Yes," Zhao said with even more terseness than usual.

Was now a good time to ask about the data drive? Xey'd taken Gowran's but hadn't given me one yet. I wanted to comfort xem, but I didn't know how. Xyr emotional shell was so thick and impenetrable.

My mind was spinning, too. I was putting plans in motion against Dr. Corto, after all, plans to nullify what she was trying to do here in Kotega. And then there was Pablo Toinette, the co-CEO of Toinette Holdings who was directing Tazia. He was going to be here, too. I would bet good credits that he would be trying to meet with Tazia. I had already recorded their holographic conversation, but if I could arrange for Gloria or Tenisha to stumble upon a covert meeting between a CEO and Orogen's spiritual advisor, that would about wrap up this job.

And shining in my mind more than any of that, the CEOs of all five companies were going to be in one room. There was a connection between them, I had no doubt. Theo's dying words, the data streaming out of the Offworld Relay, all of it pointed to something bigger, something I didn't understand. If there was any point when the CEOs went into a private meeting, I would need to get in there, to get digital eyes or ears or both.

I controlled my face and breathing and asked Zhao, "What is Mistress's role in this reception?"

"The CEOs bring their families. It's an informal gathering. Drinks, shaking hands. You'll be standing off to the side with the other Daelis."

"Seems the symbolism would be lost with people from other companies."

"It is," Zhao said while yanking particularly hard on my hair. "You're a line of security defense. Should an emergency arise, you'll be in contact with Thrace and will help get Gloria to safety."

"Surprised that Thrace isn't the one there."

"The collected CEOs don't like security in the room. Daelis are seen as symbolic, so they allow it. I'm not sure they realize that's why you're in the room."

"And where will you be, Seon Zhao?"

Zhao's hands stopped. Xey looked at me in the mirror. "Me?"

"Dr. Corto will be here, the woman causing you so much pain."

"You think I'm foolish enough to go up there? To make a scene? To think I could make any difference?"

"I think that when we're hurt or threatened, any of us, we don't always do things that are rational." Like walking away from the evidence I'd been looking for so that I could connect with my own brother. Yeah.

"I would never…" Zhao took a deep breath before continuing. "I would never risk dishonoring Mistress so."

"No matter what?"

Zhao looked me dead in the eyes. I didn't see malice there. No frustration, either. Just pure resolve. "Never. I would never."

"All right," I said. Only I was that level of foolish.

When Zhao was done, xey packed up the cosmetics and swept out of the room, leaving me with a few minutes alone before I had to join Gloria. Only then did I notice Zhao had left something behind. Sitting on the corner of my desk was a data drive. All right, then.

#   #   #

I'd been standing in the elevator for several minutes before it opened and Gloria stepped in, draped in a blood-red gown, her hair was a fountain of black woven with roses. I looked the same, of course, but on her, it was stunning. She smiled as she saw me, the sparkle back. No, not just back. Stronger than ever.

"Xyla," she said, tilting her head toward me as she entered.

"Mistress," I said. I pressed the button for Tenisha's lowest floor and then felt Gloria stand right next to me, arms touching. That wasn't an accident.

"When can we go flying again?" she asked as the elevator ascended.

"I think you'll need formal lessons before we try that again," I said, trying to keep my voice neutral.

"I think we can find time for that," she whispered back, her mouth suddenly too close to my ear. It took considerable effort not to flinch, though I couldn't keep blood from rushing to my cheeks.

I was saved by the elevator slowing. Gloria stepped away and cleared her throat, obviously shifting into professional mode right before the elevator doors opened and she strode forward toward the grand double doors that led to Tenisha's grand ballroom.

A person in a tuxedo held the door open for Gloria, and I followed her into the familiar room, though it looked completely unfamiliar now. It was the same ballroom I'd broken into. Gone was the pile of furniture in the corner draped with cloth. Instead, the room was brightly lit and populated with cocktail tables. Twinkling music was pumping in gently through unseen speakers. Tenisha was already there, directing a few staff members working on finishing touches.

"Daughter," Tenisha said when she spotted Gloria. The Kotega Systems CEO was dressed in a mauve jacket and matching, floor-length skirt. Her hair was pulled up in a more feminine look than I'd ever seen her in. "Right on time. Where is your brother?"

Gloria bowed slightly, stiff in the corseted crimson dress. "On his way, I'm sure."

"Good. Your Daeli can stand over there," Tenisha said, waving a hand toward the corner of the room near the door we'd just entered.

Gloria looked at me and nodded. I bowed, hating the corset in my matching dress, and went off to my corner. Tenisha's Daeli, Nadia, was already standing there. She nodded to me slightly as I walked over and joined her.

"Have you been prepped on what to do?" Nadia asked in a whisper.

"Yes," I said. At least I knew that Nadia was also going through this for the first time, just like me. Nadia had been with Tenisha for four years. She hadn't been present for the reception before Tenisha's own Ascension.

We said nothing else to each other, which was fine with me. Orogen and his Daeli, Tomas, entered a few minutes later. I hadn't met Tomas yet, but he was all smiles when he walked over to join Nadia and me against the wall.

"Always fun when the CEO is here, isn't it?" he said.

I smirked. Nadia shot Tomas a look and practically growled.

"Sorry," he said.

There was a brief whirlwind of activity, Tenisha making sure that every detail was in place before the first of the CEOs and their families arrived. Rae Praxis Huginn arrived first, resplendent in a silver suit trimmed with glowing magenta. His husband was on his arm, dressed in a contrasting magenta suit with silver lapels. I couldn't remember the husband's name nor the names or genders of the two adult children who followed. All were brightly dressed and boisterous in the Huginn Industries tradition.

Dr. Ariela Corto came next. She wore an evening gown of muted blue, her long, dark hair trailing straight down her back. As usual, she was alone. She'd never married. Never had a romantic entanglement hit the streams. As far as anyone knew, she didn't even have any close friends. She was all business all the time. She entered the room, accepted a drink, and stood a few meters from the Huginn contingent who were glad-handing the Siwas. She swept her gaze around the room, taking it in, her eyes barely lingering on me, but her face gave nothing away.

Zurian Toinette came next with her husband and their small gaggle of children. The Nexus CEO followed soon after, and then Pablo Toinette, Tazia's boss. He was extraordinarily tall, more than two meters, with very dark and heavily scarred skin. There were a lot of rumors about his scars, but he'd famously never clarified anything about their origins. His partner, a rotund and pale person named Claudio, was on Pablo's arm.

"There must be an army of security around this building right now," Tomas whispered.

He wasn't wrong. Thrace had told me that the entire Siwa security force was on hand guarding every entrance. Plus, every other company was bringing their own security force. There was no trust nor cooperation between the different companies' security divisions, after all. Each was here to protect their own people. The gentle music was barely covering the nonstop buzz of drones outside.

The event was exactly as Zhao had described it. The CEOs were mingling, making small talk. Each was spending some time with the Siwas, who were grouped together. There was no jockeying for position or power, however. These were all CEOs. They didn't need Orogen's ear like the Kotega families that I'd been around for weeks. They were here to meet Orogen, to congratulate him on his upcoming Ascension, and to have a few drinks.

There were no private meetings, however. In fact, the CEOs clearly avoided being one-on-one with each other. Always, there was a spouse or adult child in the conversation circle if two CEOs were together.

Several of the adult children of the CEOs were out on the balcony, nursing drinks and struggling through small talk. The teenagers were scattered around the room, each one holding up a wall and engrossed in something on their displays. The younger children were led away a while ago to a playroom. And here stood we three Daelis, watching everything play out, hearing occasional check-ins and all-clears over our comms from the security teams outside.

Pablo hadn't left the room or his partner's side. Dr. Corto hadn't given me a single glance after her initial visual sweep of the room. It was, frankly, boring.

Inevitably, whenever I think a situation is boring, it decides to become too engaging all at once. I'd been keeping an eye on Dr. Corto all night, watching for an opportunity to get her alone. She leaned in toward a server, said something, and the server pointed down a hallway out of the ballroom. Toward the bathrooms, I knew, since I'd snuck around here a while back.

At that same time, however, I saw that Pablo Toinette was excusing himself. Not leaving since his partner was staying behind, but excusing himself nonetheless. I couldn't follow them both. Couldn't eavesdrop on whatever Pablo was doing and confront Dr. Corto at the same time.

Silent circuits. I let them both go, leaving the room through different doors. I knew who I was following anyway. I didn't like having to choose, but the choice was easy. I had no idea if Pablo was going to meet Tazia or not. Knowing Tazia, she was too careful to meet him anyway. I knew that I needed to confront Dr. Corto, though. For my sake, for Gowran's sake, and for Zhao's sake. Tazia was here. Valdo was going to get me into her antique workstation. I was closing in. I didn't want to risk not being able to set things straight with Dr. Corto, though.

After a full minute went by, I looked at my fellow Daelis and said, "If you will excuse me." They both nodded slightly as I stepped out of position and followed Dr. Corto deeper into Tenisha's residence.

I moved through the hallways quickly, nodding briefly at a few members of the staff who were in the kitchen or serving. I turned toward the bathrooms. There were the larger, multi-stall bathrooms, but I saw that one of the private bathrooms was locked. OCCUPIED was lit in red. I looked to make sure there was no one around before quickly deploying my fiber-optic camera to the floor and checking under the door. Sure enough, there was Dr. Corto, sitting on the toilet with her skirt hiked up around her waist.

I retracted the camera, put on my sternest face, and bypassed the lock. I swept in and closed the door behind me in one movement.

"Who…" Dr. Corto sputtered. "What? Occupied! Stop!" Then her brain caught up with what she was seeing. Me. Standing in the small bathroom less than a meter from her. "Are you out of your mind?"

"We're done," I said.

Dr. Corto stood from the toilet, yanking up her underwear and letting her skirts drop.

"The audacity!" she was spitting and thoroughly off-kilter.

"You're done with Gowran and Zhao. You should lose my comms channel, too."

"You're out of your depth," she whispered. "You're risking your cover for some ego trip. And you don't tell me what to do. That's not how this relationship—"

"I'm not done," I said just a touch louder than I should have spoken. If someone was out in the hall, they definitely would have heard me.

The shock was clear on Dr. Corto's face. Her usual placid ambivalence was gone, shaken. But then it came rolling back along with a smile. "Decided you wanted to play the game at my level? Go on, then. What's your move?"

"You're going to leave Gowran be. He has a life. A family. He wants nothing to do with you. He certainly doesn't want to expose you."

"You talked to him. I told you—"

"Still not done," I said, forcibly interrupting her. "I know about the pregnancy. I saw the pictures."

Her face darkened instantly.

I softened my voice. "I have no judgment for that. I'm sorry you had to make that decision. But killing Gowran isn't the path here."

"He still has pictures?" she said through gritted teeth.

"Because he mourns who that child could have been. Even though he agreed with the decision, he remembers. He even remembers you fondly."

For the first time since I'd known Dr. Ariela Corto, I saw something pass over her face that looked almost like sadness. Like regret. It was gone in an instant. "I can't risk it, though. Not in my position."

I set my face and voice again. "I was afraid you would say that. But you're going to leave him be. He and his family. They're going to stay where they are and never hear from you or anyone you know. Same with Zhao."

"And why is that?"

"Zhao and Gowran both have data drives. They also have a weekly call set up. If Zhao doesn't hear from Gowran, she's going to give that data drive to Gloria, and I'm sure Gloria will be motivated to share how you were once pregnant with someone from Kotega."

"You wouldn't…" she whispered.

"And if Gowran doesn't hear from Zhao, he'll go public with the pregnancy himself. He works for a news stream after all. He doesn't want to. I had to convince him, largely by pointing out how you use blackmail to push people around like you own them."

Her face darkened more than I'd ever seen.

"And if you get the wild idea to do something to both of them, I'm on that weekly call, too. I have copies of the pictures of the pregnancy, too. And proof that you've been blackmailing the head of Gloria Siwa Kotega's house. And, of course, your involvement in creating Bastion.

"You think I'll let you—?"

"I've made this easy for you, Ariela," I spat, putting my face only centimeters from hers. "You leave them both alone, and you'll never have to worry about a thing."

"And what's to keep you, any of you, from going public with all of this?"

"We're not you. Zhao doesn't want the dishonor. You already know that if you go down, I go down with you. And Gowran?" I shook my head and stepped back. "He doesn't keep those pictures to hurt you. He keeps those pictures because of love. I wish you understood that."

She worked her jaw, staring daggers into me. After several long moments, she whispered, "Are you done?"

"You tell me," I said.

A shudder ran through Dr. Corto like she was compelling her rage to subside. She sneered and said, "Fine. Get the hell out of this bathroom."

I did, quickly and without turning my back on the CEO. The moment I was out and closed the door, she locked it behind me. I blew out a shaky breath, grateful that my legs were cybernetic. If they'd been biological, I'm pretty sure my knees would have given out.

"You did it," Bastion said.

I forced myself to put one foot in front of the next, going back out to the ballroom. I couldn't keep the smile from my face, though.

CHAPTER TWENTY-EIGHT

2 Days to the Ascension

WHATEVER I'D EXPECTED OF THE DB, the reality was something else entirely. I'd only heard stories of the lower levels of the corporations. Other than my trips down to The Mist and a recent excursion down a garbage chute, I'd never been below the 50th floor of any building. I knew that a lot of blue-collar laborers lived there. Sanitation workers, cleaners, people who earned their living by the sweat of their brow and woke each morning with aches and pains. I also knew it was a place that some people from higher floors visited for thrills, a form of poverty tourism. Particularly teenagers would dress like they imagined Mistwalkers dressed and go to the DB, thinking they were walking on the darker, more dangerous side of life.

The wide-open floor was certainly more like The Mist than anything else I'd seen in the corporate towers. No offices or apartments here. Directly to my right was a stall selling Kotega clothes at least a decade out of fashion, but each had been elaborately altered to make them fresh and exciting. Next to that was a noodle shop with the most amazing smell wafting from it. A deli sat next to that, and a fancy hat shop next to that. A curry stall was on my left. Its delightful smells were doing battle with the noodle shop. I started moving through the space, and it seemed like an endless labyrinth of life and commerce. People were crowded in, haggling and buying and selling at a frenzied pace. That was a little like The Mist.

But this wasn't The Mist. Pairs of Kotega security guards were wandering the aisles between stalls. I clocked numerous security cameras near the exits. Maybe the corporate presence was subdued, but it was here. People weren't wearing the mismatched outfits I saw everywhere in The Mist. No homebrew neural operating systems or hand-made mods were on display for sale. Everyone here worked for Kotega. They were Kotega citizens with Kotega jobs and Kotega healthcare. They bowed to each other slightly as they navigated the lowest echelons of the Kotega honor system.

They were fooling themselves if they thought this was how Mistwalkers lived.

"Where am I going?" I said to Bastion, unconcerned about being overheard in the bustle of people talking and yelling.

"I don't have a specific map of this place," Bastion said. "Valdo said he would meet us at the dumpling stall near the southwest corner."

"You don't have a map?"

"My only map is of an empty floor. Exits. Stairwells. None of these stalls are permanent. I think they change regularly."

Like a grungy farmer's market. I'd just have to wander, then. I asked, "How does Valdo even know this place?"

"A question you'll have to ask him. I have no idea."

I wandered through the maze of stalls and people, regularly brushing shoulders and squeezing past people who were friendly but seemed accustomed to having no sense of personal boundaries. I ran into dead ends multiple times and then had a hard time finding my way out. After more than 20 minutes, I finally saw Valdo sitting on a stool, hunched over a large, steaming bowl.

He was about Nox's height but built like he'd been lifting weights since he'd hit puberty. Seeing him now, it was a wonder I hadn't suspected we were related sooner. The light brown skin tone, dark brown eye color, and pronounced cheekbones were the same as mine. He even had the same straight, black hair even if he kept it trimmed short.

I sat down next to him, and my mouth started to water. I asked, "What's good?"

Valdo gave me a look that said he wasn't in the mood for small talk. He chewed his noodles, swallowed, and said, "So you found Taz—?"

"Not here," I said, cutting him off. "Not that name."

Valdo looked around like he was looking for spies. But then he nodded and focused back on his food.

"What do you want?" a stocky cook with long, orange hair asked. They were wearing a white shirt and white apron, though white was generous. They'd obviously cooked a lot in that shirt and apron, and the stains told the tale.

I glanced at the menu and said, "Vegetarian bao."

"Six?" the cook asked, referring to ounces. "More?"

"Six," I said. "Spicy."

The cook raised one eyebrow but then nodded and turned away from me.

I let a few awkward seconds slide by before I asked Valdo, "How have you been?"

Valdo shrugged.

I wasn't going to get anywhere if I didn't just dive right in. "You're still angry with me."

Valdo didn't look at me, but he chewed his food extra slowly, swallowed, and said, "Angry isn't the right word."

"Then what is?"

Valdo turned his attention toward me and said, "Why do you care? Why can't you just go back to your crazy life and leave me be? You don't need me to do your hacking. I'm sure you have people that can do that."

He was definitely angry. Despite that, he was also here. This was the opening I needed to just tell Valdo that he was my brother, that we had the same father. But I didn't want to use that as a wedge to open the door to a relationship. I didn't want him to feel trapped, forced into my life. I wanted him to want me around, too.

"I don't want to be that person, the one you walked away from. I won't say that wasn't me. It was. I made decisions that I regret. I should have known better, should have thought it through."

"But you didn't."

I shook my head.

"Vert didn't need to die. You didn't need to call in some assassin."

Maybe Vert didn't need to die. In calling Roxy to fight Vert, I'd not only gotten rid of Vert but had balanced the scales with Roxy so that she was no longer looking to kill me. I'd given her enough of a reputation bump to walk away from me.

But a man was dead because I made that decision. That was on me. I said, "Maybe not. I can't change the past. I want to do better, though."

"So you don't plan to kill…her?"

"I hadn't planned for Vert to die. Or anyone else."

"That doesn't answer my question."

I sighed. "No. I don't plan on killing anyone."

"You want my help?"

I nodded.

"Then promise me that you'll do what you can to keep her alive. Punished, yes, but alive. The entire city should see what she did. Her entire network needs to be exposed."

"What will that do to Toinette? To Ibhalism?"

Valdo turned back to his bowl and moved some noodles around. "In the short term? I don't know. But I have to believe that the truth can only benefit everyone in the long run."

It was a view full of hope and naiveté, but I had to admire it. If this was my way into his friendship, so be it. "I promise."

He nodded and returned to his food right as my bao arrived. I paid and dug in. We ate in uncomfortable silence. Once we'd both finished, Valdo said, "Come on. Follow me."

"You know this place?"

"In case you hadn't noticed, Toinette isn't the best place to get good tech, especially when you're 17."

We got up, and I started following him as we weaved through stalls. I said, "So you come here?"

"Since I was 14. Since I was able to slip out without my dad noticing."

I tried to imagine that. My memories of our dad were hazy, but I remembered him being the type of parent who would keep a close eye on his child. Not close enough, apparently. He'd left Corto Corporation without a goodbye when I was 12. I hadn't seen him again until I spied him in Valdo's mom's hospital room.

We left that floor of the DB and walked into a narrow, dark stairwell. Valdo led me down six flights before he opened the door into an apartment block. He stopped in front of a door and knocked. After a few moments, a lanky, pale person opened the door. They smiled when they saw Valdo and opened the door wider.

"Hey, V," they said. "What's going on?"

"Hey, Foss. Just need a place to chat. Private."

"Sure, sure," Foss said and stepped aside so that we could enter. "You know the way."

Valdo nodded and led me to a back room that was filled to the brim with technology. Old server racks, nanobot vats, and everything in between were stacked floor to ceiling around the room.

"We can talk here?" I asked.

"I can't find anything on this Foss," Bastion said. "Perhaps it's short for—"

Valdo closed the door, and Bastion's voice promptly cut out.

"Oh," I said.

"Faraday Cage," Valdo said. "Lost your connection to Bastion and everything else?"

I nodded. Valdo had learned about Bastion when Solomon had, when I was laid up in a hospital bed on Cirilla Island after absorbing way more radiation than any human should endure.

"We can talk here."

"How is your mom, by the way?" I asked.

Valdo tried and failed to suppress his surprise. "That's not why you called me here."

"No," I said. She'd been sick when Valdo and I met. I had stolen meds for her. "But I want to know."

His face softened. "She's doing better. She's been home for a few weeks, though she's still building up her strength."

"I'm glad."

Valdo glanced all around the room, cleared his throat, and said, "So what about Tazia? You found her?"

I told him about my job, my embed with Kotega Systems as Gloria's Daeli, and what I'd found in Orogen's quarters. As I spoke, he pulled out a handheld workstation out of his satchel and started typing notes. His parents weren't allowing him to get mods while he was underage.

"Did you take a picture of the workstation?" he asked.

"No." I hadn't because Bastion had identified it by sight, but I couldn't ask him about it now. I couldn't remember the name of it, either.

Valdo's face screwed up. "You want me to go with you, don't you?"

"The thought had crossed my mind, but no. Too dangerous. Tazia is living there, after all. I won't put you into that sort of situation if I can avoid it."

Valdo smirked. "That doesn't quite sound like the Elise I met a few months ago."

"I'm trying."

Valdo nodded and looked back to his handheld. "Then what's your plan?"

"I'm going back into Orogen's. This time, I want you on a secure comms channel. I'll need it triple-encrypted, though, protected from any monitoring that Kotega might have on their networks, the Siwa networks in particular."

"You've been using their networks, then." He started digging in his satchel again.

I deployed my data cable and presented it to him. "Want me to plug in?"

He took the cable and plugged it into the tablet. "I need access to the network settings for the Siwa network. Everything you can give me. I should be able to build a tunnel."

Exactly what Bastion and Hessod had done. I nodded and opened the menus on my display to grant him the access he needed.

Valdo started poking around on his tablet. "This Siwa network security is good. Homebrew system, it looks like. They definitely put some money into it, but it could be better. So, what's your plan for Tazia?"

"I don't have a plan for her yet," I said. "But my plan for Orogen starts by getting into that antique computer he's hiding. If I can prove that he's going to try to convert all of Kotega to Ibhalism, that he's going to merge with Toinette, even just that he's under Toinette influence, I may be able to stop him from taking over as CEO. Hopefully Tazia goes down in the process."

"Why does it matter who the Kotega CEO is?"

I sat down. "Okay, imagine that Toinette and Kotega merge. They'd be twice as big and powerful as any other company in the city."

"Okay." He was typing, partially distracted.

"First off, what happens to Kotega culture?" I said. "Or Toinette for that matter? Do they merge into some new culture? Does Kotega just convert and get subsumed? Who knows."

"Oh," Valdo said, glancing up briefly.

"It gets worse. What's to stop the combined Toinette/Kotega from forcibly taking over one of the other companies? Odds are, Corto would wind up merging with Nexus or Huginn just to push against them, but then there would be a war over the remaining company. Eventually, you're looking at the collapse of Jayu City into a single corporate entity. The erasure of so many cultures. The sheer volume of redundancies would result in mass layoffs. What's left when the dust settles?"

"I…" I could see the wheels turning. It was a lot to consider. "Wow."

"I certainly want to expose Tazia, too," I said. "Hopefully there's information on that old machine for that, but I won't know until I crack it."

He looked up from the tablet. "But you found Tazia. Isn't that enough by itself to expose what she's doing? Orogen's involvement?"

"I wish. I know she has a Kotega cover name even if she's not using it. But she's also slippery. She's better at this than I am. I need something concrete to hand to Gloria and Tenisha. If I just tell them to find Tazia, I fear she'll slip away in an instant. I have to stay a step or five ahead of her."

"She scares you, doesn't she?" Valdo was looking at me now, not at his tablet. Those worry lines across his forehead. How had I not noticed the resemblance when we first met?

"She does," I said. She'd nearly killed me more than once. She'd paralyzed Solomon, who was the best Intel Operative I'd ever known. Corto, I was worried even now that I wasn't as far ahead of her as I hoped.

"Then we need to get into that computer," he said. "I've built a tunnel. Two, actually, for redundancy. It should allow us to communicate without being observed. They won't even see that you're using any network resources."

Okay, that was beyond what Hessod had built. And much faster. I would have to ask Bastion if Valdo's tunnel was that good. Valdo disconnected my data cable, which I reeled in, smiling at him.

"What?" he said, blushing.

"I've missed you."

He blushed even harder. "Come on, we've got a city to save."

Chapter Twenty-Nine

1 Day to Ascension

"ARE YOU PREPARED FOR TODAY?" Zhao asked. Xey'd strode into the cafeteria as I was eating a leisurely breakfast with Thrace and Ridley. With a small gesture, xey'd pulled me away from my meal and off to the side of the room.

The question put a lump in my throat. Today, I was going to sneak back into Orogen's residence. The day was packed with rehearsals for the Ascension ceremony. Both Gloria and Orogen would be occupied for the better part of the day. I had to get into Orogen's today, too, since the Ascension was tomorrow. I was ready. Nox was ready. Valdo was ready. I steadied my voice and said, "Of course. And I was able to deliver that message we discussed."

"Message?" Zhao asked.

"The data drives," I whispered, referring to my little bathroom chat with Dr. Corto. "The message was received and understood."

Zhao's eyes went wide, finally understanding. Then, xyr face softened more than I'd ever seen. It was only for a moment, though. "Good, but you don't look ready for the day. You're to be upstairs in 14 minutes."

"Upstairs?" I asked, leaping to my feet and bumping the table. Plates and flatware rattled. "The rehearsals are today, why would a Daeli—?"

"Representatives from the great families are part of the ceremonies, so they are already arriving for the rehearsals," Zhao said, looking far too pleased with catching me out. For the first time, though, there seemed to be some playfulness in xem. "Did you just think this was a private, family affair?"

I ground my teeth before I said, "My mistake, Seon Zhao. I'll get ready immediately." I was out of the cafeteria and heading back to my room before xey said anything else.

"We don't have time for this," I whispered to Bastion once I was in my room, tossing my clothes off and opening my messages until I found the one that I'd missed, the one detailing my outfit and involvement in the day. "Mother of Corto."

"We could send Nox into Orogen's," Bastion said.

"He doesn't have you or the tunnel to Valdo."

"I hate that I missed your conversation with Valdo. I don't have all the details. Faraday cages wouldn't be a problem if you installed me."

"We can have this conversation later," I said. I was tired of having it, anyway. "Can you cause a fire alarm or something?"

"Nothing that would give you the hour you need for the plan. Get down to Orogen's from the roof, get what you need from that antique workstation, and back to the roof."

"This rehearsal thing is on the roof? It's still raining!" I zipped up a slimming pair of black slacks and started pushing my feet into a pair of white heels.

"I'm sure that's been accounted for," Bastion said. "And yes, it's on the roof."

"Sparks! I didn't think I was involved in this." I put on a black blazer, completing the look. No shirt. No bra. It was like the outfit was trying to undermine my plans, too. At least there were no specific requirements for hair and makeup. I ran a brush through my hair before I started touching up yesterday's makeup, which had fared decently through a night's sleep.

"We might have to trigger a larger emergency," Bastion said. "A security lockdown or an actual fire in the building."

"That would draw a lot of attention, a lot of scrutiny, particularly around the Siwas and the Ascension. And it could send Orogen to his residence."

"Do you have any bright ideas instead of shooting mine down?" Bastion asked.

"Sorry. I'm just..." Then an idea came to me, one that I didn't much like, but at least gave me a glimmer of hope. "What if I tell Gloria why I'm here?"

I expected an immediate rebuff from Bastion, but instead, he said, "Do you think she trusts you enough? Do you trust her to not eject you from the borough immediately?"

"That's the risk. I think she trusts me, especially after I saved her. She certainly wants Orogen out of the CEO chair. We have the same goal."

"Though not for the same reasons."

"But I think she would understand my reasons."

"The reasons of a Corto Intel Operative?"

I sighed. "No, but the stability of the city. The preservation of the Kotega culture, her own culture. She'll be even more motivated if she knows what I know."

"But he is her brother," Bastion said.

"I know. But it's not like I want to hurt Orogen. I can make her see that." I saw Gloria's eyes, those deep, brown eyes. I'd seen them sad, and it broke my heart. Would they be sad if I told her why I was here, why I was working as her Daeli? Or would she be thrilled? My heart dropped and then raced in quick succession.

"Maybe we should ask for Quynn's input," Bastion said.

"Yes," I blurted out without thinking. Quynn. I needed to be more concerned with Quynn's reaction than Gloria's. "Ask them what they think, please."

I waited, pacing the tiny space of my room. I needed to be upstairs in three minutes. I missed Quynn's voice. Their mismatched eyes. I wondered what they looked like today, which features they'd chosen to feel like the person they were today. And yesterday. And the day before. I had to believe that if I could see and speak to Quynn, my heart would remember how to behave. That my skin would stop warming whenever I was too close to Gloria. That I would stop noticing how she looked at me sometimes.

"Quynn wants to know how you think Gloria will react," Bastion said. "They asked about your interactions thus far."

"And what did you tell them?" I asked.

"I recounted what I've seen between you and Gloria."

I felt heat rise in my face and was glad that Bastion couldn't see it. Hopefully, Bastion hadn't noticed the chemistry between Gloria and me, or how my heart rate fluttered around her. Hopefully, he'd edited out some parts that were sure to give the wrong impression. I swallowed hard and said, "I don't think Gloria will be happy that I've been lying to her, but she's pragmatic. When she sees that our goals align, I think she might help. I'm also running out of other options."

"I'll tell Quynn," Bastion said, and then he was quiet again.

I walked out of the room and moved toward the elevator. I wracked my brain for other options, for ways I could sneak out during the summit. Maybe I could mildly poison Gloria? Make her take to her bed for a while? But I wasn't any good with poisons. Knowing my luck, I'd send her into a coma or worse.

"Quynn said that old computer has to be hit today," Bastion said. "They said to remind you that the bigger the distraction, the easier a job is to pull off."

"Then I need to talk to Gloria," I whispered as I entered the elevator.

"There aren't many other options," Bastion said.

"No better ones that I can see. Where is Gloria?"

"Already on the roof."

Sparks.

"What should we tell Nox?" Bastion asked.

"Plan is in jeopardy," I said. "But proceed with prep and await my signal."

I'd been on the roof a few times since coming here, usually just to meet with Nox or to get away from literally everyone and take in the view. It was usually a large, open area. It was only unusual as roofs go because there was very nice, faux wood flooring all over and a pair of very nice bathrooms in one corner.

Today, though, there was an enormous tent covering most of the roof, keeping the unending rain from family and staff and guests. It billowed lightly in the wind. There was a dais set up near the center of the roof, complete with a podium. Numerous large, round tables with seating were arranged around the dais. The space was sparsely decorated, but that was being actively worked on. Next to the maintenance elevator, as expected, was a huge stack of wrapped gifts sent in from all over the borough to welcome the incoming CEO.

The roof was like a hive. Tenisha's head of house, whose name I didn't know, was directing a dozen temporary workers along with the regular staff. Zhao was there, too. Xey were equally busy, which at least meant that xey didn't have time to harass me. Though xey did still throw me a cautious look when xey caught sight of me. I spotted Gloria off to one side, standing near a small table and hurriedly eating a plate of fruit.

I weaved through the workers to Gloria, gave her an appropriately deep bow, and said, "Good morning, Mistress."

Gloria nodded to me with a mouthful of something orange.

"Could we have a word, Mistress?" I asked. "In private?"

Gloria raised one eyebrow, swallowed, and said, "Can it wait? The families will be coming up soon, and there is still a lot of work to do."

"I'm sorry, Mistress. This can't wait."

Gloria looked perturbed, but she nodded. "Follow me."

I did as she walked briskly toward Zhao, who was directing several workers. As soon as Zhao noticed Gloria, xey quickly bowed. "Mistress?"

"I have to run down to my residence briefly," Gloria said. "If anyone asks, make the necessary excuses. I'll be back very quickly."

"Of course, Mistress." Zhao bowed again. Once Gloria was past xem, though, xey gave me a suspicious look. I ignored it and followed Gloria to the elevators. We were silent on the elevator ride down, though Gloria kept throwing curious glances.

The moment we entered her residence, she spun on me and said, "Okay. What is it? Are you all right?"

"My apologies for the inconvenience, Mistress. I would not—"

Gloria waved a dismissive hand. "It's just us and we're on a clock. Let's put the formalities aside for a few minutes."

I relaxed my shoulders, rolled my neck, and took a breath. Admittedly the neck rolling was partly for show. It was also to force myself to relax before I started a conversation that might lead to my dismissal from the entire Kotega borough.

"What's going on?" Gloria asked with newfound concern.

"Careful," Bastion said in my ear.

"I want to help you with Orogen," I said to Gloria.

Her face didn't react. She said, "What does that mean?"

"He shouldn't become the next CEO. You should."

Gloria took an involuntary step back, the surprise plain on her face. "It's not your place to say such a thing. You know better than that, Xyla."

"He's converted to Ibhalism."

At that, her eyebrows shot up.

"The Toinette religion. He's working closely with Toinette. They even helped him win that tournament that put him over the top with your mother."

Gloria's face changed to something I didn't recognize. Anger? Quiet fury? Determination? Without a word, she walked away toward the door. Was this it? Was she having me sent away? She touched the keypad next to the door several times and then came right back.

"What did you—?"

"Locked the door. How do you know all of this? What proof do you have?"

I swallowed hard. Here's where it got tricky. "I'm working on the proof, the definitive proof. Everything I told you is fact, but I don't have hard enough evidence to take to your mother."

"How do you know any of this? How can I believe any of this is true?"

"An Intel Operative from Toinette was running a high-level operation for months. She was posing as an evangelist—"

"Ibhalism doesn't do evangelism."

"Josephine Toinette-Deus," I said, keeping on track. "You can look her up easily enough. Though that's not her real name or her real division. She was on Cirilla for the tournament. She was blackmailing other players, implanting disruptors in their neural interfaces, whatever it took to help Orogen win."

Now Gloria was pacing, her eyes scanning the floor in front of her as she processed all of this. "How can this be? How do you know any of this? How can some…" she waved a hand and obviously swallowed whatever derogatory noun was on the tip of her tongue. "How can someone with your background know any of this?"

"I was there, on Cirilla. I was trying to stop it, but I was too late."

Gloria stopped in her tracks, her eyes fixed on me. Anger and confusion were clear on her face. Her eyes looked suddenly wet. "Who are you?"

"I'm your Daeli," I said in the most even tone I could manage.

"And?"

"And more."

"Kotega Intel?"

I shook my head.

"Then who? Who do you work for?" Her face was reddening. Her breaths were sharpening as she stared at me.

"I work for you. I can't tell you more than that."

A tear slid down Gloria's cheek as her face reddened. "Can't tell me? Me? I thought you…we… You're just going to lie to me?"

Mother of Corto. I'd told Zhao that I didn't want to hurt Gloria, but I was. It was awful, and I was struggling to keep my own tears at bay watching her suffer.

"I'm telling you everything that I can," I said. "And I'm hoping that you've learned to trust me enough to know that what I'm saying is true, that I'm here to help you, to stop Orogen from becoming the next CEO."

"Why? Why should I believe you?" her voice was quiet, but as intense as a dying star.

"I have nothing to gain from lying to you. I saw her, the Toinette Intel Operative, in Orogen's residence. He's still consulting with her. He has an antique workstation in his quarters, too, one that I couldn't immediately get into, but now I can. That's exactly the type of security that Toinette uses to secure information. Information that, hopefully, you can take to your mother."

"You broke into my brother's residence?"

I nodded.

"How can…who are…why are you telling me all of this?" Gloria's voice was edged with panic, on the verge of screaming.

"I need your help. I can't get back into his quarters during the rehearsal, not with your schedule. I'll be up there all day, and I need to get this evidence before the Ascension. I need to get to that workstation today."

Gloria shook her head, and then violently wiped away her tears. She started pacing again. "So you're here, pretending to be my Daeli just to bring down my brother? You broke into his home? You say he's gone over to some ridiculous religion? Ibhalism. So then…if that's the case…"

I stayed silent and let her work through it. Gloria was many things, but stupid wasn't one of them. And working through it seemed to be helping her rein in her emotions.

"If he's under the influence of an evangelist, then…but no, she's not an evangelist. An Intel Operative, which means evangelism is the tool. Corporate espionage is the goal. She…they…" Gloria stopped in her tracks and turned to me. "Toinette wants to bring Kotega under their control."

I nodded.

"Our culture. Our family. The entire Kotega way of life…" Gloria walked over and stood behind her chair, staring out the window over the vastness of the Kotega borough. She looked and looked, and then she shook her head and whipped her eyes back to me. "I don't believe you. This is… this is too much."

"I know. It's a lot. It's—"

"It's too much!" Her yell made me jump. She quickly looked back out the windows, and her next words were a whisper. "Stop. Stop with this foolishness. Stop with your manipulations. It's too…too cruel. I don't have time to hire and train a new Daeli, but you will remain utterly silent around me for the duration of the rehearsal."

"Gloria, please…"

"You will address me as Mistress. Or better yet, not at all." Her voice remained quiet, but there was venom in her words now. "Once the Ascension is over, I'll have no more need of you. Let's go."

She spun, tears still streaking her face, and walked forcefully back to the elevator.

I followed silently. I had more to say, but she'd made it quite clear that my words weren't going to move her. My plan had failed. I'd failed. And I'd broken Gloria's heart. Hurt her so deeply, more deeply than I'd ever wanted to.

There was no undoing this, no healing the wound I'd caused, but I refused to fail, to let Tazia win. With or without Gloria's help, I was going to stop Orogen from becoming CEO. My cover was as good as blown now, anyway. Gloria had gone from…well, however she'd felt, to hating me. So what more did I have to lose?

Chapter Thirty

1 Day to Ascension

I COULDN'T FOCUS ON ANYTHING happening for the next few hours. Gloria was being told where she needed to be, where to stand, and what to do. I followed around as the silent and obedient Daeli, fighting to hide my panic. Outside of the Siwa family and staff, there were only about a dozen other people, all representatives of the highest-ranking families in Kotega.

But all I could think about was what else I could do to get into Orogen's today. Bastion was doing research, giving suggestions, but even he was coming up with improbable or impossible ideas. I couldn't speak to him, so he was just talking to himself while I listened. I was barely containing my panic.

Gloria didn't even look at me. Whatever trust or friendship I'd engendered had evaporated downstairs. She was colder to me now than on my very first day. She didn't want me here, and I knew it. That should have been fine. She was just part of a job, right? But no, my heart was struggling with that, with her hating me. Stupid heart.

As midday approached, Tenisha spoke up, gathering all attention on herself. "Thank you all for attending today. We're going to break for lunch.

I believe we're making good progress, though we are a little behind. I'll talk with my head of house during lunch to see how we can make up time after lunch." She gestured across the roof to a series of tables that were laid out with steaming trays of food. "We'll resume in 45 minutes. Thank you all, again."

I wasn't hungry. Happens when your stomach stays in knots for several hours. But I would follow behind Gloria like a good little Daeli. That was my plan, at least, until she spun and looked directly at me. "Restroom. Now."

Oh, sparks. That didn't sound good. I followed behind her to the restrooms on the other side of the roof from the food. We entered and she made a quick check of the stalls before turning on me.

"Mistress?" I asked cautiously.

"I'm still angry," Gloria said.

I nodded and said nothing. Was she about to fire me? Call security on me?

"What's your plan?"

"Mistress?" Plan? Plan? My mind was so taken aback by the word that it didn't even make sense.

"For getting back into Orogen's? What's your plan?"

Was this a trap? I said, "I don't understand."

Gloria practically rolled her eyes before she said, "Look, I'm angry. I don't like that you lied to me, that you're probably still lying to me. I don't know who you are and that…that is such a betrayal. More than you probably realize. But I don't think you're lying about what you said about Orogen. About Toinette. I've been going through rehearsal all morning thinking about what you said. Too much of it makes sense, the way that Orogen has been acting for the last few months. The last couple of years, really. We knew about Josephine. We thought it was just a wayward romance, nothing more. I hate that what you said makes sense."

"I'm sorry, Mistress," I said.

"You need my help, don't you?"

I nodded. Was she on my side now? About to drop the other shoe and have me taken away? I though the rejection had been bad, but this confusion felt even worse.

She paced back and forth as she spoke, looking everywhere except at me. She continued. "Everywhere I go, eyes are on me. People are watching me. And if they're watching me, then you need to be there. Unless I'm in my residence, of course, and that's what you need, isn't it? You need me to be home for just a little while so that they aren't watching you, too?"

Mother of Corto. She was coming around. I felt like I could breathe again. I nodded and said, "Yes, Mistress. At least an hour."

"Stop with the mistress stuff. It doesn't sound right coming out of your mouth anymore."

I didn't know how to take that. It sounded like some strange hybrid between insult and affection.

Finally, Gloria stopped pacing and looked directly at me. "You can do it? You can get into his apartment?"

"I have already. I can again."

"Then what's your plan?"

"Do you really want to know?"

"If I can help, then I want to know."

I think my jaw hit the floor before I said, "Help? You're going to help?"

An emotion I didn't recognize flashed across Gloria's eyes before she looked away and said, "Honor help me, but I think you can help me, help Kotega. And if what you're saying about Orogen and Ibhalism is even a little bit true, I have to help you. I have to stop it. So yes, Xyla or whatever your name is, I'm helping. What do you need?"

I swallowed hard. I wished I had Quynn in my ear to guide me. Or Hessod and his seemingly endless knowledge. All I had in my ear was Bastion, who said, "Now or never, I think."

"Gloria," I said, the name beautiful in my mouth. She turned to face me again, that sparkle back in her eyes, though it was diminished. "I will need you to fake an illness or something, anything to get out of the spotlight for a while. But first, I need information about this rehearsal, about this building. I have a plan."

After I laid out the plan for her, we left the bathroom and did our very best to look like I'd been pulled aside for a lecture. Gloria held her head high as she joined the line to fill a plate with food. I stood behind her and away from the buffet table, giving my best chastised face. Zhao looked confused when xey saw it.

"Twenty minutes," Bastion said in my ear once Gloria finished eating. "I've messaged Nox that we're on. He's in position."

It felt surreal. An hour ago, I'd been silently spinning out, seeing no way through, no way to keep Orogen from becoming the next CEO of Kotega Systems. Now, I was 20 minutes away from my endgame. Once I had the information on Tazia's workstation, I was 98% sure I would have what I needed to stop her. And Gloria was on my side, ready to hand that information to her mother. A day to spare, too.

Only twenty minutes were remaining before Gloria was going to fake a stomach issue. Twenty minutes until I would finally be able to do what I do best.

"My dear guests," Tenisha's voice said over a loudspeaker, quieting the conversations and turning all heads to her on a dais in the middle of the roof. "I want to thank you all again for coming, and before we finish our rehearsal, I'd like to thank you all for the generous gifts that you brought to me and my family."

Tenisha pointed one arm to her right, and there were three piles of wrapped gifts arranged in one corner. The wrapped boxes ranged in size from dainty and palm-sized to enormous, big enough to hold a car. Or me. And I knew that behind the largest pile, the pile intended for Orogen, was the entrance to the maintenance elevator.

"Yes," Gloria said to a couple near her. "Thank you so..." Her eyes widened, and she gently placed a hand on her stomach. After her face fluttered, she resumed her smile. "I'm sorry. I'm fine. Thank you, yes, thank you."

The couple looked adequately concerned as Gloria started to show signs of some intestinal distress, right on cue.

"Now," Tenisha continued from the dais. "The man you've all been waiting for. My son and your next Chief Executive Officer would like to say a few words."

The gathered families applauded as loudly and enthusiastically as decorum would allow, which wasn't very. Then Orogen stepped up to the dais, clad in a trim black suit. His Daeli was, of course, a step behind and to the right of him.

"Honored guests," he began. "I am overwhelmed by your support, your generosity, and each of your shining faces here today and especially tomorrow. Tomorrow is a day I've been waiting for my entire life, and every one of you is so, so dear to me and my family."

"Showtime," Bastion said.

I glanced at the pile of gifts and sure enough, several people dressed in black suits were taking them away. Nox was among them. To his credit, he didn't so much as glance at me. He really was coming along as an Intel Operative. I moved my gaze then to Gloria, who sure enough, vomited right on the shoes of Darwin Kotega-Nano. She hated him, anyway.

Also, how did she vomit on cue? I would have to ask about that one later.

Darwin and a few other nearby people jumped back and looked startled and concerned. I did what every good Daeli was trained to do, which was to step up and put one of Gloria's arms over my shoulder, and then whisked her away discreetly. Orogen kept talking, likely not even aware of what was happening. Zhao was by my side in an instant.

"Mistress?" xey asked.

"I'm fine," Gloria said. "I just need to take something and lie down for a bit."

"I should take you to—"

Gloria waved a hand at xem. "I'm fine, Zhao. Xyla can see me to my room. Stay here. You have more to do here, surely. I'll be back soon, I'm certain."

Zhao looked uncomfortable but after a few moments, bowed and said, "Yes, Mistress."

Gloria and I entered the building, her arm still thrown over my shoulders. She still looked every bit the woman in distress. I guided her to the elevators and pressed the button. After a handful of seconds, one of them dinged and the doors opened. We stepped inside without a word, and then I pressed my palm to a panel near the screen. In an instant, the buttons for Gloria's floors changed from orange to blue, and I pressed the floor for her suite.

"Hold on," Gloria said, clenching her stomach.

Was she going to vomit again? Had she taken something? Was she actually sick?

"Elevator," she barked through gritted teeth. "Privacy and hold."

The doors to the elevator promptly closed, the lights dimmed, and a pair of descending tones sounded. Gloria suddenly stood up straight, the distress on her face disappeared, and she said, "Go."

Yeah. I needed to know that trick. But not now. I put one foot on the overly decorated railing on the wall and pushed up, finding the maintenance hatch for the elevator and opening it. I climbed up and out, mostly succeeding in keeping my tailored outfit from getting too grimy. I looked back down into the elevator and said, "See you soon."

Gloria nodded. I shut the hatch and leaped over the side of the elevator, landing on a support girder, and then jumped down backward to land on another. Two very tall floors down, I shimmied over to the elevator doors and pried them open. These limbs were weaker than my work limbs, but still up to the task of opening these doors. I peeked in, seeing no one in the hall, and stepped through.

As I'd planned, I was in a hallway virtually identical to the maintenance hallway Nox had led me through before. Beige walls and floor. White ceiling. Scuff marks everywhere.

"Guidance?" I said.

"On it," Bastion said as a yellow line appeared in AR on the floor leading to my right.

I followed the line carefully, checking every corner before I rounded it. It didn't take long before I saw another elevator. This one was by itself and much larger than the ones I'd left Gloria in. The maintenance elevators. I moved to the side, out of sight of anyone who might be in that elevator when it opened, and I waited.

"How are you feeling?" Bastion asked.

"Feeling? You worried about me?"

"Yes. You're distracted by Gloria."

A lump seized my throat. I croaked out, "Distracted?"

"I see and hear everything that you do. I do understand feelings. You are my friend, and I know that you're conflicted."

"No," I said. "Not conflicted. My feelings are being stupid, but it's almost over. We'll be back in Corto soon, back with Quynn. I'm good."

"You're sure?" Bastion said.

The more I kept thinking it and saying it, the more true it would be, right? "I'm sure."

After a few moments, Bastion asked, "Do you think this plan will work?"

"Never ask me that."

"Why?"

"I wouldn't execute a plan I didn't think could work," I said. "But also, you're going to jinx it if you ask questions like that."

"I didn't realize you were superstitious."

The elevator dinged twice. Before the doors could open, I whispered, "Too much luck involved in my job to not be."

The doors opened, a yellowish light spilling out and onto the floor in an elongated rectangle. I held my breath, but then Nox stuck his head out and whispered, "Star Girl?"

That nickname again. But it was better than him saying my real name aloud. I stepped forward, and he smiled when he saw me, beckoning me in with a wave. He was alone in the elevator except for a box the size of a refrigerator that was wrapped in shimmering silver paper.

"What is it?" I asked, nodding to the box.

Nox shrugged. "It's not heavy. Hopefully there's room for you in there." He pressed a button on the elevator, and then we worked together to carefully open the wrapping paper at one end. The box was made of some sort of polymer and thankfully, hinged on the end that we'd unwrapped. I worked the handle and pulled it open. Inside was a high-end dressing mirror, the type that could connect to merchants and reflect a visualization of various clothes as though you were actually wearing them. An expensive gift. And once I removed some of the Styrofoam packing, there would be plenty of room for me beside it.

"You have a plan for this packing material?" I asked as I pulled out a large, white chunk of it.

"Trash is like half of my job," Nox said. "Not all of us are wearing designer clothes and standing around at fancy parties."

I pulled out another chunk and said, "And not all of us get to move around freely without our every move being scrutinized. I practically have to dress like a Mistwalker just to leave the residence without a security detail."

"I had to clean up a toilet after two of Orogen's friends decided to do enough cocaine and Dex-Dra to kill a whale," Nox said. "There was vomit and feces on the ceiling."

I stared at Nox blankly for a moment, briefly imagining what that scene must have looked like, and then forcing my brain to stop imagining it. I grabbed and handed him the last large chunk of Styrofoam and said, "Yeah, that's worse. Can't wait to go home."

"Your lips to all the gods' ears," Nox said. He glanced at the screen on the elevator and said, "Hurry."

I did, shimmying down next to the mirror and bracing myself against it. Then Nox closed the box, plunging me into absolute darkness. I heard thumping and shuffling outside the box, probably him putting the wrapping back in place. Then the elevator dinged once. The doors opened, and I held my breath.

Chapter Thirty-One

1 Day to Ascension

THE BOX TILTED AND STARTED to roll. It shuttered over a bump, probably the transition from the elevator to the hallway.

"What took you so long?" a smooth alto voice asked.

"Accidentally hit a button on the way down," Nox said.

After a long moment, the alto voice asked, "What's in the box?"

"No idea," Nox said. "Pretty heavy, though."

Something thumped against the box a few times, and I stayed as still as I possibly could, particularly when a couple of the thumps were right against my ribs. They didn't hurt at all, but not reacting was still a challenge.

Finally, the alto voice said, "Fine. Take it to Orogen's. We're making a stack in the northwest corner of his study."

"You got it," Nox said, and we were rolling again.

I braced tightly as Nox navigated the hallways, taking several turns with surprising gentleness. Neither of us said a word. The trek eventually stopped, and the box was set down evenly again. I waited, wondering what was going on, and then I heard a door open. The rolling resumed.

Hard flooring gave way to carpet. I could tell by the feel of the box dolly's wheels reverberating up through my spine. After a little more rolling, the box went level, and the dolly slid out with a grind.

"Wait for my signal," Nox whispered.

I rapped twice on the inside of the box to let him know I'd heard. Then I heard Nox walk away and the same door open and close, though from farther away.

"So far, so good," Bastion said.

I texted back, "So far."

The door opened again, and footsteps approached. Someone grunted and bumped into the box I was in, and then the footsteps retreated, and the door closed. After this repeated a few times, Bastion said, "Orogen's speech is now being streamed through the residence. A dry run of his planned speech for tomorrow, I think. Do you want to watch it?"

"Anything of interest to me?" I texted.

"Not particularly so far, but I don't know what else he's going to say."

I had nothing better to do while I waited, so I said, "Sure."

The stream of Orogen on the roof filled most of my vision. Orogen's voice popped into my ears at that same moment as he said, "…lead Kotega with as much vision and determination as my mother and her father before me."

Applause. Too much applause for the tiny crowd I knew was up there. Someone was digitally adding more audience.

"I'm currently outlining my plan for the first 100 days of my tenure," Orogen continued. "And while I have great admiration for my mother and what she has done for Kotega Systems during her nearly 20 years as CEO, I am not her. While many of her policies will remain in place, and while I strive to lead with the same integrity, there will be changes.

"Not merely for the sake of change, I assure you, but for the spiritual health of all Kotega citizens. My mother is a woman of logic, of reason. I have done my best to absorb those lessons and will always carry that logic and reason with me, but I feel called to help lead us into a new, more spiritual future."

The crowd murmured. Behind and to the left of Orogen, Tenisha's face was placid, obviously withholding whatever she was thinking and feeling from the cameras.

"There is a place in the Kotega Systems culture for spirituality. Our ancestors knew this. A century ago, there were hundreds of temples and houses of worship in our fair borough. We have gotten away from that. We have developed a culture that looks down on spirituality rather than accepting or even embracing it, and I believe that is what is holding us back from the next precipice of greatness."

There was more applause now, fewer than before, but more enthusiastic.

"He's starting to plant the seeds," I texted.

"A bold move to make this proclamation right in front of his mother."

"Particularly bold since Tenisha doesn't like bold moves. It's been a point of contention for Gloria."

Because Gloria was more like me, often taking risks without completely thinking through the outcomes. Granted, her big risks were more about board rooms and political maneuvers than jumping off of buildings, but like me, she succeeded far more than she failed.

Another box was set down near me, accompanied by another grunt. And then another. I was starting to recognize the grunts of about half a dozen people including Nox.

Orogen continued, "I also plan to be more aggressive in our market strategies. We have held ground with our competitors in many of the most difficult sectors such as cyber, nano, and financial. I want more. I want us to take market share from Corto Corporation, Huginn Industries, Toinette Holdings, and Nexus Neuronics. I want us to at least hold steady in our struggling sectors like neural, energy, and textiles."

That got huge applause from the crowd, including from Tenisha, who smiled and nodded vigorously. This was the more standard future-CEO stuff, the big promises and market-driven speak that always whipped corporate citizens into a frenzy.

"I'm gathering my team, which I'll be announcing very soon. And we have a multipoint to make Kotega Industries as feared a competitor as we've ever been. With market share comes growth. With growth comes opportunity for everyone who lives under a Kotega roof. Our future looks bright, so very bright."

More applause, and Orogen basked in it. Pretended to bask in it, I supposed, since there were so few people actually in front of him.

A knock on the side of the box startled me. I swallowed a gasp, and Bastion wisely muted the stream. After a heart-thumping few seconds, Nox said to the room at large, "Well, that's the last one. Must be nice to be the next CEO."

"Must be," an unfamiliar voice said. "Let's go."

"When do we get dinner?" Nox said to the stranger as he strode away. Clever apprentice. That was all for me so that I knew I could exit the box.

The door closed, cutting off the rest of that conversation.

"Finally," I said aloud as Bastion closed the stream entirely.

Now was a moment of truth. I was fairly certain that Tazia wouldn't be in the residence with people coming in and out with packages, but I couldn't be sure. I stayed still and dialed up my aural implants, listening for any movement in the residence.

After five minutes went by, I knew I couldn't wait any longer. I reached up and pushed on the lid of the box. It was difficult to open with the wrapping paper back in place, but I eventually heard a rip, and the lid flew wide. I stood to my full height and carefully looked around, still wary of Tazia. My box was nearly in the middle of the stack of gifts, but there was a path out. Nox had likely arranged the gifts to make sure of it.

I climbed out, taking care to not rip the paper any more, and then carefully closed the box and tried to arrange the paper to hide the rip that I had caused. Orogen would just blame that on the maintenance crew later. Couldn't be helped. I moved quickly and silently through the hallways then, back to that hidden room.

I opened my tunneled comms channel to Valdo and said, "You there, V?"

"I'm here," he said. "What took so long?"

"Long story. On my way to the workstation now."

I passed Tazia's room on the way and saw it was empty. Bed made. Everything in order. No sign of Tazia. I reached the secret door that wasn't so secret to me anymore and opened it.

It slid sideways and I stepped inside. The familiar light flickered back on, but what was inside wasn't so familiar. My heart raced as I took it all in. The workstation was gone. The desk was still there in the middle of the room, but only a small silver disk half a dozen centimeters across and a centimeter thick sat where the workstation had been. A holographic projector.

I took a breath to settle myself and looked carefully around the room, trying to make out any signs of what might have happened. I needed to rely on my training, not my emotions. A blue light suddenly filled the room. A hologram of Tazia Toinette-Intel hovered above the disc.

"Elise," she said. "Or should I say, 'Xyla?' Such a clever girl, sneaking into Orogen's quarters. Pretending to be Gloria's Daeli. Really, it was a great plan, though I don't know how you thought it would end."

"No," I said, my voice breaking in panic. "How could you—?"

"She can't hear you," Bastion said. "I'm trying to trace the signal through the Siwa network. It's live, not recorded, but it's one-way. She's streaming to this device from somewhere."

"Elise?" Valdo said. "What's going on?"

"The workstation, it's gone," I said. I wanted to scream, to turn over tables and claw Tazia's eyes out, but the hologram was just light.

"Gone?" Valdo asked. "Are you—?"

"I'm fine, V. I'll call you back."

"How is that old man you were with on Cirilla doing, by the way?" Tazia's hologram said. "The one that I paralyzed? Did that stick? It didn't seem like he was going to be able to get back up again. I suppose that almost makes up for what you did to Vert." She spat out her dead bodyguard's name like a curse while my stomach rolled.

"Where is she?" I asked Bastion through gritted teeth.

"She's routing the stream through dozens of proxies," Bastion said. "Maybe more. I don't know yet."

"Now here you are trying to meddle in my affairs again. I shouldn't be surprised that you found your way into Orogen's quarters last week. I almost didn't notice the evidence you left, but I'm better than you. You are nothing if not determined. Foolish, but determined.

"So here's what's going to happen next. You'll never find the workstation you came back here for, so don't bother looking. Oh, what am I saying?

Telling you to not do something is like talking to a Huginn Security enforcer. Lights on, eyes open, nobody home."

"The signal is shifting and moving," Bastion said. "She's using some sort of algorithm that keeps adding proxy bounces. This might be untraceable."

"Mother of Corto," I whispered. I felt so caught, so helpless, so useless. My pulse was thundering in my ears.

"So instead of making threats, telling you to leave the Kotega Systems borough or else," Tazia continued. "I'm going to map out what's going to happen over the next few hours. First…"

The holographic stream of Tazia disappeared, quickly replaced with one of Gloria. She was in one of her private bathrooms, doubled over a toilet and vomiting in waves.

"There's the poison in Gloria's system."

That explained the look on Gloria's face. She was only supposed to fake being sick, not actually be sick. Before I could say anything, a video appeared, this one on the rooftop earlier. There was Gloria, talking to people. There was me, standing nearby. A waiter came by with a drink, and then something happened in the hologram that hadn't happened in real life. I took a drink and visibly poured something into it before handing the glass to Gloria. The video froze there, hanging in the air.

"You see," Tazia said. "You're not the only one who can manipulate video streams. Gloria is sick right now, which means that the household security is going to be reviewing video soon to find out if anyone poisoned her. Lo and behold, look what they're going to see."

I turned on a heel, determined to get to Gloria as fast as possible. If security didn't know she was sick, they would have no reason to review the video. Before I could go, however, the door to the room slid closed with a slam. I spun back to face the hologram of Tazia.

She glanced to the side before continuing, "I thought that might send you running and tripping the motion sensor. But we're not done."

Now the hologram became a video of Nox. He was in one of those indiscriminate maintenance hallways, talking to another maintenance worker that I didn't know. I took quick, deep breaths. Now was not the time for a panic attack. I'd cost Solomon his mobility. I wasn't going to cost him is nephew. Not today. Not ever.

"Your apprentice, I believe," Tazia said. "Bold of you to bring him along. So inexperienced. So young. Why, he nearly killed himself the last time we tussled, didn't he? Twice, if you count his poorly calculated confrontation with Vert at the Toinette docks."

Nox had held Vert's son hostage at gunpoint right in front of the world-class fighter. Vert had nearly taken Nox's head off. Literally. I was pretty sure that if Vert had survived his fight with Roxy, he would have gone after Nox eventually.

"While you're busy trying to save Gloria and in turn, save yourself, I'll be taking care of little Nox. I'm thinking I'll throw him out the window after immobilizing his mods. I think he'd live a full two minutes screaming all the way down before making a terrible mess in The Mist. Or maybe I'll give him hope and fight him. I haven't done that in a while. Then again, a rail gun to the face would be appropriate after the way he terrified Vert's poor son."

I was done with her. I spun again and clawed at the door that had slammed shut. I didn't recall the door being anything special other than hidden the last time I was here, but now, I saw it was a dense metal alloy that thrummed under the strain of powerful magnetic locks. I moved to the side of the door and punched at the wall but found it just as unforgiving as the door. I screamed in fury.

"And then there's your young Toinette hacker," Tazia said.

The color drained from my face. I turned to see the stream of Nox had been replaced by several images of Valdo, my brother. They were all stills, not active streams, at least. One of him at the hospital with his mother. Another of that looked like he was at someone's home, his mother and our father nearby. The last one was a blurry image of Valdo and me eating noodles in the DB only a few days ago.

"Valdo Toinette-Seventeen. Just a child, really. And from my own company." Tazia tsked. "What did you do to get that poor child on your side? Blackmail? I do hope it was blackmail. Or was it you who made his mother sick? I wouldn't put anything past you at this point."

"Don't you dare," I hissed while knowing full well that she couldn't hear me. Then I said to Bastion, "Any luck on that trace?"

"No," Bastion said. "The harder I look, the more complicated it gets. I can't get past her algorithm."

"Now, I have options with Valdo," Tazia purred. "His parents are relative nobodies compared to me. I make a few calls, send a few emails, and I could have the entire family discommended."

My stomach wobbled at the word. To be discommended was to lose your job, to lose your citizenship in the company. To lose your community and your family. I didn't know exactly what the process looked like in other companies, but in Corto Corporation, it meant you couldn't even say the person's name. It was why I couldn't say my own father's name. If Valdo and his family were discommended, they would be tossed out with nothing. Could my father transition to another company again? Difficult in the simplest of circumstances. Much harder when you had a teenage son and a sick wife to bring along.

"I'm not sure that's fair to his poor mother, though," Tazia continued. "She's one of the faithful, after all. Not sure I'd want to risk it getting out that I'd sent a sick penitent into The Mist. So maybe young Valdo just meets an unfortunate fate poking around in a server that he forgot to power down. Accidents do happen, after all, especially when someone is young and inexperienced."

I felt sick, hollowed out. My brother. My apprentice. Gloria. She was going to destroy people I cared about like ticking boxes on a form. The images of Valdo vanished, leaving me alone with the hologram of Tazia again, hovering just a little larger than she was in real life. I'm sure that was on purpose.

"Now," Tazia said. "I'm going to open that door for you. You're either going to run around trying to save all of these people, or you'll run home like a coward. Either way, you're out of my way. Fortunately for me, I'm fairly certain you'll do the former. You can't help yourself. And that's far more entertaining for me, honestly. I really do hope that whatever hole Kotega throws you in is worse than whatever afterlife Vert is facing. You deserve every agony."

Tazia's constant smile broke for a moment into a sneer. She really hated me. The feeling was mutual.

"Goodbye, Elise," Tazia finally said. "And good riddance."

The hologram clicked off and the door immediately slid open. I started to take a step out but then thought better. Instead, I grabbed the holographic projector from the desk. Then I started to run.

Chapter Thirty-Two

1 Day to Ascension

I WAS IN A FULL sprint after only two strides, bouncing off a wall with my shoulder and moving as fast as my modded legs could carry me. I held the disc in front of my face as I ran. I wasn't looking at it, but I knew that Bastion could see it. Examine it. He asked me to flip it once, turn it a few seconds later. I nearly dropped it more than once in the process.

"It's a custom creation," Bastion said. "I think there's a data port hidden behind a small panel near your ring finger."

I fumbled with the disc as I ran and found the hidden port and plugged into it. I shoved the disc into my bra since I didn't have pockets, leaving the data cable plugged in so that Bastion could do his work. Finally, I stopped in front of the door that led to the maintenance corridor. I needed to hurry, but attracting a lot of attention wouldn't help me or Gloria. Or Nox.

"Where is Nox?" I asked Bastion.

"I don't know. I don't have access—"

"—to their security systems," I said. "Right."

I took a jagged breath. My heart was pounding and not just from the sprint. Both Nox and Gloria were in danger. I didn't want to lose either. I needed to think tactically. What would Quynn say? Save the apprentice or the mark? No, not just the mark. There was more to it. My feelings were pulled to both of them. But tactically, if I didn't go to Gloria, all of Kotega security would be after me for poisoning a member of the Siwa family.

And Nox was an Intel Operative. He wasn't on Tazia's level, but neither was I. He could handle himself at least long enough to buy me some time. Then there was Valdo, my brother. He was lower on Tazia's list, for sure, since she was here and not in the Toinette borough. But still, he was in danger. His family was in danger. My father was in danger.

"Going after Gloria first," I said. "But call Valdo."

Calling Valdo started blinking on my display as I turned away from the door. I needed to go down, and I was less likely to be noticed if I descended as much as I could through Orogen's residence. I started running again as my brother connected on comms and said, "Are you all right?"

"You're in danger," I said.

"What? Me? What about you?"

"I'm in danger, too, but I need you to get to safety. Take your family and hide until I tell you it's safe."

"I…I can't…" Valdo was sputtering syllables. Then I heard a familiar voice in the background, a voice I hadn't heard in a very long time, though I couldn't make out the words.

"You have to," I said. "It's Tazia. She knows about you. She's here in Kotega now, but she said she's coming after you next. You have to run and hide. Please, Valdo. Please."

"Who is it?" my father said in the background.

"A friend from work," Valdo said.

"Do what you have to do," I said as I started down the main stairwell in Orogen's residence, taking the steps two at a time. "But get your family to safety, somewhere that Tazia wouldn't think to look for you, somewhere you've never been."

"I don't know where to start, where to go." Valdo, for once, sounded like the child he was. He was grown to the size of a man, sure. He was nearly an adult, but not quite. Fear laced his words now, aging him backward.

My heart went out to him, but I didn't have time to dwell on my feelings. My mind raced as my feet did, still bounding down the stairs. "I have a friend. His name is Echo. Off the grid. He lives in The Mist in Corto Corporation. Tell him I sent you and that you just need to lie low. He'll help—"

"The Mist?"

"Yes."

"There's no way," Valdo said. "There's no way I could convince them to go there, not even trick them. My mom is terrified of anything below the 50th floor."

"Mother of Corto," I muttered. "Do you have anywhere to go? Do your parents?"

"I don't think so."

I gritted my teeth as I thought of the one place left to suggest, though I didn't like it. "Go to my place, my apartment. I'll get a message to my partner, Quynn. Hole up there for a while. I promise I'll let you know when it's safe."

"Are you sure?"

I wasn't sure, not at all. Tazia knew my name, after all. She'd proven that she could find any information. Certainly that included my address. But it would, at the very least, put them somewhere Tazia wasn't expecting. I would be able to get there before Tazia did, once I saved Gloria and Nox. Right. Easy. But I swallowed hard and said, "I'm sure." Then I gave him my address.

"It won't be easy getting my dad there," Valdo said. "He hates Corto, but I'll make it happen."

He hates Corto. That rang through my brain, thrumming my heartstrings in the process as I finished the stairs and soon stood in front of a door that led to the maintenance hallways. It hurt to know that my father hated Corto, to hear it. If he hated Corto, did he hate me? Mom? Is that why he left? I shook the thought off. No time to go down that particular line of thinking now. I'd have to process this later. I said, "Good. Get them there. I'll be in touch."

I disconnected the call. Then, I said to Bastion, "Anything from that disc?"

"I'm fighting it," Bastion said.

"Fighting?" I asked as I worked to steady my breathing.

"As soon as you plugged in, it started erasing its memory and trying to give you a virus."

My stomach was suddenly in my throat. A virus. There was little that terrified me as much as that. The idea of a malicious program wreaking havoc on my systems made me nauseous. Those systems controlled what I saw and heard, my ability to move, to do my job or touch Quynn or interact with the world. All of that could go away or be completely out of my control if a virus took hold.

I had good antivirus software, of course. Great, even. Every Intel Operative did. Some of the better locks and workstations out there were designed to counterattack with viruses. Those were easy enough to fend off. But this was Tazia, the Ghost of Toinette. She'd nearly killed me by hacking a Stryder, which I didn't think was possible. She'd known I was a Corto Corporation Intel Operative the first time she'd ever seen me. If anyone could make a virus that I couldn't counter, it would be her.

"I have the virus under control," Bastion said. "It's the memory deletion I'm fighting."

"The virus…?" I'd heard him, but my brain just couldn't catch up.

"Elise? Are you all right?"

"You have the virus under control? How? I mean, that's good."

"Yes," he said like he was reassuring a confused child. "The virus was very sophisticated, but any virus can be beaten by enough raw computing power. When I want it, I have more of that available to me than any computer on the planet."

"How?"

"I…borrow. Lots of idle workstations in this city."

I exhaled a shaky breath and refocused. Virus contained. I'd finished catching my breath, so I opened the door to the maintenance hallway, just a crack, and immediately saw two maintenance workers and a security guard having a vape break just in front of the elevators. I gently closed the door, my eyes sweeping across Orogen's living quarters. On the opposite side, I saw a balcony lush with plants and a sweeping view of the Kotega borough.

"How many floors down to Gloria?" I asked as I moved toward

that balcony.

"Two," Bastion said. "All of them roughly double the standard height."

"So 12 or 13 meters?"

"14.4 meters."

"And how long is my grapple in these mods?" My grapple in my right work arm was attached to a thin, hyperdense cable 120 meters long. I had a feeling that these embed mods weren't as well equipped.

"15 meters," Bastion said.

"Cutting it close." I opened the door to the balcony and took four long strides, the last of which I planted on the balcony railing. I spun, fired the magnetic grapple at the metal balcony right next to my foot, and leaped out and away.

Two meters flew by, my hair and the blazer flying up around me as I fell before I caught myself against the side of the building, my modded legs catching my weight and pushing me off again. I just had to hope that nobody was right inside wondering what Gloria's Daeli was doing repelling down the side of the building. I bounced down again, and then Bastion highlighted a handful of windows in my display.

"That is the floor that Gloria is on," he said.

I bounced down to it, firming up my stance, and then I kicked off as hard as I could, swinging out half a dozen meters, and coming back in hard, bracing my legs. The thud ran up my biological spine, sending pain shooting in every direction, but the window didn't so much as crack.

"Ballistic glass," Bastion said.

"Now you tell me." I looked left and right, but there were no balconies in sight on this side of the residence. Great. I said to Bastion, "I don't have the tools I would usually use to crack this. What are my options?"

Several long seconds passed before Bastion said, "The disc."

"Disc?"

"Tazia's disc. I believe you can wedge it between the panes of glass."

"Aren't you trying to crack it?"

"I am losing that battle, and if we cannot help Gloria, then there is no point to me back-tracing Tazia's location. We already know where she is going to be very soon."

"Right," I said in a whisper. "With Nox."

I pulled the disc out of my bra, shuffled sideways, and tried to push the edge of it into the narrow gap between the panes of ballistic glass.

"It doesn't fit," I said. "And I don't have any leverage." I grunted, then I held the disc over the gap, spun slightly on my grapple cable, and stomped on the disc. The edge dented. Fortunately, the disc also wedged between the panes.

"Good," Bastion said. "Now, just—"

"I got it," I said. I straddled the disc, adjusting my cable to the right height, and kicked off hard again. This time, when I swung back toward the building, I put just one foot out, straight onto the jutting hologram disc. The disc crumpled under my heel and for a moment, I was afraid that was all the damage I would be able to inflict. But by the time my heel slipped off the crumpled disc, massive cracks appeared in the glass on both sides, an equally massive sound hitting me as they appeared.

The cracks on the right pane were bigger, so I shifted that direction and did it again. And again. The cracks grew and spiderwebbed with each try. On the third big swing, the glass gave as I hit it, my feet sailing into Gloria's dining room. The grapple cable caught on the window frame, sending me briefly toward the ceiling just as I released the magnetic grapple. I fell hard on my back, the dining room floor sending all the air from my lungs.

I laid there a moment, letting the grapple cable retract and eventually sucking in air again. Nothing makes you feel as alive as that first breath after the wind gets knocked out of you. Finally, I said to Bastion, "Any damage?"

"Your ankles and knees weren't meant for that sort of abuse, but no real damage."

I nodded and got to my feet. My back ached. Probably bruised from neck to tailbone, but at least my mods were intact. I made my way clumsily to Gloria's bedroom and her private, en suite bathroom. Sure enough, she was doubled over the toilet, heaving mucus and stomach acid into the porcelain.

"If she's been like this since you left her," Bastion said. "She has to be very weak. She could start vomiting blood soon, too."

"Gloria," I said. "You've been poisoned."

"Obviously," she grumbled without turning to look at me. "Was it you?"

"Me? No! Of course not!"

She opened her mouth to wretch again, but nothing came out. She seemed so small and frail. The color seemed drained from her entirely, her hair a tangled mess. We were both still wearing matching outfits, though both were looking worse for the wear at this point.

"It was Orogen's Toinette friend, his advisor," I said. "She sniffed out our plan."

"The operative?" Gloria asked, her eyes wide as she turned to me, still keeping her head over the toilet. Those eyes were bloodshot. Her makeup made a strange contrast with the colorless pallor of her skin.

"She's not just an Intel Operative for Toinette. She's their best, their absolute best."

Gloria vomited a dribble of yellow in response, the violent quaking of her body far too much for how little it produced. She wiped her mouth with one sleeve and slowly turned to face me. "You're an Intel Operative, too, aren't you? That's why you know all of this, why you came up with this plan. Why you're here."

I nodded, trying to keep my face steady and emotionless.

"For who? Not Kotega, that's for certain."

I glanced at my feet, then back to Gloria. "Tazia is her real name. She poisoned you and planted fake footage of me dosing your drink on the roof. Once security knows you've been poisoned, they'll review the footage and see it."

"So what's your plan? Finish me off and run away? Better I die of blunt force trauma than poison?"

Ouch. All these weeks, and she now thought so little of me. I steadied my voice and said, "We need to get you an antidote, at least some synthetic adrenaline to flush your system."

"I would not recommend adrenaline," Bastion said in my ear. "It may speed up her metabolism of the poison and exacerbate her condition."

"Wait," I said. "Not adrenaline. That would make things worse."

Gloria looked into the toilet like she was going to wretch again before she nodded and asked, "Then what?"

I took a deep breath. "Tazia is also targeting my apprentice, who is here as one of your maintenance workers. Then she's going after…" I swallowed and stuttered, but finally said, "…my brother."

Gloria looked at me again, but her face had changed. The contempt was gone. She looked pained and concerned. "Your brother?"

"Elise," Bastion said. "No. You cannot. You'll jeopardize everything you're doing here in Kotega. Keep to your cover."

"He's in Toinette," I said to Gloria. The truth came easily. It tasted sweet on my tongue, and so I just kept going, Bastion be damned. "I'm from Corto Corporation. My name is Elise. I…she…I was on Cirilla when Orogen won that tournament. Tazia helped him. Cheated. She…she made it so a mentor of mine can never walk again. Tazia got away. Now she's here, trying to destabilize the entire city."

"That doesn't explain why she hates you so much."

"You've heard of Vert?"

"Vert the Hurt? The fighter?"

I nodded.

"Of course. Didn't he die on…on Cirilla?" Gloria's eyes were darting, searching, and then grew wide and fixed on me. "Was that you? Did you kill him?"

"Yes," I whispered through the all-too-familiar guilt. "Not directly, but yes. That was my fault. And he was her bodyguard. Maybe her friend, too."

Gloria looked back at the toilet bowl. Her back arched briefly, but nothing else happened. Then she wobbled to her feet. I gently took her forearm to help her up, and she let me take some weight. She pointed back out into her bedroom. "My side table. Bottom drawer. Help me."

I did, taking much of her weight and practically dragging her over to her bed. She couldn't even stay upright without help. I started to lay her down, but she shook her head. "Bottom drawer."

"I can get it."

"It needs my handprint."

I nodded and lowered both of us to the floor. Her arm shook as she extended it, and I helped her press a palm to the front of the drawer. She felt so small and frail in my arms, not at all the strong, confident woman I'd grown to know. A small beep and click ensued, and then the drawer popped open a few centimeters.

"Now put me on the bed." Her voice was cracking. I did as she asked, the modded arms making easy work of her weight. Then I bent down and opened the drawer. It was an emergency medical kit. There were multiple vials of blood, likely her own, a dose of adrenaline, a large bag, and a dozen other small vials of various colors that weren't labeled. A hypo gun sat in the corner, ready to inject any of them into Gloria.

"Which one?" I asked, taking out the hypo gun.

"The dark blue," Gloria whispered. "Then the milky white. And the big yellow one after that."

"The blue is a hyper-oxygenator. The yellow is a bag of electrolytes. And I believe that milky white is full of nanobots, likely designed to find and eliminate toxins."

"Will it work?" I whispered to Bastion.

"I don't know the programming of the nanobots, but yes, in theory. The blue will help her stay alive while the bots get to work. After all of that vomiting, she needs the electrolytes. She'll be weak and hungry after, but I think those will keep her alive."

I grabbed the dark blue, twisted it into the hypo gun, and pressed it to Gloria's neck. "This might sting," I said.

Gloria nodded, glancing at me with something I'd never seen on her face: genuine fear. I put my other hand on hers, and she grabbed it desperately. Her fingers were like ice. I squeezed the trigger on the hypo, and with a little hiss, the blue vial emptied. Gloria grimaced, but I didn't wait. I knelt back down and loaded up the milky white, which shimmered like it was nanobots once I had it in the light. Then I injected that. Gloria's eyes went wide as the shimmering liquid took a full minute to empty into her. I felt like color was returning to the world as it returned to her. She looked flush. Her skin was warming. A tear of relief ran down my cheek.

"Are you all right?" I asked.

She nodded, still shaking and weak despite the returning color. Finally, I grabbed the yellow bag, which was larger and unwieldy once I attached it to the hypo gun. I brought it up to her neck.

"In the arm," Gloria and Bastion said at the same time.

I nodded and set the hypo down, then gently worked her sleeve up. She wasn't able to help much but seemed to be looking at me fondly, looking at me with those eyes that still pulled me in. Once her arm was bare, I pressed the hypo into the crook of her elbow and squeezed. The bag started to slowly empty, and I held the hypo in place.

"Thank you," Gloria said.

"I wasn't going to let you die," I said.

She shook her head. "For telling me the truth. For telling me who you really are, Elise."

My name on her tongue sent a shiver down my spine. I looked away from her, from those eyes. She had some truth, sure. Just enough to do what I needed her to do. But she didn't know about Quynn. She didn't know anything about my life. This was just a stupid crush, one that would be out of my life soon enough. I sighed and looked at the yellow bag, only half empty, and grunted my disapproval.

"What?" Gloria asked, her voice still gentle.

"I have to find my apprentice before Tazia kills him. I can't just sit here, be the good Daeli, and play nurse."

"You know that's not what I think of you, don't you?"

"I know I'm not a real nurse, I just—"

"As just my Daeli. You're more. You mean more to me."

I didn't look at Gloria's face. It didn't matter what I meant to her, what she felt. I had to save Nox. I had a job to do and a life to get back to.

Then, Gloria sighed and said, "Under the vials, there's a box. Take out one of the transdermal patches and stick it to my chest."

I gave her a bewildered look but then dug under the vials with one hand while I held the hypo gun steady with the other. Sure enough, I found a box, roughly five centimeters square and two centimeters thick. I sat it atop the side table, opened it, and found a stack of thin sheets the same color as Gloria's skin.

"I've never seen such a thing," Bastion said. "I don't know what those will do."

"Stick how?" I asked Gloria. "Is there a backing I need to peel off?"

Gloria chuckled under her breath. "No, they're programmed to my

DNA. Just press one to my chest, just below the collarbone."

Still holding the hypo gun with one hand, I carefully undid the strap running behind her neck and pulled the fabric down nearly to the point of exposing her breasts, which I didn't want to see. I may have had a crush, but the thought of that kind of touch still put my stomach in knots. I grabbed the patch and placed it on her chest, being very careful.

"You have to press it," she said.

I gritted my teeth and pressed my hand to the patch, pushing down lightly. I wasn't really looking at her, so I was surprised when her warm hand was suddenly on mine. I looked back at her, and that was a mistake. Those eyes. Her hand on mine. My heart fluttered in a way I didn't want.

The door to the bedroom suddenly slammed open. Both Gloria and I were startled. I spun, barely keeping hold of the hypo gun while taking my other hand off Gloria's chest and up into a defensive posture. To my relief, it was just two of the household security guards. I didn't recognize either, but the uniforms let my heart slow down a bit.

"What's going on?" the tall and pale one asked, their hand hovering near a stun gun on their belt.

"Mistress wasn't feeling well," I said. "I'm giving assistance."

"Not feeling well how?" the other guard asked, this one shorter with very dark skin. They also looked like they were ready for a fight.

"I'm fine, Adrian and Hirali," Gloria said, her voice surprisingly strong. I felt a warm hand on mine, on the one holding the hypo gun. She was urging me to let go, and I did. She took hold of it herself. "It was something I ate, I think, but my faithful Daeli has helped set me to right. I'll be back upstairs in 20 minutes."

The guards glanced at each other. Neither seemed to be put at ease in the slightest.

"Are you sure you haven't been poisoned?" Adrian asked.

"Poisoned?" Gloria said. "Whatever gave you that idea? No, just some bad shellfish. Are our guests feeling all right?"

Hirali reached up to their ear and said something that I mostly couldn't understand, though it certainly ended with, "Yes, of course."

Something didn't feel right, but I didn't figure that out soon enough.

Both guards pulled out their stun guns, metal prongs extending and electricity arcing.

I held up my hands. "What are you doing?"

"Both of you," Gloria said, some of the command back in her voice. "Stand down."

But the guards didn't acknowledge her. They didn't even look at her. They started advancing on me.

"Gloria," I said. "I don't think these two work for you anymore."

Chapter Thirty-Three

1 Day to Ascension

"I TOLD YOU TO STAND down," Gloria said as she sat up, full command back in her voice now.

The guards glanced at each other, and then Adrian said, "I'm afraid your Daeli is lying to you. Working against you. We have video proof that she poisoned you."

"Then why did she just work so hard to get me upright?" Gloria asked.

"She's manipulating you," Hirali said. "Discovered she needs you alive."

Adrian nodded and stared at me. "Can't upset the succession if you're in the grave."

I almost laughed. I glanced at Gloria, who glanced at me at the same time, her eyes rolling. I said, "Tazia really did pick the dullest nails in the box with you two, didn't she?"

The guards glanced at each other in genuine confusion.

"Oh," I said. "I'm sorry. Is she still calling herself Josephine? Maybe another name? Maybe she told Orogen to feed you that line about graves and succession?"

That's when they finally realized that I was calling them stupid, and they advanced on me with stunners at the ready. No running this time, not when I was cornered, needed to protect Gloria, and then go save my apprentice. I crouched in a fighting stance, wishing dearly that I was in my work limbs, but these would have to do.

Hirali lunged first, aiming the stunner at my face. I dodged left so that I wouldn't be closer to Adrian, the prongs of the stunner buzzing with electricity as they moved past my face. I plunged a fist into Hirali's ribcage, and they didn't even try to dodge. Unfortunately, it felt like I'd punched a reinforced wall. Hirali stumbled back two steps but looked none the worse for wear.

"Oh great," I said. "Body armor."

"I'll look for weak points," Bastion said.

I dodged another lunge from Hirali and tried an elbow break, looping my forearm around theirs and punching the outside of their elbow with my palm, but their arm was obviously modded, giving great resistance and easily bouncing back from overextension. I spun around, rolling up the length of their arm, and gave a swift, downward kick to the back of their knee. This time, the joint buckled. Hirali gave a cry as they went to their knees, but then I had to skitter back as Adrian swung his stunner in a wide arc over their fallen comrade.

I looked around for something to use as a weapon. This was two-on-one, and with their uniforms covering everything from the neck down, I didn't know what parts of the two guards were modded or biological. Nor could I see the armor that Bastion was trying to analyze. I needed an advantage, but nothing in the room stood out. Bed, side tables, lamps, armoire, dresser. Some small, decorative items that looked too fragile or light to be of any use in a fight.

Adrian charged in, and I rolled to my right, but Adrian was a better fighter than their partner. They stopped short, the charge a feint, and connected his foot to my jaw. It was a glancing blow, but enough to send me sprawling across the floor. At least that sent me away from them, so I was able to get to my feet before they resumed their attack.

Adrian jabbed with the stunner, and I parried the blow away from me, connecting with my own jab to their shoulder joint, though I only found armor. They swung the stunner back at me, and I ducked it. I swept their legs, and they neatly leaped back. As they lunged back in at me, I stepped inside their reach and connected with a jab under their chin, which sent them stumbling backward, but they stayed upright.

But then Hirali was on their feet and the two were regrouping. I was in a literal corner against both of them, and that didn't bode well for me. They were closing on me, two meters away and taking their time, watching me closely, and giving me no room for escape.

That's when something surprising happened. Out of the corner of my eye, I saw Gloria rise out of the bed. I didn't look directly at her, not wanting to tip the guards off, but I was amazed by the fluidity of her movements. Not long ago, she'd been doubled over the toilet, unable to stand or walk on her own. The combination of those hypos and whatever was in that patch must have worked a small miracle. The guards took two more steps, nearly in striking distance, before a long metal shaft, no, a metal kendo sword, suddenly crashed into the back of Hirali's head. Their eyes went wide the moment before they went flying toward me, arms akimbo, and I leaped out of the path of their fall. They were limp on the ground, the stunner tumbling away and powering down without a hand to grip it.

Adrian spun to face the new threat, but too slowly. Gloria had been practicing with a sword since she was old enough to hold it and knew more about Adrian's armor than I did. She jabbed, three quick and piercing blows to the inside of the ankle, the groin, and the throat. Adrian crumpled like wet paper, gagging and moaning and writhing on the floor.

"What was in that patch?" I asked.

"Family secret," Gloria said, her eyes still trained on the guards. Hirali wasn't moving, but Adrian was writhing. Gloria slammed the broad side of the sword into their temple, and Adrian relaxed into unconsciousness.

I looked back and forth between the two fallen guards. Both unconscious. Then I looked at Gloria. She was smirking at me in the strangest way, standing tall, that sparkle back in her eyes. Only then did I notice that my mouth was hanging open. I closed it.

"You…" I sputtered. "You're all right. How did you—?"

Before I could say anything else, Gloria closed the distance between us.

Her free hand grabbed my collar, and she was kissing me full on the mouth. Her lips were warm, soft, and aggressive. Warmth exploded in my chest, heating my face. I tasted cloves and cinnamon. Her tongue flicked against my lips, sending sparks down my spine. I wanted to lean in, to kiss back. Maybe I did for a moment, I'm not sure. Then I pushed her away, the feeling of her lips, her hot breath, still dominating my thoughts.

Gloria was holding her fingers in front of her lips, her eyes wide in obvious fear. "I'm sorry," she said. "I thought…"

"My apprentice," I blurted out, desperate to change the subject. "I have to help my apprentice."

"Of course," she said, glancing away.

I didn't know what else to say, didn't want to talk about the kiss, how great it felt, the electricity that ran through my body, or how much I wanted to kiss her again. Instead, I turned and started walking out the door. I needed to find Nox.

"Wait," Gloria's voice said from behind me.

I turned, afraid that she wanted to talk about the kiss or feelings or anything like that. I couldn't. Not now. Not ever. Instead, I saw that she was refastening the collar of her outfit, the sword lying on the bed. She wasn't even looking at me, thankfully.

"I can't wait. He's in danger."

Gloria nodded, finished with her garment, and then reached under the bed. She pulled out a second sword and tossed it to me. I caught it. It was surprisingly light, only a touch heavier than the polymer ones we'd sparred with. She picked her sword back up. "Let's go."

"Us?"

"You've barely practiced with that thing. You need me."

"But you…" I didn't know how to finish the sentence. She owed me nothing? I'd lied to her? This wasn't her fight? All of that sounded so hollow.

"I care about you," Gloria said, looking deeply into my eyes as she did. "Obviously. Whether you want me to or not. And I believe you. I believe that you're trying to help me, trying to stop Orogen. Even if you have your own motives. And I can tell you care about your apprentice. So let's go."

I smiled in spite of myself and then nodded. More than the kiss, that was the woman I was attracted to. My face flushed and I looked away before I said, "We have to find him first."

That's when some very loud klaxons started blaring in every room. Emergency lights started flashing.

"What is that?" I yelled, not that Gloria could hear me over the alarm. I couldn't even hear me.

Gloria gave me a wincing look while holding her ears. After about a minute, the alarms went silent. A robotic voice soon replaced it saying, "Emergency. Please proceed to the nearest exit. Emergency."

"Household alarm," Gloria said.

"Is that a good or bad thing?"

Gloria shrugged and said, "Not sure. Follow me." And she squeezed past me, breaking into a run as soon as she was through the door. I followed, still surprised by her speed and strength. Seriously. Whatever was in those subdermal patches, I needed some of those for emergencies.

Gloria flew from one room to the next, me close on her heels, and we were soon darting through the staff hallways. I'd only seen her in the staff area a few times, and only just outside of her residence, but it was now obvious that she knew these halls far better than I did. She took each turn with confidence until she reached Thrace's door. She put her hand on the handle, and I heard the beep of an unlock.

We were in the room, and she was in front of Thrace's security workstation in a flash. She entered a username and password, unlocking the workstation and pulling up camera feeds in rapid succession.

"I didn't know you knew this system," I said.

"I designed it," Gloria said.

"That explains why I was rather unfamiliar with it," Bastion said. "A homebrew system, though certainly a sophisticated one."

"What does your apprentice look like? Who are we looking for?"

"Short, very dark skin, close-cropped hair," I said. "He's dressed like one of your maintenance workers."

She pressed keys, and the feeds on the screen all shifted to multiple angles in the maintenance corridors. I scanned the feeds as quickly as I could, desperate to find Nox, but I didn't see him among the maintenance workers.

I hoped I wasn't too late, that he'd been able to hold of the Ghost of Toinette long enough for me to help him. I couldn't let anything happen to him.

Gloria changed camera angles and glanced at me. I shook my head, and the feeds all changed again. We repeated the process again and again, through dozens of different camera feeds covering the many floors of the Siwa compound, but I couldn't find Nox.

"Wait!" I said too loudly. I thought I'd seen something on one of the feeds. I pointed to it and said, "Go back on this one."

The feed flipped back, and sure enough, there was Nox. He was barely in the frame and barely visible in the dark room. I'd only noticed him when the emergency lights flashed, which they did again. Otherwise, he wasn't visible on the feed. I pointed at him and said, "There. Where is that?"

"Maintenance hallway," Gloria said. "Three floors from the roof. Southwest corner of the floor."

"Why is it dark? Don't those floors have motion-sensing lights just like all the other staff and maintenance hallways?"

"They do," Gloria said. "They should be on if he's in there."

"Tazia must have done something," Bastion said.

"She's hunting him," I said. "She's there. Close. We have to get there now."

Gloria was up and out of her seat in a breath. "Let's go."

I did as she asked, following her at a dead sprint through the halls. She took me through doors I'd never tried before. I didn't even know that the staff hallways and maintenance hallways connected like that, and then she was slamming the button for the maintenance elevator over and over, but nothing happened.

"What?" she muttered.

"Tazia is trapping him. Killed the lights. Disabled the elevator." I walked up to the elevator doors, wedged my fingers in, and pulled the doors open manually. I asked her, "How many floors up to them?"

Gloria looked slightly down, her eyes darting back and forth as she did some calculations. "Twelve floors."

I looked up at the darkness of the elevator shaft. Standard magnetic lift. Thick metal beams on either side that served as tracks. Occasional metal plates to serve as magnetic emergency brakes. "Almost 70 meters. That's a lot to cover and not a lot of time to cover it."

"There are stairs," Gloria said.

I shook my head, trying to remember the load ratings for my legs and the magnetics in them. "Too slow."

"You could easily climb that," Bastion said.

"Can I do it with her on my back?" I whispered.

"That depends…"

"How much do you weigh?" I asked Gloria, interrupting Bastion.

"I don't—" Gloria sputtered.

"Not a time for vanity," I said. "I need to know. How much?"

Gloria grimaced and said, "About 70 kilos. Why?"

"Combined with your weight," Bastion said. "That's technically within the weight limit, but—"

"Hold this and climb on my back," I said to Gloria as I handed her my sword. "And hold on tight. We're going up the shaft."

"The what?" Gloria's eyes practically came out of her head.

"You want to know me? The real me? This is what I do, what I'm good at. We're going up, and this is the fastest way to do it." I turned my back to her and knelt. After a few moments, she put her arms around my neck and drew her knees up on either side of me.

I rose to my feet and said, "Hey Carbon, limb status to my display."

Bastion knew the drill. I'd long ago deleted my basic digital assistant named Carbon, but it was a way to vocalize to Bastion without raising suspicions. Sure enough, the four corners of my display were soon taken up with numbers for charge percentage, joint health, pneumatic pressure, and temperature. I squatted a couple of times just to get a feel for the extra weight, and then jumped into the elevator shaft, catching one of the beams with the magnetics of my right hand and foot.

Gloria cursed under her breath, though I could hear the words clearly with her mouth so close to my ear.

Couldn't think about that now, though. Not about her breath on my skin or the memory of her lips on mine. Nope. Not the time. I lowered my weight, and then pushed off hard, up as much as possible and out enough to catch the opposite beam with the magnetics on my left hand and foot. I'd covered about three meters in that one jump. The numbers on my display looked good, so I did it again. And again. I found the rhythm of it, leaping back and forth up the elevator shaft, watching the battery percentage and joint health numbers decrease while the temperature slowly climbed.

"Are you okay?" Gloria whispered.

I grunted and kept leaping from side to side. I was getting tired. Even though the modded limbs were doing most of the work, my core muscles were working to keep both of us stable. My back was sore from the extra weight, and my trapezius muscles were starting to scream with all that weight tugging on one side and then the other.

"Three more jumps," Bastion said. "Though with each consecutive jump, you're covering less distance."

Apparently, nobody else understood that this was hard. Even in my work limbs, this would have been a challenge. I gritted my teeth and leaped again. Again. I was breathing hard. My limbs were all down below 50% charge and their temperatures were in the yellow, but not the red. I took a deep breath and leaped one more time, then looked around.

"You see the door?" I asked between heaving breaths.

Gloria's hair whipped across the side of my face as she looked around. She said, "It's above us. Maybe a meter and a half."

Losing more than a little strength with each leap, it would seem. I grabbed the rail with all four limbs so that I could turn around and face the door. Then I positioned both feet on the rail and one hand, using the other to balance.

"What can I do?" Gloria asked.

"Just hold on," I grunted. Then I leaped one more time. I had no problem making the meter and a half in one leap, but grabbing hold was another matter. No heavy, magnetic rails here to attach to. My toes caught the lip of the door, and I curled them around the scant couple of centimeters available to me. Then I scrabbled with my hands for any purchase. The doors were closed, so I couldn't grab them. The frame of the door didn't present many options, so I reached straight up and braced the heels of my hands against the top of the door frame. That held me for a moment, but I could feel the extra weight pulling me back and down into the elevator shaft. This wasn't going to hold.

Just as I was opening my mouth to yell…something, I wasn't sure what, the weight suddenly vanished from my back. I wasn't falling anymore, but I panicked, worried that Gloria had fallen. I looked left and right, and there she was, mimicking my pose. Bracing herself in the door frame.

I took a deep, shaky breath. "You scared me."

"Helped, though," she said. "You need to open these doors." She took as good a grip as she could on the top of the door frame and then placed one hand firmly behind my back.

I nodded and wedged one hand between the doors. Without Gloria bracing me, I'm not sure I would have had the leverage to make the doors move, but she helped. I was able to move them a few centimeters with one hand, then get a better grip in the larger space, and shove both hands in. The doors opened easily then.

We stepped into the dark maintenance corridor together, back to back, both of us looking and listening for any sign of Nox or Tazia as the emergency lights kept flashing every 10 seconds. Outside of those flashes, I couldn't see more than a few feet in any direction. Hallways went left, right, and straight ahead from the elevator, but I was completely turned around.

"Where are they?" I asked.

"I'll find out," she said and was no longer at my back a moment later.

I turned and saw her working a panel on the wall nearby. "What are you doing?"

"This Tazia woman turned off the lights and half of the electrical grid," Gloria said while pressing several buttons. "But as a member of the Siwa family, I do have certain system privileges."

"Privileges don't mean much when dealing with a hacker like—"

Gloria pressed her entire hand to the panel, which lit up green, and the lights suddenly turned back on.

"How?" I asked.

She gave me one of her goofiest grins. "Factory reset. Doesn't matter what she did to the system. I cleared it and turned the lights on."

"Elise?!" a familiar voice yelled from far down the hallways that ran straight out from the elevators. It was Nox, though he was nearly on the other side of the building. He was on the ground, scrambling to his feet when Tazia entered my view. She kicked Nox hard in the chest the moment he rose to his feet, sending him sprawling out of my view. She turned, saw me, and grinned. Then she waved a hand, and more than a dozen Kotega security guards poured into the hallway from behind her. They were all coming straight for Gloria and me.

Gloria looked surprised for a moment, but the surprise quickly melted into fury. "I'm guessing they don't work for me or my family anymore, either."

It wasn't a question, so I didn't give it a response. Instead, I held out a hand to Gloria, and she put the sword in it. Then I started moving down the hallway. Tactically, it was better to let them come to me, but Nox needed me. I was less concerned with fighting all these guards than with just getting past them.

"Priming all of your weapons," Bastion said. "Though you don't have many. Palm tasers, three charges per hand, though your climb up the elevator shaft means you don't have enough battery for all of them. Four smoke bombs. Your forearms are reinforced for hand-to-hand combat. You also have a single-use knockout grenade."

"The left shoulder," I whispered. "I know. But it'll knock me out, too."

"I wasn't saying you should use it, just that you have it."

"Hey," Gloria said as she jogged to catch up to me. "Going somewhere without me?"

I smiled weakly. "I hope not."

Gloria winked, then brought her sword into a ready stance. "Just like we practiced."

I wanted to thank her, but words just didn't seem like enough. I smiled and nodded, but before I could figure out what to say, Gloria focused her attention on the guards in front of us.

Right. Shut up, fluttering heart. Work to do.

As the first pair of guards bore down on us, I assumed a defensive posture, ready to block or parry, hopefully finding space for a counter after.

Gloria, however, stepped forward and to the side, sweeping a guard's leg. As they started to stumble sideways, she spun and slammed her sword into the guard's back, sending them flying into the guard I was getting ready to deal with. She hopped back, slapping both guards hard in their throats. They weren't dead, but they were too focused on coughing and trying to breathe to pose any threat.

Gloria moved forward to the next pair, and I stepped over the writhing guards to join her. She was like water, flowing around their blows, their extended stun guns, and their useless flailing one after the next. I wasn't entirely useless. As she was batting away two guards at once, a third tried to come up behind her, ignoring me as a lesser threat. I jabbed the guard behind one knee, then took a two-handed swing to the back of their head to knock them out.

But I wasn't sure Gloria needed even that. Less than a minute later, she took down three guards in as much time as it took me to bat a stun gun out of a guard's hand, nearly losing the sword in the process, and finally knocking the wind out of my guard with an overextended lunge to their gut.

Then my muscles all tensed at once, my cybernetic limbs straightened and locked. There was a pain in my lower back, hot and intense. My jaw clenched and the world grew dark. A stun gun. As an Intel Operative, you got used to seeing them. A favorite sidearm of security for every company. And once you'd felt their sting and that dizzying inability to act, you didn't forget the feeling.

I fell to the ground, my limbs twitching. My back muscles were spasming, and I couldn't unclench my jaw. I was still conscious, which was a mixed bag. On the one hand, being unconscious would have meant that I didn't have to feel all of this. But being conscious meant that I would recover faster, assuming I had the chance.

Gloria made sure that I did. She cracked the guard who stunned me in the ribs, then bent them backward. She quickly jerked the stun gun out of their grip with her free hand, spun it, and drove it into the guard's exposed neck. She followed them to the ground, making sure they kept twitching and clenching like I was for several seconds. As my flesh and mods slowly returned to my control, Gloria stood over me, taking on guard after guard, bringing each one down in turn.

By the time I was able to rise to one knee, there was only one guard left standing, very near to where I'd originally seen Nox and Tazia.

"Well," Gloria said. "What are you waiting for? All of your friends have already joined the party."

The guard fidgeted, moving their weight from one foot to the other. They glanced at Gloria, then off to where Tazia had gone, then to the rest of the guards writhing or unconscious on the ground, and back toward Tazia once more. Finally, in a thin tenor, they said, "Not for a thousand more credits." And they ran away.

Gloria extended a hand to me, which I took, and she pulled me to my feet. "You okay?"

I looked at myself, flexing my hands, rolling my shoulders, twisting my neck.

"No damage," Bastion said. "Not to my chip nor any of your systems."

To Gloria, I said, "I'm all right."

Down the hall, I heard the escaping guard make an oof sound and say "Not worth it, man. Just go."

"Who?" I started to ask but then saw Ridley come around the corner, his eyes wide with surprise.

"Ridley," Gloria said. "Good to see you. Did you see a maintenance worker, short with very dark skin, and a woman?"

But something was off. Ridley didn't look like his usual jolly self. At first, I'd chalked it up to the general horribleness of the situation, but it wasn't that. Ridley reached behind his back, and I quickly assumed a defensive posture.

"Ridley," I said. "Buddy?"

The driver drew out a rail gun, a handheld model. That wasn't for stunning, it was for killing. "I'm sorry," he whispered.

"Stand down, Ridley," Gloria said. "You are not this. Your family has more honor than this. So do you. Help me stop this woman, this interloper."

Ridley shook his head. "It's you two who are being dishonorable, trying to stop the Ascension."

"She's lying to you," I said. "She's from Toinette. She's manipulating Orogen."

Ridley just shook his head and leveled the gun at us.

Chapter Thirty-Four

1 Day to Ascension

"THINK THIS THROUGH," I SAID. "This is Gloria. I'm—"

"You're a spy," Ridley shouted. "You're trying to destroy Kotega. I can't believe I drove you here, I befriended you. We all did. You played us for fools."

I held my hands up. "I don't work for Kotega, you're right."

"What are you doing?" Gloria whispered to me.

I stayed focused on Ridley, taking an easy step toward him. I saw his gun hand wobbling slightly. He wasn't used to holding a weapon. "But everything I've done has been to help Gloria. Help Kotega Systems. That woman, whatever she called herself, she's an Intel Operative from Toinette. She's twisted Orogen's mind."

"You're lying," he said.

"Not now," I said, taking another cautious step. "She's why I'm here."

"You don't even know her name. You keep dancing around it."

"I know her real name is Tazia Toinette-Intel. Josephine Toinette-Deus is one of her aliases. Orogen gave her a Kotega cover, but I don't know what it is. Do a quick search for Josephine, though, go ahead. She was quite public. Lots of pictures."

"This is a trick." Ridley was glancing between Gloria and me. He was confused. Unsure. Nervous.

"It's not. You didn't know my name, but we are friends. You're a good man, I know it. Please just look her up on your display. One picture."

Ridley swallowed hard, his eyes still dancing between Gloria and me.

"Please, Ridley," Gloria said. "One look."

Ridley gave a quick nod and said, "Ronin, image search Josephine Toinette-Deus." His eyes focused on the middle distance. In that moment, I considered attacking, using the distraction to disarm him. But this was Ridley. He was confused, not evil. Not turned. A few seconds later, his eyes went wide. He let the weapon drop and clatter to the floor. He crumpled to his knees, pressing his forehead to the floor.

"I'm so sorry, Mistress," he said, his voice shaking. "I have dishonored myself and my family. I am a fool."

In an instant, Gloria was with him, kneeling and pulling him off the floor. She wrapped him up in her arms. "It's all right, Ridley. It's all right. It was an honest mistake. You were being honorable and loyal to Kotega. I can never fault you for that."

"I'm so sorry, Mistress," he said, tears streaming down his face as he let himself be held.

"Gloria," I said, relief colliding with urgency. "My apprentice."

Gloria pulled Ridley to arm's length and looked him in the face. "I need you now, all right? So does the rest of Kotega. Security is compromised. I need you to keep them from the roof, all right?

Ridley nodded, struggling to compose himself. "Of course, Mistress. I'll do what I can."

"Not alone, he won't," a familiar voice said from the end of the hall. It was Thrace, a trickle of blood coming from a gash on his forehead. He was holding an assault rifle. Carmela was next to him, a heavy frying pan in her hand and a splatter of blood across her apron that didn't look like it came from the kitchen.

Gloria readied herself for a fight as the pair trotted toward us but soon relaxed. They weren't here to attack us. I'd never been happier to see a security guard. Or a cook.

"I don't know who infiltrated our security," Thrace said, "but when I find them, I'm going to bury them. First alarm of any kind in the household in three years, and we're betrayed by our own security." He gave a slight bow to Gloria and nodded to me. By Corto, was I glad to see him.

"I think Elise," Gloria said, gesturing to me, "is first in line to bury someone."

"Elise?" Thrace asked. Carmela's face twisted up in confusion.

"Long story," I said. "Gloria and I are headed to the roof."

"You three need to keep security off of us," Gloria said.

"Absolutely, Mistress," Thrace said, the question of my name neatly put into a box or forgotten. The guy was a professional.

We turned and resumed our chase, our duo turned into a group of five. I felt better already. We sprinted up the stairs, only to find a small group of security guards standing in front of the last stairs up to the roof. They looked downright hungry for a fight.

Fortunately, we were more than up to the task.

"Down," Thrace yelled, and Gloria and I dropped to our knees. The assault rifle barked, three bursts of five or six shots. Half the guards dropped in an instant. Then Thrace yelled, "Go!"

We engaged. Thrace used the same technique that the rest of the guards used, only he was better. He led the Siwa house guard in training drills, after all, so he wasn't just their teacher but knew their weaknesses. Ridley wasn't nearly as trained but was scrappy and his arms were long. Carmela proved just as deft with a frying pan in a fight as in the kitchen, wrecking several stun guns and cracking skulls with surprising skill. Within a few minutes, we had overwhelmed the security guards that Tazia had turned.

"Go," Thrace said between heavy breaths.

Gloria did a quick check of the three, making sure nobody was seriously hurt before we proceeded, crossing another T-junction toward the stairs.

As Gloria and I started up those final steps, though, we heard a cacophony of footsteps approaching. Thrace took aim and fired down the hallway, around the corner from where I could see. I heard bodies drop, but footsteps continued.

"I'm out," Thrace yelled, tossing the rifle over his shoulder to hang on his back and pulling out a pair of batons. The three of them were brave, but only one experienced fighter between them. If we left…

My thoughts were interrupted by the rattle of gunfire. Thrace, Ridley, and Carmela ducked. The guards out of sight hollered, their footsteps suddenly sounding random and confused. The gunfire continued until another familiar voice yelled, "And stay down!"

Gloria and I exchanged a surprised glance.

"By all the gods, am I glad to see you," Thrace said.

I looked around the corner to confirm my greatest surprise. Zhao was walking down the hallway, stepping over bodies and the few living security guards cowering and prone, their hands behind their heads. Xey were carrying an assault rifle and had two others slung over xyr back. Xey looked just as comfortable with the weapons as Thrace, too.

"How?" I started to ask but didn't know how to finish the question.

"Didn't xey tell you?" Ridley asked. "Zhao served with planetary defense for, what? Three years?"

"Five," Zhao said, handing Thrace a clip for his weapon. "Just like my mother and her father before her."

I did know that, but I still hadn't expected Zhao coming down that hallway looking like a commando. I looked xem square in the eye, waiting for xyr judgment. To my surprise, Zhao gave me a slight nod. No smile, but no sneer. No foul words. I didn't wait for more. I couldn't.

"We'll hold the stairwell, Mistress," Thrace said, loading the clip and prepping his rifle.

"I know you will," Gloria said from a few stairs up, quickly looking at each of them in turn. "I'm proud to know you all, to have you on my staff, on my side. Wish us luck."

"Luck," Zhao said.

I bowed to them, to all of them, hoping it showed them just how thankful I was to each of them.

Gloria nodded to me and said, "All right. Let's go get your apprentice."

Chapter Thirty-Five

1 Day to Ascension

WE HURRIED UP THE STAIRS, climbing nearly ten meters before we reached the door to the roof. I paused, terrified of what I was going to find on the other side of the door. I took three deep breaths to compose myself and then opened the door. I expected those throngs of people, Kotega's highest society and most prominent families screaming or cowering, Tazia's fury on full display against my apprentice. Instead, there was no one. Drinks were left half-finished on cocktail tables. Hors d'oeuvres were strewn across the rooftop. Chairs were overturned.

"What happened?" I whispered, looking around intently for any sign of Nox or Tazia.

"The evacuation," Gloria said.

"You just couldn't leave well enough alone, could you?" Tazia's voice rang out across the rooftop.

I turned and stepped around the corner to see her standing over Nox. He wasn't moving. I stared for a few moments just to make sure he was still breathing, dread gripping my heart like a vice. He was, though blood trickled from his lip and eye. I refocused on the Ghost of Toinette. I said, "You know me. Never one to just walk away."

"You could have left. Could have told your apprentice to do the same. Could have avoided all of this, but you're just too much a fool."

"Careful, meddler," Gloria said to Tazia as she stepped around from behind me. She held her sword down at her side, but I could see the relaxed readiness coursing through her body like a predator ready to pounce.

"You already lost, Gloria." Tazia pronounced her name like she was spitting poison with each syllable. "You can just go back downstairs, back to your life of vast privilege and, admittedly, far less responsibility since you won't be the next CEO."

"And lose everything I know? Every bit of culture that Kotega has built? I have no desire to follow your cockeyed religion."

Tazia shrugged. "I could care less if you follow Ibhalism. A means to an end. This city is already an illusion. Culture? Corporate identity? Lies. We're all just cogs in this machine, somehow believing that we're important, that we're all different. We're data points. If not for me, for this, even that would be lost. I'm saving all of us."

Despite my best efforts, I felt the color drain from my face. I recalled my brief time at the top of the Offworld Relay when its custodian had shown me the data flowing from our planet to the mysterious Gibbingson Holdings. Every purchase made in Jayu City broken down to demographics. Millions of citizens, each making multiple purchases each day, all of it streaming across the cosmos as information. Data points. Did Tazia know?

"People like you will always find a rationalization for their actions," Gloria said, taking a step closer to Tazia.

Tazia didn't move when she said, "You've never met anyone like me, girl. But your new friend has. Your Daeli. Xyla, isn't it? Except that's not really her name. Hasn't she—?"

"Elise has told me quite enough," Gloria said, still moving toward Tazia, flowing slowly toward her with her shoulders squared. "Enough about herself and your plans. Why don't you step away from her apprentice and give me the satisfaction of putting you on the ground?"

A flicker of surprise crossed Tazia's face, but it was quickly replaced with a sneer, and she stepped away from Nox. As Gloria brought her sword up into a defensive posture, Tazia shrugged off her cloak, revealing her modded arms, heavily built. Much more heavily than last I'd seen her. She balled up fists, and half-meter-long blades extended from her forearms. The two circled each other, each taking careful steps and never taking their eyes off one another.

When the violence started, I nearly missed it. I wasn't sure who moved first, but in a blink, blade clashed against blade, then again and again. Tazia's movements were electric, like lightning striking over and over, one blade and then the next. But Gloria flowed like water, seeming to move much slower, but catching every blow, parrying them away as her feet swept and scurried. Then Gloria shifted, spun, and counterattacked. Again, she didn't look as fast, but her blows were fierce and kept Tazia on her back foot.

I ran around the fighting to Nox, keeping one eye on the combatants as I kneeled to check on my apprentice. I found multiple cuts and bruises, already visible despite his dark skin. I reached into a small compartment on my forearm and brought out smelling salts, wafting them in front of his nose for a moment before his eyes flicked open. He breathed deep and waved an arm in front of his face, trying to banish the terrible ammonia smell.

I tossed the salts away and took hold of his wrist, gentle but firm. "Hey, hey. It's me, Nox. It's Elise. I've got you."

"How?" he muttered. "Where?"

"Still on the roof," I said and gestured toward the fight with a nod. "I had to tell Gloria more than I wanted, but it seemed to work."

Nox lifted his head, wincing in pain. Once he saw them fighting, though, his eyes grew wide. He smiled a little, which made a fresh rivulet of blood open on his lip. "She's done now. Her plan exposed, fighting the other Siwa sibling. How is she going to get out of this one?"

I gave Nox a smile back, though I didn't feel it the same way. If anyone could get out of anything, it seemed like Tazia Toinette-Intel was the one to do it.

"What is it?" Nox asked.

I didn't want to unload these thoughts on him, though. I asked, "Are you all right? Hurt beyond what I can see?"

"I'll be fine," he said. "Nothing permanent." He started to sit up but winced even harder and laid back down. "Not much use right now, though."

"Then just stay here. I'll take care of this."

Nox nodded. I stood back up. The fight was still raging, Tazia and Gloria taking turns on the offensive and neither showing signs of slowing, but I knew that couldn't last. Tazia was modded to the gills just like I was, probably more. Gloria's mods were minor, intended to make sure she wasn't given a competitive advantage. That meant she was going to tire far quicker than Tazia.

Then something dawned on me. That lack of mods also meant that Tazia had to be stronger and faster than Gloria. Train your biology all you like; you can never rise to the level of good cybernetic limbs. That meant that Tazia was holding back, playing with Gloria, wearing her down. I adjusted my grip on the sword Gloria had given me, and as soon as Tazia's back was to me, I leaped into the fray.

I brought the sword in low and fast, aiming for the side of Tazia's knee, but she side-stepped, and I nearly took out Gloria's kneecap instead. Tazia adjusted her stance, taking in both Gloria and me in her peripheral vision, fighting each of us off with one hand a piece. She was moving faster now, much faster than when she'd been fighting Gloria alone. I hated being right sometimes.

"She must have incredible neural processors," Bastion said. "Her eyes are tracking independently, her focus fully split."

I risked a glance at Tazia's eyes, and sure enough, only one eye was looking at me, the other was tracking Gloria, giving Tazia an unnatural, cross-eyed look. It made my skin crawl. I paid instantly for my change of focus, however, Tazia's arm blade throwing me off balance and swiping deeply through my left leg, the blade twanging off the metal structure below the polymer skin.

I rolled through the fall, coming up to my feet and reengaging, but I was too slow, too inexperienced. For all of Gloria's skill and training, she also seemed to be flailing against a whirling dervish of blades and fury.

"You're both outmatched," Tazia yelled, echoing my thoughts. "But this is rather fun!"

"Three cameras all just turned on," Bastion said, his voice urgent in my ear. "They're on a barely secured private network. Not Kotega security."

Though my focus was fully on Tazia, Bastion lit up the three cameras in my display, all glowing neon green. In my periphery, I saw one directly behind Tazia, one over Gloria's shoulder on the same side, and one over mine.

Turned on? By whom? Friend? Foe? Given her neural processors, was this Tazia herself, somehow manipulating things even while battling two of us?

She gave me an answer soon enough. As I swung my sword toward her face, she ducked, and my sword made contact with Gloria's. Tazia spun and rolled, engaging both of us from the other side. Gloria and I attacked, and Tazia parried both blows so that our swords struck each others' again. And she did it again. And again. If I wanted to doctor some video to make it look like I was fighting Gloria, like I was trying to kill her, it was a good way to do it.

"Disengage!" I yelled and backed three steps away.

Gloria clashed with Tazia once more, nearly losing her balance when my sword wasn't there to be led to, but then she righted herself and moved back as well. Her chest was heaving. She let the sword fall to her side in obvious exhaustion. She gave me a quizzical look but didn't keep her eyes off Tazia for long.

"She's playing us," I said. "Filming this so she can set me up later."

"Clever," Tazia said. "I already have enough, though. I'll just have to kill both of you. Don't worry, though. Kotega Systems will be left in good hands when you're gone. Orogen Siwa-Kotega, Chief Executive Officer of Kotega Systems and devout follower of Ibhalism ushering Kotega Systems into a bright new balance between fate and chaos, kneeling only to the prophets. Preserving Little Sekhmet Settlement."

"We need help," I said to Bastion, though loud enough that anyone could hear me. I didn't care where the help came from, just so long as we got it.

"Should I contact Hessod? Gustin?" Bastion asked.

"Call Huginn security for all I care," I whispered. "We have the Ghost of Toinette. She's threatening to upend the entire city. Cover be damned."

I re-engaged Tazia, firing a smoke bomb at her feet and lunging in the same breath. I didn't know the extent of her mods, but I was hoping a little smoke would make it harder for her to track me. Harder to track Gloria, who was the bigger threat.

I was wrong. Tazia caught my lunge, spun me around, and then drove a blade through my upper right arm. Too low to hit Bastion's chip, fortunately, but the stab and twist made that arm drop uselessly to my side. Then a foot hit the middle of my back and sent me sprawling away. I groaned and heard the rapid-fire clash of metal on metal. Then a scream. Gloria's scream. And Tazia's laugh.

I turned over and rose to my feet. I couldn't see anything through the smoke. "Thermals," I said to Bastion. "And how bad is the arm?"

My vision instantly changed from regular sight to a spectrum of colors representing gradients of hot and cold. Tazia was still standing, her biological parts a warm orange, most of her modded limbs a cooler green, though her joints were nearly red from effort. Laying on the ground was Gloria, mostly orange with only minor fluctuations in color.

"The arm is irreparable," Bastion said.

"Palm tasers still primed on the left hand?"

"Of course, though you only have enough charge for two hits."

I picked up the sword from the ground. My right hand had dropped it when it fell dead. "Is this conductive?"

My vision briefly switched to something else, something I didn't know how to read. It was a different gradient of colors, certainly not based on heat. Then the thermals came back a moment later.

"It is, yes. Why?"

"I need you to time the taser discharge. Fire it when I make contact, even if it's with her blades."

"Clever, indeed," Bastion said. "Understood."

I ran back into the fray, roaring like a beast. I wanted her to hear me, to turn her attention from Gloria. I fired two more smoke bombs right at Tazia's chest as I ran, just to maybe put her off balance, give me any advantage. She swatted them away, my thermal barely keeping up with the motion. Once I was close enough, I jabbed with the sword, a blow better to block or parry than dodge.

Her bladed arm swept up to meet the sword, and Bastion did as he was told. Tazia diverted the blow, but the moment our blades touched, my taser fired. Tazia's arm jerked away, and she rocked back a few steps, snarling.

"Enough of this!" she bellowed.

I took the best defensive stance that I could with one arm, but it did me no good. She raised her left arm, palm open toward me even though she was two meters away. Then my vision turned to static, and I was on my back. Something had hit me in the face. I dropped the sword and reached up to find some sort of goo there.

"What is it?" I yelled, grateful the goo hadn't covered my mouth.

"Unknown," Bastion said. "Hold your palm in front of your face. Stop touching it. This would be so much easier if you would just install my chip!"

My heart was rattling in my chest, my breaths coming fast and uncontrollably. I was fighting down panic at my newfound blindness and losing, but I did as Bastion asked. I heard a hiss, and my vision started to come back, groups of pixels materializing like spots.

"Charged conductive gel," Bastion said. "Thank goodness."

"On my face?" Charged conductive gel had many industrial applications, none of them relevant to my job, but I'd never heard of it used as a weapon. I was going to have to remember that.

"It's brilliant," Bastion said. "Temporary interference with any electronics it comes in contact with. And when fired as a projectile, it has sufficient enough mass to send an opponent toppling. Good thing you had a spray of adhesive dissolver in your wrist."

"Good thing." It was a basic tool, and one I was suddenly glad that I'd included in these limbs. I sat up, my normal vision slowly returning through the haze of evaporating gel. But now, I couldn't see Gloria. I didn't hear any fighting. Then the wind was picking up, the rain around the tent almost going sideways for a moment. The smoke wouldn't last long. I wasn't sure if that was a good or bad thing, but I got to my feet just the same.

"One more time," I said. "The taser and the sword."

"It did very little last time," Bastion said.

"I have a different follow-up this round." I started running again, sprinting a few meters and yelling again.

"Foolish woman," Tazia said through the smoke. I was just beginning to see her outline as I approached, swinging the sword. This time, she dodged, and a foot caught my shin. I rolled, dropping the sword and grabbing my left shoulder as I popped up. I pulled at the joint, and it came a way, a small whine emanating from the knockout grenade.

I spun and tossed it at Tazia's feet, holding my breath. There was no point, of course, the knockout grenade was a combination of gas, sonics, and EMP designed to knock out anyone in the vicinity. Habit made me hold my breath against at least one part of it.

But the grenade didn't detonate, not there, at least. Tazia was just too good. The smoke was clearing, and I was able to barely see Tazia easily swing one of those blades, knocking the grenade off of the roof before it even hit the ground. It sailed over Nox's prone form and into the Kotega night. The boom came a moment later, distant and muffled by the rain.

I fell to one knee, out of tricks. Gloria came into view, the smoke almost gone, and I discovered what Tazia had done. Gloria was bleeding from multiple cuts on her face and chest. Her left hand was gone, though the stump wasn't bleeding. At least some of her was modded, even if it was difficult to tell outwardly. She was barely holding her sword with her right hand. She was shaking all over.

Tazia bent down, picking up my discarded sword, and the Ghost of Toinette smiled in a way that drained all of the light from the world. "Thanks," she said. "She can't die by my blade, after all."

Her eyes still trained on me, that terrible smile plastered in place, Tazia held the sword high aloft and then brought it down with all possible speed. I closed my eyes. I couldn't watch, couldn't bear witness to Gloria's death. I awaited the sickening sound of a metal sword smashing and slicing through flesh and bone, holding my breath.

But that wasn't the sound that rang out. Metal clanged on wood, a sharp contrast to the metal-on-metal clangs of before. I opened my eyes, but it wasn't Gloria who had caught the blow. Tenisha Siwa-Kotega, matriarch of the family and CEO of Kotega Systems, was standing over her daughter. She was holding a still-sheathed sword over Gloria's face, a shield against

Tazia's blow. With a flick of her wrist, tossed aside Tazia's stolen sword and shoved the Ghost back in one motion.

"I don't know who you are," Tenisha said. "But you will not lay a hand on my child."

Chapter Thirty-Six

1 Day to Ascension

"MOTHER, STOP!" OROGEN YELLED, BREATHLESS as he burst out of the stairwell onto the roof, desperate to catch Tenisha.

Tazia had stood upright, genuine surprise on her face for a few full seconds before she put her mask back in place. Tenisha held her sword, scabbard still on, level and aimed at Tazia's face.

"Who are you?" Tenisha said.

"Ask your boy," Tazia purred.

"I'm asking you."

"Mother," Orogen said. "This is Sana, my friend. My advisor."

"Anyone who would try to murder your sister," Tenisha said without taking her eyes off Tazia, "is not your friend."

Tazia took a step backward and tossed a glance at me, then another at Nox. She was surrounded, though neither I nor Nox posed any real threat, not compared to Tenisha. I could see the wheels turning, Tazia trying to figure out her next move. She wanted Orogen to succeed as CEO. Souring him in front of the current CEO would have the opposite effect.

"I just foiled an assassination attempt," Tazia said. "The alarms throughout the residence, the evacuation of the roof, and your daughter's unexpected illness just before, doesn't any of that seem a bit convenient?"

Tenisha glanced down at Gloria, who was struggling to sit up, but the CEO's sword didn't waver. She held it steady and level.

"She lies," Gloria croaked.

Tenisha's eyes fixed back on Tazia. "My daughter says you lie. What proof do you have that you tell the truth?"

"I can vouch for her," Orogen said, staying a full meter behind his mother, his wide, panicked eyes dashing back and forth between Tazia and Tenisha. "She has been aiding me, watching my back for months. I brought her in because I suspected something like this would occur."

Tenisha ignored him. "Gloria, why are your Daeli and this maintenance worker also bloodied? Where is your security detail?"

Gloria opened her mouth, but I could see panic plain on her face. The answer was long, complex, and the political ramifications were even more complex.

"My name is Elise Corto-Intel," I said, saving Gloria the trouble. I pointed at Tazia. "I'm an Intel Operative, and I'm here to stop this woman."

Orogen's jaw dropped. Tenisha's face twisted in surprise, though she didn't take her eyes off Tazia.

I said, "Her name is Tazia Toinette-Intel, and she's been working to subvert Kotega Sys—"

I was cut short by a snarl and Tazia lunging toward me with both blades, swallowing the distance between us in three strides. I dived out of the way but felt sharp pressure from my left leg, my dive stopped short, and I hit the ground hard. I looked down to see one of her blades driven through my leg just below the knee, alarms flashed on my display, and then Tazia pulled me toward her, her other blade drawing back.

My sword was gone. I clawed at the ground and swung at any part of Tazia that I could reach, but it was no use. I threw my forearms in front of my face and neck, bracing, but another blade flashed in, diverting Tazia's blow.

Then several things happened at once. A leg swept Tazia's, putting her on her back. As her arm flew up, I was yanked off the ground, that blade still running through my shin. With a sharp clang, I fell to the ground, alarms still flashing on my display. I rolled away from Tazia, from the flailing of limbs and blades. Once I was two meters away, I saw that one of Tazia's blades had broken off in me. I grabbed it and pulled it out. Then I took in the scene.

Tenisha had unsheathed her sword and engaged Tazia. Tazia was fast, her neural processors allowing her to use her limbs and eyes independently. I had no idea what mods Tenisha had, but since she was a Siwa, they were certainly minimal. Tenisha had training though, decades of the best training, and she was making Tazia look as foolish as Tazia had made me look.

Tenisha kept perfect form, her body sideways, sword at the ready, her other hand out and holding the scabbard as balance. She hopped easily to dodge blows, parried with minimal effort, and occasionally jabbed quickly, piercing flesh or mods with each tiny movement. She wasn't on the attack, however. She was letting Tazia lash out and pay each time she overextended. Finally, Tazia screamed and flew at what she thought was an opening. She was wrong. Tenisha moved like a refined version of Gloria, and then her sword spun, arcing several times as she made a slow turn.

Tazia stumbled, her weight unbalanced. The arm with the broken blade fell uselessly to her side, dark coolant flooding down from two gaping wounds. The other arm fell off entirely just below the shoulder. Tazia spun, looking back and forth at both arms in bewilderment. Before she had a chance to say anything, however, Tenisha approached and made one fast swipe at the Ghost of Toinette. Coolant gushed from both of her thighs. She fell back on her rump.

Tenisha swiped the sword hard down and to her side, flinging off drops of coolant and maybe some blood. She resheathed her sword and said, "Judging by your actions, it would seem our Corto infiltrator hit close to the truth. How close, I wonder?"

"Mother, please," Orogen said. He hadn't moved, and he looked terrified. Terrified of what? His mother or Tazia? Or of his future falling apart? Had he been duped, too?

"You will remain silent until I ask you to speak," Tenisha said.

"Mother," Gloria said with a strain.

Tenisha softened like she suddenly remembered Gloria was there. "Are you all right? Do you need a medic?"

Gloria shook her head before she said, "Please listen to Elise. I think she's telling the truth, that she knows what's going on."

"You think?" Tenisha said.

"She saved me from poison, then fought beside me. I haven't had the chance to confirm anything, but her story makes sense."

Tenisha turned to me. "Explain this, then."

A lump rose in my throat. This woman, this CEO, who was skilled enough to make the Ghost of Toinette look like a child with a toy sword, had turned her gaze on me. She wanted the truth. I was saved by Orogen who took that moment, the moment his mother was looking at me and away from him, to turn and run.

I don't know if it was his clumsy and loud footsteps or my own gaze moving to him, but Tenisha turned. Her shoulders fell as she saw him, then she said, "Security, full lockdown, authorization Tenisha one one Gloria seven Orogen."

I heard no response, but there were either security forces in the residence still loyal to Tenisha and the Siwa family or some very clever automated system in place. SIWA NETWORK FAILURE suddenly lit up on my display.

"Oh…" Bastion said, his voice cutting out. "I…she…"

Right. He'd been using a tunnel into the household network. He was probably struggling to connect via my comms array.

Orogen pounded the call button for the elevator, but the button only blinked red. He looked back, his eyes wide, and then ran to the nearest stairwell, but the door didn't open. The doorknob wouldn't yield.

"Don't do this," Tazia said. For the first time since I'd known her, she sounded frail. Weak. "The wheels are in motion. Just let them spin."

"What wheels?" Tenisha said, still staring at her worthless son.

"The wheels to save this city. This entire planet."

"You're mad. How? How did all this happen?"

Tazia sneered at the CEO but didn't say anything.

"Orogen has converted to Ibhalism," I said. "This woman was posing as an evangelist in order to do it, to convert him or someone like him."

Tenisha looked at me, her face unreadable. She set her jaw and said, "From the beginning."

I told the story from the first time I'd run into Tazia in the Toinette borough, back when I only knew her as Josephine. I laid out her involvement in the tournament, helping him win, and why I was here with my apprentice to stop her. Throughout, Tenisha kept her face impassive, moving her gaze between all of us in turn as the story moved. As I got to the present, to the twists and turns of tonight, the CEO held up a hand.

She looked at Tazia and said, "Why Orogen? Why my son?"

Tazia stayed silent. As I'd told my story, Orogen had drawn closer, listening intently himself. Disbelief was plain on his face. I was right. He'd been fooled by Tazia, too. He had converted to Ibhalism with his whole heart, had believed that Tazia was named Josephine and was his advisor. His friend. No one likes finding out that they've been played for a fool.

"Mother," he whispered. "I'm so sorry."

Tenisha held up a hand again. She turned to Nox, who was sitting next to me now. "And you are who she says?"

Nox nodded. "Nox Corto-Intel. Apprentice."

Tenisha looked at Gloria. "And you vouch for this story?"

"As much as I can," Gloria said. "Elise saved me. Fought beside me."

Tenisha sighed. "Political untangling aside, I can confirm their identities later. The story will be harder, but…" She looked at Tazia now, unbridled contempt plain on her face. "This one's aggression makes one thing undeniable: my son let a viper into our home. You nearly killed my daughter. You poisoned my son's mind. You even raised a hand to me."

"You're too late," Tazia said again with a sneer.

"Too late?" Tenisha said. "Why? Because I have announced that Orogen will be the next CEO? Because you tricked him into following the Toinette faith?" Tenisha knelt down to eye level with Tazia, though kept out of reach. "I am still CEO of Kotega Systems. The next CEO is who I say it is. So long as I sit in that seat, I can change who follows."

"Mother?" Orogen said, stepping closer to her.

"You would doom us all," Tazia hissed. She'd been saying things like that. I'd thought they were the strange, sociopathic justifications of a madwoman. Now, though, I had to wonder what she meant.

"Doom us how?" Tenisha asked.

Tazia grinned. "You know exactly how."

Tenisha's eyes narrowed. "This isn't some standard Toinette Intel operation. Your VP wouldn't dare. Who do you work for?"

I didn't wait for Tazia to not answer that question. I said, "She's working for Pablo Toinette. Directly. I saw them talking over holo. The other Toinette CEO is out of the loop."

Tazia's eyes went wide. Tenisha's head whipped back to her, and she said, "The Cabal…"

Cabal? What cabal? What did that mean?

"At least someone is trying to save us," Tazia said, "trying to stop them from ending this doomed experiment."

"Be silent," Tenisha whispered, though I could just barely hear her.

"You know what's coming, what's ending. It's only a matter of time before Gibb—"

Tazia didn't get to finish, though. Tenisha brought her sword up and slammed the butt of the hilt squarely into Tazia's forehead, knocking her out cold. She slumped sideways and fell fully to the ground.

But Tazia was about to say Gibbingson Holdings, I knew it. That name kept popping up. And Tenisha knew. She heard what I did and stopped it.

Tenisha's shoulders fell. She made the saddest sound that I'd ever heard, somewhere between a sigh and a groan. She walked over to Gloria, all of the earlier grace and elegance gone from her. She looked drained of life. She gently handed her sword to Gloria before turning to Orogen.

"I wasn't supposed to be CEO, you know," she said. "My brother was older, which still mattered a little back then. He was also my father's favorite. My father was the CEO for four decades. Did marvelous things for Kotega Systems. This residence, in fact, was his idea. He did much of the design and oversaw the construction."

"Warren Siwa-Kotega," Bastion said in my ear. "The second-longest tenured CEO in Kotega history. The company was floundering before he took over and was posting record profitability and growth by the time he stepped aside."

"What are you going to do, Mother?" Orogen croaked.

Tenisha continued. "My brother, Lahyard, had all the best tutors, had successfully guided the acquisition of an off-world processor company to bolster our Neuro division, and had made a great case to be the next CEO. I, on the other hand, didn't really want the job.

"Rather different from you and your sister, I think. We had two other siblings, as well. The youngest, your aunt Patrice, wanted to be CEO but was far too young to be in the running. Your uncle Lucas and I, on the other hand, had different aims. Lucas always wanted to be a musician, a dream that he made real."

"Lucas Siwa-Kotega is about to retire from the Kotega Philharmonic," Bastion said. "He's been principal violinist for over 15 years."

"I wanted to be an actor," Tenisha said. "I wanted to grace the stages and the streams. I'd been taking acting classes since I was four. I did well in my studies, of course. And I'd guided our Security division well for a time, but leadership didn't call to me the way it called to Lahyard. He wanted it, needed it like the chair was made for him."

Tenisha glanced down and away. She took a deep breath before she continued. "He wanted it too much. That's always the problem with power. Those who want it should not have it. But often, those who don't want it don't know how to wield it, don't understand the pressures that come with it."

She looked off into the distance as she spoke. "Lahyard had been making backchannel deals with Nexus Neuronics. He'd been trading our cybernetics tech for their neuro tech, artificially inflating the division's advances. He'd made the acquisition to cover the sudden and otherwise inexplicable technological advances.

"But he didn't cover his tracks well enough. Honor and ambition rarely mix well, and when someone gets so far in front of their own feet because of their ambition, they forget how powerful honor can be in our company. Lahyard, like some before him, assumed that everyone around him was as ambitious as he, that they craved success and advancement to the detriment of all other things. Like he did. He was wrong. Three neuro engineers blew the whistle on him."

"I've never heard this before," Orogen said.

Gloria looked just as confused as her brother.

"Neither of you have," Tenisha said. "Very few in Kotega Systems have. Father made sure of that. If it had become public, the dishonor wouldn't have just ruined Lahyard but tainted the family. We might not have been able to hold onto the CEO's seat in the face of that."

After a long silence, Orogen asked, "What happened?"

Tenisha looked at her son, her gaze unwavering. "Lahyard was exiled. There was a very public display, which you two have seen recordings of, of Lahyard announcing that he was taking a different path. My place in the succession was announced with all possible fanfare. And Lahyard left."

"Where did he go?" Gloria asked.

"I don't know," Tenisha said. "He was quietly discommended. Maybe he went to another company, to The Mist, or to a different planet. We never spoke of him publicly again. His dishonor was too great. We'd avoided the damage, and that was enough."

"They buried this well," Bastion said. "I cannot find a record of Lahyard after that press conference. Wherever he went, Kotega Systems buried it. He must have changed his name, maybe even changed his face."

Tenisha was staring at Orogen now, her face expectant and sad at the same time. Several minutes went by before the full meaning of Tenisha's story washed over Orogen. His eyebrows shot up and then his entire face fell.

"You can't mean…" he said.

Tenisha nodded and said nothing. I couldn't imagine being in her shoes, banishing her son over a mistake. He'd been tricked by the Ghost of Toinette, the best there was. There was no shame in that. But in Kotega, where honor meant so much…

"No," he said and started pacing. "I can't. I won't just vanish. I won't be tossed to The Mist or shipped off to some other company or world. This is my home. These are my people. I am their shepherd. I might even be a prophet!"

"Oh, Orogen," Gloria said, as quiet as she was sad.

"There has to be another way," Orogen said. "I have not dishonored myself or our family. I have done everything you've asked of me, everything demanded of me. Finding religion, finding true faith is not a dishonor."

Tenisha sighed. "You brought a spy into our home. There is no dishonor in finding faith, even faith outside of Kotega. There is dishonor in falling prey to manipulation, to becoming a pawn for a rival company. You are not fit to lead this company or this family. And if this gets out to the wider public, your dishonor will ruin us."

Orogen stopped pacing. He took a wide stance and stared at his mother. "This is my home. I'm not going into exile."

"Brother," Gloria said, her voice a plea. A tear slid down her cheek.

"Don't you act like this isn't exactly what you wanted!" Orogen spat at Gloria. "All you've ever wanted was the CEO seat. I earned it. I did everything for it. You're getting it by default."

The color drained from Gloria's face. I opened my mouth to say something, to defend Gloria. She'd also done everything for it, had earned it just as much as Orogen. But this was a family issue, a sensitive one that neither Nox nor I had any business really being privy to, but here we were. My voice would not be welcome.

The three Siwas were silent for a while. Tears were streaking Gloria's face. Orogen was pacing again, furious and thinking his way through it. Tenisha stood passively, watching her son. Waiting. Finally, Orogen stopped in front of his mother again.

"There has to be another way," he said. The fire was gone from his voice. It sounded like begging.

Tenisha darkened, looking sadder than before. "I know of only one other way. An older way."

Orogen shot a look at Gloria. Gloria's eyes fell to her mother's sword, cradled against her chest. Her face crumbled then, and she hugged the sword close, as if trying to keep it from entering the conversation.

"No…" I whispered to myself. I heard Nox gasp.

"I don't understand," Bastion said. I couldn't bring myself to explain it. He would surely understand soon enough.

Tenisha walked over to Gloria and grabbed her sword. Gloria held fast, though it didn't look like a conscious effort, not a real resistance to her mother, but only to what taking that sword meant. Tenisha pulled the sword from its scabbard, leaving the ornate wood firmly in Gloria's grasp. Gloria's mouth was tight, tears still streaming as she gently shook her head, begging for another way.

Tenisha turned back to Orogen and carefully took the three steps to him. She held out the sword, hilt-first, no malice or aggression in her stance or face. She looked distraught but determined. Orogen took a step back from his mother. She closed the distance with him. He took a step back again, shaking his head. Tenisha advanced again.

"I can't. I won't," Orogen said, his voice shaking. "This is ridiculous. You can't expect me to take that sword. This isn't the dark ages."

"The blade or exile," Tenisha said. For the first time, I heard a tremor in her voice.

Orogen turned away from his mother, and I saw tears streaming down his face. He suddenly looked so much like his sister. Those same eyes, glistening. My heart went out to him. It was an impossible decision, an unfair one. No one in Corto Corporation would ever be made to choose between death or exile. But this wasn't Corto. I looked away. His tears weren't mine to witness. I focused instead on Gloria, watching from several meters away. I wanted to hold her, to tell her everything would be all right.

Then her eyes suddenly went wide. She dropped the scabbard with a dull thud and brought a hand to her mouth. She screamed through it. I turned back to Orogen just in time to see a dozen centimeters of Tenisha's sword sticking out of his chest. He was looking down at it, staring in disbelief, like he didn't understand what he was seeing. Then Tenisha quickly pulled the blade back, flicking her son's blood from it in one fluid motion.

Tears were gathered in the eyes of all three Siwas now. Orogen fell to his knees. Then he fell forward, his eyes still open as he breathed his last.

"I'm so sorry, my son," Tenisha whispered. Her hands were shaking. Her eyes were wet.

I looked down at Nox, who was staring at the scene. I gently placed my hand on his elbow and turned him away. We looked off into the Kotega night, letting the remaining Siwas grieve without our prying eyes.

"What now?" Nox asked in a low voice.

"I don't know," I said. I hadn't thought that far ahead. Tazia's threat was gone, but our covers were blown, and we were in the heart of the Kotega borough. We'd also been privilege to not one, but two major secrets of the

Siwa family. As battered and far from home as we were, I didn't see a good way to escape.

We remained there in silence, the night filled with Gloria's wailing and the soft patter of rain on the tent and roof.

"Jump?" Nox said.

"Do you have the tools to do that? Because I don't. Plus, my limbs are half dead."

Nox shook his head.

"I don't see a viable escape route for you, either," Bastion said. "Not with your current tools and the damage that both of you have sustained."

"I think we're at the mercy of Tenisha and Gloria," I said.

After several minutes, Gloria calmed. She was speaking to her mother though I couldn't make out the words. I could have dialed up the sensitivity of my aural mods but decided against it. Gloria had lost her brother. Tenisha had done the unthinkable, killing her son. Whatever words they needed to keep from Nox and me, they deserved to keep private.

"Elise," Tenisha finally said. "And…Nox, was it?"

We both turned around to face the surviving Siwas. "Yes," he said.

Tenisha took a deep breath, looking over both of us before turning her gaze to Tazia. "This one is going to be thrown into the deepest, darkest hole we have. And let me assure you, that is a very dark and deep hole. People will forget her name, forget that she existed. Toinette will never know what she did here, only that she failed. And only if they ask."

"She'd probably prefer death," I said.

"Maybe, but no. There would be some honor in that, some measure of sacrifice. I won't grant her that. She led my son down a path to dishonor. His blood is on my hands, and that is because of her. I will ensure that she lives a long and miserable life."

"And Pablo Toinette?" I asked.

Tenisha turned back to me and arched one eyebrow. "There will be a discussion. And that is information you should not share, either of you. It's dangerous information to know."

"Danger from you?"

Tenisha smiled, but it wasn't a happy smile. "No, not from me. The

Cabal…it's my name for them, for forces working against the entire city. They're dangerous, more dangerous than this sad woman who tricked my son."

The Cabal. Forces. Forces that crossed the five companies, I would bet. And they were connected to this mysterious Gibbingson Holdings. Tenisha had the information I was seeking. I had to wonder if all of the CEOs did, if Gloria soon would.

"As for you two," Tenisha continued, looking at Nox and me with an inscrutable look.

My heart dropped. It was in her power to put Nox and me in that same deep, dark hole. Tenisha glanced back at Gloria, nodded, and looked at me again. She said, "I leave that in the hands of the next Chief Executive Officer of Kotega Systems."

My relief was palpable. It wasn't a guarantee of freedom, but I was certainly less afraid of Gloria's judgment than Tenisha's.

"On a personal note, thank you," Tenisha said. "Whatever drove you to infiltrate my company and my home, you brought all of this to light. Saved Gloria's life, from what I understand. I cannot say that I'm happy with any of this," she looked at Orogen's body, her face hardening. "But even worse things would have occurred if not for you."

Then, Tenisha turned away from us and strode over to Tazia, her lips moving, talking to someone on her communications implants. Gloria stood, her makeup a wreck from tears as she limped over to me.

"I'm so sorry," I said once she was close.

Gloria's response was a nonverbal war of emotions. She set those eyes on me, tears still threatening to brim over. One side of her mouth quirked up like a smile, but then it all fell apart to more sadness. "My brother was a fool," she said. "But he was still my brother. I never wanted this."

"I know," I said.

"As for the two of you," she said. "We need to talk."

Chapter Thirty-Seven

IT WAS NICE TO HAVE one last ride in Gloria's limo and only barely because of how comfortable it was compared to a Stryder. The fact that I wasn't on my way to the deepest, darkest hole in Kotega was highest on the list of reasons it was nice. And Nox was next to me for the ride, gliding comfortably back to the Corto Corporations borough after some mild medical treatment.

"Looks like you get the big chair after all," I said, trying to lighten the mood. I realized too late that was the wrong thing to say. "I'm sorry, so sorry it ended like this."

Gloria looked back briefly at her fallen brother. "When we were kids. I must have been eight or nine, maybe. We would play up here. He liked to pretend he was one of you, an Intel Operative. He thought it was all sneaking into buildings, knocking out security guards, and making elaborate escapes, usually involving helicopters."

"Helicopters?" I said.

She chuckled. "Yeah, like on the old streams. Can you imagine? Neither of us had ever seen a helicopter in real life. I think there's one in a museum in Nexus, but he was convinced that was how Intel Operatives got around. I was never allowed to be one, of course. I was his analyst. Or once he was pretending to be on the job, I had to play all of the security guards that he would beat up. He didn't actually hurt me. He was so gentle back then. Back before either of us thought about what being the CEO means, what honor really means to a family like ours. I miss that little boy most of all."

"It's not fair," I said. "The weight of an entire company, an entire culture on your shoulders. No family should have to bear that much of a burden."

"And yet, we do," she said. "I should have expected this, for Mother to invoke the old ways. We haven't needed them for a long time, but we were taught them. Taught our history. Most of it. Orogen didn't leave her with much choice."

"There's always a choice," Nox said with unexpected venom.

Gloria gave him a hard look. "That's easy coming from Corto. Do you even know who your grandparents or great-grandparents were? How far can you trace back your lineage? How little does it mean to you?"

I placed a gentle hand on Gloria's wrist and a firmer hand on Nox's chest. They both backed off. "It feels extreme to us," I said to Gloria. "But I get it. As much as I can, at least." I then gave Nox a hard look.

He looked at his feet and said, "I'm sorry for your loss."

"It would seem," I said to Gloria again. "We're at your mercy."

"My first real test," she said. "And I have to do it before our security forces arrive to take Tazia away and clean up this mess."

"We won't go quietly," Nox said. "If that makes any difference."

We were just leaving the Kotega Systems borough, nothing changing apart from the faces on the ads that covered the buildings. Same products. Same slogans. Kotega faces changed to Toinette faces. Next would be Huginn, and finally Corto. I wished the limo was just flying over Drakon Bay, a more direct route. But Ridley was keeping to established traffic lanes. Nothing to draw attention.

"What are you thinking about?" Nox asked.

"Hmm?"

"You look like you're a light year away."

I smiled and looked out the window. "Did you make any friends in Kotega? Any real connections?"

"Me? No. Not my type of people. No ambition, you know? I worked with a dozen people, all older than me, and none of them could even dream of a bigger life. They worked for the Siwas, for Corto's sake. They saw the height of ambition every day but were perfectly happy to come to work, clean toilets or fix stuff, and then go home and watch their streams. Every day."

"Not quite the thrill of jumping off buildings, is it?"

"Or pretending to be someone else for a while?" Nox said. His voice had softened.

I looked at him, and he gave me a commiserating smile. He'd pretended to be someone else, too, of course, but he knew. I smiled back at him, a sad smile, and then looked back out the window.

"You miss her already," Nox said. "Don't you?"

Gloria smiled wryly and said, "I need your word that everything that happened here won't be getting out to the general public, particularly the public in Kotega."

"I understand," I said. "And you have it."

"I need both of your words." She looked at Nox now. "It would ruin everything, make this all for nothing."

"I get it," Nox said. "My word, too."

Gloria looked back and forth between us as though considering our answers before she nodded, her face still somber, and said, "Then you're both leaving. I'll have Ridley fly you to the Corto borough, the first landing pad that he sees. You're on your own from there."

"Forgiving Ridley?" I asked.

"Not yet," she said with a smirk. "But I trust him to drive you."

"Thank you," I said, unable to contain the smile that spread across my face. Nox did the same.

"Can we talk?" Gloria asked, nodding toward the edge of the roof. I nodded and followed her away from Nox, both of us limping. Once we were a few meters away, she reached down and took my left hand, the one that still worked.

"Gloria..." I said, hoping I could head off whatever she had to say. Keep her from talking about the kiss or feelings or...

"Let me say this, please."

I should have just walked away, but I nodded. I let her take my hand and lead me away from Nox. She stopped, still holding my fingers. She said, "You don't have to go. I don't know your life back in Corto. You have your apprentice, family, certainly some other people who need you, who would miss you. I get it. If you stayed, though…if you stayed here with me…"

I was shaking my head already. I didn't want to hear more. I didn't want to let that fantasy play out in either of our heads. "I can't," I said.

"Can't? Or won't?"

I looked her in the eyes. I knew what she was really asking. Was I unable to stay here or was I choosing to go home, choosing to not be with her? I kept my gaze as neutral as possible before I said, "Both. I care about you. I want all the best for you. And I'm going home. I have a life there, people that I love. People that I choose. I'm sorry."

It was hard to tell if newfound sorrow washed over her. Maybe that was just me inflating my importance in her life. She was so sad already over the loss of her brother, I think my rejection was just a pebble perched on a mountain. She slowly nodded and let go of my hand.

"I'm here," I said to Nox. "That should be enough What did she say to you?"

He smiled in a way that made me wonder if he was blushing. I envied the darkness of his skin in that regard. His face would never announce to the world when he was embarrassed. He said, "She just told me to look out for you, and…"

"And?"

"Nothing."

"What?"

Nox sighed. "To make sure you stay away."

"Oh." Stay away. Like twin daggers aimed right at my heart, twisting with each syllable.

"I don't think it's for the reason you think, though. I don't know much about that stuff, but I think…I'm not sure she'd be able to keep to her word if you showed up again. To keep to our bargain. Me? No problem. You…?"

"Neither of you can come back here, though," Gloria said. "I don't just mean the residence. It'll be hard enough to explain the two of you

disappearing to the rest of the household staff, the ones who are loyal to us."

"I understand," Nox said.

Gloria looked at me. Those eyes again. Those blasted eyes. Nox really didn't get it.

"That's the bargain we're making," Gloria said. She'd rolled her shoulders back and taken the distinct thunder of a CEO. "I let you leave. You say nothing to anyone of what happened here. And neither of you ever returns to the Kotega Systems borough. I'll send a communication to your CEO myself insisting on it. Whatever the job, they cannot send either of you. If you're caught here, you'll join Tazia."

"Agreed," I said.

"Agreed," Nox echoed.

"You might be the luckiest woman alive," Bastion said.

I looked out the window again. We'd made that bargain, and I'd done so in good faith. I needed to leave Kotega and Gloria behind just as much as she needed me to leave. More. I had Quynn. Gloria would find someone. Someone better. I had no doubt of that.

"Hey," Nox said.

I focused on him, giving him a warning look to not push me on this.

"I'm glad you're here. I'm glad you chose Corto. I know I'm not at the top of your priority list, but you're my mentor. I'm glad you're still my mentor, Star Girl."

"Me too," I said.

"Me three," Bastion said, breaking his long silence. He hadn't said anything since we'd been on the roof of the Siwa residence.

Ridley dropped us at the first landing pad he spotted in Corto Corporation, just like Gloria had promised. He never lowered the partition or said a word to either of us. As soon as we were out of the limo, the door closed and the sleek, black vehicle quietly rose and sped off back toward Kotega.

"Smells like home," Nox said.

I took a deep breath. We were both several kilometers from our apartments, both barely outside of Huginn Industries and much closer to the salt smell of the bay than where we lived, but he was right. There was a coppery smell to the air mixed with that saltwater breeze. The rain was still coming down, but it felt different somehow. It felt like home.

"Go home, apprentice," I said without a hint of an order in my voice. "I plan to enjoy being in my own bed for a while. You should do the same."

Nox gave me a strange smile before he nodded and strode off toward a Stryder that was landing on the other end of the landing pad. I watched him take off and go. Standing on that landing pad, the sky finally starting to clear, the events of the last month came over me in waves.

"Bastion?" I said.

"Yes?"

"Ridley. Thrace. Carmela. Zhao. We left them to hold the stairwell, to watch our backs. Are they-?"

"They're fine," Bastion said. Carmela and Ridley were treated for minor injuries at a clinic. Everyone else is fine."

That was a small relief. I asked, "Do you think they'll hate me?"

Bastion was silent for a long time before he said, "Maybe a little. But only for a while. You saved their culture. This city. They'll know that eventually."

Or they wouldn't. I thought it but didn't say it. Sometimes that was the job, to do something daring while the entire city sleeps in their beds, unaware.

Then a few minutes later, my own Stryder arrived.

#   #   #

When I was a teenager, I landed an ensemble role in a musical that ran for three full months. I'm pretty sure my mom pulled some strings to get me the part. I wasn't a very good singer and had no ambitions for the stage. I think she was trying to keep me from jumping off buildings with my friends. We see how well that worked in the long run.

Anyway, I wound up loving it more than I thought I would. I made some great friends, and that theater started to feel like home after a month of rehearsals and three months of performances.

Along came closing night. My mom had cried when she dropped me off. Everyone was acting really weird, hugging longer than normal, talking like we were never going to see each other again, and generally being way too emotional. And these were a bunch of actors who ran pretty hot emotionally anyway.

I remembered standing backstage, getting ready to go on with the rest of the ensemble. After three months, it all felt perfectly normal. And yet, it was closing night, making everything feel strange, foreign, and final. It was that juxtaposition that finally brought tears to my eyes. The mundane and the extraordinary happening at the same time was just too much for me.

That's what it felt like walking into my building, riding the elevator, and walking the dozen or so meters to my front door. I realized rather late that I should have texted or called Quynn to let them know I was coming home, but I'd been distracted. Guilty that my thoughts had been more on Gloria than Quynn.

Before I could put a hand on the door to the apartment, Bastion said, "You have an email from Gustin."

"What does it say?" I asked.

"Better you read it yourself, I think."

That sounded ominous. "Okay. Show me."

Elise,

Welcome home. Tenisha Siwa Kotega just announced that Gloria will be the next CEO of Kotega. Orogen has "taken to temple," whatever that means. I can't wait to hear the story of how it happened. Debrief tomorrow, 06:00.

Good news and bad news. Bad news first: you'll no longer be reporting to me soon. But that's tied to the good news. The CoC doesn't report to someone like me, after all.

Great work.

Gustin

CoC. The Cloak of Corto. I hadn't even thought about that for so long. That was going to be me. I was succeeding my mentor, Solomon, as the next Cloak. It was something I'd dreamed of for over a decade, but it tasted sour right now. Maybe it would sweeten over time, but right now, it was just too much. I took a deep breath, put a smile on my face, and opened the door.

I expected to see Quynn home. It was almost 19:00, so they should have been settled onto the couch watching a stream or nestled at their gaming station, immersed in some video game or another. A normal evening. Quynn was there, sure enough, but I'd forgotten that I'd also sent Valdo and his family here. It took me a few breathless moments to compute that, to see Valdo, our father, and his mother sitting on our couch, watching the news with Quynn.

Then someone else came into the room from the kitchen, someone who rarely came over and really, really shouldn't be there at that moment.

"Elise Corto-Intel," my mom said, spitting every syllable of my full name at me. "So good of you to finally join us. Please, come in. I came over to see how Quynn was doing, to check in on them since you were off on business. What do I find? Him. HIM! The one person on this entire planet that I should never have to see in my life, and he's here in your living room. What in the name of Corto were you thinking?"

Chapter Thirty-Eight

I STOOD THERE WITH THE door still open, my mind tripping over itself. I hadn't seen my mom and dad together in the same room since I was 12. Quynn had never met my dad. Valdo had never met my mom. Here was a collection of people that didn't belong in one room together, let alone my living room. My mom was still ranting as I locked eyes with Valdo. My brother who didn't know he was my brother. Except now, I'm sure he knew. I don't know how long they'd all been in this room together, but from the looks of it, certainly long enough to air out some truths. Valdo looked so confused. Happy, maybe? Disappointed? I wasn't sure. This was certainly not how I wanted him to find out.

"What do you have to say for yourself?" Mom asked, still standing by the door to the kitchen.

"Everyone is safe," I said to the whole room though my eyes were on Valdo. "The threat is gone."

"What threat?" Mom asked.

I sighed. "Can we sit down?"

My mom's face turned a shade of red that told me she was about to yell. The red was a powerful contrast to the silver dress she'd worn today.

"You said you would stay calm," Quynn said to her. They were standing next to our viewscreen, which was muted, but showing the news. A fire following an explosion a couple kilometers from here. Had they all been watching that before I came in? Quynn shifted their weight, staring daggers at my mother. They'd chosen a particularly feminine look today with lots of curves and very dark skin. Those eyes, though, those eyes were home. Those eyes were real love, not just some crush.

"I'm calm," Mom said. She totally wasn't calm.

"I'll explain as much as I can," I said. "I'm going to sit down."

I sat down near where Quynn was standing, though they barely looked at me. I really just wanted to sit on my couch and talk to my partner and decompress from the long time away, but that would have to wait.

"Valdo and I met a couple of months ago in the Toinette borough," I said.

"Part of your job?" Mom asked, spitting the last word like it was a curse.

I nodded. "He wound up helping me. I swear, running into him was complete chance. I didn't even know he existed before then. I certainly didn't know who his father was."

"How long?" Valdo said.

"How long have you known?" my father asked, putting a hand on Valdo's knee to silence him. I didn't like that one bit. In that moment, I realized how old my father looked. Taller than me, he had slightly darker skin and dark, bushy eyebrows under his thick, salt-and-pepper hair. He'd grown softer over time, his muscle giving way to a small gut.

"I've known since I brought the meds to the hospital," I said.

Even though they were sitting on the couch, my father spun on Valdo. "That's how those meds showed up? Her? You made a deal with an Intel Operative? What did you do? What do you owe her?"

"Bentley," Valdo's mother whispered. I saw where Valdo got hit height, there. She was shorter than any of us, plump and pale. "I wouldn't be sitting here if not for her."

"Bentley?" my mother asked through a barking laugh. "You left us and chose the name Bentley? How ridiculous."

Valdo's mother gave mine the nastiest look imaginable, but my mother didn't even seem to notice.

My father spun around to look at his wife, though some of the venom was gone from his voice. "I don't care what she did. Valdo lied to us. An Intel Operative for Corto? We don't know what she—"

"She's right here," Quynn said. "And she's your daughter. I know you love your new family, but she still has your blood in her veins. You chose to leave her behind, but she didn't make that same choice. And you're in her home, so a little more courtesy would be nice."

I struggled to fight down a smile as my father blushed and took a sudden interest in his hands.

"And why did you leave us, huh?" Mom asked. She was still standing, looking imperious and nervous at the same time. "I woke up one morning and you were just gone, half your stuff gone with you. Three weeks of human resources investigations before they told me that you'd left Corto Corporation, discommended. You're right in front of me now and I'm not allowed to say your old name, which was much better than Bentley."

My father's face darkened and closed off, but his wife put a hand on his knee. "Tell them. They deserve to know," she said. "It's long past time."

He looked at her, and his face slowly softened. He looked old. Sad. He stood up and walked across the room, nearer to the windows overlooking the Corto Corporation borough before he started speaking. "I was a coward," he said. "I went to a conference. You remember? The one in Huginn? One of those few cooperative meetings between companies to discuss the next steps in neural interface developments, ethics and neuro or something like that."

"Why would I remember that?" Mom said with all possible vitriol. Seeing both my parents in one room made me wonder how I didn't inherit either of their rageful streaks.

"I met Imelda. I couldn't help how I felt about her, though I certainly had control of myself. How I reacted. I know that. But nothing happened. I came home to you all."

"For all the good it did," Mom spat.

"Please, Mom," I said.

She shot me a look with almost as much contempt as she held for my father.

"I'm mad at him, too," I said. "But I want to hear what he has to say."

She sighed, crossed her arms, and focused her attention and wicked gaze on my father.

"We stayed in contact. Email. Text. I thought it was just a silly crush, one that would pass given enough time. That Imelda would just become a friend. But I started looking into Ibhalism, too. I hadn't even realized how much I'd been missing a spiritual aspect to my life. Corto Corporation is so rigidly secular. They nearly worship the founder and the company. That's not real spirituality.

"But Ibhalism called to me. It made sense. Then I started to see the mighty hand of Corto politics in everything around me. The tight grip on our lives trying to keep chaos to a minimum. It felt so forced, so unnatural. It left no room for the spirit, not for me anyway. I saw it when I was at work, on my commute."

"Even in our home?" Mom said, though she sounded sad instead of angry.

My father, for his part, looked ashamed when he said, "Yes. Even at home." He took a deep breath and a long pause. "I should have been better, been braver. I should have talked to you, both you and Elise. I should have explained myself. But I was a coward. I packed my things over three days and then left in the middle of the night. I knew it was wrong, but I also knew that the outcome would be the same no matter what. To leave Corto Corporation is to face discommendation, to lose your family and everyone you know. It was never an easy decision, but it was the right one."

"Right for you," Mom whispered. She glanced at me and then away. Tears were threatening to spill out of her eyes. Yeah. That was the reaction I inherited.

"You're right," my father said. "And I'm sorry for that. I'm sorry for how I left, how duplicitous that was, but I'm not sorry for leaving."

"And you welcomed him into your home," Mom said. She was looking at her hands, fidgeting with something, but I knew she was talking to me.

"I was trying to keep them safe," I said, standing up. "I can't tell any of you the circumstances, but Valdo was in danger. Valdo and his family. I wasn't excited about harboring the man who left us, but I was determined to save three people who didn't deserve to be put in danger like that."

Mom looked at me. She was still angry, but she was listening, taking it in. I could see a glimmer of respect in her eyes.

"Thank you for that," Imelda said.

"And Valdo," I said, turning to him. I wanted to apologize and say so much, but the look on his face told me to save it, that this wasn't the time or place. So, instead I said, "I'm so glad you're safe. All of you."

"So what happens now?" Mom asked. "One big, happy family? Should I expect to see these three on Founder's Day? Are we going to partake in some idiotic Toinette religious holidays now?"

"Stella," my father said.

"Don't you dare," Mom said, advancing a step and raising a threatening finger toward him. "You don't get to say my name. You don't get to do that. Never again."

"Stop," Quynn said before I could. "This was a case of really bad timing followed by a conversation that needed to happen. Now it's over. Everyone go home."

Mom crossed her arms again and donned a smug smile, glaring at my father.

"I mean everyone," Quynn said while looking directly at my mom. We were going to pay for that later, but I was glad, so glad, that Quynn had put their foot down.

It was Imelda's turn to stand now. "Quynn is right. We should go. Thank you for your hospitality and your protection, apparently. I'm so sorry that this happened, that all of this happened." She started for the door, and my father followed close behind, careful to keep his eyes off my mother.

"Before you go," I said to Valdo. "Can we talk?"

He glanced at his parents. My father looked disapproving but then looked to Imelda, and then he kept walking out of my apartment.

"We'll be back at the landing pad when you're ready," Valdo's mother said, and then she left as well.

"So I'm to be treated like that Toinette trash?" Mom asked once the door was closed, apparently not caring that Valdo was still in the room.

"Not at all, Mom," I said. "But trust me when I say that I've been through a lot the last month, this conversation included. We'll have lunch soon. Many lunches, I promise. I love you, Mom."

That seemed to break the flood of her anger, finally. She sighed and shook her head. "I never thought I'd see him again. For years, it was all I wanted. Just to see him. But now…"

"I get it, Mom. I really do. But you don't have to see him again."

She smiled sadly before she grabbed her bag, hugged Quynn and me, and left.

"I'll give you two some space," Quynn said. They grabbed my hand, a strange mix of worry and relief on their face. "I'm glad you're home."

"Me too," I said. "And thanks."

Quynn went into our bedroom, quietly closing the door behind them. I gestured for Valdo to sit down, but he didn't wait.

"You're my…sister? Why didn't you tell me?" he asked.

I ran a hand through my hair. "When I found out, standing there outside of your mom's hospital room, I was shocked. I…I hadn't expected to see my father again. Ever. In Corto Corporation, when someone leaves for another company, defects, then they may as well be dead. We're not allowed to speak their name again. His leaving stunted my mom's career forever. I had to work out of the shadow of that for years. And you didn't want to see me, didn't want to speak to me."

Valdo opened his mouth to speak, but I held up a hand.

"And I get it. I understood. The person I was on Cirilla, the decisions I made, I'm not proud of them. But I knew that you needed time. Space. Maybe you thought I was pestering you anyway, but it's because I didn't want to lose you entirely. I've never had a sibling. I always wanted one, but it never happened. And then I found you."

"You could have told me the other night, down in Kotega."

"It didn't feel like the right time. I'd finally gotten you to talk to me, to return a call and see me face-to-face. I didn't want to mess anything up. I was hoping to become your friend, to atone for how I behaved on Cirilla, and then tell you."

"You didn't think telling me might make me want to get to know you better, to work through our issues? I've never had a sibling, either. After we first met, I wanted to be you. The life you live, it's so different from mine. It's a life I never even considered. I wasn't even mad, just terrified that you might be a bad person, that I was caught up in something…something awful."

"I'm sorry for that," I said. "And yeah, I did consider just telling you. But I didn't want to take a risk, didn't want to you think I was lying just to leverage you. So many what-ifs ran through my head, so many of them went poorly."

"As poorly as this?" he asked, gesturing around the room.

I blew out a breath. "Some. Some worse. Plenty went better, though, for sure."

"Your mom sure was pissed."

I shrugged. "Your…our dad left Mom and me in the middle of the night. I was 12. No note or goodbye or anything. She's been holding onto that for almost 20 years."

"I had no idea."

"He never talked about it? About us? About Corto Corporation?"

"Not to me. I knew he didn't like Corto, but I just thought that was corporate loyalty."

I sat down on the back of the couch and glanced out the windows. It was the deep dark of night, the only illumination coming from the towering ads that covered most of the skyscrapers around us. Hard to imagine how someone could hate this place, how they could leave it all in the middle of the night, let alone leave their partner and child.

"Maybe," I said, still looking outside. "I've been hanging onto some of that rage, too. He left me as much as my mom. It changed our lives, and not for the better. I knew that if I told you, I'd be welcoming him back into my life. Not as a father or anything like that, but he's a big part of your life. There would be no avoiding him. Not entirely."

Valdo didn't say anything, and after a while, I turned to look at him. His mouth was hanging open, his gaze transfixed on the view screen.

"Valdo?" I asked. "Are you—?"

"Elise," Bastion said in my ear. "The news."

At that same moment, Quynn burst out of the bedroom, their eyes wide and frantic. "Elise," they said and pointed at the viewscreen. "Look."

I turned and there was my picture on the viewscreen, hovering over the shoulder of the news anchor. That didn't make sense. That couldn't be me. I was too confused to panic.

"Unmute," Quynn said.

"…still trying to confirm the authenticity of these recordings, but they paint a stark and terrible picture of one of Corto Corporation's own as a killer and someone who far exceeded their mandate as an Intel Operative. A warning to our viewers: the following footage is disturbing."

The anchor and my picture were replaced by a familiar scene from an unfamiliar angle. It was the feed from a security camera overlooking the back of the Saga Freya, the yacht I'd fought Theo on, his father's yacht. I knew what came next, what happened. Those events haunted me. My heartbeat thundered in my ears. I couldn't get enough air. The footage was from the end of our fight, the water from the enormous pool exploding everywhere, tossing a mangled Theo onto the deck. Then there was me, limping my way out of the pool, slowly approaching Theo, and then the green sparks flying out of his head. He dropped lifelessly to the ground.

The anchor was back, and my picture was replaced with that of Theo. "The man that Elise allegedly killed in that footage was Theo Huginn-Intel, son of Sinclair Huginn. We don't know anything more at this time regarding why Elise was there or why she murdered this young man."

"What is happening?" Quynn asked. I had no answer. Not that I could get enough breath to speak.

"This is in every borough," Bastion said. "Every news stream and all over the Net."

"We are just starting to comb through hundreds of hours of footage," the anchor continued. "And thousands of still images dating back years, detailing numerous activities, all of them with Elise's name attached to them."

The anchor stopped talking and looked into the middle distance for a moment, obviously seeing something on their display. "This is surprising," they continued. "It appears that the recent failure of the Offworld Relay may have also been caused by Elise Corto-Intel. Our techs have found images of her there the day that it went dark, and I believe we may have footage of—"

"Turn off viewscreen," I yelled. The enormous screen went dark and silent.

"How?" I said between shallow, quick breaths. "I don't understand."

"Tazia," Bastion said, his voice now coming from the speakers in the apartment since everyone present already knew about him.

"Can't be," I said. "She's been thrown into a cell in Kotega, she—"

"It was automated," Bastion said. "You just received an email, routed through a dozen false accounts, but she signed it with her name. There's a video."

"On the big screen," I whispered, terrified of what I was about to see. But I had to see it.

"Elise…" Bastion said.

"The big screen!" I yelled.

Bastion paused before the news stream was replaced with what looked like a still image of a server. Not just any server. The one surrounded by explosives that I'd found in the Toinette borough. But it wasn't in the same room, but a different, equally nondescript little space.

"Elise," Tazia said in voiceover. "You just never learn. In the unlikely event that you actually stop me, you'll get this video right after I send every news outlet in the city a little present. What comes next is on you."

An instant later, the server lit up, little red lights flashing rapidly all over it. Then it exploded. That explosion and fire on the news, that was the server. She'd moved it into the Corto Corporation borough. The video blinked out, and the news stream came back, my face hovering over the anchor's shoulder.

"Elise," Valdo said in a cautious whisper. " What does this mean?"

"It means…it means…" the word came to my mind, but I couldn't bring myself to say it. Couldn't deal with it.

Quynn's hands were suddenly on my shoulders, their face close to mine. "Elise. Elise? We're going to be all right. We'll get through this."

Get through this? How? My face all over the streams, all over the city. My operations suddenly in the public eye. No one could be an Intel Operative if everyone knew their face. Corto Corporation would toss me to The Mist. Discommended.

"Elise?" Valdo said. "Elise. What does this mean?"

"It's over," I said, failing to hold back tears. "My career. My life. It's all over."

Acknowledgements

This book, more than any before it, was an arduous task. Putting Elise so firmly outside of her comfort zone put me firmly outside of mine. If you missed Quynn and Hessod being around for much of the book, trust that I missed them even more. Helping me through all of those difficulties was my wife and alpha reader, Christy Arnone. She read the book not just once, but twice, and deserves a lot of credit for helping this book be what it is.

While Katie Salvo started this journey for The Jayu City Chronicles, my thanks go to Stephanie Hansen for picking up the torch and carrying it so very well as my agent. And of course, thank you to Jason Henderson and In Churl Yo at Castle Bridge Media for their continued faith in Elise and her adventures.

As always, I would not be the writer I am today without the time I spent pursuing my MFA at the University of Missouri-Kansas City. So, I have to thank Hadara Bar-Nadav, Christie Hodgen, Michael Pritchett, and Whitney Terrell for their teachings, patience, and sage advice during my time there. Reading their works always brings me back to basics when I begin to stray and reminds me of when it's okay to break those rules, too.

To so many friends-turned-fans that keep me going during the quiet months of writing. Claire Jarman and Vanessa Davis in particular are the best cheerleaders that an author could ask for. They're amazing friends, too.

CASTLE BRIDGE MEDIA RECOMMENDS...

If you liked this book, you might also enjoy reading the following titles from Castle Bridge Media available on Amazon or by order at your favorite book store:

The 23rd Hero
By Rebecca Anne Nguyen

ANIMAL CHARMER
By Rain Nox
Animal Charmer
Magic & Melody

Austinites
By In Churl Yo

Bloodsucker City
By Jim Towns

SOUL CATCHER
By Don Sawyer
The Burning Gem
The Tunnels of Buda

THE CASTLE OF HORROR
ANTHOLOGY SERIES
Volume 1
Volume 2: *Holiday Horrors*
Volume 3: *Scary Summer*
 Stories
Volume 4: *Women Running*
 From Houses
Volume 5: *Thinly Veiled:*
 The 70s
Volume 6: *Femme Fatales**
Volume 7: *Love Gone Wrong*
Volume 8: *Thinly Veiled:*
 The 80s
Volume 9: *Young Adult*
Volume 10: *Thinly Veiled:*
 Saturday Mournings
Volume 11: *Revenge*
Volume 12: *Ripped From*
 The Headlines
Edited By Jason Henderson
and In Churl Yo
*Edited By P.J. Hoover

Child of Dark Water
By E.G. Rand

Castle of Horror Podcast
Book of Great Horror:
Our Favorites, Top Tens
and Bizarre Pleasures
Edited By Jason Henderson

Cherry Dark
By R.L. Wilburn

Dream State
By Martin Ott

Dominic
By Lee Guzman

FRENCH DECEPTION
By Janice Nagourney
A Forgery in Paris
A Forgery in Lyon
A Forgery in Marseille

FuturePast Sci-Fi Anthology
Edited by In Churl Yo

GLAZIER'S GAP
Ghosts of the Forbidden
By Leanna Renee Hieber

Hellfall
By Jay Gould

Isonation
By In Churl Yo

JAYU CITY CHRONICLES
By Chris M. Arnone
The Hermes Protocol
Necropolis Alpha
The Cordelia Solution

THE PATH
By David Bowles
The Blue-Spangled Blue
The Deepest Green

Junk Film: Why Bad
Movies Matter
By Katharine Coldiron

Nightwalkers:
Gothic Horror Movies
By Bruce Lanier Wright

MID-LIFE CRISIS THRILLERS
18 Miles From Town
By Jason Henderson
Lost Angel
By Sam Knight
Ties That Kill
By Deven Greene

THE PATH
By David Bowles
The Blue-Spangled Blue
The Deepest Green

Strange Shape of Love
By Herta Feely

SURF MYSTIC
By Peyton Douglas
Night of the Book Man
Dark of the Curl

The Thing That Happened
When We Were Little
By Caroline Kelly Franklin

Tick Town
By Christopher A. Micklos

Yesterday's Tomorrows:
The Golden Age of
Science Fiction Movies
By Bruce Lanier Wright

THANK YOU FOR
SUPPORTING INDEPENDENT
PUBLISHERS AND AUTHORS!
castlebridgemedia.com